THE SHADOW OF THE GODS

THE PANTHEON WAR: BOOK ONE

ALSO BY ALYCE CASWELL

Standalone Titles

Love and Lockdown

*The Eyes of Charon**

Jen Cooke Novels

Dealing with the Demon

The Galactic Pantheon Series

The Tortured Wind

The Twisted Vine

*The Flickering Flame**

*The Shifting Ice**

*The Whispering Grass**

*The Creeping Moss**

*The Galactic Pantheon Novellas***

*The Adventures of Grace Pendergast, Galactic Reporter***

*novella

**collection

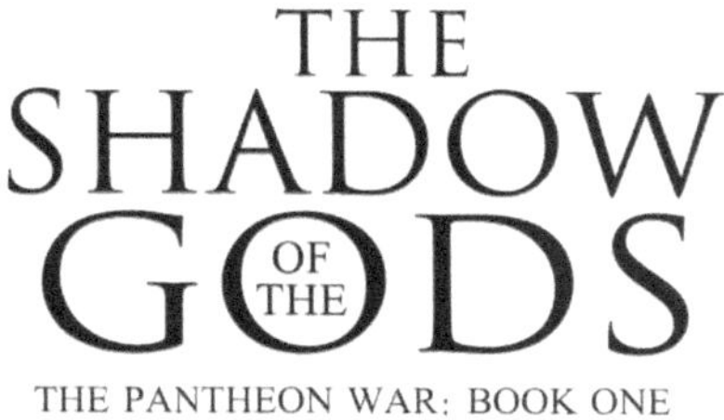

THE SHADOW OF THE GODS

THE PANTHEON WAR: BOOK ONE

ALYCE CASWELL

ISBN: 978 1 922807 00 7 (EPUB)

ISBN: 978 1 922807 01 4 (Print)

Cover design by Biserka Design © 2022

Once upon a time, humans spread far and wide across the galaxy, colonising worlds and mingling with other species. They were welcomed by their galactic neighbours in those early days, because they discovered that all of them shared a common deity: the Creator God.

Humans soon became so numerous that one god was not enough to care for them. The Creator God begat more than fifty divine children, the sub-level gods and goddesses of the Galactic Pantheon, each with their own domain to rule over. There is a god of deserts, a god of rainforests, a goddess of fire...and so on.

Most beings live their entire lives in the shadow of the gods.

Once you leave that shadow, there's no going back.

ONE

The pirate vessel was parked between her and the planet. Easily three times the size of her own starship, the looming bulk did not lumber forward and engage her in a lasfight. It simply sat there, unbothered by her scowl, doing its best to mimic a black hole with that dark paint job and a complete lack of plexiglass panels.

Expensive. Deadly. And definitely going to give her a headache.

Captain Ami N'uni had already assumed her usual position; she was standing in front of the viewport on the bridge of her ship, her mane of brunette hair pinned sharply away from her face. Her preferred outfit hadn't changed in five years—the loose white shirt with the puffy sleeves, the faded denim jeans studded with useless but pretty shards of metal, the scuffed black boots, and the chunky leather belt that held her lasgun.

Ami thought she cut a fine figure in this get-up. The shirt clung exactly where it needed to—potentially distracting to her opponents, but practical enough that she could still move fast. Not that she made a point of meeting any of her opponents in person. But she'd known that she would have to face this particular opponent at some point.

Admiral Julius Kratis had a massive beef with her.

You'd think she was shitting in his slippers, not rescuing slaves from his ships.

Ami's cargo vessel, the *Free Ride*, was embarrassingly small and its hull was a patchwork of grey and brown metal from various repair jobs. The *Free Ride*'s unusual shape—it looked like a hand with a thumb positioned beneath four merged fingers—never failed to announce Ami's arrival. Possibly because the 'thumb' was actually a heavy lascannon capable of punching through most shields, perfect for threatening the pirates and slavers she came across in the void of space.

It usually comforted Ami to know that, at a moment's notice, she could run back to her chair, wrench the manual controls out of the left armrest, and leap to another system.

But today, even though her feet were planted directly beneath her shoulders and her spine was straight, she felt a fragment of worry detach from a hidden place inside her, riding blood vessels up into her brain where it implanted itself. And grew.

'Smart fucker,' her only crewmate, Avurn Singh, muttered from the weapons console.

'Language,' she murmured, though she didn't quite have the mental capacity to inject any disapproval into her tone. She kept her green eyes at half-mast.

The ten-year-old boy sighed dramatically and went slack in his chair. A clump of charcoal hair flopped over his sepia-toned face, hiding both the purple freckles he'd inherited from some alien ancestor and his impatient grimace. 'I accompany you to avoid being lectured by my sister. Please don't you start. It seems we did not encounter retribution from Julius earlier on our run because he knew to lie in wait here above Ilbb. And he was smart enough to keep his distance so he wouldn't trip the Chippers' planetside sensors.'

Avurn took perverse delight in the shock on the faces of their allies and enemies alike whenever a visual communications link revealed that he had been crewing the weapons console, targeting their ships with the lascannon if need be. Avurn, with his unbroken voice, could pretend to be a human adult of any gender when a conversation was verbal only.

Ami *should* have been more concerned about showing Avurn the seedy side of the galaxy, but his sister had given him a personal shielding device—and Avurn always managed to keep out of trouble, even when they docked and left the safety of the *Free Ride* behind. Avurn had a habit of embarking on solo adventures. Ami wasn't sure she wanted to know what he got up to, because he'd warned her never to ask.

'Can we send a message to the Chipper outpost without Julius getting wind of it?' she asked, tapping a finger against her lip. She winced when she felt a flake of skin detach. The dry environment on her ship really wasn't friendly to her complexion and she'd forgotten to use her face creams again.

'Yes, I can connect us to the outpost on a secure link,' Avurn answered, but he didn't move towards the communications console. A third person should have been crewing it, but Ami had never found someone willing to fill it in return for exactly zero pay. And she wasn't sure she could trust anyone else.

Avurn knew a lot about the galaxy and how it worked—which often led to him saying things she didn't want to hear. Like now. 'Do remember, Ami, the Chippers don't exactly have a ship at their disposal. They'd have to use Xan's vessel. They won't, however, since he is a contractor and will ask them to pay him extra for the service. And you know my brother-in-law prefers to regale everyone with his past escapades rather than admit to the fact that he can't fly in a straight line anymore. He is frequently inebriated.'

'I suppose there are benefits to having a backup pilot who's underage on most worlds,' Ami said.

Avurn snorted. Most residents of Carton City, the desert planet's only permanent settlement, spent their time at the bar, watching the drama vidshow that was Xan and Jensa's marriage. Jensa enjoyed the attention and played into it, much to Xan's exasperation.

Avurn, since the wedding, had been allowed his own unit next to theirs. This was done less for Xan and Jensa's privacy and more because Xan wanted to be able to claim that he had no knowledge of Avurn's untoward activities. Xan had chosen to become a contractor for the Chippers instead of serving a lengthy prison term for his past crimes. He wanted to keep his posterior out of a cell. Understandably.

'Concentrate,' Ami scolded herself.

The destruction of her ship was not the preferred outcome for her or her opponent. Julius would want to plunder the *Free Ride* before he sold it for scrap—or maybe he'd keep it for his pirate fleet. And he would have something nasty in mind for her and Avurn.

Slavery, most likely. A fatal end wasn't off the table either.

If Ami had to choose? A quick lasbolt to the head, thanks. Because slavery, which had very recently been the future awaiting the people riding in the hold of her ship, was a fate worse than death.

The legality of slavery varied across the galaxy. If slaves were allowed on a world, then the Chippers couldn't do a starking thing about it—the Galactic Law Enforcement Agency was an independent organisation and could only enforce the laws of a planet's governing body, not change them. And even if a planet had made slavery illegal, then a Chipper would actually have to be on hand to witness the violation. There weren't enough of them to cover an entire galaxy.

The Chippers stationed at the outpost on Ilbb never had any spare coin-chips; most of GLEA's funds went towards paying their agents (and their cheaper contractors) to provide safety and order. Not all grateful worlds could afford to donate money to the Agency. It was, of course, much more economical to let someone else tackle the far-reaching slavery issue.

If Ami didn't mention the laws she'd broken elsewhere, the Chippers would keep letting her use Ilbb as her base of operations.

But they weren't going to be happy if she started a war in orbit.

'Hail him,' Ami said, nodding her head towards the other ship, which was steadily filling the viewport. 'Don't want Julius to get bored and start strafing the planet.'

'He'd have a hard time hitting anything.' Avurn snickered as he moved to the communications console. Once he'd dropped into the seat anchored there, he swiped a single finger over the sensor pad in front of him. 'Carton City is but a small speck—and there are only scattered nomadic tribes on the rest of the planet.'

Static washed across the viewport, leaving in its wake a toothy leer. Julius was a Hiktai, a reptilian species with green scales, flexible legs that allowed them to stand or crawl comfortably, and an evolutionary urge to protect their hives—in Julius' case, he considered himself a hive of one. Even the captains in his fleet couldn't count on him to help them out of sticky situations.

Ami might be human, but Carton City was her hive, thugs and Chippers both, and she sure as stark wasn't going to let anyone endanger it.

'Admiral Julius Kratis,' she greeted.

'You done fucked up this time, N'uni,' Julius said cheerfully. 'We got you on vidcam! Stealing the merchandise right out of one of my ships. And my fleet's registered to New Sydney. Gonna get you in real trouble, that.'

Ah. Stark. New Sydney's government did have laws against slavery, to appease their nearest neighbours in the same system, but the punishment was a paltry fine. Theft, however...they took a dim view of that and perpetrators got tossed into the maw of a terrifying creature when it emerged from the ocean's depths. Luckily for Ami, New Sydney folk *really* loved their loopholes.

'So do you want me alive or dead?' Ami asked.

Julius clacked his front rows of teeth together. 'Alive, but I think you'd rather be dead.'

'You can come collect me in person and gloat to my face,' Ami suggested. 'I have a docking port free.'

'You starker! You'll blast me the moment I step on board.'

Ami laughed. 'Well, it would absolve me of the theft, wouldn't it?'

That little loophole she planned on using? Kill whoever first accused you of the theft and suddenly there's no accusation—or crime.

Julius shook his head furiously. 'No, you will surrender yourself and enter *my* docking port. I will give you five minutes to comply. Be a single nanosecond late and I'll slaughter twenty percent of the slaves you stole from me.'

Ami cursed softly. She waved her hand at Avurn, indicating for him to cut the link, and once again the viewport was filled with Julius' monstrous ship.

What was she supposed to do?

The people crammed into her ship's hold deserved the freedom she had promised them.

'Julius will not entertain the notion of trading your life for theirs,' Avurn warned her. 'They're worth more than we are.'

Ami rubbed her temples. 'I know. And even if we do manage to get off a few shots with the lascannon, that shield is practically impenetrable. As for taking him out when I exit the docking port... forget it. He's got a whole crew over there with itchy trigger fingers.'

'No, he doesn't. He's alone.'

Ami dropped her hand and lasered in on Avurn. He was hunched over, shrinking down in his seat, suddenly looking his age. A boy caught in the act of doing something wrong.

'Av?' she asked.

'I can only sense one lifesign over there,' Avurn said quietly. 'That entire ship can be crewed by a single being. Julius has a well-equipped vessel, granted, but he's the only one on board. No doubt he relies on the appearance of having a sizeable army when he only has a handful of captains in charge of automated ships. Such hubris. There is a chance we could overpower him.'

Ami's words were slow, suspicious. 'Our sensors can't penetrate that hull.'

Avurn expelled a forceful sigh that sounded as though it had been yanked out of his mouth along with several teeth. He held out his left arm, reefing up the sleeve of his jumpsuit. Avurn's preference for wearing the colour black had often been a source of amusement for Ami, especially since he lived on a desert planet, but now even his expression was bordering on dark. He didn't yield his secrets easily and why he'd kept this one was obvious.

The bump in the hollow on the opposite side of his elbow was thumbnail sized—and surrounded by angry red lines that twisted their way up towards his shoulder. He'd inserted something beneath his skin.

'I have a chip,' Avurn said, his eyes never meeting hers.

Ami wrapped her fingers around her lasgun, the leather grip worn down to the metal because it was second-hand, not from her use of it. She was a terrible shot. 'Av. Chippers have chips. That's why we call them...anyway, their chips go in the temple, not the arm.'

'Can't really risk discovery by putting it there, can I?' Avurn chortled. He sounded much more like his usual self now. 'It gives me the same powers they have: I can manipulate the universe's energy to create forcefields, and I can sense the energy that life-forms exude. Except I amped my chip up—you won't *believe* how poorly designed theirs are, with such basic settings—so I'm pretty powerful.'

'Avurn! Stark!' Ami clenched her jaw, feeling stress twist inside her abdomen. 'You're wearing a chip you stole from GLEA! That's a serious offence and if the agents on Ilbb see it—'

'I didn't steal it, I created it myself,' Avurn said, scowling. 'Granted, I did steal a chip so I could reverse-engineer it in the first place...'

'*Avurn!*'

'Captain!' Avurn shot out of his chair. He stabbed a finger towards the viewport. 'I can help! So let me.'

Ami could already hear the tongue-lashing she'd get if Jensa ever found out what her brother had been up to. Catching a lasbolt was a much less painful option, frankly.

Ami drew a deep breath, momentarily swamped by stress-induced nausea. 'Alright. Two of us versus one particularly nasty pirate who has more lasguns than he does limbs. How do you propose we get out of this mess, Av?'

Avurn grinned.

TWO

'It seems Captain N'uni is going to surrender herself to Kratis,' Second Lieutenant Pina-Sai said, once the unsecured link being Webcast between the two ships cut out.

His quickening breaths visibly ghosted across the viewport. The climate control system on their small, egg-shaped ship was faulty and had left them shivering in a temperature that was more appropriate for an icy moon. The ship badly needed repairs, though Private Kieran Krendasta wondered what, if any, help the outpost on Ilbb could offer them. Ilbb barely had any buildings, let alone starship facilities.

Finding a reputable mechanic was also going to be a problem. Most of the planet's residents were criminals using Ilbb as a hideout —the agents posted here had made it their mission to introduce the shady characters of Carton City to the ways of the Creator God.

Kieran wasn't sure how successful they'd been. People tended to take the Galactic Law Enforcement Agency for granted and didn't always feel inclined to repay their services with coin-chips or worship of GLEA's approved god. Kieran had mentioned his thoughts on this to Pina-Sai once, and the lieutenant had been quick to remind him that they shouldn't expect anything in return for helping people.

Everything they did was done in service to the Creator God. Every agent was grateful to be carrying out his will and protecting his mortal children.

Kieran didn't feel particularly grateful. The Creator God was starking useless.

Pina-Sai was bent into an awkward shape in the cramped cabin, though even if he had been afforded more space (and the budget to acquire a vessel with said space) he would not have used it.

Almost seven feet tall to Kieran's five foot eight, Pina was not considered that unusual when among humans—even if he did stand out. But he had been raised on Lentaria, which was primarily populated by a blue-skinned, four-armed species that were all markedly shorter than Pina. His family had married and bred with humans for several generations, resulting in his tall stature. Full-blooded Lentarians had refused to speak to Pina until he'd adopted a permanent hunch that lowered himself to their level.

The only signs of his ancestry were the slate-grey eyes without any obvious pupils—and that peculiar braying laugh. Something Kieran didn't hear very often.

Pina's peppery hair was tightly cropped, exposing the chip in his temple, and his beard was kept tidy, as was required by the Agency. He had chosen to join GLEA, a predominantly human organisation, which should have solved his problems, but he was often overlooked for promotion—no doubt due to the painful and rather public breakdown of his marriage.

Agents who were married rose much quicker through the ranks, because of the potential offspring they could bring to the Agency. Those families unable to conceive naturally were encouraged to merge their DNA in approved clinics to create their children. Divorce was heavily frowned upon.

For all the difficulties in his life, Pina was a very patient man.

Kieran tried not to feel resentful about being paired with Pina. His superiors had said something about them being 'suited'—frankly, they were both infamous screwups. No decent agent wanted to be associated with either man.

Their latest mission had been a glorified babysitting assignment on Unanda and they'd been on their way back to Gerasnin when their ship's main console had started glitching. Things had got progressively worse after that. And of course their leapdrive had chosen to malfunction and strand them *here*.

Kieran had accidentally glanced at the dust-blown planet twice. A cube of ice seemed to be nestled against the nape of his neck, sending tendrils of frigid water down his spine.

He'd managed to avoid any deserts for a full Old Earth year.

Pina moved his avid gaze from the viewport to his companion. 'What do you think we should do, Kieran?'

'Assist Captain N'uni,' Kieran replied.

'Oh? To avoid touching down on Ilbb for that little bit longer?' Pina asked, his lips curling. 'I will admit to being somewhat attached to this portable refrigeration unit, since it has lasted several months longer than most ships I've been assigned. But it's no longer comfortable *or* habitable. Your dislike of warmer climates is no reason to stay up here and freeze to death.'

Kieran narrowed his eyes at Pina, but managed to maintain a respectful tone. 'No, sir. It's clear that we will board and help the captain.'

'It's clear, is it?' Pina echoed, his fingers fidgeting and overlapping each other on his knees. Kieran knew this meant that Pina was anxious and fighting the urge to wrap his hands around a glass of something strong. 'What reasoning have you used for your assumption, Kieran?'

Unease gnawed a chasm into Kieran's stomach.

Here we go again, he thought.

'It's just a feeling, sir.'

'A feeling?' Pina pressed. 'Or a vision of the future in which you see us helping her?'

Kieran looked away, pained. No agent could see the future; it wasn't one of the powers their chips gave them. But he had seen things. Mostly nothing useful, just snippets of daily life. Occasionally it was something to do with a mission. The Agency had dismissed these incidents as simple deja vu—even after that disaster on Fintaz.

Kieran now had a reputation for being unstable. He'd given up on applying for officer training because the answer was always an emphatic no.

It was safer to pretend he had *feelings* instead.

Pina pursed his lips and nodded. 'No need to explain yourself. We will assist.'

Kieran stared at him. 'What? No lecture about how we don't have the ability to perceive the future?'

Kieran brushed his sandy-brown hair off his face (he really needed to get it cut—the agents on Ilbb would frown at how shaggy he had let it become) and tapped the protrusion on the temple that housed his chip. It was a small, insignificant bump, but sometimes he lay awake in bed for hours, wondering why the chip felt so cold beneath his skin. Other agents never seemed to lose sleep over it.

Pina frowned. 'I am not our superiors, Kieran. While they might say you cannot possibly see the future...we are followers of the Creator God. Who knows what his plans are for us? The chips we use are mortal in design, hardly as potent as a divine gift. And there are already so many sub-level gods out there giving away powers like candy. I would be surprised if the Creator could not do the same.'

Hard to argue with that logic, Kieran mused.

Agents of GLEA gained their abilities through the use of tech—and only because the Creator God allowed it. Worshippers of the desert god, the Desine, were given their so-called 'Magic' upon birth. They could wield immense power without any artificial aid and were able to summon vast sandstorms, howling monsters that ripped skin from bone.

Monsters that claimed you, body and soul.

Kieran swallowed, bringing much-needed moisture back into his mouth. 'You are never going to re-earn your old rank, Lieutenant. Being paired with me is bad enough for your reputation. Once people get wind of you actually *believing* me...'

'I am a divorcee, so I'd say your reputation is the one taking a battering,' Pina said as he began to steer their ship towards the pirate vessel. Even if the sensors on that monstrous bulk had been fooled by their basic cloaking device, Kratis would certainly notice when they attached themselves to one of the docking ports on his ship.

'Your divorce *has* caused issues for you,' Kieran agreed. 'Or maybe your career stalled because you are incapable of learning any discipline in your old age.'

Pina flicked him a grin. 'Old! Fifty is nothing for someone of Lentarian stock. I've at least a hundred Old Earth years left.'

'I'm glad I won't live that long,' Kieran said, fighting to keep his own grin off his face. 'Imagine being paired with you for a century. It's a miracle I'm still sane after a single Old Earth year.'

'If you had a rank, I would bust you from it just for disrespecting your elders!'

Silence soon fell between them, Pina requiring more focus as he hacked one of the docking ports on the pirate vessel. Kieran lacked his finesse with invading an opponent's systems, never mind that GLEA provided them with third-party software that was *supposed* to be user-friendly.

'Got it,' Pina said as their docking tunnel extended and clanked into place.

Kieran and Pina both moved to the hatch, running their hands over their belts and ensuring that their lasguns, personal shielding devices, and communicators were present and secured. Relying on a chip alone had been the death of many an agent in the past.

Kieran glanced down at his violet jumpsuit and grimaced.

Their bright clothing wouldn't exactly help them move undetected through the ship, most likely decked out in the neutral greys favoured by most designers, but it was their official uniform. Pina had two gold strokes over his right shoulder, indicating his rank—something Kieran knew he'd never have.

He was even more of a screwup than Pina was.

Kieran unclipped his lasgun from his belt, feeling the soft gel-based handle readjust inside his tight grip. He pressed his other hand to the airlock and sent his awareness through its twin on the other side of the tunnel.

His lips were already moving. 'No lifesigns in the corridor. Safe to disembark.'

'Do you have a plan?' Pina asked, squeezing Kieran's shoulder, a gentle reminder not to blunder into the situation—as he had done so many times before.

Kieran laughed shortly. 'You're the lieutenant, Lieutenant.'

'My career advancement might have stalled, but that's no reason for you to give up your own goals, Kieran,' Pina said calmly. 'Since you have so far shown no interest in marriage or breeding, which would fast-track you through the enlisted ranks or perhaps gain you a spot in officer training, we must build your strategic skills to a level that will impress our superiors. This is *your* mission to lead.'

'You just don't want to be the one responsible if we fail.'

'Possibly.'

'Oh well, I can only get us killed,' Kieran said, then shook off Pina's touch and slapped the sensor pad beside the airlock. He hurtled through the docking tunnel an instant later.

'Kieran...!'

Pina cut short his rebuke and chased after Kieran, swearing.

AMI WALKED out into enemy territory, arms wide, bare palms offered to Admiral Julius Kratis.

He was shorter than she expected and his four lasguns (one in each of the clawed feet he wasn't using for balance) were indecently long. If he was human, Ami would have said he was compensating for something. That kind of comment would have no effect on him. Hiktai were a hard species to read, but he had to have a weakness. Everyone did. Ami was willing to bet that even the gods had weaknesses that could be exploited.

Julius raised a lasgun and fired.

The ensuing lasbolt blatted against the wall beside Ami, though did no damage to the metal plating. She didn't need the reminder to play nice. He'd already put in her in a vulnerable position by stipulating that she could not exit the docking tunnel with a lasgun or a personal shielding device.

Julius threw a pair of lascuffs at her feet. 'Put those on.'

'Afraid of one harmless little human, are you?' Ami sneered, bending down on one knee. She scooped up the cuffs. 'Pathetic, but not surprising. You know I can hijack this ship as soon as I get my hands on the controls. Bet you never learned how to fly it. You rely on all those automated systems, don't you?'

Julius snarled. 'Put 'em on *now*. Then tell me the code to open your docking port. No funny business, N'uni.'

'I was thinking of trading me for my cargo?' Ami batted her eyelashes. 'Pretty please?'

'No trade and no more stalling!'

'Get one of your minions to cuff me. Oh.' Ami managed a giggle, but she was going to have to rinse the taste of it out of her mouth later. 'You don't have any minions on board, do you. It's just you, all alone on this big clunker. I guess most people laughed when you asked them to join your little so-called fleet. They must know you keep being outwitted by a human with only one lascannon attached to her shitty ship.'

All four lasguns rose in unison. 'You wyvern, I'll—!'

Julius fired. The lasbolts tore across the space between them—and hit only air. Then the bolts bounced away, striking and scoring the nearby bulkheads.

'Shooting before you finish your sentence?' Ami tutted. 'Now that's just unsporting.'

'I said no personal shields!' he roared.

Ami's response was to wave her very empty hands. She hoped the frantic hammering of her heart wasn't too loud or obvious. Gods, she could have just *died*.

Yep, definitely got a temper on him, that's Julius' weakness, she thought. *As for my weakness? Poking the wyvern, that's what. Can't believe I trusted Av to block any bolts with his supposed powers that I've never seen him using. Shit. I forgot how reckless I can be when I'm backed into a corner.*

Ami hurled the cuffs back at Julius. They hit the stretch of scales beneath his vinyl jacket and bounced onto the floor.

'Put those on and get some extra cuffs for your other appendages,' she ordered. 'Oh, and while you're at it, toss me your lasguns.'

'Chipper!' Julius hissed, his slitted yellow eyes full of venom.

'Do you *see* a chip on me?' Ami smirked. 'Nope, I'm just the woman who's going to shove you into a lifepod and strand you on the planet below. Then I'll put out word on the Web that you've had to abandon ship. This giant eyesore will disappear in a matter of hours—good luck identifying the thief from down there.'

His throat crackled and popped as he laughed at her.

Not the intended reaction. Ami resisted the urge to mop the bottom of her shirt over her damp forehead.

'ACTIVATE DEFENCE SYSTEM!' Julius roared.

Alarms started screaming.

Julius grinned broadly, until his maw opened far enough to reveal his second and third sets of teeth. 'Even a Chipper can't deflect this many lasbolts.'

'Av...?' Ami called.

The boy skidded into view from around the corner.

He'd hung back inside the docking tunnel earlier, sneaking aboard once he'd hoodwinked Julius' systems so they wouldn't notice his presence. Ami had told him to keep out of sight, but Avurn had warned her that he could only create one forcefield at a time and he would join her inside it if he had to. As for the shielding device his sister had given him, Ami had quickly discovered that Avurn had long ago sold the 'ancient and disgustingly inferior piece of tech' because he'd needed the money to fund the construction of his chip. Gods help them.

'Ami, we are starked!' Avurn shouted.

The bulkheads shifted around them. Metal panels withdrew, exposing their deadly secrets, and within seconds the corridor was studded with hundreds of lasguns—and oh shit, they sprouted from the ceiling too.

Ami reached for the weapon stashed at the small of her back. She wasn't a great shot, but even at this range she ought to be able to hit Julius—

The corridor exploded with light and noise.

Ami hit the floor. She lay there, dazed and winded, watching as the lasbolts bounced off the invisible barrier that stood in front of Avurn's outstretched hands. He towered over her, all four feet of him, a force to be reckoned with. It was as though they were encased inside a plexiglass bubble, safe from anything Julius could throw at them—but they couldn't escape the acrid tang of ozone coming off the lasguns.

Avurn grunted as he struggled to maintain the forcefield and his arms began to tremble; a Chipper conducted the universe's energy through their hands when using their powers. But Ami was sure she had never seen any of them wield *quite* this much energy before.

Ami rolled onto her knees and staggered up onto her feet. Julius was still flashing that toothy smile, surrounded by a maelstrom of death, gleefully clacking his claws against the steel flooring. Not a single lasgun dared to fire at him.

'Av!' Ami said. 'How much longer can you keep this up?'

'We shall see!' Avurn replied. 'Hopefully until my virus takes out his weapons systems—and those systems were very easy to access!'

The lasguns, as though hearing the desperation in his voice, suddenly drooped in their sockets. The ensuing silence was somehow louder than the cacophony the weapons had been causing moments earlier.

'ACTIVATE!' Julius said, lifting one pair of feet to kick a nearby bulkhead. 'Stark you, keep firing!'

Ami felt fingers brush past the small of her back.

Lasbolts shredded their way through Julius' scales. He staggered back against the wall, throwing a mangled look of disbelief at them. Smoking holes swiftly replaced his eyes. He hit the deck. Hard.

Avurn lowered Ami's lasgun, his expression grim.

'You killed him!' Ami cried.

'The opportunity presented itself,' Avurn said flatly.

The echo of nearby footsteps reached them. Avurn flinched and turned towards the sound, the lasgun rising once more. His hand was frighteningly steady.

Ami withdrew from him, trembling. There was so much she wanted to yell into his stony face, but only one sentence fell out of her mouth. 'You said...you said there was no one else on board.'

'I was wrong. It happens. I'll kill them too.'

'Av—no!' Ami lunged for the lasgun.

Avurn's expression shifted from defiant to startled when his finger slipped on the trigger. The weapon discharged.

'Oh stark,' the boy said faintly.

Ami swung her eyes in the direction the lasbolt had gone. Standing in the centre of the corridor was a man in his mid-twenties, his rigid stance emphasising his perfectly sculpted form (even the relaxed fit of his jumpsuit couldn't hide *that*). Stark, he was hot.

Ami would have attempted to buy him a drink, if not for the current circumstances.

He had both hands thrown up in front of him, the lasbolt hovering mere micrometres from his fingers, evidently kept in place by a forcefield. He gently nudged the bolt to the side, targeting one of Julius' mounted lasguns and effortlessly destroying it. He wielded his powers with much more precision than Avurn had.

Ami looked at the newcomer's right temple.

Yep, definitely a chip there.

Not that she needed to see it, since his uniform was a giant purple clue.

'I'm glad I wasn't too late,' the Chipper said, then glanced at the corpse on the floor. His lips twitched. 'Well, I think he would disagree.'

Ami was too stunned to let the hysterical laugh escape.

THREE

Kieran didn't waste time trying to come up with an elaborate plan.

While Pina grappled with a console in a vain attempt to shut down the defence system, Kieran made his way towards the three lifesigns he could sense further along the curved corridor, clustered near another docking port. Pina hadn't answered when Kieran had asked him if he could deactivate the lasguns in time—they were springing up all along the corridor like the rapidly spawned flowers of Ti'slo'a Prime—and had instead shouted at Kieran to just *run*.

Kieran had obeyed without question.

His personal shielding device deflected the lasbolts hailing down on him, until it failed with a whine and a whiff of smoke. But by then he didn't need it. A small forcefield caught the only bolt that came close to ending his life—which, surprisingly, hadn't come from the ship's weapons. Those lasguns were now offline, though Kieran seriously doubted this was due to Pina's efforts, given how frantic the lieutenant had looked when they'd parted.

Kieran took stock of the scored floor and bulkheads, eyebrows raised.

Both the captain and the boy should be dead.

As for the pirate, he shouldn't be on the floor. His automated weapons would have recognised his biometrics and should not have targeted him.

The lasgun in the boy's hand, however...that'd do it.

'I shot Julius,' Captain N'uni said and yanked at the weapon.

The boy stubbornly held onto the lasgun for several seconds, only relenting when she hissed something into his ear. It sounded like she was invoking the wrath of a relative on him.

Captain N'uni's gaze was defiant when she turned back to Kieran. 'This ship is registered to New Sydney. Admiral Julius Kratis accused me of stealing his property, so it's perfectly legal for me to kill him to render said accusation null and void. If you have a problem with me ridding the galaxy of someone who considered living beings his property, then I'm going to have a starking big problem with *you*.'

'He dealt in slaves?' Kieran paused. Her starship was close enough that he could get a read on the energy inside it. He detected twenty lifesigns. 'Why would you bring them here, Captain?'

'No one looks on Ilbb for escaped slaves,' she said. 'It's a wasteland where criminals go to disappear; snitches don't last long down there. And unlike most seedy ports, it's not watched by slavers. Anyway, I help these people catch a ride to wherever they want to go from here. Some even assimilate into the local population.'

She was trying to distract him.

She was doing a starking good job of it.

Kieran indicated her companion. 'I believe the minimum age for humans on a starship's crew is eighteen Old Earth years.'

'Not on Ilbb,' she fired back. 'And that's where my ship is registered.'

The boy lifted his chin. 'Even so, there are few captains who would refuse someone as valuable as me. Mentally, I'm quite advanced. My body has not developed at a similar pace, but my predominantly human genetics are to blame for that.'

Kieran frowned heavily, until his vision went almost grey. There was a buzzing sensation in his right temple, where the chip rested, when he focused on the boy. It was not unlike what he felt around other agents when he tried to link his powers to theirs. He'd always had trouble doing that.

Kieran was less powerful than every other agent he'd ever met— discounting that one bizarre and horrifying incident on Fintaz—but he had resigned himself to this after more than two decades of disappointing his superiors. An agent's power levels could be due to the chip they had been issued with, or even a minute glitch in their brain chemistry.

But even someone with Kieran's limited capabilities could still sense the concern in the boy's energy.

'He shot the pirate,' Kieran stated.

Captain N'uni hooked the lasgun onto her belt and stepped out in front of the boy, palms offered: both a gesture of peace and a plea for Kieran to listen.

'Please don't arrest Avurn,' she said, a wobbly smile sketched across her features. 'I might be a shit shot, but no one on Ilbb will testify to that, mostly because they love to help anyone avoid GLEA's prison cells. They'll back me up. Secondly, it was self-defence, which *might* be one of those New Sydney loopholes. And lastly—his sister would never forgive me.'

'Ami cannot continue to liberate slaves if I am incarcerated,' Avurn declared, frighteningly solemn for someone so young. 'Can you imagine her trying to navigate the perils of space without me? She only managed to transport foodstuff before I came aboard!'

'Av, you're not helping!' she said.

Kieran closed his eyes. *Creator God, now would be a great time to finally reveal that you give a shit about me. Tell me what to do. Just a hint. Anything.*

Silence.

Kieran studied Ami closely. She was beautiful, but he couldn't allow that to affect his judgement. Still, he didn't think she or her crewmate were lying about their activities. Those twenty souls on Ami's vessel—he could feel their hope, feel them reaching out for an intangible, uncertain future.

The communicator on his belt spat out Pina's shrill voice. 'Kieran! A self-destruct sequence just activated!'

'Av?' Ami asked.

The boy nodded grimly. 'It would be Julius' style to rig a self-destruct sequence to his lifesign.'

'You little starker!' Ami snarled and kicked the pirate's corpse, flipping him over onto his back. She yanked open the vinyl jacket he'd been wearing. An ugly device was cratered onto the Hiktai's torso, covered in lights that were winking furiously as the ship's self-destruct counted down.

She swore again. 'Shit! Is your ship fast, Chipper?'

'We'll take yours,' Kieran said instead of answering outright. He ripped the communicator off his belt. 'Pina, get to this docking port. Now!'

'The pirate captain?'

'I dealt with him,' Kieran replied.

Suspicion laced Pina's words. 'And by "dealt with", you mean...'

'He's dead.'

'Kieran! Do you even *want* to repair your tarnished reputation?'

'Just get over here!' Kieran barked and cut the connection.

'Thank—' Ami began.

Kieran turned his back on her and bolted towards the nearest docking port. He didn't check to see if she and the boy were following him. He had an awful feeling that he wasn't running from them or the self-destruct, but from the fact that he had, yet again, done something to endanger his position in the Agency.

Would they finally kick him out? Toss him headfirst into a galaxy he'd never had to navigate alone?

He had been given to GLEA's Orphanage Division as a baby. He'd never known any other life. But maybe it would be safer for the Agency if he was gone—and safer for everyone in the galaxy if he wasn't constantly being sent out on missions.

Who am I kidding? he thought as he ran. *They didn't even punish me for that massacre on Fintaz.*

They should have killed me.

ILBB ORBITED two of three suns in a trinary star system, but fortunately the celestial giants weren't close enough to kill anyone who stepped outside. It was, however, starking bright on the planet's surface. Sunlight here could last two to three Old Earth days. There were rumours of vegetation hidden amongst the rocks that dotted the desert, but Ami had never seen anything growing on Ilbb and nor had she bothered to scour the blazing dunes for any evidence to the contrary.

Ami shaded her eyes with a hand as she scanned the area between her designated landing pad (it was a patch of sand marked by four steel posts blasted into the bedrock by Xan Jones, so it might as well be called a landing pad) and the squat building that belonged to the Chippers. No thugs in sight. Good.

Behind her, Avurn was leading Ilbb's newest residents out of the *Free Ride* and towards the bar, where freshly minted IDs were waiting, courtesy of Tends—Carton City's best forger and only bartender.

Tends was a large, bronze-skinned human who considered

everyone they met to be their children, though it was said they already had a brood somewhere out there in the galaxy. Their white-streaked hair spoke of some life experience, but Ami didn't know if any of it involved children. She'd never looked Tends up on the Galactic Database—or anyone else in Carton City for that matter. Most of them used aliases. Even Xan Jones and his pal Denton Dashing were guilty of doing it.

Both Xan and Denton had been operating as warlords when the Chippers caught up with them. They had become GLEA's very first contractors over a decade ago (they were paid, but not very well) and were charged with helping Ilbb's minuscule Chipper population protect Carton City from the desert tribes who lived beyond the dunes.

It wasn't unheard of for GLEA to need extra firepower and bodies on the beat, particularly as there were more planets than Chipper outposts. And not everyone wanted to sign up to the Agency, exchanging their freedom for a purple jumpsuit and a life governed by rules. The Chippers had chosen to bulk out their numbers with reformed criminals.

Xan and Denton had been a very successful trial run, it seemed.

Carton City had come under attack more than once during their tenure on Ilbb. However, if Ami's friend Ralcha, who lived in a tribe outside the city, was to be believed, Xan and Denton had ignited the most recent clash. With permission from their Chipper employers, they had squashed several shelters out in the desert by landing Xan's ship on top of them. The residents of those shelters had not been amused and had banded together, using their Desine-gifted abilities to bury several of Carton City's buildings beneath giant piles of sand.

Privately, Ami thought the protracted conflict stemmed from the fact that the tribes worshipped the desert god, who was definitely not GLEA's preferred deity.

Never mind that the Desine, like the many other sub-level gods across the galaxy, was one of the Creator God's immortal children, created for the sole purpose of helping their father look after his creation. Humans, mostly. They had multiplied to the point of becoming the galaxy's most prevalent species.

Avurn waved at Ami from the entrance of the bar before vanishing inside. When planetside, Avurn was unofficially employed by Tends and paid by the hour.

If the Chippers had ever bothered to visit the bar, they'd have realised that the boy was serving booze. Not that they could do anything about it. Ilbb lacked a governing body. The uncontested Chipper presence on the planet granted it some basic laws, such as murder being illegal, but nothing complicated—that is, nothing about underage employment or underage supply of alcohol.

'Carton City,' Ami said, waving her hand around. 'Pretty obvious how it got the name.'

The two Chippers—Private Kieran Krendasta and Second Lieutenant Pina-Sai, as Ami had discovered after some hasty introductions—had followed her down the boarding ramp of her ship (it sloped over the lascannon, once it managed to groan its way open).

'It does look like someone dropped metal cartons wherever they felt like it,' Kieran said, nodding at the town.

'And someone bothered to add street signs!' Pina-Sai said, then brayed with laughter. The distinctly inhuman noise (*Probably got some Lentarian heritage,* Ami thought) sounded way too similar to the alarms on Julius' ship. 'Thug Alley? Denton's Driveway? How can anyone tell the difference between a driveway and a street—it's all just sand.'

'I don't know the story behind Thug Alley, but Denton's Driveway is a more recent addition.' Ami grinned. 'It's a long-running joke. Denton can't afford a hovercar or a place to stash it, but he has a couch to crash on thanks to Allen Smith, our local e-paper reporter. Allen runs *The Carton City e-Post*.'

Allen had tried his luck at being a mediaist, one of the flashy Webcasters who glitzed up the news until it was practically fiction, but he'd landed himself in hot water by revealing intimate information about a government official on a world where it was illegal to do so. Since then, he'd turned to writing only, hiding his face and using an assumed name ('Smith' was a common family name on Ilbb—there were so many of them one could be forgiven for thinking they were related). This was standard practice for e-paper reporters, who preferred a degree of anonymity.

Ami supposed it was a lot easier to investigate shady dealings when no one knew what you looked like.

'You have a dedicated e-paper?' Kieran's lips curved, a smile reluctantly replacing his grimace. 'What in the Creator God's name could he possibly have to write about?'

Ami shrugged. 'Allen's inventive. I can't wait to read his report on Julius nearly blasting me and mine to bits. Maybe I should offer myself as a reliable source.'

'Keep your silence, Captain N'uni, for this is now a GLEA matter,' Pina-Sai said firmly. 'You can return to your ship. Your services are not presently required and if they are we will send word for you.'

With that, Pina stalked off towards the outpost, the settlement's only stone-based building. Already the local Chippers were spilling out to welcome him. They were a singular swarm of purple, somehow even more blinding than the blistering sand that filled the street. Above them, the vidscreen bearing GLEA's symbol (five gold slashes on a purple background) flickered unsteadily.

Ami grabbed Kieran's arm before he could follow his superior. 'You won't get in trouble, will you? For supposedly killing Julius?'

Kieran's expression became hooded. 'I don't care what they do to me, so long as I get to leave this world quickly.'

'Is Carton City that bad?' Ami laughed.

Kieran opened his mouth, then closed it. He looked lost, vulnerable, and deeply afraid. Ami's hand left his bicep and rose to his face, her palm hovering beside his cheek. Her fingers grazed the skin concealing the chip that enabled Kieran to perform his tricks. His eyelids shuddered but never quite met.

Ami had no idea why she was touching him. Or why he was allowing her to do it.

'Are you okay?' she asked softly.

Kieran blinked—then jerked away from her. He shot a frantic look over at the other Chippers, but they were busily talking to Pina, the taller man bending over as he explained the reason for his delayed arrival.

Kieran kept his voice low, but each word struck Ami as though he was shouting. 'Okay? I'll never be okay. No matter how many lives I save, it still doesn't make up for the ones I took.'

'But you're in the service of the Creator God, right? If it's for the good of the galaxy...' Ami trailed off when she saw the unshed tears shining in his startling blue eyes.

'Killing is a last resort, we must always attempt to capture a criminal first,' Kieran murmured. 'I have killed thirty people in as many seconds. My superiors said that I couldn't possibly have done it, since my power levels are so low. They absolved me. But I'm still a murderer.' He shook his head. 'I have to go. It was nice meeting you, Captain N'uni.'

Ami was unable to stop herself calling after him, 'If you have time later, come find me at the bar. I'll shout you a drink. And lend you a pair of ears. I'll listen.'

He paused, but didn't turn around. 'I may hold you to that.'

Ami watched him walk away and resisted the urge wistfully. It had been three Old Earth years since her last romp in bed (she'd been twenty, old enough to know better than to sleep with *that* particular man) and stark, that uniform looked good on him.

Physical attractiveness aside...haunted was exactly her type. She wanted to kiss away Kieran's pain and put him back together.

No one had done that for her. But she could do that for him.

Ami knew there was no point in hoping that something serious would develop between them. GLEA preferred their agents to marry and reproduce with fellow agents, since those who were born into the Agency were more likely to conform to its ways. Putting your hand up for the duty of breeding was the fastest way to get promoted.

Kieran was still only a private, which meant he hadn't gone through officer training or grabbed himself an enlisted rank. He had a long way to go inside the Agency.

But he wouldn't get very far if something kept holding him back.

Ami raised her gaze to the clear sky above her. 'Creator God, I don't think your agents are looking after Kieran Krendasta very well. If you won't make them do it, then I swear to you I will. Just try and stop me.'

Ami knew it was dangerous to provoke a god. Some of the sub-level gods were downright vindictive if you called upon them (Oceania, the water god, was to be avoided at all costs), but she'd never heard of the Creator God doing or saying anything to his creation. Not since he'd left the galaxy in the care of his godly children.

Made her wonder why GLEA even bothered to serve him.

'Not going to stop me, huh,' Ami mused as she headed for the bar. 'Didn't think so.'

FOUR

The whispers had started again.

Kieran did his best to ignore them, but that meant having to focus on every single syllable being uttered inside the outpost's meeting room. He gave his report, so did Pina, and then the five resident Chippers (none of them were wholly human, which made Kieran feel, for the first time in his career, like the odd one out) began passing judgement from their chairs, which were arranged in a pentagram.

Kieran eyed them. They all had higher ranks than him, with the authority to oversee two hundred agents between them, but they must have pissed someone off to get posted to Ilbb.

'Ah yesss, do not worry about the ship,' Major Nexis Yetz said, waving a long green appendage that Kieran initially mistook for a stick instead of an arm. He wasn't overly familiar with Xifisa, the genderless insectoid species to which Yetz belonged, and hadn't even met one before today. He also had no idea where Yetz's chip had been inserted, because there was no telltale bump anywhere on zir head.

'It was an old model,' Yetz continued. 'It would have been too expensssive to repair—and it is perfectly reasonable that you had to deal with the pirate in that manner.'

'Reasonable? Is it, though?' demanded a dark-skinned woman, the spongy purple tentacles on her scalp weaving this way and that. Her height would match Pina's if she was standing, which was impressive.

Kieran breathed a sigh of relief.

Finally, *finally*, he was going to get what he deserved.

'Do not interrupt me, Lieutenant Ryn,' Yetz said and tilted zir pyramid-shaped head at a disapproving angle. A human-like gesture, no doubt used to set zir audience at ease. 'Thisss is a ssspecial cassse.'

'Oh, because he's a delicate, misunderstood young man who *hasn't* spent years immersed in our ways?' the lieutenant demanded, crossing her arms.

Kieran had heard about her from Pina, who considered Sies Ryn a fair agent, even though she was standoffish to most people. Her uniform contained two gold strokes on one shoulder and a separate stroke on the other; she was a first lieutenant, a single rank above Pina. Her midnight-black boots were so polished Kieran could see his reflection in them.

'Your sssarcasm is not welcome here, Lieutenant,' Yetz said. 'Kieran has indeed ssspent years in ssservice to the Creator God. We mussst ressspect that. He was given to the Orphanage Division as a baby and has no family. There would be no placcce for him in the galaxy if we ssstruck him from the Agencccy.'

'Kieran still hasn't recovered from what happened on Fintaz,' Pina added, deftly ignoring Ryn's fierce expression. 'That is the root cause of his defiance. He needs professional therapy, as I can only do so much to help him. Though I will keep trying, regardless.'

Kieran threw a frown in his direction. Pina raised his

eyebrows in response, as though daring Kieran to challenge him. He had spent an entire Old Earth year trying to convince Kieran that Fintaz could be left in the past—but Pina wasn't exactly the best role model. If those benders of his (and the slurred monologues that accompanied them) were any indication, Pina had trouble moving on from the things he'd tried to leave in his own past.

Pina had improved, even thrived, during their partnership. He hadn't touched any alcohol in months. Kieran wished he could have made some progress of his own.

I'm sorry, Pina, I'm a lost cause, Kieran thought.

He stepped forward. 'Major Yetz. I killed a man. I should have incapacitated him instead. You are well within your rights to take out my chip and strike me from the Agency. Being a member of the Orphanage Division does not give me special protections.'

'Kieran!' Pina sighed gustily. 'Major Yetz, please. Do not let him persuade you.'

'Listen to Krendasta, sir,' Ryn countered. She was nodding. 'He knows he isn't passing muster among us. He's desperate for us to toss him out, since he is too much of a coward to leave of his own accord.'

Kieran stiffened.

Pina turned to her, his gaze beseeching. 'Sies—Lieutenant Ryn, we should not discard Kieran when he needs us the most.' He gestured at Kieran. 'He is in pain. Can you not see it? Can you not sense it in his energy? If he is forced to leave GLEA, he will no longer be supported or cared for. He needs me—he needs the guiding hand of the Agency.'

Ryn huffed. 'The Agency can't afford to keep liabilities like him on the payroll.'

'Enough!' Yetz ordered. 'I have sssent word up the chain of command and have been informed that the Head General himssself will have the final sssay in thisss matter. Ah, there is his responssse now.'

The console on the side of Yetz's chair had started flashing. Ze flicked one stick-like arm across a sensor and text immediately scrolled across the techpad that was suspended over zir lap with the help of protruding cables. Kieran nearly laughed. Head General Zareth Sins, the current elected leader of GLEA, couldn't have deemed Kieran that important if he wasn't even bothering to announce his fate via a verbal communicators link.

The Head General was the only being who could terminate any agent, no questions asked. His decisions were always quick. Always for the benefit of the Agency.

Please, Kieran begged silently. *Please, please, please.*

An insidious voice crept into his mind, louder and harsher than all the other whispers. *Yes, yes, let them kick you out. Then you can come back to me.*

Kieran gritted his teeth. *Shut up.*

The whisperer did not obey him. *I am the only one who under-stands you. The only one who can help you.*

I won't listen to you, Kieran snapped, hoping against hope that he was arguing with himself. Any other explanation was too fright-ening to contemplate. *You're not real.*

Then who stopped you killing every single living being on Fintaz? the whisperer challenged.

Kieran started when he felt Pina's gentle touch on his shoulder. Pina always seemed to know when Kieran needed—and wanted—some reassurance, no matter what he said out loud.

Kieran nodded his thanks. Pina smiled encouragingly in return.

Yetz lifted zir triangular head from the techpad. 'The Agencccy will not lose one of itsss own today. As we do not have the budget for a replacccement ssstarship, it has been ruled that Private Kieran

Krendasssta and Sssecond Lieutenant Pina-Sssai will join our outpossst. They remain partnered, for now.'

'No, no, no!' Kieran burst out. '*Fuck!*'

'Kieran, calm yourself,' Pina murmured. 'This outpost is under-staffed. What if Kratis' underlings come to this system, seeking retribution? It will be alright, Kieran. Fintaz was not your fault. You are not endangering anyone by being here.'

'Yes, I starking am!' Kieran cried, shrugging off Pina's hand and staring wildly at the others. They would not survive the inevitable carnage. He could already see them reduced to their bones and exoskeletons, completely stripped of blood, skin, and scales. The image was so vivid in his mind he was sure it was one of the visions of the future he was so often cursed with, not just a fearful imagining. 'You don't get it! None of you get it! You're all going to die!'

Ryn's eyes narrowed. 'Terminate the tantrum, Private. You are still an agent of GLEA. Act like it.'

His heartbeat was loud and frantic in his ears, a stampede that threatened to trample him. But once more Pina laid a hand on his shoulder—and Kieran found that he could breathe deeply again. How did Pina manage it? Always presenting himself as calm and in control, even when he wasn't. It was a valuable smokescreen that had no doubt kept Pina from being thrown out of GLEA on more than one occasion before he gave up drinking.

'My fellow agents,' Kieran began, grateful that Pina was at his side. 'The last time I was in a desert climate, people died. Because of me.'

'Nonsenssse,' Yetz said. 'It was those desert-powered sssand fleasss. They attacked you and killed themselvesss in the processss. Foolish humansss.'

'That's not what happened,' Kieran gritted out.

'Kieran, no agent can create or control a sandstorm, you know this,' Pina said in that patient, unhurried tone of his.

'I thought you believed me!' Kieran snapped, jerking away and heading for the main access corridor.

Pina chased him down, only catching up to Kieran after the exterior door had already opened. Ilbb's eternally arid air began to fill the atrium, a confronting contrast to the cold, sterile climate that was strictly maintained inside all of GLEA's buildings.

Pina adopted a whisper, even though the other agents couldn't hear him from the meeting room. 'I do believe you, Kieran. I believe you have visions of the future. I believe that the Creator God would grant such visions, but never a power so destructive and violent. It wasn't you! It wasn't. I can't...I can't fathom that you would be able to...'

'You can't fathom it because that would mean you've been trying to save a murderer,' Kieran said darkly. 'That you befriended a monster.'

'Kieran, wait—'

Kieran stormed out of the outpost, his fists clenched at his sides. He didn't look back.

AMI WATCHED Avurn carefully and wondered how she'd never noticed it before.

One time, his serving tray should have gone flying when a pair of the local thugs tripped him. But it skated through the air undisturbed before returning to his steady grip. Avurn bounced into the back room, grinning to himself.

Another time, he staved off a drunk and weaving Denton, whose heavy bulk should have crashed into the boy. Avurn threw up a hand, his teeth gnawing into his lip. Denton appeared to hit a pane of invisible plexiglass before toppling backwards. Avurn, having avoided the fate of being transformed into a human pancake, dusted himself off and stepped over the body in his way, ignoring Denton's request for a fresh tankard.

But despite his stolen powers, Avurn still managed to get himself into trouble with Tends, who had noticed that some coin-chips from the register were missing. Ami quickly doused her smile when Avurn sprinted towards the exit, chased by both his incensed sister, Jensa, and an exasperated Tends.

'Who'll serve us now?' wailed Denton, after he'd managed to crawl into a booth that Xan had scored earlier. Denton's copper beard was slick with alcohol.

Xan's expression was perfectly deadpan. 'We could always ask Petria to do it.'

'Stark that!' Denton exclaimed in horror, standing up and nearly falling back down again the moment he was upright. 'I'm gone! Don't you dare tell Petria I was here.'

He tore out of the bar. Ami had tried to warn Petria, who she'd saved from slavers on a previous run about two years ago, that Carton City's limited supply of decent men could result in poor decisions. But Petria had taken a liking to Denton Dashing. He really wasn't worth the effort and was terrible in bed, but Ami hadn't said any of this out loud because that would mean admitting to making that mistake herself.

Denton—and the rest of Carton City—had assumed that Petria would move on, given enough time. But she hadn't.

During a very public spat in the bar one night, Petria had accused Denton of returning her feelings. He hadn't denied it. Because he couldn't. Seemingly, this personal revelation of his had terrified him so much that he'd been running away from Petria ever since.

Petria let him run. She seemed sure that Denton's love would eventually overwhelm his fear, that he just needed space. And besides which, she had plenty of things to occupy herself with in the meantime. Petria had made many friends among Carton City's unsavoury characters and was in the midst of expanding the import/export business she'd created.

If Denton knew she was the reason the price of his favourite beers had gone up, he didn't let on.

'Sorry,' Ami said to her companion. 'You have my full attention now. This place is like a free drama vidshow. I don't like to miss a single episode.'

Chief Ralcha, who looked no different from most humans in Carton City, shrugged. 'I am glad I have no idea what you're talking about. My people live a simple life in the deserts, worshipping the Desine, using the dunes for shade in our search for sustenance, finding our entertainment in our surroundings.'

Ami eyed Ralcha. She was sure he was having her on again.

There were two empty glasses on the table in their booth. Neither of them had been touched by the Yabul chief, who disliked the sour pom juice Ami favoured and had instead been drinking the water in the horn-shaped flask hanging from a strap on his shoulder. His tattered brown cloak and crude wooden spear made him look a lot like the sort of person Xan and Denton were paid to keep away from Carton City. Xan had given Ralcha an intense stare earlier, but he'd stopped Denton from causing trouble because he knew that Ami and Ralcha had an arrangement.

Ami could see where Ralcha's cloak had fallen open, revealing trendy black leathers that were so shiny and new they had to be imported from elsewhere. Ilbb's native fauna had more colourful hides than that. Ami was also pretty sure the spear was meant to lull his enemies into a false sense of security, since his belt carried more than one lasgun. Recent, deadly models.

Ralcha was quite adept at pretending to be a primitive tribesman when it suited him.

Ami slid a finger around the rim of one of the empty glasses, frowning. 'This Desine of yours—he's not going to get mad at me for dumping new people into his territory? People who don't worship him?'

Ralcha shrugged. 'He would have made his feelings clear by now if he did not like it.'

'Are you sure?' Ami demanded. 'I'm responsible for the lives of the people I save. I don't want to piss off some sub-level god who might hurt them to get at me. And I've heard your Desine has a nasty streak.'

Over half the beings she'd rescued had opted for an obscure life among the desert tribes on Ilbb, which was a good deal safer than wandering back out into the galaxy with the same faces that could be recognised by the slavers who supposedly 'owned' them. New IDs could only do so much. Most people couldn't afford the reconstructive surgery needed to alter their appearance.

Stark, Ami could barely afford to pay Tends for those IDs in the first place.

Some of the folk who walked off the *Free Ride* wanted to take their chances with the multitude of planets out there and Ami couldn't blame them—Ralcha seemed happy enough, but he was fourth-generation Ilbban and fifteenth-generation Desine worshipper. He didn't know anything else.

Though, judging by his knowledge of lasball tournaments, he was no stranger to the Web.

Ralcha patted Ami's arm. 'The Desine watches over everyone inside his domain, even those who were not born here. And any slaver who comes to Ilbb will certainly meet their match in the Yabul.'

'You'd need a pretty good anti-bombardment shield to repel the lascannons on a starship,' Ami said.

Ralcha blinked slowly in response, as if he hadn't heard her. It was tempting to repeat herself, but she knew he wouldn't confirm or deny her suspicions. He never did.

Ami paused, looking down at his hands. Strange, she'd known Ralcha for four years (ever since she'd encountered him quietly returning Xan, who was drunk and had passed out somewhere in the desert) and yet it was only now that she noticed the matching faded lines that ran diagonally across his palms.

Ralcha smiled when he noticed the direction of her gaze. 'My binding scars. My bound-one—what you City Dwellers call a spouse—and I shared blood before one of our priests. It is a marriage custom among my people, but I will gladly perform it for you myself when you find the one who steals your heart.'

Ami's own smile was wistful, sad. 'Never going to happen.'

'My offer stands, regardless,' Ralcha said, a twinkle in his golden eyes. 'I'll send someone to your bartender friend tomorrow, to guide anyone who wishes to join my tribe. You may come to the Yabul any time you choose, Ami. I would be happy to welcome you as one of us.'

Ami swallowed. She couldn't accept his kind gesture.

Gods, she wanted to. But what she had done...could never be forgiven. She didn't deserve a family.

When Ralcha stood, he was immediately the recipient of lewd insults from the bar's unsavoury denizens. Ralcha bowed towards them and flicked his fingers, as though bidding them farewell. Piles of sand leapt off the unswept floor, skittering into the tankards his opponents were clutching. Soon there was more sand than alcohol in their mouths. They shoved their tankards away, complaining about their hard-earned coin-chips being wasted on grit instead of grog.

'No refunds!' Tends said, re-entering the bar with a cowed Avurn at their side. 'You lot were stupid enough to anger a Desine worshipper. In fact, I should be charging you for the sand since it came off *my* floor!'

Chuckling, Ralcha made for the exit and quickly had to step aside to allow someone else to storm in.

Kieran Krendasta's blue eyes were turbulent when they landed on Ami. She nodded her head slightly and he came to her, filling the side of the booth that Ralcha had just vacated.

'What can get me blackout drunk the fastest?' he demanded.

Ami looked over at the bar and saw that Avurn was back at work, watched closely by Tends. She lifted a hand. 'Av! Get me a Minty Madness over here.' She shuddered. 'Xan is obsessed with them. Personally, I find them too sweet.'

Kieran wrapped his hands around the tankard as soon as it arrived—and then knocked back the drink in one go.

Ami stared at him, mouth hanging open. 'Uh. You're supposed to savour those.'

He blinked rapidly. 'Wow. I'm already light-headed.'

'I see the purple folk didn't kick you out,' Ami noted, using one of her cups to indicate his temple. 'Probably should lay off the booze, though. I've heard the chip malfunctions when you've got too much alcohol in your system.'

Kieran set his tankard down, frowning. 'I have spent the past year trying to convince the Agency that I did something awful, but they refuse to punish me. Instead, they insist that I need more understanding, more allowances, more Pina-Sai following me around and whispering words of encouragement. It might have worked, if I'd continued to avoid deserts. But now I'm stuck here. Even Pina doesn't believe me. I thought he did. I thought...'

Kieran shook his head in agitation. His hair, long enough to smother her fingers if she ran them over his scalp, bounced with the movement. Ami clenched her hands together to stop herself following through with that oddly innocent fantasy.

'Talk to me,' Ami said. 'You can't frighten me off, Kieran. I've seen, heard, and even *done* some of the worst things anyone can possibly do in this galaxy.'

They locked gazes. She thought he would refuse to unburden himself, but he must have sensed how sincere she was with that chip of his.

Kieran released a long, tortured breath. 'Alright. But I'll need another one of these drinks.'

'Av!' Ami called.

Once his request had been accommodated and the tankard stood empty in front of him, Kieran leaned across the table, his blue eyes like lasbolts, effectively nailing her to the seat. 'One Old Earth year ago, I was sent to Fintaz. It's mostly covered in tundra, but there's also a large desert—Ilbb reminds me of it, actually. Same beige-coloured sand. Same heat. Same...*whispers.*'

A shudder passed through him.

'The local authorities requested GLEA's help,' Kieran continued, his voice dropping to a murmur as he slipped into his memories. 'Someone was targeting worshippers of the Creator God, entering their houses and stealing priceless items—stuff that was meant to be auctioned off, with the proceeds being donated to the Agency.' Kieran laughed shortly. 'Of course, GLEA wasn't going to sit by and let that happen.'

'Of course not,' Ami said dryly. 'Have to make sure your wealthiest donors still have that wealth to donate.'

'Exactly,' Kieran agreed. 'So I was sent along with a team. We staked out several houses and the one I was watching turned out to be the target. I chased the thief into the desert and was ambushed. Turns out it was an entire syndicate responsible for the thefts and I'd just landed in their nest.'

He hesitated, so Ami gently prompted him, 'But it wasn't something you couldn't handle, I'm guessing, since you're alive to tell the tale.'

Kieran grimaced. 'My abilities...are not particularly impressive. And even the strongest agent can only deflect so many lasbolts.'

'Sounds like you should have had backup,' Ami commented.

'It was foolish of me to proceed alone.' He sighed. 'Especially since I...I knew I would be ambushed.'

'Wait, you went and got ambushed for the fun of it? Some Chipper you are.'

'No, listen!' Kieran said, frustration lacing his words. 'Agents can't see the future. The chip only lets us touch the energy of things that already exist, not what *might* exist. But I had a vision that showed me there were several people involved and that they would attack me if I followed the thief back to their base. I told the other agents that we should stay together, stake out the house I was assigned to as a team. They said I was just nervous. Jumpy. There was only ever one thief caught on the security vidcams. They made me doubt myself. Made me think I was crazy.'

'That's not the first time you had a vision and no one believed you,' Ami guessed.

Kieran nodded. 'Correct. But the repercussions were never this severe. Anyway, there I was, surrounded by lasguns in the desert...'

FIVE

The nearest star was high in the sky, a blistering ball of heat and fury. His uniform clung to his back, glued there by perspiration. Kieran swallowed and his tongue grated over the roof of his parched mouth. Both of his temples, not just the one housing the chip, throbbed angrily.

Starking wyverns! Kieran thought. *Why did I listen to my fellow agents? Why did I believe them instead of my own instincts!?*

A human male emerged from the pack, decked out in a silver cape and matching hat—the clear leader of this set-up. He chortled when one of his minions handed him Kieran's personal shielding device and lasgun, both outdated and laughably small. 'You Chippers have spent centuries trying to reach the Creator God with those fancy chips of yours. You've never heard so much as a peep. No one has, not since he fucked off and left us at the mercy of his godly children. But I suppose now you'll finally get to find out if he's really been paying attention to you.'

Wind streaked past Kieran's face, scrubbing sand over sweat.

They hadn't cuffed him. There was no point. An agent funnelled their power through their hands, but any forcefield he created wouldn't last long against that many lasguns. A more powerful Chipper might hold out for fifteen minutes. He'd be lucky to manage five. And he doubted they'd agree to give him back his personal shielding device.

White-hot panic flooded his veins. He needed a weapon. He needed...*something*.

He reached out in desperation, but he didn't expect an answer.

Countless whispers, sharp as knives, found his mind and burrowed into it, scraping and stinging as they went. Kieran shook his head from side to side, but they persisted. Perhaps he truly was crazy. First the visions. Now these voices.

He watched the sea of lasguns rise around him.

This was it, then.

Kieran held up his hands, conducting the universe's energy into a small shield. He would gladly have welcomed the company of those 'starking wyverns', to strengthen and expand his forcefield. But they had derided him. And now he was going to die because of them.

No, let us help, the whispers said. *Use us. It is your right. We can give you the power to destroy your enemies.*

Creator God help him, he had no other option.

He gave in to the delusion.

The criminals laughed at him, the foolish agent who had gone looking for trouble without any backup. They didn't see the dark shadow smothering the dunes behind them, thrown down by an immense sandstorm the size of a city, brewing to its full height within seconds. But they heard the roar. A sound that struck fear into their hearts—and Kieran's.

They turned and shouted, pointing up at the storm. Kieran

could do nothing. He had surrendered himself to the whispers. They had claimed him. He could only stand there and let the surge of power blast through him.

The leader bellowed orders and frantic voices flew back at him in response, every coherent word lost to the violent winds. Maybe the thieves were trying to retreat.

But they were too late.

The sandstorm descended, howling as it came in for the kill. Kieran fell to his knees and his whole body arched, his ensuing scream swallowed by the funnel of sand that swirled around him. His hands were wrenched towards the sky, if one remained overhead at all, and he was bent so far back he was sure his head must nearly be resting on the ground.

Bleached bones danced around him. Jaws detached from the thieves' skulls, jerking up and down as though the dead men were silently laughing at Kieran.

This couldn't be happening. This couldn't be real.

And this raw, intense power...it filled him to the brim and then kept going, until he thought he might explode and pass into the afterlife. The Creator God should have received his soul and condemned it. He should not have escaped justice. He should have died. But he didn't.

The murderer still lived.

Kieran screamed again and the storm screamed with him.

Fury ruled him now. He'd been pushed to the edge long before he'd fallen from it. His fellow agents hadn't listened to him, hadn't believed him when he'd needed their belief the most. But what had he expected? To them, he was an embarrassment, a delusional screwup. Nothing he did ever seemed to change their minds. He was so tired of trying.

Sand skittered along the streets in the nearby city, finding and reporting back to him the exact locations of the other agents on Fintaz. They were hunched down in the gardens of grand houses, waiting for a thief that would never come.

They were mere insects, waiting to be crushed beneath his boots.

I want them to pay for this, he thought.

We understand, said the whispers. *We will destroy them all. Every living being inside the city.*

Horror and clarity struck Kieran, a double punch. The storm had already killed thirty beings and was intent on ripping the skin from thousands more.

'STOP!' he cried.

We are doing this for you, the whispers insisted and they continued with their mission, heedless of his pleas.

He felt the storm shift and grow, a seething mass hungry for revenge, bloated from the emotions he had unwittingly fed it. He held up his hands, but the reins of power slithered out of his grasp. Kieran collapsed onto his back and rolled over, trying to get onto all fours, but exhaustion flattened him in moments. He tasted sand and desperation on his lips. This storm was his doing. His responsibility. He had to stop it.

First, he called for the Creator God.

And heard only silence.

But then Kieran found a silvery cord inside his mind, one so thin and frayed he dared not hold onto it too tightly as he rowed himself towards the end, where he knew—*he knew*—there was someone who could put an end to the carnage.

Help me, help me! he cried.

How did you find me? a voice roared back at him, frantic, confused—and delighted. *No, don't answer. I do not care how, only that you did. What is wrong? Why are you so afraid?*

Kieran wavered. But only for a moment. *Please. Please stop the storm. I can't let it kill them.*

He lost consciousness before his request could be granted.

Kieran woke hours later, when GLEA's search party found him surrounded by blood-stained sand and the bones of his enemies. There was no one else to take the blame. His fellow agents wiped clean their horrified expressions with orchestrated concern, as important to their image as their starched violet uniforms. Kieran only had the bottom half of his jumpsuit left and struggled to hold it up to his waist as he clambered to his feet.

He hurriedly checked himself over. Still as pale as ever, his skin bare of burns or blisters. A miracle from the Creator God, the other agents said, that he had survived an attack from sand fleas, the scum who bowed to an inferior god.

'Don't you get it?' Kieran shouted. 'I killed them! I killed them!'

'The chip does not allow you to create sandstorms,' one of his colleagues reminded him. 'And you have been monitored for sand flea powers ever since you were an infant, as we do with all those who have questionable origins. You've never shown any signs of such heritage or you would not still be among us. It wasn't you.'

Kieran's throat was still raw from screaming, but he kept arguing, his anger fuelling each and every word. 'There was no one else here. No one else who could have done it. I'm telling you—I pulled down a storm and killed them! Just starking believe me for once!'

'Is it possible?' another agent wondered. 'To trap a storm inside a forcefield and move it?'

'Yes, it starking is! It must be!' Kieran cried, gesturing around. 'Look what I did—that's proof enough!'

'Kieran, you've been through a terrible ordeal...'

'You are not powerful enough to do something like this...'

'By the Creator God's will you have survived...'

'It must have been one of those sand fleas trying to defend themselves and they lost control of their powers...'

And now Kieran could also hear Pina's voice in his memories, though they had not been partnered then and nor had they met. 'It wasn't you! It wasn't.'

Kieran knew otherwise.

SIX

'I don't hear the whispers in space,' Kieran said, resting the rim of his tankard against his bottom lip. 'But now that I'm posted to Ilbb, they're...God, I'm stuck here. And people are going to die. There will be nothing left of this place—no structure left standing, no one left alive. Except me.'

He stared down into his drink, surprise streaking across his features.

'What?' Ami asked, wondering how he'd gone from warning her about the imminent destruction of Carton City to looking as though he'd suddenly found the Creator God at the bottom of his tankard.

He laughed. 'The voices. They're growing quieter, even the loudest of them. No wonder Pina used to drink so much.'

Ami reached across the table and tugged the tankard away from him. 'Planning to drown out the voices along with your sorrows? Not a good idea. You haven't even got to the hangover yet. Minty Madnesses are *brutal.*'

'Wouldn't you do the same?' Kieran asked. 'If you'd killed thirty people by calling down a storm to rip the skin from their bones?'

Ami cupped her hands around the tankard, her dry palms greedily absorbing the droplets condensing on the metallic surface. 'I've done stuff that haunts me, but I have enough trouble paying for fuel, let alone a crutch. Besides, wallowing? Nope. Running from my problems is more my style.'

Kieran rubbed a thumb over the skin concealing his chip. 'Do you have another trip planned soon?'

Ami pursed her lips. She felt compelled to help him, but she wasn't sure she knew how. 'Why, you want to jump aboard? I can't stop you killing people with a freak sandstorm—and I won't lie and say the possibility doesn't terrify me.'

'Good,' Kieran said. 'It should terrify you. But as I said, I don't hear the voices in space.'

'I can try to avoid worlds with deserts, but I frequently stop in here—it's my homeport,' Ami told him. She grinned. 'Plus, Jensa would kill me if I didn't bring Av back once in a while.'

'Major Yetz would probably appreciate it if I continued to report in,' Kieran mused.

'Will ze even let you leave Ilbb?'

'We'll find out tomorrow,' he said and stood, heading directly for Xan's booth, where the contractor had already amassed an impressive collection of empty tankards.

Ami sighed. *Good one, Ami. Let the hot Chipper with the scary powers get hooked on booze.*

Huh. It hadn't occurred to her *not* to believe him about said scary powers.

Maybe it was because she saw that same pain in her own eyes whenever she looked at a reflective surface for too long.

A serving tray hit her table and she looked up into Avurn's thunderous expression. He snapped, 'You cannot bring a Chipper on board! He'll rat me out the nanosecond he catches a glimpse of my chip!'

'Av, he told his people he killed Julius,' Ami said. 'I hardly call that ratting you out.'

Avurn crossed his arms over his pristine apron. 'And what if he discovers *your* ghastly secret?'

'Get back to work, kid!' Tends called from the bar, saving Ami from having to answer her crewmate.

———

PINA-SAI WAVED his hand over the sensor pad on the wall and light blasted into the cells. The human male known as Xan Jones cursed and clawed his slick black hair over his face, shielding his eyes from the worst of the glare. Pina could muster no sympathy for him. The cells in the outpost were comfy by galactic standards; they even had beds. Pina had ended up in far worse places, before *and* during his time with GLEA. He had a much more colourful past than Kieran could possibly imagine.

'I am told you usually consort with Denton Dashing, your fellow contractor,' Pina noted, then jerked his head at the cell's other occupant, a crumpled mess of violet fabric and greenish vomit. 'I see that Private Krendasta took Dashing's place in tonight's misadventures. This vice of yours isn't something you should be passing onto others.'

Xan's scowl was so wide it escaped his matted hair. 'Vice? Now listen, Lieutenant. The local crims on this world respect me because of my high tolerance. They don't do any shady shit when I offer to drink with them—and if I have to sacrifice my health and my wife's good opinion to keep them from committing yet another crime, you bet I will! At least it's better than your tactics. Ranting on and on about the Creator God does stark all and you know it!'

'Alcohol interferes with our chips and nullifies our abilities,'

Pina explained calmly. 'I am concerned. I do not want Kieran's career to suffer.'

Xan chortled. 'Ha! I think it's pretty obvious his career's already in the shitter. Why else would Kieran agree to go tearing off into space with Ami? And that was before he got drunk, by the way.'

'He did *what?*'

'It's the starking truth, Creator God as my witness,' Xan said, holding a hand to his heart.

Pina closed his eyes for a moment, swallowing the bevy of curses he wanted to unleash. 'Running from his problems, then drinking them away when they catch up to him.'

'Yeah, wonder where he learned to do that?' Xan mused. 'Don't think it's something you Chippers teach at them temples of yours on Gerasnin.'

'I am not supposed to be in here,' Pina said tightly. He indicated Kieran's crumpled form. 'Look after him, Jones. He'll feel awful when he wakes up and he will need a decent dose of sympathy—something I cannot give him when our superiors are watching.'

'Kieran's been under my protection since he touched down on this planet,' Xan said solemnly. 'I swear it. And now that he's managed to keep up with me on a bender, he'll be my friend 'til the end of time. Lots of perks with that.'

'I can imagine,' Pina said, suppressing a shudder.

After dawdling his way through the outpost, which was quiet and filled with the gentle energy of slumbering agents, Pina stepped outside into a frigid embrace. He did not roll down the sleeves of his jumpsuit, merely studied the stars. True night didn't always occur here on Ilbb and rarely during the correct Old Earth hours, as the three suns infrequently coordinated with each other, so Pina intended to enjoy the pleasant darkness while he could.

His sigh steamed into the air. 'Stark it, Kieran. I am not supposed to be your role model.'

For a year, they'd been paired together. A very deliberate decision by their superiors. Even though they hadn't explained their reasoning, it was obvious to Pina. Kieran Krendasta had needed a stabilising influence—and Pina-Sai had needed someone he could look after, someone he had to stay sober for, someone to remind him that he could save lives, not just endanger them.

He'd done well at the start of their partnership, determined to prove to his superiors that he could pull himself together. But it hadn't lasted. Mere weeks after Pina had met Kieran, a mission had sent them to a world recovering from a series of landslides, where one of the first displaced victims they'd met had looked eerily similar to a girl Pina had failed to save when pirates had attacked his former posting.

His arms had felt instantly fatigued, as though her broken body was still weighing them down.

So Pina had ended up in the seediest bar imaginable, attempting to wash away the memories with something that could have cleaned the hull of the ancient starship they'd been assigned. He'd thrown himself into a bar brawl, his chip no longer working because of the alcohol in his system, and had allowed more punches to come his way than what he dealt out.

He'd always been too late, too tall, too *something*.

Kieran found him afterwards. Understanding had lit his blue eyes, as though he could see right into Pina's past, and Pina had wondered if that wasn't impossible, because this was a young man who claimed to see the future, though no one believed him.

They'd sat together beneath the bar's flickering neon lights while Pina had explained, haltingly, why he'd had taken up drinking.

'You stopped trying to feel anything after that girl died,' Kieran had guessed. 'Because it hurt too much.'

'Yes. And now I have to work even harder to numb the pain, erase those feelings.'

'Pina, I don't think the beings in this galaxy want unfeeling bots to save them. They deserve to be helped by someone who cares.'

Pina's braying laugh had drawn far too much attention, but he hadn't been able to stifle it. 'My husband, Jon, he said something very similar. After a while, he accused me of not feeling anything for him either. I guess I didn't help matters much, taking any far-flung posting I could, leaving him behind so often.'

Kieran had listened, had let Pina talk himself into the right decision, to give up alcohol completely. Not for any future strangers he might save—no.

He'd done it for the young man who needed someone to keep him on the right path.

'Listen, Kieran'—Pina had grabbed him and pulled him in close—'you have to feel. It was a mistake to wall myself off, I know that now. Don't drink this stuff. *Feel.* And for stark's sake, never imbibe while on duty. Too many people rely on us and we cannot let them down.'

Even now, beneath a blanket of stars on a very different world, Pina had to remind himself that he needed to feel. Kieran might worry him and cause him sleepless nights, but his colleague had made him laugh again and had given him the companionship that he would gladly feel a hundred years' worth of pain to keep.

'How can I help Kieran, Creator?' Pina asked quietly.

The Creator God would not answer. He never had, but he did not need to. If there was help to given, it would arrive in some veiled way that did not reveal the Creator's hand. Pina shook his head, appalled at himself for being so direct with his god. He turned to re-enter the outpost.

A tunnel of light shot down from the sky and struck the sand in front of him. Pina threw an arm over his eyes, blinded and astonished, his knees trembling as he prepared to drop onto them and sing the praises of the one he served—

His path is unique and no other being can take his place, said a deep, fatherly voice, one that Pina trusted implicitly. *He cannot be imprisoned here, inheriting only hate and fear. He must have other influences in his life. He must accompany Captain Ami N'uni.*

Pina tumbled onto the ground, gasping, darkness pressing in around him once more. His fists dug into the sand as he lay there, unable to move, unable to process what had just happened. He should have been thanking the Creator God for answering him, for bestowing him with such an honour. But all he could do was...breathe.

Slowly, strength returned to his limbs. He wobbled onto his feet and managed to walk back inside, his steps lethargic and uncertain.

He could not tell the other agents about his incredible experience, because they would not believe him—it had been centuries since a member of GLEA had been blessed with a divine visitation. And the message itself? Letting Kieran go off and do his own thing with a young ship's captain and her even younger sidekick? It was laughable.

'Is this how you feel, Kieran?' he wondered. 'When you have those visions of yours?'

It occurred to Pina, as he climbed into the bunk above Sies Ryn's, that the best thing he could do was learn how to present a convincing argument to his fellow agents, without referring to a seemingly impossible vision. Then he could teach Kieran how to do the same.

And when he had accomplished that, he would finally convince Kieran that the incident on Fintaz was not his fault. It was simply an excuse to stray from the path the Creator God had given him.

SEVEN

Ami yanked the pillow down over her ears and cursed soundlessly. Some of the phases she wanted to shout were so crude and graphic she doubted even Avurn had learned them yet—and Jensa would not forgive her for passing on that knowledge.

The pillow flew off Ami's head and sailed against the wall. Avurn stood inside the doorway, hands outstretched, a scowl forcing his lips apart and exposing his gritted teeth.

'No need to show off,' Ami grumbled.

Stark it. She'd forgotten to change before going crawling into bed and her shirt definitely wasn't fresh. Not to worry—there were five identical clean shirts in her closet. Her jeans, still on the floor where she'd hurled them, had sand crusted onto the ankle cuffs but they could survive without a wash cycle for a few days yet.

As for Ami herself? A cold shower was in order, especially after the fun dreams she'd had starring a certain Chipper. She did *not* need distractions like that. But if she was honest, those fantasies were far more welcome than the usual nightmares that saw her stranded in some dark, empty place from which there was no escape. She feared that endless oblivion more than anything she encountered in her waking hours.

'The Chippers have requested our presence,' Avurn said. 'Krendasta ratted me out.'

'I'm sure you'd be locked up in the cells with Xan and Denton already if that was true,' Ami retorted, throwing the blanket off her legs and swinging her feet onto the floor. Carton City's contractors spent more time in the outpost's cells than they did in their own beds—or on Allen's couch, in Denton's case.

Avurn tipped his head to the side, lips pursed. 'Hmm. I did allow fear to subvert my thought processes, didn't I? Tidy yourself up and meet me outside in ten minutes.'

'Or what? You'll use your chip to hurl things at me?'

'No, I try to avoid annoying you too much,' Avurn replied. 'Because if pressed, you might inform my sister of my activities and I'd rather not cause her any more concern. She has had enough trouble in her life...'

The silence stretched between them.

Ami nodded just once, showing she understood.

It had been six years since she'd freed Jensa from pirates who'd kidnapped her with the intention of selling her to the highest bidder. Ami would not have known anything about her situation if an orphaned four-year-old child hadn't hacked his way onto her ship and informed her that he required her services.

Ami had hesitated, then only seventeen and running from her own problems.

Avurn had responded by blackmailing her, threatening to inform certain people of her whereabouts if she didn't help him.

Before that day, Ami had only ferried inanimate cargo. The pay hadn't been great; the emotional pay-off had been even worse. Ever since then, she'd been juggling barely profitable goods runs with the rescue of vulnerable beings. All because a little boy had shown her how to use her ship's lascannon to coerce the galaxy's scummiest wyverns into cooperating.

Ami smiled fondly.

Avurn's scowl returned in full force. 'Stop that. I don't need the chip to tell me when you're getting sentimental about our first meeting.'

'Scram, Av,' Ami ordered. 'Before I try to do something stupid, like hug you.'

He obeyed, muttering about how he could have picked any ship's captain that day.

Ami rolled her eyes, but her annoyance dissipated when she slid into her private ensuite (the facilities afforded to the ship's captain were only marginally larger than the communal bathroom) and found that Avurn had left her a box of hyponeedles on the chrome wedge that served as her vanity. They were a welcome sight. She made use of one immediately.

'These are heavy-duty meds, Avurn,' Ami murmured. 'You little starker.'

If anyone else had dared to track her cycle, they'd already be eating vacuum. Coming from Avurn, though...it was a nice gesture. Even if his motivation was more practical: the *Free Ride* needed at least two functional crew members. The contraceptive implant did wonders for most human women by halting their cycles, but for Ami it only made her period slightly less of a warzone.

Yawning, she entered the shower cell and prayed that the Creator God would let her have hot water for once. To her relief, the holes in the ceiling spat lukewarm liquid at her instead of the icy pellets she'd been expecting.

Ami allowed her mind to wander. She supposed she could understand why Avurn's sister had latched onto Xan, a decade her senior, so quickly after arriving on Ilbb—Jensa had needed someone to fill the hole left by her parents, someone who made her feel safe and loved. Irresponsible though he was, Xan was kind to Jensa and seemed to enjoy taking care of her. Their marriage might not be perfect, but it was comfortable.

Ami's parents...now there was a disaster, on a planetwide scale. Quite literally.

'...AND the captain of the *Free Ride*, Ami N'uni, is clearly doing the Creator God's work, by helping those the Agency cannot,' Pina said, turning to face each agent, arms spread as though he could unite the opposing factions in the meeting room by pulling them together inside a loving embrace. 'It was the Creator's will that our ship's leapdrive malfunctioned near Ilbb just as Captain N'uni needed our assistance. Are we to stand by and let her serve our god in our place? Without doing what we can to help her? No! With that in mind, I propose that Kieran be assigned to the *Free Ride*.'

Kieran looked up from the floor, where he'd seated his gaze the moment Pina had stepped forward to address their superiors. Pina had already sent word to Ami and her crewmate, without seeking prior approval, that the agents of the outpost wished to speak with them. His unorthodox actions had caused something of a stir.

'No, this is foolish,' Ryn interjected. 'Carton City needs every available agent on hand to deal with those Desine worshippers.'

Major Yetz raised two of zir spindly arms. 'Peaccce, Lieutenant Ryn. We should be mindful of the coincidenccces that come our way, as they could be the work of our Creator.'

'I don't think our god made Krendasta drink himself stupid last night!' Ryn said. 'He's a liability.'

'All the better to sssend him away from temptation,' Yetz countered.

Kieran frowned slightly and not just because of the raging

headache he'd earned last night—along with the inability to use any of his powers. A mere two hours ago, Pina had picked him up off the floor of the cell and explained that the chip's functionality would return, once Kieran's system had expunged the foreign chemicals.

Of course, Pina had then lectured him severely for his lapse in judgement (Kieran hadn't dared to bring up Pina's previous drinking habits—the lieutenant had managed to stay sober for several months, which was an achievement). Xan had copped his own lecture when he'd given his communicator details to Kieran. The contractor might seem a useless drunkard to most people, but there was something about him that Kieran liked.

Pina grinned over his shoulder at Kieran as frenzied discussion erupted around them.

Much as Kieran was pleased to see that his friend looked happier than he had in the full year they'd known each other, he didn't trust the sudden excitement in Pina's eyes; they were bright silver this morning, instead of their usual fusty grey. Kieran's stomach twisted.

Mercifully, that was when Ami arrived, Avurn in tow.

Kieran released a sigh of relief, which earned him a severe side-eye from Ryn—clearly the most dedicated agent Ilbb had to offer. She had already shown that she was capable of quoting, word for word, GLEA's most obscure rules. She had joined the Agency about the same time he had graduated from the Orphanage Division, but she was much closer to Pina's age. Many agents entered the Creator God's service later in life.

Major Yetz's arms snapped disconcertingly as ze rubbed together the bristly knobs that capped the ends of zir limbs. 'Ah. The captain herssself. And her...crewmate. I am not very good at guesssssing the ages of humansss, but he doesss seem a bit young.'

'I keep him out of trouble,' Ami replied.

'I am sure you take thisss responsssibilty quite ssseriously,' Yetz said.

Ami's lips twitched, but the smile Kieran suspected she was hiding didn't surface. Avurn could take care of himself, if Admiral Julius Kratis' (now vaporised) corpse was any indication.

'So what are we all here for?' Ami asked.

'My superior is about to assign me to your vessel,' Kieran informed her. 'Or I believe so, anyway.'

'How'd you swing that?'

'They are colluding against us!' Ryn said, the stubby purple tentacles on her scalp growing jagged with agitation. 'This is a set-up, Major, so that Krendasta can his avoid his duties on Ilbb.'

Major Yetz slapped the armrest of zir chair so hard that one of zir limbs actually splintered, though ze didn't seem too concerned by this. Multiple conversations fell apart immediately.

Yetz focused all pairs of zir tiny ruby eyes on Kieran. 'Be honessst, Krendasssta. Is thisss the challenge that will bring you fully back into the fold?'

Kieran looked at Ami, at the tight-fitting jeans and the loose shirt with a plunging neckline that drew his gaze. This wasn't the first time he'd encountered a woman as attractive as her, but she certainly was the first outside of GLEA violet.

Kieran wanted to escape Ilbb. But he also craved her presence.

He felt as though he had been crawling through an endless desert in search of the one thing that could quench his thirst. And here she was.

'Yes,' he answered.

Yetz didn't sense the lie. The chip enabled its wearer to read the energy of other beings, including very strong emotions, but deception could, more often than not, slip through undetected. Kieran hoped no one in the room had an olfactory organ that was sensitive enough to pick up the sweat gathering between his shoulder blades.

'It is sssettled then,' Yetz said with a decisive nod. Even though the human gesture looked odd on ze, it contained enough gravitas and finality that Ryn huffed and said no more.

Kieran couldn't help but grin at Ami. She offered him a wry smile in return.

Then her eyes slowly slid down his form.

Kieran's temples pinched as the vision blinded him, flooding his mind with images of her hands on his chest. He could even feel her fingertips raking hot lines over his skin. *God.* The vision cleared as quickly as it had arrived.

Kieran focused on the wall instead of her, hoping he could forget those exhilarating sensations—and knowing there was not a starking chance that he'd succeed.

Once he was outside, with only Pina for company (Ami and Avurn were already striding towards the *Free Ride*, debating what their next destination should be), Kieran rounded on his friend. 'Pina! What in the Creator God's name made you do that? Not that I'm ungrateful, because I really can't stay here on Ilbb, but you took a huge risk just now. Why?'

Pina drew himself up to his full height, something he never did. 'I had a revelation. A vision, if you will.'

'Lieutenant...' Kieran said warningly, wondering if Pina was making fun of him.

Pina patted Kieran's shoulder. The gesture was a lot more tentative than usual, almost reluctant, as though Pina was afraid to say what was on his mind. 'You are not the only one who has been blessed by Creator God. Last night, he gifted me with a visitation.'

'You did this because he told you to,' Kieran surmised, squinting at his colleague. One sun had cleared the horizon already. Another horrifically hot day had begun.

'No, Kieran! No! I want what's best for you.' Pina's aghast expression grew even clearer as the second sun began to rise. 'I will heed the Creator God's words, but not solely because it was he who spoke them. You have supported me during some trying times of my own. It would be remiss of me not to return the favour to a friend, someone who was there for me in ways that no other...' Pina paused. Kieran suspected he was thinking about the other agents GLEA had paired him with before Kieran had been hurled into his orbit.

'You are like family to me,' Pina went on. 'And on Lentaria, saying it makes it so. You are my brother. I have declared it.'

Kieran swallowed. 'Lieutenant, I'm a monster. A murderer.'

'You are my brother,' Pina said, shrugging off those other labels. 'Go. Leave this place. Do what you need to do. I'll be here when you return.'

Kieran stared at him. Pina's decision to enact the Lentarian custom was a thoughtful, heart-warming gesture, but Kieran was sure he wouldn't have done it if he truly believed Kieran about what had happened on Fintaz. Pina still saw him as a victim, not an instigator.

But Kieran had been alone for so, so long and he had always wanted to know what it was like to have a family.

Brothers had their disagreements, didn't they?

'Goodbye, Pina,' he said.

'Safe travels, Kieran.'

EIGHT

The *Free Ride* broke free of the chains gravity had wound around its hull while it had sat despondent on the sand, awaiting its captain's instructions. Ami stroked the chrome running above the controls on the left side of her chair. She smiled. Then Avurn started muttering about the low fuel supplies, Kieran started asking questions, and that persistent rattle somewhere on the bridge started up again—only the last of these would be silenced by the smooth vacuum of space.

Ami glanced at the lasgun on her belt and grimaced. She had adamantly vowed that none of her opponents would ever lose their lives. Just their livelihoods.

Admiral Julius Kratis was a massive blip on her record.

Avurn must have noticed her looking at the weapon, because he piped up, 'Ami, you really shouldn't be carrying that if you don't intend to use it. It will be much better served on my belt. Do you not agree?'

Ami cleared her throat. 'Absolutely not. We have a Chipper on board, Av.'

'I will remind you that our homeport is Ilbb,' Avurn returned. 'There is no law there restricting the age of someone carrying a lasgun. He has nothing to enforce.'

Ami transferred her frown onto Kieran. He had chosen to stand behind the safety railing that curved around the bridge, instead of seating himself at the weapons console despite her suggesting it. If she needed to threaten someone with her ship's giant lascannon, Avurn would have to take the controls. And she wasn't sure she trusted him to do that anymore.

'Avurn isn't wrong,' Kieran said with a shrug.

'Don't encourage him, Kieran,' Ami snapped. 'He shot Julius. I don't care that you took the blame. He still did it. Also, you might want to avoid New Sydney for a few years, until the statute of limitations runs out, just in case there isn't a handy self-defence loophole you can use—should have let me wear that one, huh. Don't suppose GLEA's going to advertise your involvement in Julius' death, are they?'

Kieran swallowed. 'My superiors maintain that everything we do is done in service to the Creator God. If they've kept quiet about agents breaking laws, that is the reason.'

'Of course it is,' Ami said dryly, but didn't push. It was clear that it bothered him. 'And anyway, it's in *my* rules—no killing allowed.'

'Yes, you have impressed this upon me many times before,' Avurn groused. 'You know, Ami, the slavers and pirates we let go? They continue to carry out their dastardly deeds. And they continue to improve their weapons in anticipation of future encounters with us.'

Ami held in the exasperated sigh. Barely. 'Kieran, don't you dare let him sway you with his logic. Killing is bad, okay?'

Kieran turned away, his gaze lost to the scattered stars beyond the viewport. She wondered what he saw out there. His past, probably. That day on Fintaz.

'Stark,' Ami said. 'Kieran, that was thoughtless of me…'

His shoulders relaxed, just slightly. 'You cannot excuse my actions and continue to berate Avurn for his.'

'Exactly,' Avurn added. 'His kill count is high enough that I will need to destroy two small pirate vessels to catch up—depending on crew sizes. Although, the incident on Fintaz is still in dispute. Justifiably so. He doesn't seem to have the required power levels.'

'How does he know about that?' Kieran demanded.

Ami bridged her hand over her brow. She could feel pressure building inside her skull, despite the hyponeedle she'd used earlier for her cramps.

'I didn't tell him anything,' she said. 'But I'm not surprised he knows.'

Avurn was anything but careless. He'd revealed his knowledge of Kieran's background deliberately—perhaps as an attempt to unsettle Kieran and get him to leave the *Free Ride*. Ami seriously doubted that Kieran could be convinced to return to Ilbb. She also wasn't keen on the idea of stranding him there, since Carton City might not last very long if she did.

Ami tilted her head towards her crewmate. 'Avurn reads. A lot. Except his idea of light reading is to hack into systems and peruse everyone's secrets. I prefer adventure zines myself, but Av won't touch those. Fiction's boring, he says. Too predictable. Whatever. I like predictable—it's safer. Look, he's been doing it since before he could walk, according to Jensa. It's not a habit I can get him to break. He doesn't *want* to break it.'

'You have been more than happy to use my hacking abilities in the past,' Avurn said, then poked his tongue out at her. Ami mirrored him, mostly because she was pleased to see that he was capable of exhibiting *some* immaturity.

The moment passed. Her crewmate was back to his usual staid self.

'Are we going to investigate the latest tip from the Trading Post?' Avurn asked, straightening in his chair at the communications console. 'There is a suspicious shipment headed for Aurus. Unsurprising, really—they recently forced all Chippers off the planet and rumour has it they're building up an army. You need bodies for that. Conscription works faster than waiting for volunteers.'

'Trading Post?' Kieran echoed.

Avurn waved a hand towards the bottom-right corner of the viewport. Ami knew better than to assume the gesture was casual—the Trading Post probably *was* in that section of space.

'An antiquated space station,' Avurn explained. 'Stowed inside an asteroid belt in the Solence System and only a couple of days away in leapspace. If you want to trade goods and information discreetly, that's where you conduct your business. Ami and I receive tips about the slave ships docked at the Post in exchange for a paltry sum.'

Ami snorted. 'Paltry sum—as in, most of what we earn on our foodstuff runs. And of course they charge us an extra "convenience fee" to send the tips over the Web, don't they!' She shook her head, remembering the amount she'd paid for the Aurus tip. 'Don't quit GLEA, Kieran. You'd be lucky to get a handful of coin-chips as a member of my crew. It'd be much less than what you earn now—and that's saying something.'

'It has been some time since we docked at the Trading Post,' Avurn noted.

'Do you need to visit there often?' Kieran asked Ami.

'No, we try to keep away, we don't want to look like regulars,' Ami replied, kicking a leg up and resting it over her opposite knee. 'Otherwise our enemies would jump us the moment we docked. And it wouldn't be safe for our sources if they became associated with us—but it's not like I want to visit the Post often anyway. Some space station. It looks like a giant beer can with seven uneven spokes sticking out of it.'

Avurn smiled thinly. Ami knew this meant she was wearing on his patience.

'This latest tip is already two days old,' he said. 'Which means they are well on their way to Aurus. We must act now if we mean to intercept them in orbit. Might I also remind you, Captain, that we need fuel. Not urgently, but it is a concern.'

'Any suggestions, Kieran?' Ami asked, swinging her chair in Kieran's direction. 'Any...*foresight* on the matter?'

Kieran shook his head. 'No foresight. I do not have your experience, so I'll simply observe this time.'

'Careful, you might pick up some of my bad habits,' Ami said, grinning. 'I have a lot of those, by the way.'

Stark. Had she just been flirting with him?

'Do you want Kieran on the bridge when we make contact?' Avurn asked, throwing a frown at the Chipper in question. 'The moment a slaver or pirate sees him in that uniform, they'll panic and try to take a shot at us. They might even get lucky. Our lascannon might be decent, but our shields are not.'

Ami pursed her lips, then nodded sharply. 'Good point. Okay, it's a six-hour leap to Aurus from here. Kieran, would you mind waiting out in the corridor after we exit leapsace? Until you're needed?'

'Needed?' Avurn echoed. 'Whatever for? We don't need him.'

He tapped his fingers on the crook of his elbow, a very deliberate gesture. His chip was hidden by the long sleeve of his jumpsuit, but if he straightened out his arm enough, the protrusion might just show through.

Ami narrowed her eyes at him.

Kieran was the one who broke the tense silence. 'If your

previous methods continue to work, then there will be no need of me.'

'Yes, no need for any power slinging,' Ami agreed, giving Avurn a significant look, which the boy seemed intent on ignoring. 'But, Av, how long are we going to get away with relying on our big bad lascannon? A Chipper can do a lot of things that we can't.'

'You believe that a man in a purple jumpsuit can persuade them to hand over their cargo?' Avurn snorted. 'Highly unlikely.'

'My ship, my rules,' Ami said. 'Which means I have the final say. You can always stay on Ilbb, you know.'

Avurn scowled and said no more.

KIERAN WAITED IN THE CORRIDOR, watching the action through the open doorway leading to the bridge. The viewport showed the angry, blotchy face of a teenager, one who didn't take kindly to being Ami's latest victim. By the sounds of things, Ami had crossed paths with this particular captain before.

'I *knew* it! I starking knew it!' the teenager ranted. 'I knew someone at the Post would rat me out.'

'Who says it was someone at the Trading Post, Captain Larry?' Ami asked calmly.

She stood in front of the viewport, hands clasped behind her back, boots firmly planted on the deck. If not for the two crossed fingers being kept out of Captain Larry's line of sight, Kieran would have thought Ami entirely confident.

He had been surprised when she'd asked him if he'd had a vision. Usually he preferred *not* having them, but he was disappointed that he couldn't help Ami on this occasion.

'We put in at the Post to buy supplies two days ago—the timing is pretty starking suspicious!' Larry snapped. 'Someone there sold you the info. Who was it?'

Kieran caught a brief flicker of concern in Avurn's expression. Then the boy stood and lifted his chin, projecting a level of imperiousness that could have cowed royalty on certain worlds. 'It was foolish of you to dock there, Larry. The Post requires a manifest and a full description of a ship's cargo, which you gave freely. Anyone could have hacked that information.'

'Shut up,' Larry snarled, his accusing finger filling a good half of the viewport. 'You're a starking kid. You don't get to talk to me like that.'

'You are a mere four years my senior,' Avurn said, raising a hand over his head to indicate the difference in their heights—unfortunately for Larry, it seemed that Avurn was steadily gaining on him. 'Perhaps I should inform your homeport that they have on their register a captain who is not only underage, but is also engaging in the slave trade? You really should have picked a different planet, with different laws, when you registered your vessel.'

Larry's face purpled.

'Gods, Av, really?' Ami muttered. She waved at the viewport, a cue for Avurn to cut the link; Larry's image dissolved into stars an instant later. 'Check that our shield's capacitors are working, unlike the last time we tangled with this starker. Ugh, that was a close one, wasn't it? Larry's lasguns are starting to grow hot.'

Avurn leapt into the chair connected to the weapons console. He slapped the sensor pad. 'The shield is functional, but is it operating at an optimal level? Doubtful.'

The ship shuddered around them. Judging by the small beads of sweat gathering on the side of Ami's face, this was definitely something Kieran should be worried about. Avurn announced that he was funneling most of the ship's power towards the large lascannon that jutted out beneath the ship. It was very telling that Ami didn't order him to prioritise the shield instead. She jerked a hand in Kieran's direction, an unmistakable cue.

Kieran moved onto the bridge. 'I take it you need my help.'

'Yep, a lot sooner than I thought I would,' Ami said. 'We can't let it be known that someone at the Post gave us the info. Once this gets out, our sources won't help us anymore.'

'Then I'll take the blame,' Kieran said. 'This is now a GLEA-sanctioned operation.'

Ami smiled. 'I was hoping you'd say that.'

She sauntered over to the communications console and delicately swiped one finger over the sensor pad. Larry's back loomed in front of them; it seemed the teenager was in the middle of a swear-laden rant. He spun back around, scowling, then started chewing out whoever had left the communications link open.

'Captain Larry,' Ami interrupted. 'A moment of your time, please.'

'What?' Larry snapped.

Ami indicated Kieran, who was standing behind her. 'I thought I'd introduce you to the being responsible for your current predicament.'

Larry paused, taking in the purple jumpsuit—and the bump on Kieran's temple, which would have been quite obvious if the bridge of the *Free Ride* was magnified on Larry's viewport.

Kieran put on his sternest voice, emulating Major Lorne Lavine, one of the teachers he'd had at the temple on Gerasnin. 'You didn't think that GLEA would continue to ignore your activities, did you? Your ship is registered to a planet with laws that forbid slavery, something which Captain N'uni's crewmate handily pointed out to you.'

'A Chipper! A starking Chipper!' Larry spat, his eyes darting from side to side. 'You lot don't mess with us—you don't have the guts. And you're too skint to chase pirates across the galaxy! You only have the funds to take out small-time crims.'

Kieran lifted both his hands, palms offered to the viewport.

'What are you doing?' Larry's voice sharply rose in volume.

'I am generating forcefields around each of your ship's lasguns,' Kieran said, smiling pleasantly. 'So that when you fire them, the bolts will be deflected and blow holes in your hull.'

'You—you can do that?' Larry squeaked.

Avurn coughed loudly. He seemed to be having trouble settling on an incredulous wide-eyed stare or a disapproving frown.

'Av!' Ami called. 'Our lascannon can blow a hole in their shield, can't it?'

'Ah yes, our sensors indicate that theirs is one of the weaker models,' Avurn said smoothly. It was impossible to tell if he was lying.

Kieran tilted his head towards the viewport. 'I suggest, Captain Larry, that if you don't want to end up in a cell on Gerasnin, you will allow us to relieve you of your cargo.'

'All of it? The foodstuff too?'

'Have to feed our guests, don't we?' Ami remarked.

Larry snarled. The viewport cut to starry space once more.

Within moments, Larry's ship started coasting towards them, a docking port lit up on its starboard side. The multiple lasguns studding the vessel (all pitifully small when compared to the lascannon affixed to the bottom of the *Free Ride*) folded away into the hull.

'You starking liar!' Avurn burst out, seemingly unable to keep it in any longer. 'No Chipper can manage that feat. You can't generate that many forcefields, not on that scale and not from that distance. Certainly not without the help of other Chippers. But...' Avurn's expression grew thoughtful. 'I am impressed with your chosen tactic.'

Kieran released a hiss of air. 'I have learned that some people aren't fully aware of what an agent can do. We were lucky. I don't have any power right now. My chip's out.'

'Booze still in your system?' Ami questioned.

Kieran winced. His tongue felt dry, furry. 'It seems I need more than a day to recover.'

Ami sighed and unclipped her lasgun. 'Alright then. I'd better go with you to the docking port and provide backup. Av, call me before you blast anything.'

'What good is he if he can't use his chip?' Avurn said.

Kieran caught and held the boy's gaze. 'You may have noticed that Captain Larry capitulated without seeing any proof of what I can do. We are taught not to rely on the chip in every situation. Our tech isn't unreliable, but it isn't infallible either.'

'You're afraid of using your powers,' the boy accused.

'Av!' Ami said. 'Shut up.'

'I'm right, aren't I—you're afraid,' Avurn taunted, leaning back against the weapons console, his lips twisting. 'What happens when we need those powers of yours, Chipper? What happens when people need your help? Will you stand by and do nothing?'

Kieran turned away, stowing his shaking hands beneath his belt.

NINE

The off-loading of Captain Larry's unwilling passengers took significantly less time than his consignment of bananas from Sunda-far. Larry himself carried a few of the crates into the tunnel connecting the ships' docking ports and sneered at Ami and Kieran each time he came by. After he'd brought the last crate to them, he said, 'So the Chipper is letting us go. Very kind of him. Or maybe he doesn't have the power or the authority to take us in.'

Kieran leaned against the airlock on the *Free Ride*'s side of the tunnel. 'Or maybe you're a nice, easy target and I'm looking forward to coming across you again.'

Ami smiled and blew a kiss at Larry, who responded with a crude gesture. Kieran lifted one of his own hands, either a farewell or a threat, and Larry immediately retreated several paces, fear widening his eyes. He was still brave enough to demand answers.

'But who was it?' Larry shouted. 'Who ratted me out to the Chippers?'

'How large is your crew?' Kieran countered just before the

docking ports disengaged and the airlocks sealed, the tunnel collapsing between them.

'Good one,' Ami said approvingly. 'He'll be side-eyeing everyone on that ship for a good Old Earth year.'

'Back to Ilbb?' Kieran asked.

Ami nodded. 'Yep. Need to get these folks to safety as soon as possible. My contact is the chief of a tribe based there.'

She paused, evidently waiting to see his reaction. Kieran shrugged. He hadn't come across many of those who worshipped the Desine, the desert god, and if one of them was helping Ami resettle survivors of the slave trade, then they couldn't be as bad as everyone in Carton City seemed to think they were.

But that wasn't what was really bothering him and she knew it.

Kieran blew out a breath. 'Very well. I can stomach Ilbb for one night, but any longer than that and the whispers could overwhelm me. I'd rather your crewmate didn't hear about those. I'm sure he'd find some way to use them to denigrate me and my abilities.'

'Av's a shit,' Ami said, laying a hand on his arm. 'Don't listen to him. He'd use a lasgun to solve all of his problems if I let him.'

Kieran closed his eyes for a mere moment, but it was a moment too long. He saw the leering skulls of his victims on the backs of his eyelids. 'I wish this one incident hadn't encumbered me forever...I want to use my abilities in a way that makes up for Fintaz, but I'm always afraid that I'll kill everyone on sight.'

'It'd be a good thing if you can learn to make do without the chip,' Ami noted. 'That's if you're still set on getting tossed out of GLEA. I suppose that might be safer for everyone, actually. No powers, no danger—right?'

'I used to *help* people with my powers, I used to save and protect them. Not kill them. And that...' Kieran hesitated.

'That made it worth having the chip?' Ami's hand rose to hover between them, two of her fingers bending to indicate his temple.

Unable to stop himself, he leaned into her touch, nestling his cheek against her palm. Her breathing hitched.

'Yes,' he said softly. 'Without the chip, I am nothing.'

Ami retracted her hand. She gave him a swift nod and turned away, heading for the hold where her new passengers were waiting. Judging by the frantic voices bouncing up the corridor, she would need to calm them down before she explained their new situation. Already the *Free Ride* was moving out of range of Captain Larry's reappearing lasguns, guided by Avurn who seemed to be quite capable of taking Ami's chair when he needed to.

Kieran remained by the airlock for several minutes before he finally sought sanctuary in the tiny cabin that had been allocated to him.

BY THE FOURTH time the *Free Ride* had regurgitated Kieran Krendasta in as many weeks, Xan Jones figured he had Kieran's routine pinned down—get the night patrol over and done with, get to the bar, get drunk, get dragged to the outpost by an exasperated Second Lieutenant Pina-Sai, then get punished by the higher-ranked losers with yet another night patrol to be carried out the next time Kieran made planetfall.

'Night patrol' was a misleading term. A shitload of those patrols had to be undertaken when all three suns were out. Keeping to Old Earth hours removed some of the confusion of galactic travel, but Xan didn't like how it messed with his sleep patterns.

He had been doing the night patrols with Denton ever since they'd first arrived on Ilbb. They had to ensure that the city's indistinct boundaries were not crossed by any unwanted 'sand fleas' (Xan privately despised that term), something that hadn't happened in a couple of months, admittedly because Denton hadn't gone out and antagonised the nearest tribes lately. Xan occasionally took the heat for those excursions, even though Jensa begged him not to.

Xan wished Denton would pull his head together—and soon.

'Any idea why you Chippers are so set against the desert folk?' Xan asked Kieran one night as they traversed the narrow alleyway behind the bar. 'Seems to me that the Agency ignores most sub-level gods and the people who worship them.'

Though Ilbb's dusk wasn't due for at least ten Old Earth hours, Xan knew he'd be trading words with the local crowd soon enough. Even the harshest daylight couldn't keep them holed up in the metal boxes they called home. He'd actually helped the thugs drill their own well so they could avoid asking the Chippers for the use of theirs (no crim wanted to be beholden to them for *anything*), but that hadn't convinced large chunks of Carton City to stop trying to mug him. Xan thought the thugs a pretty ungrateful lot, considering how hard it was to find water on Ilbb.

Although, that might have had more to do with luck than skill on his part.

Kieran frowned, shadows creeping across his expression. 'I'm not sure why the enmity is so strong. Or why it's lasted so long. Those who follow Oceania, the water god, cause far more trouble than any of the desert-based tribes.'

'Could be the Desine has a beef with his dear old Creator dad,' Xan said, then perked up when he saw movement at the end of the alley. 'We've got company. Say hello. Be nice.'

The thugs swarmed into view and ringed the two humans, lasguns and sneers out. To Xan's relief, they were Siv's people. They generally didn't shoot themselves up with drugs that might shorten their tempers.

Xan was impressed that Kieran hadn't reached for his weapon or tried to create a forcefield—the kid's personal shielding device was still broken and the replacement Major Nexis Yetz had ordered wasn't due for months. Most Chippers would have raised their hands the instant Siv appeared. The kid had guts. But guts weren't always an adequate substitute for brains.

Admittedly, Xan didn't reach for his own lasgun either, a much heavier piece that he kept strung across his torso. Oh well, his guts had kept him alive this long.

'Hello,' Kieran said. There was a noticeable twitch at the corner of his mouth, as though he was trying not to smile. The kid—*stark it, Xan, you've only got six years on him*—was enjoying himself. 'I'm told I should be nice to you.'

'Heard them Chippers can't use their powers when soused,' Two-Eyed Siv, the leader of the gang, rasped. 'What good is he against sand fleas if he can't throw up a shield or shoot straight?'

Two-Eyed Siv was a moisture-craving Jezlo (Ilbb had been her last choice for a hideout, obviously—it was *everyone's* last choice). All Jezlos had two beady eyes, so Xan wasn't sure how she'd earned that moniker. Really, Siv should have had a name that referenced her missing tentacle.

'So why don't we just blast 'im?' added one of Siv's minions.

Kieran opened his mouth, presumably to tell them he hadn't had a chance to get a drink down his throat yet. But Xan knew that response wouldn't save the kid later, when he really did get sloshed. No way was he going to let Kieran make himself a tempting target.

Xan clapped a hand onto Kieran's shoulder. They were a similar height, which Xan approved of—not that he'd choose a companion for that reason. Absolutely not. 'Hey. Kieran's with me. I trust him. And he doesn't think he's too good to be seen drinking with us, unlike the rest of those purple starkers. Look, we could stand here nattering all night—or Kieran and I can get this patrol over and done with, so we can all enjoy a drink at the bar. My shout.'

'Denton coming?' Siv asked.

'He's got the dawn shift,' Xan replied, shrugging apologetically.

'Which means he's trying to decide between Allen's couch or that feather-filled bed Petria's always boasting about.'

'Poor woman!' Siv clucked in amusement. 'She won't get any action for months.'

Though the Jezlo didn't give any verbal orders, she and the thugs began to fade back into the shadows of Thug Alley, resuming their futile wait for unsuspecting prey.

'You handled that well, Xan,' Kieran said.

Xan patted the lasgun covering his chest. 'Don't let this beauty fool you—my true weapon is getting people to talk. And if I get them drunk enough, they'll tell me all their darkest secrets.' He nudged Kieran's side with his elbow. 'Don't worry. You never tell me anything.'

'You collect blackmail material?' Kieran mused.

'Nah, not my style.' Xan shook his head. 'They're wanted crims, sure, but a lot of them need a friendly ear instead of a prison cell. Okay, we've got murderers and even worse scum in Carton City, I'll grant you that. But there's more than a few folk who only stole food so they wouldn't starve. They can't contact their families on the Web without being traced back here, you know? Sad.'

Kieran studied Xan for a long moment, as if he could see right into his soul, which made the contractor feel mightily uncomfortable.

'You have access to GLEA's criminal records,' Kieran stated.

Xan didn't see any point in denying it. 'No one questions it when a Chipper contractor looks into the families of wanted criminals, do they?'

'You wouldn't be able to help the people here, if you didn't work for GLEA,' Kieran said quietly, seemingly lost in thought.

Xan chortled. 'Don't go spreading it around, but I'm a big old softie.'

Later, Xan parked Kieran's comatose form in a secluded booth at the bar, despite Tends' protests. Xan figured this was a better option for Kieran than the outpost. The kid deserved to get his lectures from Pina-Sai only, not the entire brood. Pina seemed to genuinely care about Kieran. He must know the reason his friend drank himself stupid.

Xan didn't know that reason yet. But he was working on it.

He wanted to help the kid, stark it. Too bad he was often nonsensical himself; drinking erased the pain, if not the memories. One day Xan hoped he'd forget watching a storm-tossed ocean steal his mother from him...but this was not that day.

He returned home after one of the nearby stars had set and encountered a grumpy Avurn. His young brother-in-law blew through ten whole minutes demanding that Xan spend some time with his wife, because when Jensa was bored she liked to sneak into Avurn's unit to clean it. Xan waved the boy off with a vague promise to do so, pretended not to hear when Avurn muttered something that sounded suspiciously like 'I have not yet shot you on account of you being responsible for my sister's happiness', and then entered his own cosy unit.

Jensa was just waking up.

Xan, smiling, went to join her in bed.

TEN

'Stark, stark, *stark!*' Ami said on their fifth run.

'What's wrong?' the ship's resident Chipper asked, standing from his chair so that he could approach Ami.

Kieran had finally agreed to crew the weapons console—Ami had won him over by pointing out that it was safer to be strapped in during a lasfight, but she suspected he knew the real reason for her insistence. She felt increasingly uneasy when she saw Avurn sitting there and that could interfere with her ability to focus at crucial moments. And besides, before Kieran's arrival, Avurn had needed to fling himself between both consoles. A dangerous manoeuvre, given that Avurn had to unstrap to manage it. The *Free Ride* wasn't one of those fancy ships that had magnetised hoverchairs on the bridge.

Avurn's cheeks were puffed out so much it looked like he was about to explode from the effort of not saying 'I told you so'. He knew exactly what had gone wrong.

Ami sighed. 'We're too late. This tip was days old. Av, don't you start. Please.'

'Now what was it you said...' Avurn stroked his chin, uncannily mimicking a university professor they'd rescued one time. 'Ah. That's right. You said we didn't have enough room in the hold to go after these pirates immediately. I disagreed with your decision, you'll recall. We could easily have crammed more bodies into the corridors and living quarters.'

'Did you seriously expect me to endanger the people we already had on board?' Ami demanded.

Kieran held up his hands, palms out. They'd been away from Ilbb for two Old Earth days, long enough that his powers should have recovered from his latest bender. But he didn't need to generate a forcefield. The gesture worked just as well as if he had used the chip; it forestalled the brewing argument and gave him the opportunity to ask, 'What happens when you're not able to intercept a shipment in space?'

Ami refused to wilt beneath his gaze. 'We leave it. Too risky.'

'You don't report it to GLEA?'

'Even if—and that's a big *if*—these folks are being taken to a planet with laws against slavery...' Ami shook her head. 'The Chippers don't have the resources to rescue every single individual. I wouldn't trust them to do it anyway. Look, this ship was bound for the Enocian Harem. Aren't there a bunch of staffed temples on Enoc already? GLEA should have noticed that the Harem has been importing unwilling workers. Or maybe it's in their best interests *not* to notice.'

'You think the Agency turns a blind eye,' Kieran stated.

Ami gave him a careless shrug, hoping her energy wasn't Webcasting just how hopeless she felt. 'Well, Enoc's one of the richest planets in the galaxy. Most people there have deep pockets— and GLEA needs their donations to fill the gap when the funding from their little side project, TerraCorp, falls short. You got another explanation?'

Kieran opened his mouth, then closed it again.

It was common knowledge that TerraCorp, a terraforming company with a sketchy past, was a subsidiary of GLEA. And it was no secret that due to a bevy of competitors, TerraCorp had been struggling to make enough of a profit to fill the Agency's coffers.

Finally, Kieran managed, 'No agent would use the Enocian Harem if they were aware of this. Slavery is illegal on Enoc. The Agency does not condone criminal behaviour.'

'But you lot can and will enforce the laws on a planet where slavery *is* legal,' Ami said dryly. 'Kieran, I've met a lot of folks in violet jumpsuits and they're not always the best advertisement for GLEA. You Chippers might think you're closer to the Creator God and so-called perfection, with those chips of yours, but you're just as mortal as the rest of us.'

'There is no point in dwelling on something we cannot change,' Avurn interrupted. He was impatiently tapping the communications console. 'We should check in with our sources at the Trading Post. They may have received word of another shipment elsewhere.'

Ami rammed her fist into the side of her chair. She missed the vital controls in the armrest, mostly because she'd performed the gesture so often.

'Stark it,' she growled. 'Stark it, stark it. I hate this, I hate—'

She broke off when she realised that Kieran was kneeling beside her, his hands closed over her fist, cushioning her knuckles against the next blow she so badly wanted to land.

'Can we break them out of the Harem itself?' he asked.

Gods, he looked completely serious.

'What? With one'—Ami glanced at his belt—'*two* lasguns, a boy who sold his personal shielding device to fund his dodgy activities, a starship captain who can't hit a wall at twenty paces, and a Chipper who may or may not be sober? And let's not forget that your own shielding device is still broken, Kieran! This is completely beyond us.'

'Impossible, insane...' Avurn stroked his chin again. He didn't even have bristles, for stark's sake. 'Ingenious. They won't be expecting it.'

Ami swallowed. Her tongue reluctantly unstuck from the roof of her mouth. 'Threatening someone at a distance with a lascannon is one thing. Busting into a building is another thing entirely. We have no experience with planetside retrieval! And we have no idea what type of resistance we'll encounter. Security personnel, automated systems—stark, even a confusing layout. We won't even get past the front door, Av. Maybe Kieran can convince his lot to do something about it.'

Avurn chortled, but a dark undercurrent lurked beneath his words. 'Please, Ami. You know that asking the Chippers for help has never yielded the intended results. Why do you think I came to you all those years ago? They ignored me when I asked them to save my sister—because they were too embarrassed to admit that they *couldn't*. They're chronically understaffed and always leaking coinchips. Some of them even take bribes. They can't be trusted. No, it's up to us.'

Ami turned to ask Kieran if there was a trustworthy agent on Enoc he could contact, but he was half slumped against her chair, gaze distant. Ami had the impression that only a shell remained while his mind was lost somewhere out there in their vast galaxy.

A vision of the future? Maybe. But it also looked like a good way to get killed, being distracted like that.

Good thing I'm here to watch this back, Ami thought. *And his sides. And his front...*

Avurn hadn't noticed Kieran's strange behaviour yet. He was hunched over the communications console, a boy on a mission. 'There are privacy laws on Enoc that make obtaining information somewhat difficult. But I can get you the layout of the Harem, Ami. I can get you anything.'

Ami didn't tell him to stop. Avurn was the best weapon she could throw at tech-based obstacles. As for performing impossible feats...she knew a certain being who had some experience with that.

'Kieran?' she prompted.

When his eyes alighted on her, they were twin blue voids, completely lacking any pupils. Ami baulked, but she didn't look away. It wasn't fear that kept her frozen in place—it was his fingers clenching hers, each knuckle so tight they were dredging up bones that formed prominent ridges over the backs of his hands.

She leaned in, pressing her forehead against his, the frightful heat of his skin scorching hers.

'Come back to me,' Ami whispered.

Kieran blinked and abruptly released her hands. He stood, floundering, clearly unsteady on his feet.

'Vision?' she asked.

His voice was rough. 'Yes.'

'Do I want to know what you saw? Are we going to horribly die if we attempt a rescue?'

'No one is going to horribly die,' Kieran replied. His eyes were now back to normal and a smile was flitting along his lips. 'At least, not today.'

Avurn cleared his throat. 'Care to elaborate for those of us being unfairly kept in the dark?'

Ami shrugged and propped her leg up over her knee, knowing she had no right to feel so relaxed—it was strange, terrifying even, that she trusted Kieran this much after five short weeks of knowing him. 'Might as well let Av in on your secret, Kieran. He'll figure it out himself if you fly with us long enough. And if this does work, then your unique gift will prove that it has a place here on my ship and in our future plans.'

Ami clenched her jaw, steeling herself for an argument, but Kieran didn't provide one. Frankly, she needed to know if his visions could be useful or if they were just a distraction.

Gods, he was enough of a distraction himself.

Ami swallowed. 'Right. So what did you actually see, Kieran?'

'...BUT he can't be having visions of the future,' Avurn insisted. 'The chip makes it possible to read existing energy—so that one might discern how many lifesigns are aboard a vessel, for example— but it doesn't allow its wearer to predict the future. That energy doesn't exist yet.'

'Shut up, Av,' Ami said, rubbing the tiny communicator she'd stashed inside her ear. The gesture looked completely casual to an outsider and, as an added bonus, sent static screaming into Avurn's identical earpiece.

She and Kieran walked arm in arm, leisurely climbing the marble steps that led up towards the Enocian Harem. It was a beautiful building, palatial in nature, and its glittering white dome looked like it belonged on some icy world. But instead of being surrounded by snow, the Harem was bordered by an eclectic selection of buildings made from glass and stone. Stunning works of art for people to live and work inside. There were no factories on Enoc—not because the planet didn't have any natural resources, but because those who could afford to live there didn't want pollution ruining their view.

Ami looked down at her attire and barely managed to stop herself shaking her head in disgust. Her fuchsia dress stretched from her armpits to midway down her thighs—and yes, there were real gems studded everywhere on the shimmering fabric. It took her a lot of effort not to hitch the starking thing up or tug it towards her knees.

'May I ask where you found that on such short notice?' Kieran asked out of the corner of his mouth.

'My closet,' Ami answered, smiling in what she hoped was an enigmatic way. 'You never know when you might need to escort a Chipper into the most expensive brothel in the galaxy. Do I need to give you some pointers on how to behave once we're inside?'

Kieran laughed. 'What makes you think I haven't visited a brothel before?'

'Uh, let's see…there's that obsession with in-house breeding you folks seem to have.'

'Not all of us are celibate outside of attempted procreation, if that's what you're thinking,' Kieran said, still sounding amused. 'And would it surprise you to know that many agents have chosen to start families with partners outside the Agency, even though it hampers their career advancement? Besides, places like the Harem always ensure that contraceptive implants are operating at optimal levels. If we're to indulge externally, the Agency prefers it to be done where breeding cannot occur.'

Ami kept her eyes ahead. It was a good thing he didn't know what she was *really* thinking. He was wearing his usual purple jumpsuit and scuffed boots, but it was increasingly difficult not to imagine him without either, splayed out before her and completely hers for the taking. Unfortunately, that delightful image wasn't a vision of the future.

I really need to get laid, Ami thought. She scowled at the Harem. It didn't have a sign because it didn't need one—and external advertising was considered too crass by the galaxy's wealthiest denizens. *Too bad I'm not here to have fun.*

A human male in a three-piece suit stood beneath the ornate archway marking the entrance, shaking hands with those beings who could return the gesture and giving a warm verbal welcome to those who lacked limbs. He scrutinised Ami for several agonising seconds, disapproval lining his brow when he noticed that her dress was no longer in fashion—but a smile rapidly spread over his face when he saw that she was accompanied by a Chipper.

GLEA's agents were exactly the kind of people the Enocian Harem wanted on their side, especially if they had just accepted a shipload of trafficked beings. Slavery was illegal on Enoc and only royalty could escape prosecution here.

Funny how planetary rulers could get away with the worst shit.

Ami hastily dropped that train of thought. Nope, too late. Each and every scar that was streaked across her back tightened and burned, a phantom snap of pain that lingered. She badly wanted to lean against a wall and breathe deeply until her heart stopped racing, but she suspected that wouldn't help maintain her wealthy socialite cover.

'We have a special selection available for you this afternoon,' the man said to Kieran, ignoring Ami. 'Your companion is welcome to indulge as well.'

'The Agency continues to appreciate your generous hospitality,' Kieran responded.

Ami squashed the irrational urge to slap the grin off his face.

She instead let her gaze drift towards the high ceiling, picturing the concealed air ducts that supplied fresh, sweetly scented air to the Harem's vast array of nooks and crannies. Up there, somewhere, was Avurn, dodging discovery while no doubt sneaking peeks into secluded rooms to see what people were getting up to.

Avurn was probably having the time of his life.

ELEVEN

Avurn Singh was, in fact, vastly unbothered by what the Harem's occupants were getting up to. After extensive reading and research on the matter, he realised he didn't much care for sex. Whether this was because of his body's age, or because he would never be interested in the act, it didn't really matter.

What bothered him was this recent development: Kieran Krendasta suddenly announcing that he'd had a vision showing the pirates' victims (how he knew it was the same people from the Post's tip was up for serious debate) being introduced at a special debut event. A brief glance at the Enocian Harem's schematics had apparently been enough for Kieran to locate the room they were—would be—in.

Of course, Kieran couldn't say with certainty if they would succeed with their rescue mission, just that no one would die.

His visions, if they did exist, weren't terribly useful.

Ami had told Avurn about what Kieran had seen before he was ambushed on Fintaz, but Avurn had felt the need to point out, 'That is hardly evidence of foresight. He could have had a nightmare that coincidentally came true. And the Harem would not parade our targets about tonight, when they've only just been brought in, recently captured. These people are not going to smile and service clients without complaint.'

Ami's face had swiftly darkened. 'There are ways to make them smile, Avurn. You know that. You know who my parents are and what they did to me.'

Kieran had returned to the bridge at that point, providing a timely interruption. It had been somewhat amusing to see the Chipper stop dead and stare at Ami, who was squeezed into that flashy dress she'd grabbed in some disreputable market on an even more disreputable world. It would be highly impractical in a lasgun fight and Avurn had told her so. Often. But when had his disapproval ever kept her from doing something rash?

Ami had ducked her head and blushed in response to Kieran's appraisal.

It had been hard for Avurn not to roll his eyes at that.

Kieran was a temporary problem. Ami would go to bed with the Chipper, immediately get him out of her system, and then she'd stop being distracted at inopportune moments. The Denton Dashing fling hadn't lasted longer than ten minutes. Not that he knew about that one, of course.

Avurn paused, remaining flattened against the cool, metallic surface of the air duct. He could have sat up if he'd wanted to, since the duct was large enough to admit adult humans (cleaning bots were outlawed galaxywide because of those troublesome bot uprisings in the past), but he fancied that keeping low made him look more stealthy. Like the spies in those vids he watched in the safety of his own quarters. He would never admit to indulging in *fiction*. It should have been beneath him.

Absently, he tugged on the sleeve of his jumpsuit, even though it hadn't ridden high enough to reveal his chip—and there was no one around to see it anyway. He needed to kill this habit. And fast. The gesture looked too suspicious.

Like he was hiding something.

Avurn tapped the pads of his thumb and middle finger together, activating the sensors injected inside them. They projected a bar of light that swept across his skin, filling every line and smothering every bump, until the schematics he'd hacked from the Harem's poorly protected server covered his palm.

Techpads were so archaic and such devices (along with their secrets) could be stolen.

Avurn would only lose his ability to scour the galaxy for information if someone sliced off his hand. Not an entirely impossible event, but he'd have bigger problems than Web access at that point.

The schematics showed him that his destination featured an antechamber that led into a theatre, complete with stage and seats. That such a room existed, matching Kieran's vision, could be mere coincidence. As could the fact that the Harem's greatest concentration of lifesigns, according to Avurn's chip, were to be found there. But then one of his fingers beeped discreetly; there was an update on the server, announcing that the room had been assigned to a special debut event. No casual clients allowed.

Interesting. Very interesting.

Most lifesigns in the room were clustered in the antechamber, though there seemed to be ten souls backstage, presumably waiting to make their entrance. Avurn didn't sense any fear or anguish in their energy. Quite the opposite, actually...they felt rapturous.

Ami had told him to provide backup, if necessary. This order was basic, leaving far too much room for interpretation. He supposed she wouldn't approve of him laying explosives in a duct set against an exterior wall, but *someone* had to create an exit strategy that didn't involve fighting their way past the Enocian Harem's expert security guards.

What would Ami do without him? Honestly.

AMI AND KIERAN were promised a range of things—drinks, canapés, utmost discretion—by their guide as they were led to the debut event. A cheerful Jezlo wobbled over to greet them when they arrived, bowing at her midsection and telling them that they were just in time. She shut the wooden doors to the corridor with a distinct clunk.

Ahead of them lay an archway, the theatre beyond it currently veiled with twinkling gold cloth. The antechamber was identical to the one Kieran had seen in his vision, but he'd leisurely waded through those silent images so he could examine them more carefully. In real time, everything seemed to be moving very rapidly and the room was so much noisier than he'd expected.

Kieran swept his eyes over the small crowd in the antechamber, recognising politicians and famous vid actors, but there were others whose sources of wealth were not as obvious. One human woman stood off to the side, arms crossed, expression hard. She looked decidedly out of place, as did the flicker of silver he saw beneath the right cuff of her charcoal pants. A prosthetic leg. He wondered why she hadn't replaced it with a better model, one that had pale brown synthflesh to match her skin tone, because as an attendee to this event she surely must have the means to do so.

She caught his gaze. Her eyebrows rose.

Kieran turned back to Ami, grinning as though they were sharing a private joke.

'Sense anything?' she asked.

'Ten extra lifesigns in the theatre, as expected, but there's only one person who strongly objects to being here.' He tipped his head slightly. 'That woman in the pantsuit. I get the impression this whole thing is distasteful to her.'

'Hmm,' Ami said, an affable smile fixed in place. 'Could be she's got a partner who likes a bit of extramarital excitement and doesn't care for it herself, but came along anyway to keep them happy.'

'Could be,' Kieran agreed.

Ami's cheeks tightened. 'And just because someone feels like they're happy to be here, that doesn't mean they are.'

'Are you saying I shouldn't trust what my chip is telling me?' he asked.

Her eyes, usually a warm sea green, now possessed the darkest, coldest depths Kieran had ever seen. 'There are ways to force people to smile.'

'True,' Kieran said, though she clearly meant something more serious than threats. 'How can we be sure that the beings backstage need our help?'

'Leave that to me. You just do your bit and throw your weight around as our resident Chipper.' Ami pursed her lips. 'Also, it'd be nice if you shielded us from any stray lasbolts. I kind of need to stay alive, so I can make sure that Avurn doesn't take over the galaxy or something.'

Kieran chuckled. 'I almost want to see how he'd manage it.'

'Oh gods, me too,' Ami admitted.

Mournful, echoing notes donged from speakers hidden inside the walls. The Jezlo who'd welcomed them gleefully pulled the gold cloth covering the archway aside, an invitation for the Harem's favoured clients. Ami and Kieran joined the stream of beings filing into the theatre. No one made use of the seats. They milled about in front of the curtained stage, practically vibrating with impatience as they waited for the Harem's newest employees to be presented to them.

The Jezlo darted out of sight, presumably to check on things backstage. She reappeared within moments and slapped her tentacles together. Right on the cue, the strip lighting overhead dimmed. The donging gave way to tinkling chimes.

Then the curtain whispered into the wings, exposing the stage.

Ten beings paraded themselves before the audience, their smiles bright, their lifesigns radiant with unbridled joy. Kieran watched them closely, sensing nothing untoward and wondering if he was somehow reading the wrong energy. He fought the urge to tap his temple as though his chip was some malfunctioning gadget.

Ami grabbed his arm, nails digging into fabric and flesh.

'They're drugged,' she hissed. 'Can't you see it?'

Kieran couldn't, honestly. But she was the one who had years of experience with this sort of thing—and she'd believed him about his visions and how dangerous he could be, if forced to remain on Ilbb. She deserved the same amount of trust that she had given him.

'We need to put a stop to this,' Kieran said. '*Now.*'

Ami stroked her earpiece. 'Avurn. It's time.'

The mystical twinkling in the background cut out. The overhead lights blazed again, illuminating the crowd and chasing away any of the shadows they could have used to hide themselves.

Avurn tumbled out of a nearby grate, landed on the stage, dusted himself off, grinned around at everyone—and then produced Ami's lasgun from his belt. Ami hadn't had a suitable place to stash it on her person and weapons weren't exactly favoured in the Harem; Kieran had been allowed to bring his in because the Harem hadn't wanted to discourage a Chipper from using their services.

'Don't fret,' Avurn ordered everyone. 'I am not here to relieve you of your valuables.' He sighed. 'Unfortunately.'

THE ROOM ERUPTED WITH PANIC.

Stark it, Av, Ami mentally groused as the boy tossed the lasgun in her direction (she'd been afraid he would keep it, despite the plan). *Great way to introduce us and make sure no one sends us an invite to anything ever again. Wait. Never mind. I don't want to be invited to this kind of party anyway!*

Meanwhile, Kieran had stepped forward and taken command of the room, forming a calm eye in the middle of a bloated, heaving storm. His lasgun and uniform did most of the talking for him. It also didn't hurt that he cut a fine figure in that purple jumpsuit. Ami caught more than one set of approving eyes.

She didn't appreciate that hot whoop of jealousy in her gut.

'Please remain calm,' Kieran was saying. 'This is a GLEA-sanctioned operation. I apologise for the interruption and for the zealousness of these...contractors.'

Contractors. As if they had dark, seedy pasts. Well, Ami did have one of those. Avurn was still working on his. Wait, where did that kid—

Ami relaxed slightly. There he was, standing beside Kieran.

Avurn's usual dark jumpsuit looked menacing next to Kieran's brighter outfit and the boy was markedly shorter than the Chipper. But no one in the room dared to challenge him. Avurn had easily made it look like he too possessed Kieran's authority—complete with stern, disapproving frown.

Time to stop staring and do her part.

Ami hauled herself up onto the stage and addressed the Harem's newest members. 'We're here to help you. Stop dancing.'

They froze as if they were trapped inside a vid that had just been paused. Slowly, they relaxed, abandoning the ridiculous gestures that hadn't quite matched the swaying of their bodies. Arms and appendages dangled by their sides. Hair and fur trembled. But their smiles remained fixed in place. Ami's heart clenched. Hitting someone with Rapture was a downright shitty thing to do—being under the influence was bad enough, but coming out the other side was even worse.

Once the drug wore off, you hated yourself.

'Anyone who was kidnapped by pirates and got jabbed with a hyponeedle recently'—Ami cast a quick look around and pointed—'go stand against that wall.'

Ten beings shuffled across the stage.

Avurn cleared his throat. 'The opposite wall would be better.'

Ami gave him a suspicious look. He did not explain himself and she was frankly too afraid to ask.

'Stand against the opposite wall,' Ami corrected, indicating the change of location with a wave of her lasgun.

Soon all of the Harem's debut members stood with their backs to the—hopefully—safer wall, still beaming brightly. Two of their number had managed to squeeze tears out of their eyes, which suggested that their doses had either been too weak or were wearing off. Kieran stared at them, then at Ami, his lips forming the silent question.

'It's a drug called Rapture,' Ami announced, stomping her boots on the stage and making sure she had everyone's attention. 'It forces you to smile and be happy and you'll do anything you're told, because you know you'll *enjoy* it. It's a compulsion. You want to keep feeling good and obeying commands sets that off—no matter how awful those commands are. And no one's the wiser, unless they ask you the right questions. It's starked. I wouldn't hit my worst enemy with this shit.'

Avurn's voice was quiet. 'Even the ones who put you under?'

Ami shuddered. 'Even those starkers.'

'How long does it last?' Kieran asked.

'Several hours,' Ami replied. 'Enough time that a client might not realise their chosen employee isn't lawfully willing. Though I wonder if anyone here cares. I bet you were all in on it.'

'Of course not!' and 'preposterous notion!' were two very popular phrases that started echoing throughout the theatre.

Kieran turned away from Ami and scanned the Harem's patrons with his eyes and, presumably, his chip. His search ceased when his gaze reached the Jezlo who seemed to be in charge of the event.

'My chip isn't infallible, but I'm not sensing any strong shock from her,' Kieran observed. 'I don't think she's a mere attendant. It's a disguise in case something like this happens, allowing her to discreetly slip away. But we won't be letting her do that. She probably used the Harem's funds to obtain the slaves and I wouldn't be surprised if she's high enough up in the hierarchy to hide the purchase from her colleagues.'

Ami glanced at Avurn. 'What's the deal with the wall?'

'Explosives,' he said simply.

She wasn't surprised—in fact, she'd kind of been banking on it.

'Blow it,' Ami ordered.

Avurn raised his eyebrows. 'Really? You're condoning the destruction of private property?'

'Av, I'm really, really pissed off right now and I'm in the mood to do some damage.'

Kieran's expression remained neutral, though Ami caught an approving glint in his eyes. 'The financial loss might make the Harem conduct more extensive checks on their employees in future. And we need to get these people out of here as soon as possible—in case the pirates return and attempt to recapture them for another buyer.'

Avurn clapped his hands together. Not a harmless gesture, knowing him.

Ami had a single moment to hold her breath—and then the exterior wall exploded, raining debris all over the room. Kieran threw out his hands, his ensuing forcefield halting a jagged chunk of plastered concrete; Ami was relieved that nothing too large had flown in anyone's direction. The pirates' trafficked victims weren't injured by the blast, though some had their hair painted grey by dust. They suddenly looked decades older than they were. More of them had started crying, tears spilling over their smiling lips.

'Go, go, go!' Ami said, then remembered she had to be more specific. She gritted her teeth. 'Climb out the hole in the other wall! Once you've done that, you will follow me directly to my ship, which you'll board, and then I'll fly you off this planet and take you somewhere safe.'

They began scrambling towards freedom.

This was of course the moment the doors to the antechamber burst open, admitting a group of humans in purple jumpsuits who hurtled through the archway and into the theatre. All of them bore lasguns, personal shielding devices, and grim expressions.

'The Harem's famed security personnel called for external backup, most disappointing,' Avurn said. 'I am, however, impressed with the rapid response time of the Chippers.' He elbowed Kieran in the side. 'But you did cause a scene in front of their wealthiest donors. How embarrassing for them. They must be *very* keen to strike you from the Agency now.'

Kieran's laugh sounded hollow to Ami. 'I doubt that'll happen. Go with Ami and the others.'

Avurn tossed the Chipper a wild grin over his shoulder as he raced off. Instead of immediately joining her crewmate, Ami hovered in the gaping exit that had been blasted into the side of the building. She watched Kieran set his lasgun on the floor. He then planted his knees beside the weapon and bowed over, fingers laced behind his head. The very portrait of a man surrendering to his fate.

'Private Kieran Krendasta,' he identified himself. 'Accompanying Captain Ami N'uni, under orders from Major Nexis Yetz. No one was harmed during this rescue operation, but I need to make a report to the highest-ranking agent available.'

Ami suppressed a laugh and hurried away. Major Yetz was going to *love* being thrown under a hoverbus. Though the major was no friend of hers, ze had conveniently forgotten to investigate whether or not Ami had broken any laws on her runs. Ze knew she'd rescued countless beings that would have otherwise suffered.

But Yetz had zir limits. And so did zir superiors. Ze was definitely going to ban Kieran from riding along with her now.

Stark, it had been fun while it had lasted.

TWELVE

Kieran hadn't quite believed that Head General Zareth Sins himself was on Enoc when his fellow agents told him. GLEA's elected leader was too busy to personally speak with each individual agent and had probably delegated any consideration about Kieran's future after the death of Admiral Kratis to a trusted general. Pina had never met Sins and Kieran doubted Major Yetz had either.

Kieran had expected to get into *some* trouble, given that the Enocian Harem contributed generously to GLEA's coffers.

But even the events on Fintaz hadn't landed him in this much hot water.

Head General Sins was a human male with flawless ebony skin and his hair, mostly grey with a single stubborn streak of brown, was thick and severely slicked back. Sins kept his hands clasped behind him as he took in the breathtaking view of undulating lilac oceans, the arched window giving the impression that this room of the temple flowed right out into the sky. The heavy purple clouds on the horizon were darker than Sins' uniform, seeming like an ever-present, if distant, threat. It wasn't yet night-time on Enoc; the only visible stars were the gold ones sitting on the Head General's shoulders.

Sins turned to regard Kieran, his face so rigid it could have been caved from stone.

Kieran paused, not sure where to stand. There was no desk in the open-plan meeting room, no barrier to keep between himself and his superior. The soft reclining seats, purple silksein trimmed with gold, looked tempting but he didn't dare find comfort in any of them.

'I have heard that you will do anything to get us to cut you loose,' Sins said.

'Most days,' Kieran agreed. 'But not today.'

'And why is that?'

Kieran managed to keep his eyes from sliding to the floor, though he wondered if he should be showing more deference. 'Over the past five weeks, I have helped people, those whom the Agency might not have been able to help—and perhaps even those who sought an agent's assistance only to be ignored. I will not apologise for my actions.'

'Upon your discovery of this particular situation,' Sins remarked, 'you should have informed a higher-ranked agent on Enoc and given them the opportunity to take action.'

Blood rushed into Kieran's cheeks. He tried to mimic Pina's calm, but the tremble in his voice lasted far longer than he would have liked. 'Yes. I should have. But I was concerned that it would alert Chi—agents who might have benefited from the exploitation of these people. Our Agency is no stranger to the Enocian Harem. And not every being is impervious to bribery.'

'I have looked into the matter. Your fellow agents were not involved.'

'They weren't aware of it, then,' Kieran noted, glad that Avurn had been wrong about other agents taking bribes. This time, anyway. 'Or they'd have been doing something about it. Right?'

Sins' gaze was sharper than a blade's edge. 'How did you know that those beings at the Harem needed help? I am told they had Rapture in their systems, masking anything in their energy that might have clued you in to their plight.'

'My companion, Captain N'uni, has some experience with the drug,' Kieran answered.

'And what of the boy's involvement?' Sins asked, head tilted to the side, as though evaluating Kieran and finding him wanting.

'I'd rather not disclose any information on that matter.' Kieran kept his arms pinned to his sides. He realised he was prepared to leave GLEA, right now, and he was serious about it for the first time in his life, despite the previous attempts he'd made to get thrown out. 'You should be thanking me, because if this had been discovered by mediaists or an e-paper reporter before I dealt with it, you would have had to do some fast thinking to preserve our image, given that it occurred right under our noses. Sir,' he added as an afterthought.

Sins stared at him for some time. Then he threw his head back and laughed. 'Good God, Krendasta, you remind me of a friend of mine.'

'Sir...?' Kieran repeated, this time confused.

The Head General moved away from the window and lowered himself into a chair. He indicated the one beside him. Kieran dutifully took it, though he remained perched on the furthest edge from Sins.

'The rainforest god, Bagara,' Sins clarified, rubbing mirthful moisture from his eyes. 'I am on speaking terms with Bagara and have dealings with two more sub-level gods. Go on, be shocked and appalled. The leader of GLEA, the most devout follower of our Creator, consorting with his godly children? Perish the thought.'

'No, it...it makes sense,' Kieran said.

Sins raised an eyebrow. 'Oh?'

'There had to be a reason that certain worlds claiming a sub-level god as their patron were not high in our priorities,' Kieran explained. 'You yourself insisted on GLEA helping everyone, not just those who worship the Creator God, when you were elected to your position. You would not abandon those planets or your principles. So you must have an agreement with specific sub-level gods and only help when they ask it of you.'

Sins nodded. 'Correct. We are all children of the Creator God, mortal or otherwise, and we should work together to keep peace among the stars. I was once more open about it. Now I must be more discreet. Most of my generals are no longer in favour of tolerating other gods.'

Kieran didn't envy Sins. The Head General's position relied on the votes of the Agency's most senior members. Sins would have to constantly balance doing what he thought was right with what was popular. Did that mean he didn't agree with having to marry and breed?

The Head General remained unmarried, after all. He had joined GLEA long ago, before the Agency became concerned about its deteriorating numbers.

'So you see, Kieran,' Sins went on, 'I completely understand about using unorthodox allies to cover the gaps in GLEA's reach. I commend you on the outcome of this operation, though it did perhaps cause more chaos than it needed to. I will assume the chaos was due to the actions of your civilian companions and not a lack of planning on your part. Do us both a favour and don't disabuse me of that notion.'

Silence stretched between them, not an uncomfortable one, but Kieran couldn't relax completely into the chair.

He swallowed. 'If I'm not in trouble...'

'...then why are you here?' Sins finished, the humour fading from his expression. 'I have read into your history with the Agency, though I was pressed for time and possibly missed a few details. I'm quite happy with Major Yetz's decision to assign you to the *Free Ride* and I believe that is where you should stay. No, I wanted to make an offer to Captain N'uni: a more varied selection of planets where freed slaves can live, under the watchful eyes of gods who provide greater protection than I can.' Sins smiled again. 'I would personally recommend worlds with rainforests. You do know that the rainforest god considers himself the god of lost causes and casualties? Bagara will even help those outside his domain.'

'I had heard that rumour,' Kieran murmured.

'Take heart, Krendasta, for we are not facing this galaxy alone,' Sins said warmly and stood. An unmissable cue, but Kieran remained seated. 'I'll send a list of planets to Captain N'uni shortly. Tell her to charge any expenses relating to your, ah, retrieval missions to the Agency.'

'I can tell her. Not sure she'll agree to do it.'

Kieran suspected she would, given the lines that crossed her forehead whenever she sat down in her ship's small kitchenette to go through the sums. But he didn't want Sins to assume that Kieran made the final decisions on the *Free Ride*.

'Ensure that she does,' Sins instructed. 'One last thing, Krendasta—you'd better requisition a new personal shielding device before you leave. I suspect you'll need it.'

Kieran reluctantly stood. This was an opportunity he'd never have again. If Zareth Sins wanted to help people by using all available tools and methods, then surely—no. Kieran shook his head. He needed to stop inviting ridicule and stop talking about the visions, not bring them up with the man who signed off on all of the Agency's promotions (though how much input he had beyond giving his approval was up for debate).

Does this mean I actually want a rank? Kieran wondered. *I think I do. If I rise high enough, then maybe I can change things...*

'General, do you work with the desert god?' he asked suddenly.

His heart sank when Sins shook his head. 'No. I've heard he's out of reach, even to his siblings. Some sort of family feud we're not invited to. I'm starking glad we *aren't* invited.'

Kieran headed for the door.

Sins' words beat him there. 'Why do you ask?'

Kieran performed what he hoped was an adequate shrug. 'Just curious about the god who looks after Ilbb. It's Captain N'uni's homeport, so I'll be spending a lot of time there.'

'It's wise to take note of whose domain we're operating in,' Sins said, nodding approvingly. 'We need to work together, gods and mortals alike, if we want to make a real difference in this galaxy. Countless beings depend on us. And we depend on you, Kieran. Don't give up on the Agency now.'

'I won't, sir,' Kieran promised. 'Not yet, anyway.'

'That's all I can ask.'

Once he was alone in the corridor outside, Kieran released a long, tortured breath and felt his heart restart. Head General Zareth Sins had not been what he'd expected and that was a good thing. But now there were even more questions creeping into his thoughts, unbidden and unwanted. If Sins could speak to the gods and they spoke back to him, did that mean they conversed with other mortals as well?

The voices. Is the desert god speaking to me? Why? Should I tell the Head General?

NO! That single word carried the fury of a thousand sandstorms.

Kieran froze. 'It's you, isn't it.'

No answer this time, but Kieran could sense a distinct presence in the corridor, one that exuded potent, deadly energy. A gust of blistering wind abruptly slammed into him, through him, past him—Kieran gasped, took a step back—and then a vortex of sand appeared, swirling up from the tiled floor and building a featureless form that failed to grow eyes or a mouth. A sub-level god had arrived.

Did they all look this terrifying?

'What do you want from me?' Kieran demanded, forming tight fists in the hopes that this would stop his hand shaking. It didn't work.

Stop running away and stop ignoring me!

Kieran ground his teeth together. 'I don't suppose you'll leave me alone if I ask you to.'

You used your powers and called me to you. And now you are in danger. They will come for you. You need my help.

'They will come for...' Unease prickled its way along Kieran's spine. There was something horribly familiar about all this, but he couldn't place it—a memory, flitting out of reach. 'How can you help me?'

Fingers emerged from the god's sandy form and pointed at Kieran's chip. *You need to remove that first. Then I will tell you everything.*

'No,' Kieran said, his anger churning and roiling in his gut, the perfect counterbalance to the icy fear that had taken purchase inside his veins. 'I am an agent of GLEA. And you are not going to take that from me.'

Kieran nearly laughed at himself. He wouldn't have said this several weeks ago (stark, probably not even a day ago), but he'd seen the good he could do, the people he could save when no other agent was able. The Agency might not promote him if he didn't marry and breed, but they weren't going to throw him out. Even as a private, the lowest possible rank, he could still do *something*.

Ami and Avurn needed him. He was useless to them without the chip.

He drew a breath, gathered his strength—and then stormed right through the sandy figure. It collapsed and scattered over the floor.

Kieran kept going, not daring to look back, his feet pounding the tiles even faster than his heart was beating. But before he could make it to the hoverlift, a roaring furnace chased him down and pinned him against the doors. He slapped his hands on the gleaming chrome surface, trying to push himself away from it, but the pressure intensified.

The doors to the hoverlift opened and Kieran suddenly sagged. He was now alone in an empty corridor. Not a single speck of sand remained.

'Are you alright?' the agent inside the hoverlift asked.

Kieran wasn't sure how to answer.

He hurried inside and swiped the sensor pad, refusing to talk or make any eye contact until he reached the ground floor.

THIRTEEN

Ami lowered her techpad and clutched it against her chest, hiding the lines of text streaming across the screen—a giant list of potential safe havens and associated contacts, courtesy of the Chippers. 'The Head General told you that I could offer any of these planets to our passengers? And that whenever we're on a "retrieval mission" we can charge our expenses to GLEA?'

Kieran nodded, running a hand through his shaggy hair and messing it up even further. He looked frazzled. Ami couldn't blame him. Being confronted by someone capable of deciding—possibly destroying—your future would scare anyone shitless.

The sun was setting behind Kieran, darkening the lilac horizon, and stars were beginning to speckle the sky.

It was almost...romantic.

Avurn's voice exploded out of the entrance to the *Free Ride*. 'Go away! I do not care if you are grateful that I saved your life. Do not waste any more of my time with your incessant chatter. You saw me blow up a wall today and don't think I won't do the same to you if you continue to aggravate me. Begone!' A pause, then—'Ami! Please tell me we've got enough coin-chips for fuel.'

Ami mirrored Kieran's neutral expression for barely a nanosecond, then both of them started laughing. When their combined mirth had died down, far sooner than she'd wanted it to, Ami released a sigh. 'Much as I like GLEA paying for my fuel, it's...it's not enough. Saving handfuls of people...mopping up after the bigger crimes...'

'You don't have the resources to do more than that,' Kieran told her gently.

Ami shifted on her feet, agitated. 'I know. But I wish someone would destroy every Rapture factory in the galaxy. I know where most of them are, actually. On Rochaccia. That planet has an ongoing civil war, so both factions sell slaves and drugs to pay for materiel and mercenaries. You Chippers can't touch that one—you don't have enough people to take on a problem that size. And all that shit is not illegal there.'

Kieran regarded her for several long moments. 'You can't blame yourself for failing to do something that is impossible.'

'I'd like to do more than the bare minimum, Kieran. Just once.' Ami snorted. 'Look, I now have a Chipper on board who can predict if we're all going to horribly die on certain missions. Maybe we *can* do the impossible and save everyone. The two of us against the galaxy.' She rolled her eyes when Avurn began shouting at yet another passenger, apparently because they'd asked to see a menu. 'Three. Can't forget our little trigger-happy friend.'

She was glad Avurn hadn't needed to use his powers in front of Kieran in the Enocian Harem, but she supposed it was only a matter of time. That discovery wouldn't go well for anyone. The boy was dangerous when cornered. Ami reached for her lasgun and found it missing. She was sure she had fastened it to her belt after leaving the Harem, but then again...Avurn had been underfoot all afternoon.

Ami shivered as the cool evening breeze washed over her. She was tempted to board the *Free Ride* to escape it.

But then Kieran gave her a smile that warmed her from nape to navel. 'General Sins told me that GLEA has used unorthodox allies in the past.'

'Unorthodox could mean "way more efficient at getting shit done",' Ami noted. 'Huh, I'd get way more shit done if I had an army at my beck and call. There's millions of starship captains and mercenaries tearing about the galaxy, but they're way out of our price range. Unless I can use GLEA's coin-chips to convince them to take down the rulers of Rochaccia...how much can I expense at any given time?'

'I'd rather we didn't try that,' Kieran said. 'Since I have no desire to be kicked out of GLEA...for now.'

'Alright, well, let me know when you do want to get booted and then we'll try it.' Ami tilted her head from side to side, trying to work out the kinks in her neck. 'Anyway, I'd like to get back to the usual routine of aiming my lascannon at other ships and threatening the captains who were stupid enough to pull in at the Trading Post. Much easier. Much less chance of things blowing up in my face.'

'And less chance of the whispers finding me. There must be a desert somewhere here on Enoc or he wouldn't have...' Kieran trailed off.

Ami frowned, concerned. 'Are you okay?'

For a moment, he seemed on the verge of telling her something important. Ami leaned into him, shielding him from the wind, hoping her desire to help him was emanating from her in waves, loud and clear enough to be received by his chip. Gods, she was a hypocrite. Expecting him to share his secrets when she would never return the favour.

Kieran jerked away from her. His lasgun was out in his hand before Ami could even blink. He slapped his new personal shielding device and took a step forward, carefully positioning Ami behind his body and the humming orange sphere encasing it.

The intruder took her time, ambling up the boarding ramp with her arms spread wide, revealing (or pretending) that she was no threat. She stopped when Kieran twisted his spare hand, clearly preparing a forcefield. Ami recognised the woman as the one Kieran had pointed out to her in the Enocian Harem.

'Easy there,' the woman said, then flashed a smile. 'I wondered if I could get a statement for my report. The Head General is still refusing to see me, so I will need to get my information elsewhere.'

'Mediaist,' Ami hissed.

The intruder cleared her throat. 'No. I'm an e-paper reporter. I don't reveal my sources or provide any images of them. The safety of the people who help me is paramount.'

Kieran deactivated his shielding device and drifted back to Ami's side, keeping his silence. She should have been grateful that he wasn't trampling all over her authority, but she missed Avurn's less tactful way of dealing with unwanted presences. Not that Ami would ever use a lasgun to solve her problems. Stark, it was tempting. But there was too much blood on her hands already.

'Name,' Ami ordered.

'Grace Pendergast,' was the answer.

Ami narrowed her eyes. That name was definitely familiar. Grace Pendergast was a famous and faceless enigma who dug out information that her peers couldn't find or didn't want to reveal.

If this woman really was who she claimed to be, then she was the first great e-paper reporter, the one that Allen styled himself after back in Carton City. Though no images accompanied her stories, Grace Pendergast had been proven to be right too many times to ignore—stark, the whole galaxy considered her their 'champion of the truth'. She'd been on the beat for about twenty Old Earth years, so either she'd started in her late teens or she'd had some starking good work done on her face.

'You'll get nothing out of us,' Ami said. 'Cut your losses and leave. Now. Or should I let your readers know that you were hanging out in the Enocian Harem, desperate to get your grubby little hands on slaves?'

'I was doing research for a story,' Grace replied, her voice as smooth as highly buffed chrome. 'One that explores the connection between the galactic slave trade and the civil war on Rochaccia. Until today, I was under the impression that the Chippers were not intending to do anything about it. Is this now a priority for the Agency?' she fired at Kieran.

'You will have to ask my superior,' Kieran said simply.

'And who is that, Private Krendasta? Head General Zareth Sins —or the captain here?' Grace enquired, a glint in her eyes.

Ami clenched her jaw. The adrenaline from earlier was fading. She clapped a hand over her mouth, but it was no good. The yawn escaped—and drew the reporter's attention right back to her.

'You look familiar,' was Grace's next attack.

Cold fear flooded through Ami and the adrenaline reignited. It wasn't beyond the realm of possibility that the e-paper reporter had recognised her. Avurn had scrubbed Ami's details off the Galactic Database and she had filled out since her time on Rochaccia, but she'd been in all those starking Webcasts.

Ami glanced at Kieran. He didn't question her or the sensations he must be receiving through his chip. He nodded slightly and pressed his hand to the small of her back. As he began to steer Ami towards the hatch, he called over his shoulder, 'This vessel has exterior vidcams. If you don't want images of your face being given out to mediaists, Ms Pendergast, then I suggest you step away. I seem to recall that you prize your anonymity.'

Grace backed down the ramp, but she didn't look concerned.

Ami knew this was only a small, short-lived victory. The reporter would find them again. And next time she might not leave.

As soon as they were safely inside the *Free Ride*, Ami slammed her hand against the sensor pad on the wall. After a worrying groan and an angry hiss of hydraulics, the ramp reluctantly clanged into place.

She grumbled under her breath, then forced a tight, painful smile. 'That was nicely done. And I think I'll ask Avurn if he can look into actually installing those external vidcams.'

'I've spent too much time with Pina-Sai,' Kieran mused. 'His calm, patient manner seems to be rubbing off on me.'

'Oh gods, I'm in trouble,' Ami said.

Kieran blinked at her.

'I was hoping my good qualities would start rubbing off on Avurn, so that he's not...well, not so *him*.' Ami laughed and shook her head. 'I feel like I'm picking up his gung-ho habits instead. Some guardian I am. Jensa is going to kill me.'

'I'm here to ensure she's the only one who has the chance to do that,' Kieran told her.

'You've added yourself to her firing line, by the way. Maybe I should have warned you not to jump on board. Now, about earlier...'

'You mean your reaction to Pendergast possibly recognising you?'

The awkward pause was mercifully obliterated, thanks to Avurn shouting at someone to stop touching sensors in the hold.

Ami gritted her teeth. 'I can't talk about it. At least...not now.'

She expected suspicion, curiosity, and a whole lot of prying. A part of her craved it. Her past haunted her, constantly chased her. It was hard dealing with that shit alone. But could she share that much of herself with him? Gods, she wanted to.

Kieran bowed his head briefly. 'I understand. There are things I can't...deal with, let alone discuss.'

She had a feeling he didn't mean that day on Fintaz.

'Oh good, we can both suffer in silence,' Ami said cheerfully. 'Denial is going to be *so* healthy for us.'

'And not distracting at all,' he added.

His expression was innocent, but there was a twinkle in his eyes. Ami grinned and sashayed down the corridor, heading towards the bridge.

Maybe a little distraction wasn't such a bad thing.

FOURTEEN

Kieran woke a nanosecond before the ship jolted, throwing him out of bed. He flattened his body to the floor as the *Free Ride* bounced around him, his quarters small enough that he was able to brace himself between the wall and the platform that served as his bed. Pain shot through his elbows and knees as he rode out the increasingly violent shakes, each one worse than the last. He started counting them. Three, six, nine—and then the ship abruptly settled.

Kieran leapt off the floor, futilely grabbing at his jumpsuit. He gave up and left it hanging from his waist. This situation seemed a little more alarming than a wardrobe malfunction.

He made it out into the corridor. The ship chose to reward his efforts with a savage lurch that threw him against a bulkhead. Ami stumbled past, shouting assurances towards the hold and no doubt hoping their passengers would take the hint and stay down there. She wasn't wearing her jeans and appeared to be in yesterday's shirt, judging by those soup stains.

'Are you awake yet?' Ami asked, chortling.

'That remains to be seen,' Kieran replied and fell into step behind her.

Both of them stopped dead when they hit the bridge. The viewport was filled with twisted blue and green ribbons, all swirling chaotically as the world that was their canvas rolled faster and faster, like a lasball thrown down a hill. It took Kieran a moment to realise that the ship was the one moving, not the planet.

Ami turned to the person in the captain's chair. 'You should have woken me when we came out of leapspace, Avurn! You know the re-entry is getting bad.'

'Ami, I told you that disabling the alarms was not going to make the stabiliser problem go away.' Avurn sounded almost bored.

Kieran hooked his hands onto the bridge's safety railing, wishing he had at least ten other agents with him, though he wasn't sure that even a combined shield could save the *Free Ride*. It wasn't unheard of for agents to perish in starship accidents. Their forcefields worked best against lasbolts or small projectiles—shielding something this big from something as uncompromising as gravity...it was too much for mortal beings.

Ami swung a too-wide grin at him. 'So I don't suppose you Chippers want to cover the bill for these repairs?'

Kieran grimaced and tightened his grip on the railing when the ship heaved again. 'I assume General Sins meant refuelling and minor fixes. This seems considerably worse.'

'It is,' Avurn said, uncharacteristically succinct.

The ship rocked even harder. Kieran caught Ami when she tripped and went flying backwards. Her palm skidded along his bare chest as he grabbed her arm, bracing her against his body. She looked up at him, her green eyes filled with not fear, but something else, something that completely consumed her energy, something his chip couldn't accurately translate. Whatever it was, it singed his senses and left him wanting more.

Kieran guided Ami over to the communications console. He suspected that any attempt to pry Avurn out of the captain's chair would be tantamount to suicide.

An intensifying rattle demanded his attention. Kieran cast an eye around for the source of the sound, noting that the panel concealing the fire extinguisher was loose. He had a forcefield ready before the panel detached and hurtled its way across the bridge. It froze in midair, caught and contained by his powers. The panel dutifully flew into his grip. Kieran exhaled.

'Nice trick,' Ami said. 'Now get yourself strapped in.'

Kieran dropped into the bridge's only vacant chair and wedged the panel into the tight gap between his thigh and the weapons console. He swiped the sensor responsible for activating the straps, but they didn't appear. Ami shouted at him to slam the console with his fist. Kieran obeyed. A high-pitched whine answered him, then the straps circled his form and cinched themselves against his chest.

He could sense lifesigns on the planet, scattered into pockets of concentrated habitation—villages, towns. Communities that wouldn't exist without starship access. But all he could see through the viewport were vast mountains and valleys, covered in rocks and massive trees. Hardly a safe place to land. None of them would escape unscathed.

Kieran only spotted the dark patch of asphalt when branches began whipping the belly of the ship.

'Stark, that landing pad is small,' Avurn muttered. 'Kieran, we need to have strong words with your Head General—this does not appear to be the most prudent location to off-load our passengers. I know it was the first one on the list he sent us, but maybe it was ordered by risk, not by proximity to Enoc.'

'Av, just land the starking ship!' Ami snapped. 'And don't you dare get yourself killed. Jensa would never let me hear the end of it.'

Kieran craned his head over his shoulder and saw the smirk

twisting Avurn's lips. The ship was now steadier (even if it was still bouncing across the canopy of the rainforest) and it did seem to be slowing, enough that Kieran could make out distinct trees instead of an endless green blur. He reached for Avurn's energy, to confirm that the boy was feeling more confident about their predicament—only to hit a wall of static.

'Be quiet! I need to concentrate!' Avurn said. 'Do you want us to *die?*'

Kieran shot a look at Ami. She hadn't said a word either, so he wasn't sure who Avurn had been lecturing. Her jaw was clenched and her fingers were gouging holes into the padded arms of the chair at the communications console. He found her energy a lot easier to read. She wasn't afraid—she was angry. He knew this was not how she'd choose to go, with so much undone.

'Brace!' Avurn shouted.

The ship became eerily silent as it drew closer to the asphalt, but it didn't break apart or collapse when Avurn fired the thrusters. There was a small, feeble bang, one that Kieran had heard on previous landings. He took that as a good sign.

Ami closed her eyes briefly. A drawn-out sigh bled over her lips.

Kieran punched the relevant sensor on his console and waited for the straps to reluctantly shrink out of sight before moving over to Ami. He touched her arm. 'Are you alright?'

She laughed. 'Yep. Just wishing I could afford a better ship.'

'Even if you could,' Avurn said, leaping over the safety railing and heading for the doorway, 'I'm sure you would still disable "those starking alarms" and put us all at risk. My sister wouldn't like hearing about that, would she? I guess I can forget to mention it—if you let me sit in the captain's chair more often.'

'Avurn!' Ami scolded, but she was smiling. 'Are you trying to blackmail me again? Because you're doing a starking bad job of it. If

Jensa thinks you're in too much danger on this ship, you'll just end up trapped on Ilbb.'

Ignoring her, Avurn bounced out of sight and down the corridor, hollering for their guests to make a hasty exit if they didn't want to go through another landing like that.

Kieran had heard the story about how Ami and Avurn had met during a quick meal scarfed down in the ship's kitchenette (squeezed into a corner in the hold, with two foldaway chairs set into a bulkhead, it was hardly an ideal location for leisurely dinners). Avurn had been four years old at the time. That hadn't stopped him blackmailing Ami, thirteen years his senior, to help him—and he'd even accompanied Ami during her poorly planned, if successful, attempt to rescue Jensa.

Avurn was a lot more than he seemed. A lot more.

Kieran frowned. Neither of Avurn's temples held a chip. It would have made more sense if the boy did have one. Kieran had encountered static-like interference when linking his forcefields with other agents' or when trying to sense their energy, but never around people outside of the Agency.

Was his chip glitching? Causing him to feel something that wasn't there?

Kieran sighed. It had been days since he'd had a drink, but the effects that alcohol had on his powers could be cumulative. He would need to ask Pina.

'You hearing voices?' Ami queried, interrupting his thoughts.

'Should I be?'

She waved casually towards the viewport. 'This planet is mostly covered in rainforests, with extensive savannah zones near its magnetic poles, but there are some areas with slightly sandier soil. I don't know if that qualifies as desert, though...'

Kieran swallowed, his throat suddenly so dry that it chafed.

The desert god had found him on Enoc, in the stone corridors of its largest temple, which in turn had been surrounded by an urban sprawl and purple oceans. Kieran wasn't sure how quickly the desert god could follow him across the stars—and he didn't want to linger in one place too long to find out.

'Have you ever wondered why it only happens near deserts?' Ami asked.

Kieran did his best not to flinch or correct her. 'Why do you ask?'

Ami stretched, groaned, and slowly unfolded herself from the chair. She glanced around the bridge, no doubt checking to see if any other panels or fixtures had come loose. Rattled was not how Kieran would have described her. No, there were better words.

Determined. Tenacious. Beautiful. *Saviour.*

'It's confusing, is all,' Ami replied, forehead creasing. 'I've never heard of a Chipper pulling down a sandstorm, but I suppose it's possible. A storm's a lot bigger than some debris though.' She nodded towards the fire extinguisher panel, still standing upright against the weapons console where Kieran had left it. 'But you've told me you're not particularly powerful. So how did you do it? It's not like desert-based powers don't exist, but GLEA monitors all of its agents to make sure none of you have the Magic...'

Her gaze fell to his chest. Kieran looked down at himself, remembering that his torso was bare. He didn't feel embarrassed by her appraisal and nor did he tell her to stop; he simply waited until her eyes reached a more appropriate level, then gave her a questioning look.

Ami's lips slowly curved. 'I'm starting to think that having a Chipper on the bridge is very distracting.'

'Only starting to?' he asked, grinning back at her.

'So you don't just have visions—you can read minds too, huh?'

'No, but I do know when someone is checking me out.'

Ami snorted with laughter. 'Should I feel offended that you

didn't return the favour? You haven't looked at my legs once.' She pulled her shirt further down to her knees. 'Well, I thought you didn't. But now I wonder. I was a little too *distracted* to notice you noticing me, wasn't I? Right, that's enough flirting. We should go out and find whoever it is we're meant to be dealing with.'

'We should,' Kieran agreed and leaned in close, seeking her. Seeking more.

Ami held up a hand, intercepting his chest. She gave him a gentle push. 'Kieran. I get it. I know how easy it is to latch onto the first person who gives you the attention you've wanted so badly for so long. Don't let gratitude be the only reason you're into me, okay? Look. I've been down that road. You'll regret it.'

'It's not the only reason.' He chuckled. 'I have seen your legs, after all. But what impresses me most is how much you do for others, how many risks you take for those who can never pay you back. You deserve more than gratitude. You deserve admiration.'

'Ah, stark,' Ami murmured. 'You shouldn't say shit like that.'

'Why not?' he asked.

'You don't know me. You don't know what I've done. The lives I've taken.'

'I know about the lives you've saved.'

She hesitated. 'There are some things you can't fully atone for.'

'Believe me, I know,' Kieran said.

They shared a long, loaded look. Then Ami turned away, her tone flippant once more. 'I better get some pants on—and make sure Avurn hasn't stolen my lasgun. Again. I really need to deal with that kid. Little starker.'

Kieran lingered on the bridge after she left, privately acknowledging that she had a good point, that he didn't really know her.

But he did know that he couldn't stop thinking about her.

FIFTEEN

'Av, you have got to stop polishing the floor of the bridge,' Ami said, snapping the third and final buckle of her belt into place.

Avurn stopped at the bottom of the ramp, staring up at her. 'Why? We have an image to maintain. A polished floor sets us apart from the scum we tangle with.'

'That floor is so reflective I'm seeing faces from my memories swimming on it.' She stalked past him, her boots clanging on the ramp before thumping onto asphalt. 'And one of these days, I'm going to see arms—right before they pull me down into oblivion.'

Avurn blinked. 'You're poetic today. But we don't have time to indulge your sudden burst of creativity. According to the list the Head General sent you, our contact's name is Micadei Rforine. I'm not sure we should trust him.'

'Your chip tell you that?'

'No, I performed a simple search on the Web—either he's using an alias or his identity was never entered into the Galactic Database to begin with.' Avurn's lip twisted. 'I am trying not to rely on the chip, because Kieran might sense me using it. Perhaps you should order our resident Chipper to read our contact's energy.'

'I just might,' Ami muttered.

The man in question looked to be barely out of his teens and his eyes were a similar shade of green to Ami's, though his were filled with mischief instead of the exhaustion Ami was used to seeing in the mirror. His beige cargo pants and button-up shirt were the perfect complement to his dark copper hair and warm amber skin. For some reason, he was waving energetically at Ami, as though her appearance was the highlight of his day. It could be that he was excited to help victims of the slave trade. At least, she hoped that's what it was.

Ami waited until Kieran had reached the bottom of the ramp before she left her ship's shadow. As they walked, side by side, she said quietly, 'I've never dealt with anyone outside the Trading Post or Ilbb before now.'

'And you're wary of someone my Head General has recommended,' Kieran guessed. 'Because the Ch—the Agency wasn't aware of the situation at the Enocian Harem.'

Ami smiled. 'You can say it, you know. *Chippers*.'

'You, Captain N'uni, can be a bad influence sometimes,' he said.

'Only sometimes?'

'I wouldn't mind being under...your bad influence more often.'

Stark. This thing between them was about to go supernova and Ami wasn't sure she could stop it—or even if she wanted to.

They'd only made it halfway across the modest landing pad when Micadei Rforine came racing towards them. Ami stiffened. Kieran held out a hand, palm down and presumably forcefield-less, letting her know that he sensed no danger. That or he could deal with it. Micadei opened his arms—Ami flinched in anticipation— but he lobbed his embrace on Kieran instead. The Chipper turned a beseeching expression towards Ami who quickly transformed her laugh into a cough.

Micadei reared back to slap both of Kieran's shoulders. 'This is awesome! When Aunty Grace said she'd run into you, I could not believe it—'

'You know this guy?' Ami asked.

Kieran shook his head. 'I've never met him before in my life.'

'Oh, that's right, we don't know each other,' Micadei said, deflating. Then his grin came flooding back. 'Yet! I'm Micadei, by the way. Ever since I received Captain N'uni's message, I've been busy speaking to a whole bunch of villages—and all of them are happy to help you out! This is just the sort of thing that will make Bagara proud of me and, well, it's not been easy living in his shadow—'

'Bagara's the name of the rainforest deity, right?' Ami clarified.

Micadei nodded, beaming. 'He does not care who you worship. Once you're in his domain, you're immediately under his protection.'

'Reminds me of something Xan Jones told me,' Kieran mused. 'He said that I'd qualified for his protection the moment I landed on Ilbb. And I apparently earned his friendship until the end of time because I kept up with him in the bar when we first met.'

Ami raised her eyebrows. 'I'm impressed. That's a pretty serious offer, coming from Xan. How many Minty Madnesses did you do that time anyway?'

Kieran frowned thoughtfully. 'Eight.'

'Shit,' Ami said. 'No wonder Xan likes you.'

'Um, hello?' Micadei interrupted, biting his lip, possibly afraid they'd forgotten he was there.

Kieran's gaze unfocused for several moments and Ami held her breath, waiting for him to unearth something frightening in Micadei's energy. But then Kieran shrugged. 'You seem like an honest person to me. I'm sorry we haven't met before.'

'But we have now!' Micadei said cheerfully. 'We'll get along great, I just know it.'

Kieran's lips twitched. Ami fought back another laugh, grateful that she wasn't the one on the receiving end of more exuberance than a single human could possibly contain.

This Micadei was *exhausting*.

Wait a minute. Hold up. Ami needed to check something. 'Aunty Grace, huh. That wouldn't happen to be Grace Pendergast, would it? Famous e-paper reporter, champion of the truth, kind of like a wyvern hunting down prey when she's chasing a story?'

Kieran stilled beside her.

'Um.' Micadei started wringing his hands. 'Well, she *is* my aunt. But I won't tell her you're here. I promise.'

'Come on, Kieran,' Ami said, turning back to her ship, her pulse thudding in her ears. 'We need to get the stark out of here before that reporter catches up to us.'

'You're running low on fuel,' Kieran reminded her in an undertone.

Stark. He was right.

'We've got fuel!' Micadei said. 'I can give you fuel—all the fuel!'

'I sensed no malice from General Sins,' Kieran commented. 'He wouldn't have recommended this world without good reason. And I believe that Micadei will keep our presence here a secret, despite his connections.'

Ami grabbed his hand and pulled him away to have a quick, possibly heated, discussion about who was actually in charge of their so-called retrieval missions. But Kieran stopped short, her arm growing taut between them.

'The whispers,' he said, panic flitting through his blue eyes.

'What are they saying?' Ami asked.

'They don't like Micadei. They say he's an enemy.'

Ami shook her head in disbelief. 'So you're going to trust the voices that made you call down a storm and kill a bunch of people? Really?'

'No, of course not! But it…it wasn't supposed to happen if I stayed away from deserts!' Kieran finished angrily. 'Is nowhere safe? Will everyone around me always be in danger? I'll never be able to set foot on a planet again!'

'I won't let you hurt anyone,' Ami said, reaching out to smooth the lines gathering on his face. His eyes closed and he leaned into her touch, his skin warm and slick, though she wasn't sure if it was due to fear or the humidity.

Kieran abruptly flinched away from her. 'What's your solution? How can you stop the voices—stop *me*? You can't! Nobody can!'

'I got you out of that vision you had about the Harem, didn't I?'

Ami loved it when he smiled, especially when she was the cause, but then it was gone, wiped away by worry.

Kieran nodded slowly. 'I won't refuse your help, Ami, but I don't think it will be that easy in future. I know I can't trust him— the voices,' he corrected, and Ami had to restrain herself from asking what *that* was about. 'I trust General Sins. And I trust Micadei. What you see is what you get. His energy is as bright and unfaltering as a young star and it's…it's a nice change. I don't sense that from most people.'

'It's not normal to be that happy,' Ami said, eyeing Micadei warily. 'But I'll trust your judgement on this one. We'll drop off our passengers, fuel up, and split. We can always check in on them later, to see if they're okay. I really don't want to wait around and give this guy's aunt a chance to jump us. And if she shows up before we leave? I think even I could manage to hit her with at least one lasbolt.'

Kieran looked down at her belt. 'I think Avurn has taken your lasgun again.'

'Oh for stark's sake,' Ami said, then stormed off. 'Av! What are you playing at? This planet has laws restricting the use of lasguns! Laws you fell under the moment you left the ship!' She threw her next words over her shoulder, not particularly caring where they landed or who heard them. 'It's illegal for someone his age to carry that here, right?'

'Is it?' she heard Kieran ask.

'Well yes, but...' Micadei indicated the group of nervous beings who were keeping close to the *Free Ride*'s hull. 'Your crewmate helped these people and will probably continue to help people. So I guess I'm saying...I saw nothing.'

That clinched it for Ami.

If Micadei was going to overlook a small infraction for the good of others, then he couldn't be a complete waste of oxygen. And 'Aunty Grace' hadn't made an appearance yet. That was another point in his favour.

Frankly, it was a huge relief to know that she didn't have to fly all the way back to Ilbb every time she rescued a new batch of beings.

She was a mortal, not a god.

She couldn't afford to squander any of the limited lifespan she had left.

THE *FREE RIDE* drank thirstily from a fuel pump positioned on top of an extensive underground pipe system that Kieran would not have expected to find on Bagaran, a planet without extensive trade links. He kept an eye on Micadei, who was flitting about and reintroducing himself to the planet's newest arrivals, telling them all for the tenth time that they could change their mind about which village they had chosen for their new home.

Ami and Avurn were having a disagreement, something about

the hull integrity being compromised by a loose stabiliser. Kieran decided not to listen to that. He was going to have to board the *Free Ride* regardless, to escape the Desine, and he preferred denial to anxiety.

'Waiting for someone?' Kieran asked when Micadei paced past him again, practically vibrating with nerves. 'Your aunt, maybe?'

Micadei blinked. 'What? Oh! No. She's already here on Bagaran. Except I made sure she didn't know you'd landed yet.'

'Glad to hear that,' Kieran said. He hadn't seen another starship approach Bagaran's sole landing pad, but it was possible the mediaist had a much faster ship at her disposal and had arrived on the planet ahead of them.

Micadei nodded absently. 'I'm doing my best to hide your presence. My aunt is the least of our worries.'

Kieran swallowed. The whispers were muted for now, but they hadn't gone away. He hoped the refuelling wouldn't take much longer.

Kill him, the Desine's louder voice suddenly hissed. *Kill him! His father deserves to feel the same pain that was inflicted on me!*

Kieran took one step back from Micadei, then another.

'Kieran?' Micadei asked, concern erasing his carefree smile.

Strangle him with his own starking vines—

Kieran hooked his shaking hands onto his belt. 'Don't come near me.'

'Okay?' Micadei sounded confused. 'But you look awful?'

Panic squirmed in Kieran's gut and he staggered towards the *Free Ride*, only managing to remain upright for several more seconds before he fell to his knees. Sweat slithered over his forehead and dripped onto his fingers. The asphalt swam in front of him, heaving and roiling like molten rock.

Kieran spat bile. This cleared the bad taste in his mouth, but it did nothing to expunge the presence infiltrating his mind.

He sensed Micadei's approach, heard the rasp of his bare feet, and blindly scuttled away. 'Stop! I don't want to hurt you.'

'Why would do you that?' Micadei asked quietly, but he didn't come any closer.

'I don't know!' Kieran exclaimed.

He should die! I will not be the only one without! howled a searing desert wind.

'NO!' Kieran said.

He couldn't fight a god alone—but he wasn't alone, not anymore. There was one person who could save him. He called her name.

Ami's cool fingers slid beneath his chin. He focused until her words drowned out all else. 'Those voices won't leave you the stark alone, huh? I'd blast the lot of them with my lascannon if I knew where to aim it.'

'I'm going to hurt him!' Kieran stabbed a finger towards Micadei's pale face.

Ami grabbed Kieran's hand and folded both of hers around it, eyes wide. Belatedly, Kieran realised that he could have unleashed a forcefield without meaning to. He winced. That had been stupid and reckless. If he could bring down a storm by accident, he needed to be far more careful with such casual gestures.

'No, you won't hurt Micadei,' Ami said sternly. 'Because I'm here and I'll get Av to shoot you if I have to.'

A laugh escaped Kieran, startling him and apparently the Desine too because the god's presence withdrew from his mind. 'And Avurn would do it, no questions asked.'

Ami attempted a smile, but it looked increasingly brittle.

'We need to get out of here,' Kieran said. He leaned heavily on Ami as she helped him to his feet, then nodded at Micadei. 'I'm sorry. I won't be able to see you again. It's for your own safety.'

Oddly, Kieran didn't sense any surprise from him. Just crushing disappointment.

'I understand,' Micadei said. 'I can't protect you. Not from them.'

'And who exactly are we talking about?' Ami demanded.

Micadei didn't answer her. He faced the opposite direction and crossed his arms. Ami cursed and ran for her ship, yelling at Avurn to fire up the thrusters. The boy didn't ask any questions. He immediately disappeared up the ramp.

Kieran lingered, watching Micadei. 'What do you know that I don't?'

'Umm, just enough to make things worse,' Micadei said, refusing to meet his eyes. 'You'd better go. If they haven't found you yet, if you don't know what's going on and your thoughts can't betray you, then you're safe. Well. Sort of. You're less safe than you were. I won't draw attention to you by saying something I shouldn't. But if you still want to risk it, Aunty Grace is the one who knows everything about everything. You should ask her.'

'Not happening,' Kieran said and sprinted towards the *Free Ride*. Before the desert god could take control of him. Before he could harm an innocent man.

The boarding ramp was already closing. Kieran leapt onto it and didn't look back.

SIXTEEN

The third vessel they'd intercepted in the past week loomed before them, its hold packed with lifesigns—the *Free Ride*'s sensors and Kieran's chip were in agreement on this one. Technically, it was also the first vessel of the week. Ami had only tangled with Captain Jackson five days ago and it seemed the pirate hadn't learned her lesson.

Ami ignored the pointed look Avurn was giving her from the communications console—she couldn't give him the opportunity to voice his opinion on her refusal to kill their opponents, since it would only undermine her authority—and instead aimed her hard gaze at the young woman whose face was filling the viewport.

'Captain Jackson, you know how this goes,' Ami said and locked her arms behind her back, stiffening her stance. She couldn't afford to relax, even if Jackson was an easy mark. 'Unless you've forgotten the usual procedure since we last saw each other. Which would be quite a feat.'

'You're lucky she's as broke as us,' Avurn muttered. 'Or those lascannons of hers would be fixed by now. Our shield is barely operational as it is.'

Ami gave him a curt wave, the signal for him to shut up and let her do the captaining on her own starking ship. She then jerked her head at Kieran, who stood beside her, suitably solemn and silent. 'As you know, I have a Chipper on my crew, so if we have to board you, you're going to have fun catching the lasbolts his forcefields throw back at you.'

But she wasn't going to let that happen.

Kieran had a functional shielding device again, but knowing GLEA it would probably crap out after a couple of minutes—and he'd explained that he could only generate a forcefield big enough to cover his torso, which made Ami secretly glad Avurn had a chip that enabled him to do much better (he had shielded them both on Julius' ship, after all). But despite Kieran's repeated claims that he wasn't very powerful, there was always the chance that he would suddenly invite a sandstorm on board and Ami had that down last on her list of 'things I want to see inside a starship'.

'Yeah, yeah, we'll get a docking port open,' Captain Jackson groused. 'Stay still and we'll come alongside you.'

'Kieran,' Ami ordered.

He left her side without question. He had his lasgun out and his shielding device was already activated, in case he met resistance in the docking tunnel.

Captain Jackson started unleashing a stream profanity aimed at Ami's parents. Ami did not disagree with Jackson's assessment of her mother and father, even if the pirate didn't actually know who she was insulting. Avurn killed the viewport's vidscreen, once again revealing the jagged coral-like vessel in front of them.

'Yep, you are definitely too young to learn some of those words,' Ami told Avurn.

'That's not why I cut her off,' he said tightly. 'I just finished hacking Jackson's onboard ledgers. The taxation laws on the world where her ship is registered demand meticulous records. It's a good thing I'm a speed reader.'

'Av.' Pressure mounted against Ami's temples. 'What are you getting at?'

Avurn stood and moved directly to the weapons console. Ami bit back an order for him to keep away from it; in Kieran's absence, someone *did* need to sit there. Avurn slipped into the seat, explaining, 'Captain Jackson recently took out a significant loan. The reason listed is "short-term employment". Any crewmembers pulling that many coin-chips will undoubtedly have combat training.'

'She could be planning to use that loan to hire a good mechanic,' Ami said, though her heart was plummeting faster than a starship in freefall. 'She does need to repair those lascannons...'

Avurn huffed, clearly unconvinced. 'I told you it was suspicious that Jackson had already stocked up again, but you insisted on chasing this tip anyway.'

Her earpiece buzzed. Ami slapped it. 'Kieran?'

'Ami, I don't see any slaves on Captain Jackson's vessel.'

'Vision?'

'Yes.'

Ami squinted at the ship drifting across her viewport. It was taking Jackson twice as long to dock as last time and Ami had assumed it was because the pirate captain was stalling to be petty. But maybe there was another reason.

'Who are these twenty extra lifesigns then?' Ami asked.

'Mercenaries,' Kieran answered. 'They are well armed. I can't hold off that many.'

Ami brushed a finger over her earpiece, muting her side of the link. It would have been nice if the *Free Ride* had a functional intercom system, but she couldn't justify spending the coin-chips to repair it if individual Web-connected devices still worked.

She turned to Avurn. 'Two people with chips can pool their powers together and make bigger a shield, can't they?'

Avurn shook his head. 'I will not reveal myself to Kieran.'

'Av! He needs your help.'

'No, you will not persuade me—and there is no point in exposing myself when we can easily put them out of commission *for good*,' Avurn snapped.

The lascannon was warmed up and ready for action. It was the usual precaution. Just in case someone needed to fire the weapon, though that very rarely happened. But dread hardened inside Ami's stomach as she watched Avurn.

'Ami.' Kieran's voice came through her earpiece again. 'What do you want to do?'

'We're leaving,' Ami said, after de-muting the device. She knew her ensuing sigh would force some static down the link. 'We'll catch up with Jackson next time.'

'When she has had a chance to repair her lascannons?' Avurn demanded. His fingers were so rigid they were forming arches on the console. 'When she is finally ready to reduce us to insignificant dust? No! We cannot waste this opportunity.'

'Av—'

Ami stretched out a hand to stop him, but she lacked a chip and Kieran wasn't on the bridge to do it for her.

The very large and very powerful lascannon affixed to the bottom of her ship fired.

An explosion lit up the bridge.

'NO!' Ami cried.

She fell. Her knees hit the deck; pain flared but quickly became a distant ache. Hot, dark anger blinded her, stole her breath, caused her heartbeat to throb in her ears. When she regained her senses, she found that her fists were anchored to the floor. She couldn't move. She *shouldn't* move. Because what she really wanted to do was wrap her fingers around his tiny neck, that little shit—

'No one will mourn them! They were pirates and mercenaries!' Avurn was arguing somewhere nearby.

'Stay away from the console!' Kieran roared back at him.

'Ouch, that's some grip you've got there.'

Avurn's voice had wobbled as though he was actually *afraid*, so Ami looked up and saw that Kieran had both hands out in front of him, Avurn struggling to move while two separate forcefields kept his wrists pinned against the bulkhead beside the viewport. Avurn's arrogance had been completely wiped away. In its place: a child's panic.

'Enough!' Ami rasped. 'Let him go.'

Avurn slid down the wall and his feet touched the floor, but he stayed where he was, a hand clasped over the sleeve that hid his own chip. His eyes were wide.

Ami supposed it was easy to see Kieran as harmless. She'd lost sleep over the past few weeks, wondering how he had moved that sandstorm on Fintaz. She hadn't seen him accomplish anything on a similar scale. But his forcefields, though small and unimpressive compared to what Avurn could produce, were still very effective.

Kieran stepped back and positioned himself beside Ami. He didn't ask any stupid questions, like if she was okay (she wasn't) or if she wanted him to intercede (Avurn was *her* problem). He simply stood there while she used him to climb back off the floor.

'You,' Ami snarled, pointing at Avurn, 'are going back to Ilbb. And I'm going to tell your sister exactly what you did.'

'I rid the galaxy of a repeat offender!' Avurn shouted.

Ami held onto Kieran, worried that she'd topple over again. She sucked in a breath, then noisily released it. 'You think you're so smart and ahead of the game, Av, but you're not. You don't care about the consequences of your actions. You don't see the bigger picture. And frankly, that's a big weakness for someone who I suspect has designs on taking over the entire galaxy. Shit, Av!'

'But Jackson won't hurt anyone ever again!' Avurn exploded, surging forward—and stopping abruptly when Kieran lifted a hand, though it seemed the Chipper had only done it as a warning. The gesture carried no forcefield. 'We need to kill these fuckers, not send them merrily on their way!'

'Av,' Ami said, his name a weary whisper.

The boy glowered at Kieran. 'It's this starking Chipper. If he can see the future, which is no longer the absurd notion I thought it was, then he might be able to infect your mind with some other power lurking in his arsenal. It's not impossible. Nothing's impossible. He has to go.'

'Watch out, Av has a chip!' Ami blurted, knowing exactly where this was going. She gripped the lasgun on her belt, which was thankfully still there, but she couldn't bring herself to pull it on her young crewmate.

'You betrayed me! You ratted me out!' Avurn howled.

And then he struck, hands extended. Kieran pulled Ami away, neatly sidestepping the invisible blast that hit the empty air beside them. He effortlessly called up a forcefield of his own before Avurn could launch another attack. Ami darted behind the safety railing. This was definitely not her fight. She watched as Kieran advanced on Avurn, brushing aside the boy's next few frantic attempts, each one slower than the last. Avurn retreated, much too late, and he futilely slapped at the bulkhead as new forcefields held him against it.

Kieran turned back to Ami, his raised arms remaining steady. 'That explains why I feel so much static around him. But how he did get a chip? I don't see one?'

Ami cut off her laugh before it became hysterical. 'He made it himself, by reverse-engineering one of yours. It's in his left arm, in the crook of his elbow. You should cut it out.'

'No starking way!' Avurn said. 'Fuck the fuck off!'

Kieran tipped his head to the side, frowning. 'He would just make another one.'

'Yeah, I don't need a vision to see that coming,' Ami said with a snort. 'Probably thought he was untouchable because of how much he boosted the chip's settings, but clearly years of training can outdo power levels.'

'His control is poor,' Kieran noted. 'He relies on speed and brute force, without taking the time to properly craft the universe's energy. This can work in certain situations, granted—if you're lucky enough to get it right the first time. But subsequent forcefields will vary greatly in shape and in power. They can even become intangible and practically useless, as you just saw. It's an unreliable method.'

'Give me a year and I'll be pulling ships out of the sky!' Avurn ranted.

Ami rubbed her forehead. 'Stark it, Av, I thought I was making progress with you. I guess not. Maybe you'll never change.'

'My superiors will want to remove the chip,' Kieran said, edging his way across the bridge, towards Avurn. He went no further when the boy lobbed a glare in his direction. 'Or they might offer to bring Avurn into the Agency, to give him the training he needs.'

Avurn didn't like the sound of that, judging by the fresh expletives he launched at them. He followed this up with a diatribe about how Kieran's presence on the ship had ruined *everything*.

'Kieran's presence has done more for us than your starking chip ever did,' Ami pointed out. 'Especially since you won't use it in front of other people—which is most of the time!'

Avurn grumbled something under his breath and went slack

against the bulkhead, breathing heavily. All the fight had gone out of him.

Kieran lowered his hands to his belt and bowed his head. 'I'm sorry I used so much force. I expected...greater resistance from you. Had you trained on Gerasnin, you would have easily overpowered me—your forcefields have the potential to be *very* strong, if given better foundations. I think it would be best if you developed your abilities.'

'I am *not* setting foot in one of GLEA's temples,' Avurn growled.

'You won't need to.' Kieran pressed his lips together. 'Ami, if he's going to have a chip, he needs to know how to use it properly. I can teach him.'

Ami stared at Kieran. 'Seriously? You think this is a good idea?'

'Well, it's an idea at least,' he conceded. 'Avurn can help me create a larger shield than I could ever manage alone.'

'Okay, that might be useful,' Ami said, already envisioning the possibilities. How many more people could she save with Kieran and Avurn working together? 'But he'll take over the galaxy—shit, the entire universe—if we're not careful. Can you make sure you cut his chip out *before* that happens?'

Kieran studied Avurn for a moment and then shook his head. 'I won't need to. I am sure the Creator God will render it useless in that case. The chip enables its wearer to touch the universe's energy, but only because the Creator God has allowed that connection to form. It is a privilege that can be revoked at any time.'

'He's not my god, that starker can't tell me what to do,' Avurn muttered.

'Hey, respect that starker or you could lose the powers,' Ami warned him. 'Now sit yourself down and have a good, long think about your future.'

Avurn pouted, actually pouted. 'And what future is that, exactly?'

Ami gritted her teeth and swallowed the first few words that came to mind. 'Either you're going to be stuck on Ilbb with only your chip for company—or you're going to be out here in space with us, learning how to use the starking thing and doing your best to act like a decent human being. I'm not holding my breath, mind.'

'So what experience does *Private* Krendasta have with training junior agents?' Avurn asked archly and crossed his arms, standing just that little bit taller. Clearly, he was feeling more confident.

'You don't have a lot of choices, do you?' Ami threw at him and spun on her heel. What she really needed was an excuse to leave the bridge, some sort of distraction to occupy her so she wouldn't do or say anything she'd regret later. She knew exactly who could help her with that. 'Kieran, I need you to come check something out in the hold with me.'

Kieran immediately followed her. He didn't seem surprised when Ami pulled him into her sleeping quarters instead. He maintained his silence while she shed her clothes; he even gathered up her shirt and jeans so he could fold them for her. She knew the exact moment he glimpsed the scars on her back, because his gaze swept up to hers, completely missing the more interesting parts of her anatomy.

Anything could have caused those scars and he could draw his own conclusions. But she was just so tired. Tired of dealing with it alone. Tired of hiding herself from him.

She bent her elbow over her shoulder and gestured down at the thick ridges crisscrossing her flesh. 'Laswhip. My own father. Mostly because I refused to join in when he was tormenting his slaves. But that wasn't my only transgression. One time, he whipped me after I warned some visiting mediaists that he planned to trap them on the planet and enslave them. Another time, it was because

I apparently sided with my mother over something. Laswhips weren't her style. She preferred to lock me in a room without food for a week. I should be grateful her punishments were so merciful, she said.' Ami rolled her eyes. 'But she's no better than him. She deals in slaves too. So many lives ruined because of them.'

Kieran's eyes glittered with tears on her behalf. Ami envied him. She hadn't been able to cry in years and sometimes she wished she could. Crying always seemed to help Jensa feel better; a few tears and suddenly she could confront Xan about what he'd done to upset her.

'Is that why you've dedicated yourself to saving people?' Kieran asked. 'To make up for what your parents did—what they still do?'

Ami shook her head. 'No. I have my own shit to atone for. They got sick of me baulking at their lifestyle and hit me with Rapture. I… couldn't stop myself. I'd resisted them for so long and I thought they'd never find a way to wear me down, but I was too weak to fight the drug. I used the laswhip on the slaves they brought before me. Some survived. Others I whipped until they died. And I *enjoyed* it.'

'The drug caused that reaction, you know how it works,' Kieran said.

'I keep telling myself that. Maybe one day I'll believe it.' Ami rubbed her eyes, but the tears refused to come. 'I escaped. Stole this ship. Started ferrying goods. I was in a bad place, so I guess Av showing up to blackmail me was the best thing that could have happened. I managed to save Jensa—it was stupidly easy, all I had to do was threaten to shoot the slavers' ship, because no one had ever challenged them before. Okay, maybe someone had, but not with such a giant lascannon. Anyway, I realised that's what I wanted to do. Target the slavers and the pirates who work for them—and save the lives they want to ruin.'

She saw the tension in his shoulders, saw his desire to come over and offer her the comfort she definitely didn't deserve. But Kieran stayed seated on the bed. Relief and disappointment warred inside her gut, a potent mix that made her instantly nauseous.

'You're from Rochaccia,' he guessed. 'And if Pendergast recognised you...'

Ami's throat tightened, but she knew she had to keep going, had to get the full story out in one go or she'd lose her nerve.

'Yeah,' she said. 'My parents paid a bunch of mercenaries to help them invade a planet, which they renamed and started ruling. Set themselves up as the legit governing body on Rochaccia, so the Chippers couldn't arrest them. Things went pretty well for a while. They got to do horrible shit together.' Ami laughed darkly. 'But then they got divorced and wanted the other's share. That's how the civil war got started. It's still going. Thing is, one of the laws they made stipulates that Rochaccia can only be inherited by someone who is chosen by the planet's rulers. Plural. *Rulers*. They both chose me. Probably thought I was easier to manipulate than some stranger, I guess. If one of them dies, I get their half of the planet and whatever's in their treasury—which will make me very valuable to the last one standing.'

Ami drew a long, steadying breath. 'I have to keep running. I can't get caught. Because my parents will dose me with Rapture, to turn me into the compliant heir they want, and I won't be able to stop them. I got lucky with a weak dose last time. That's how I got out.'

Too afraid to look at him, in case his face was full of pity, Ami fled into the cramped ensuite, sealing herself away inside the even smaller shower unit. The water hit her cheeks, the way her tears never would. Her sobs remained dry, barren.

She pressed her forehead against the filmy chrome wall and waited for the filth to wash off her.

It never did.

SEVENTEEN

Kieran stayed where he was at first, unmoving, hunched over on the thin foam mattress. Ami was beating herself up over something she still couldn't change or control, but he had no advice to offer her. He had very little control over his own life. What could he give Ami except empty reassurances? Should he leave?

He heard her sobbing and shifted awkwardly on the bed.

Then he made his decision.

He stripped off his jumpsuit, passed through the screeching door of the ensuite, and stood in front the shower unit for barely two seconds before the access panel slid open and Ami's hand emerged. He took it, squeezing into the confined space beside her. Lukewarm water streamed over them like miniature, translucent ropes, binding them closer together, until her back was pressed against Kieran's chest. His chin found a perch on her shoulder and he kept his hands flat on her stomach, making sure they didn't slide around too much.

Kieran offered himself, his support, anything but words. None of them seemed right.

After a few minutes, her body started shaking and he fretted—

until he realised that she was laughing. Ami twisted slightly and used the new angle to grin at him. 'Every single one of the guys I've been involved with bailed before this point. They were always happy to take the sex, never the side order of angst and regret. But I guess you're stuck here. No escape in the vacuum of space, huh.'

Kieran tightened his hold on her. 'You know me better than that. You know me better than anyone else in this entire galaxy.'

'Actually...yeah, I think I do. And that scares me. It scares me even more than the dark oblivion my nightmares keep stranding me in.' Ami cleared her throat, banishing the unsettled whisper that had claimed her voice. 'Listen, before you get any ideas—I'm better off alone. Too bad you don't have that luxury. You've got to snare yourself an Agency spouse if you want to get anywhere with your career. You're still a private. Have you picked anyone yet?'

'No, not yet,' Kieran answered, withdrawing to touch the sensor on the wall.

The water cut out. Long seconds passed before the drying system reluctantly activated, blowing cold air over them. Kieran shivered. So did she.

'What happens if you can't find someone you actually love?' Ami asked. 'Will you just marry whoever's convenient?'

Kieran aimed his gaze at the moisture-beaded wall, unable to meet her eyes. 'Even if I did marry someone to gain a promotion, I'd refrain from intercourse and request that we merge our DNA to procure children, like they do for those couples and groupings who are otherwise incapable.' He sighed. 'But I...I don't want to raise a family with someone I don't feel anything for. It seems unfair to the child, even it helps to fill out GLEA's ranks.'

Ami slapped the shower unit's access panel aside and stumbled out, lurching her way into her sleeping quarters. Kieran followed, steadying her, then stepped back when he became acutely aware of their mutual nakedness. It hadn't bothered him earlier. Their time in the shower cell had been intimate, not sensual. But now, standing beneath the brighter strip lighting of her main cabin, he could see the shadows sliding away from her body, leaving space for his touch. Kieran swallowed.

She snagged his hand. 'Sit down. Let Av stew a bit. The kid needs a chance to do some self-reflection. Well, he needs a starking brain transplant, but those never turn out the way you want them to.'

He knew it was easier for her to say all that rather than just ask him to stay. But this situation was verging on inappropriate, especially since his desire for Ami was now very apparent. Kieran waved vaguely in the direction of his groin. 'I am not sure if I should...'

'We're both adults, Kieran. And I can keep my hands to myself. If you can,' she added, grinning.

He raised his eyebrows: a question.

She copied the gesture: a challenge.

Laughing, Kieran sat beside her. He waited, still as a statue, while she pulled a thin sheet up from the end of the narrow bed and wrapped it around them both. Ami rested her head against his shoulder and said, 'I'm glad I told you everything. Even if it was exhausting.'

Kieran pressed his lips together. 'There's something I want to tell you. It's only fair, given what you've shared with me.'

'Ooh, this sounds juicy,' Ami said, wriggling as she got comfortable.

'Hardly,' Kieran said. He marvelled at how easily she fit against him and how comfortable he felt in her presence. 'You know about the whispers. There's one voice that's the loudest—and he is not the god I would have chosen to allow into my mind.'

Ami blinked at him. 'You have a sub-level god in your head?'

'Well, not in it,' Kieran said, unable to temper his smile. 'That's just where I hear him. Anyway, the desert god appeared to me in the temple on Enoc and, well, seemed intent on making me leave GLEA. Then on Bagaran, he wanted to use me—use my body or my powers, I'm not sure—to kill Micadei. I barely stopped the Desine accomplishing that, thanks to you. And now I'm afraid that when he catches up to me again, he'll make me do something...something worse than what happened on Fintaz.'

'That won't happen, not while I'm around,' Ami vowed.

'Ami...' Kieran paused when her fingers slid through his and squeezed her hand in gratitude. He wondered if she also felt sparks ignite from that simple touch. 'I don't want to lose my chip. I can use it to do some real good out here with you and Avurn, and I finally know that this is why I'm in the Agency. To help those my fellow agents can't. Or won't. This is probably what Major Yetz hoped would happen when ze allowed me to leave Ilbb.'

'Ze isn't as clueless as ze pretends to be,' Ami agreed, then performed an exaggerated sigh. 'You just had to have a bigger tale of woe than me, didn't you. I'll trade you: my parents for the desert god.'

'Don't tempt me.'

'Kieran, I haven't even *started* to tempt you.'

He turned towards her and gently cupped her face. 'You probably should start. I already have.'

'So I guess we aren't keeping our hands to ourselves anymore, huh.'

Kieran breathed in sharply, about to ask if he could kiss her, but then she moved forward and answered his unspoken question with her lips.

Chaste at first, the kiss deepened as Ami leaned further into him, her palms skating over his chest, her fingers drawing hot lines across his skin—just like in the vision he'd had weeks ago in the outpost on Ilbb, he realised. Was this thing between them inevitable? He wasn't sure. So far his visions had shown him flashes, brief snatches of events—such as the gathering they had crashed in the Enocian Harem. He'd known they would survive that. But what if he'd seen their deaths? Could he have stopped it? Could he change the future?

Their lips parted.

'Avurn has probably stewed long enough,' Ami murmured.

'I'll check on him,' Kieran said, kicking off the sheet and standing from the bed.

Ami didn't follow him. 'Kieran...I want to return to Ilbb. I usually would have stopped in by now—and my sources at the Trading Post haven't sent me any more tips to chase. I've got nowhere else to be.'

Kieran knelt and scooped his uniform up from the floor. He was very aware of her eyes following his backside as he shimmied into the jumpsuit. He smiled, taking far longer with the manual zipper than he needed to (only senior agents had automated uniforms), but then he had to turn around and acknowledge what Ami had said. 'How long we are staying on Ilbb?'

'Couple of nights, so Jensa doesn't complain about not seeing Avurn enough.'

'Can I sleep on the ship?' he asked quietly.

'Sure. Stark, I'd understand if you wanted to stay on board the whole time. But I know I can't keep you away from the bar.' Ami dropped back against her nest of ratty pillows, arms linked behind her head. 'Too bad you'll end up soused and soft. I guess I'll have to relieve this tension on my own. Unless you want to stay sober for me and risk the Desine finding you...'

Kieran bent down and kissed her. He hadn't meant to, but she inspired impulsiveness in him and he enjoyed it, enjoyed her company, enjoyed being able to tell her everything. When he drew back, he sensed mischief and desire blanketing the pain and misery she carried around in her energy every single day.

'Don't tempt me,' he murmured.

Ami's lips curled.

TENDS KEPT one eye on their techpad and the other on the patrons milling about their bar. So far they had spotted twelve spelling mistakes in the latest issues of *The Carton City e-Post* and their screen was annotated with the corresponding corrections. They intended to send it off to Allen before dinner and then they'd head to bed early, leaving Avurn in charge. It was handy having a worker who could terrify the thugs into paying. Avurn might only be ten years old, but he always had that glint in his eyes...and he was a superb blackmailer.

Tends caught a glimpse of their reflection in a (surprisingly) clean glass and smiled. The bar had been awfully dreary before Jensa had donated her mother's saris to them (Jensa had said the garments evoked too many painful memories; Tends had initially asked for the saris because they'd worried she might come to regret the loss). It was easier to wear something cheerful and eye-catching instead of trying to brighten up the nooks and crannies that held darker secrets than the patrons who liked to hide in them.

Admittedly, Tends had another reason for wearing the saris.

Denton Dashing, who was tenaciously proud of his archaic opinions, would take one look at Tends, mutter something about them needing to 'pick one and stick with it, don't confuse folk', and then leave. Any evening without Ilbb's most difficult customer was a good one. If Denton didn't spend so much of his money in the bar, Tends would have banned him outright.

There were very few worlds left that still held Denton's views— it narrowed down his planet of origin significantly. Tends was certain they could find out the most intimate details of Denton's life if they tried. It was what they did. Had done.

Before Carton City had stopped being a last resort and became their only option.

'Get your mitts off my money,' Tends said idly.

'How did you know I was here?' Avurn demanded, hands on his hips and definitely not reaching into the coin-chip drawer set beneath the register console. No, not this innocent little boy with his cherubic smile. 'Or even on the planet? The *Free Ride* landed five minutes ago.'

'Magic,' Tends replied. 'Kind of like what those Desine worshippers have.'

'Sure. And I've suddenly decided to join the Chippers.'

The boy was already glowering and he hadn't even put on his little white apron, which would probably have been incinerated long ago if Tends didn't pay him extra for the 'humiliation' of it. Tends wanted their servers to look professional and privately thought the apron was adorable on Avurn, but never dared to mention it—especially not at a time like this, when the boy was a tiny thundercloud threatening to explode into a full-blown cyclone.

Tends dropped their techpad onto the counter, loosened their stance, and shifted into Bartender Mode. 'What happened this time?'

Avurn viciously yanked his apron out of the cupboard beside the register console.

'My esteemed captain and that Chipper she foolishly trusts,' Avurn practically growled, 'had a go at me after I blew up a ship with pirates and mercenaries on board. All of whom were participating in the slave trade, I might add. Ami and Kieran have taken it upon themselves to *strand* me here until I agree to restrain myself in future. Can you imagine possessing that much audacity? They are not my parents. My parents are dead. And they will be too if they don't stop treating me like…like some irresponsible child!'

'Av, my dear boy,' Tends said, knowing their ample beard wasn't going to smother their grin completely, 'I know it's easier to kill someone than to give them a chance to correct their behaviour. But we all deserve that chance. Every living being. And believe me, taking lives is not something that should be done lightly. It takes a toll on you, no matter what you tell yourself.'

'Yes, I suppose you would know, given your past,' Avurn said.

Tends wasn't surprised that the boy had looked into them, but they were fearful about what it meant. Avurn was the type of being who'd fool you into thinking that he was letting you off the hook… when what he was really doing was waiting for the opportune moment to ask for something in exchange for his silence.

Avurn hesitated, his fingers frozen on the ties of his apron. 'Tends, I…' The boy looked distinctly uncomfortable. 'I really appreciate what you have done for me. This job has funded many important projects of mine and your wisdom has always given me more than mere food for thought. If Denton Dashing says anything about your sari today, even under his breath, I will water down everything he orders.'

Tends stepped forward to help Avurn with the apron, deftly tying a double-knot and not adding a single bow or flourish, though they were sorely tempted to. 'Av, adulthood is something you earn when you've collected experiences, not years. Don't be afraid of making mistakes. You'll get more experience that way.'

Avurn stared at Tends, apparently flummoxed. 'I'm allowed to make mistakes?'

'They won't define you so long as you learn from them,' Tends replied. 'Now shoo. Allen's just entered and I know he's itching to have words with me again.'

'He should ask you out instead,' Avurn grumbled and was gone before Tends could remark on that. They didn't watch the boy scurry off, instead scanning the booth where Ami was sitting. She was a good influence on Avurn, but sometimes Tends wondered if she remembered that her companion was still a child in many ways.

Allen made a beeline for the counter. 'Tends! I know you're itching to correct my spelling and grammar, so we might as well get it over with!'

Tends didn't have the patience to deal with Allen—or the fact that their many decades of only being attracted to dangerous thugs had been so abruptly dismantled by the arrival of an infuriatingly harmless e-paper reporter. At least it was easy to dismiss the possibility of anything happening between them, since Allen let Denton sleep on his couch. Tends had no interest in pursuing Allen so long as this went on. The contractor had been given many chances to change his behaviour and Allen was inexcusably naïve if he thought Denton wouldn't squander this one too.

Tends waved in Avurn's direction. 'The boy will take your order, Allen!'

Ducking into the back room, Tends began to prepare a large case of bottled Minty Madnesses. The order had come through very recently, a rush job, and the bartender intended to deliver.

EIGHTEEN

Kieran was already onto his third Minty Madness. Not that Ami needed to count the tankards to know a coherent conversation wouldn't be forthcoming. A diagonal smile was slashed across his features, his pale cheeks bloomed with colour, and he was waving an unsteady hand at the bar.

Avurn eyed Kieran distastefully when he stopped by with Kieran's latest order. 'A tragic waste of a chip, if he's going to interfere with it like this.'

'Says the boy who's definitely tried a Minty Madness in his time,' Ami shot back.

'I was not going to wait years to see what all the fuss was about,' Avurn sniffed. 'I still do not understand the fuss, by the way. And since I loathe making a fuss myself, I promise to be more mindful about the consequences of my actions in future.'

'Good, I'll see you on the *Free Ride* in two mornings' time,' Ami said.

Avurn opened his mouth, then sealed it, trapping whatever retort he had stowed away in there. He nodded curtly, but maintained a cordial tone. 'I've procured more of the meds you require—I noticed you were running low—and I would have done so regardless of the outcome of this conversation, but I'm sure you do not believe me.'

He marched towards the counter, his strides stiff and short. Ami sighed. She didn't think her problems with him were over, not by a long shot, and she felt a weight settle over her heart. Gods, what was she going to do with him?

'You're not listening! You never listen!' Avurn's sister snapped in the next booth over.

Xan was quick to defend himself. 'That's rich, Jensa! I do my fair share of listening, but you're too busy accusing me of things to actually listen to *me*.'

Too many interested pairs of eyes were heading in that direction. Avurn spun back around. He now wore a dark expression that threatened all manner of unpleasant punishments in store for Xan if he kept upsetting Jensa. Nope, this wasn't Avurn's problem to solve; it was theirs. Ami quickly shook her head, trying to dissuade him.

'Do something or I will!' Avurn mouthed at her.

She hung herself over the wall dividing the two booths and gave Xan a wave. 'Hey, Xan! Get your butt over here. Kieran needs some company. I'm buying.'

Xan didn't need to be told twice; he'd heard those last two magic words. Ami made space for him on the cracked vinyl seat and then hovered at the entrance to the booth, watching Kieran's personality dissolve even further, replaced by the carefree drunkenness that Xan had mastered long ago. Kieran began regaling Xan, who cheered in all the right places, with tales of his latest adventures aboard the *Free Ride*. Ami wished she could put a stop to Kieran's unhealthy dependence on booze, the consequences be starked, because he had so much life in him when he was sober, so much drive to save people and solve the galaxy's ills.

This...this sloppy, boastful facsimile wasn't him. It was a shield he had erected to keep the voices at bay. The desert god had forced Kieran to become his worst self. Again.

Ami's earpiece buzzed and she immediately swiped it. 'Ralcha.'

'Ami! I saw your ship pass over us.' He sounded far too chirpy for her current frame of mind. 'Am I to assume that you have some new arrivals for me?'

'No,' Ami said, casting a furtive glance around the bar—in case there happened to be a stranger lurking nearby. Say, an eavesdropping sub-level god. 'I need to ask you some questions, though. To help with my retrieval missions.'

'I'm intrigued that anything I say can be used in your missions,' Ralcha mused.

'Intrigued enough to make the journey to Carton City?'

'I'll be there tomorrow morning.'

Ami flicked her earpiece, disconnecting the link, and resisted the urge to smack her palm against her forehead. *What are you doing, Ami? You can't take on a god...even for him.*

Ami sat down opposite Jensa, who was still fuming. This booth wasn't any better than the one Ami had just left. The battered carbon-fibre walls that kept the seats and table hidden from view looked as though they hadn't been repaired in generations. Tends had never attempted to spruce up the place in the six years Ami had used Ilbb as her homeport.

Ami cleared her throat. 'Sorry about lending away your husband. But I figured you didn't want to keep having that conversation with him.'

Even while downcast and in tears, Jensa Kaur Jones was beautiful. Her eyelashes were naturally long and when she walked the movement was so graceful she seemed to be floating. Many people had tried to befriend her—even Petria, who'd wanted an exercise buddy—but Jensa preferred to run alone, carving out solitary circles in the sand around Carton City. Jensa often claimed that running helped her forget things she didn't want to remember. Ami wondered if that'd work for her too. Probably not. She couldn't forget her parents while they were still hunting her.

'Xan's an idiot,' Jensa said. 'A massive idiot. And if he thinks I'll let him go on these GLEA-sanctioned stealth patrols into the desert, where any sand flea could kill him...'

'The Chippers are sending Xan and Denton out there, to spy on the tribes?' Ami asked incredulously. *Ralcha and his people won't like that. They will retaliate and I can't blame them.* 'That seems...dangerous.'

'It is!' Jensa cried, her fingers wound tightly around the mug in front of her. Coffein, by the smell of it. Jensa never touched alcohol and Ami wondered how long she could remain married to a man who imbibed far too often. 'I just want him here. With me. So we can have a baby. Then everything will be fine. You'll see.'

'Jensa, it's probably best if you and Xan get yourselves sorted before you complicate matters with a kid,' Ami said, trying to keep her voice light and devoid of judgement, even though she was storing shiploads of it in her gut. 'Things aren't sorted, are they?'

Jensa's flawless white teeth needled her bottom lip. 'He doesn't listen. I keep trying to tell him I feel trapped. He always makes the big decisions and of course I let him do that, because he's the one who makes the money.' Her eyes blazed. 'And don't say I need a job. Can you imagine getting a job *here*? Tying me down in Carton City? This isn't where I want to raise my child.'

Ami gave her a noncommittal shrug and didn't point out the glaring problem. Xan Jones was still doing time as a contractor; there were too many years left of his sentence. But Jensa deserved to be cut a little slack, given that her parents had been killed in front of her and she'd become a teenage victim of trafficking. She'd also been the one who had thought to stow Avurn in a cupboard the moment the pirates had boarded her family's ship—a selfless act that had been meant to save him, not create an opportunity for him to rescue her.

'None of that's important now anyway,' Jensa said, beaming.

Ami stared at her.

'I want to know how you feel about that handsome Chipper,' Jensa continued and tipped her head towards Ami's previous booth —which Xan had just tumbled out of, laughing uproariously. 'You blasted out of here two months ago looking like crewmates and now you look...like something else.'

Ami drew a shaky breath. When the air finally escaped her lungs, she realised she needed a friendly ear as much as Jensa had. 'We shared so much with each other. I hope it wasn't *too* much.'

'I've always wondered if the chips make them better in bed,' Jensa said wistfully. 'Xan's rarely sober enough to give it a go and I can't help it if my eyes start to roam. You must give me more details. How was it? How was *he*?'

'Jensa!' Ami hissed. 'We haven't...what we shared was better than that.'

Jensa arched her eyebrows. 'Really?'

'Really.'

Ami rubbed her temples. Avurn's heavy-duty meds were still in her system, thanks to her uterus' most recent tantrum (four whole days early, for stark's sake), but even they couldn't stave off this particular headache. She'd only known Kieran for a couple of Old Earth months! It shouldn't have happened this fast. But then why did it feel so right? She wanted him to always be on the bridge of the *Free Ride*, supporting her in her attempt to atone, and she wanted to stand beside him on countless worlds across the galaxy. The desert god would be the missile and she the shield that stopped him.

She couldn't imagine a future without Kieran. But if she told him this, there was a chance he would say she didn't have any part in *his* future. Because he might literally see it.

Ami settled for shrugging instead of trying to explain.

Jensa clucked her tongue. 'Be careful, Ami. Don't get too attached. He's going to want to marry inside the Agency and have little GLEA babies, isn't he?'

Ami waved a hand at Tends, who had chosen a very convenient moment to emerge from the back room. 'Hey, I need a pom juice and a coffein refill here! And can I get two Minty Madnesses over in Kieran and Xan's booth?'

'Oh, Av really hates those,' Jensa said. 'I'm glad. He stopped pestering me about trying them after I gave him one.'

Ami sidestepped the first few words that sprang to mind. 'Speaking of Av...'

'I know he has problems,' Jensa said quietly. 'But I can't parent him. He won't let me. He doesn't respect me enough to listen to anything I'd say—but he respects you, Ami. You're the only adult who has any kind of impression on him. That's why I let him risk his life on that ship of yours. You did get the stabilisers fixed, didn't you?'

Ami held in the despairing groan. *Great. I couldn't stop him blowing up a ship full of people and yet I'm still his best chance at turning out even halfway decent.*

KIERAN THOUGHT he could probably come up with a melody to go along with the bassline that his temples were drumming out as he eased his way back to consciousness. When his vision cleared, he blinked up at the disapproving frown that was blocking the sky—no, the ceiling of his quarters aboard the *Free Ride*. Not the person he'd expected to see.

Kieran recalled very little from the previous night, but he was sure that Second Lieutenant Pina-Sai hadn't been the one to carry him back to the ship.

In fact, he was having flashbacks about Avurn creating a force-field to hold him upright, because Ami had found him too heavy to manage on her own. Avurn had cursed the whole time, especially when he'd lost control of his powers and sent Kieran slamming into the sand face first. Then the boy had hissed into Kieran's ear that he'd better teach him something worthwhile or Kieran would have to sleep where he fell in future.

Kieran was unable to kill the smile that these memories evoked. And he was unable to feel any regret about last night's choices, even while besieged by an awful hangover, because he hadn't heard or seen anything that might resemble the desert god.

He frowned, recalling the presence he had felt on the other side of his door all through the night—Ami.

She had stood guard there, to make sure the Desine didn't come for him, and he'd found it impossible to contrive a convincing argument for her to leave, because his cabin had been spinning around him. It had been hard enough trying to get out of his jumpsuit. Which he apparently hadn't managed, because he was still wearing it. Sort of. It was mostly wrapped about his hips and legs.

Oh, that explained how he'd ended up on the floor.

'Good morning, sir,' Kieran greeted as he sat up, rubbing his lower back. 'Does Major Yetz wish to see me?'

Pina sighed deeply. 'Oh, Kieran. Is this my fault? What sort of role model am I? Why did I not teach you more sensible coping mechanisms?'

'Am I in trouble?' Kieran asked. He scuttled around, looking for a fresh jumpsuit—and ran into the one Pina was dangling in front of him.

'No, but you should be,' Pina said, dropping the item of clothing. Considering how creased it was already, Kieran didn't complain. 'You were supposed to report in as soon as you landed. Instead of doing your duty and assisting Dashing on a night patrol, you insisted on selfishly drowning your sorrows. This is not the path the Creator God chose for you.'

Kieran reared back onto his haunches. 'Really? If he doesn't want me to stray from that path, then he should protect me. Stark it, Pina...' He closed his eyes for a moment. 'He shouldn't be forcing Ami to do it in his place. She has no way of protecting herself, let alone me.'

'What are you talking about?' Pina demanded.

'Nothing. At least, nothing you'll help me with.'

'Kieran, you know I believe you about your visions,' Pina reminded him.

'So does this ship's crew!' Kieran said, bracing himself on the bed as he stood. 'And I've used my visions, Pina, I've used them to save people. The way the Agency never let me.'

Pina nodded encouragingly. 'That's good, Kieran.'

'But I should still keep my mouth shut when I report in?' Kieran knew he shouldn't be unleashing his anger and frustration onto Pina, but stark it, everything was so much easier when he was far from this fucking planet, its outpost full of stuffy Chippers, and that endless, deadly desert.

'If it means that Major Yetz will continue to allow you to travel with Captain N'uni, then yes,' Pina replied, folding his arms. 'The galaxy needs you out there.'

Kieran turned away from Pina, ripped yesterday's jumpsuit off his body, and tossed it onto the bed. 'I know I'm needed! I know I can't quit! But I shouldn't have to pretend...I shouldn't have to hide. I don't have to hide who I am with her.'

'The Agency is where you belong in the end, not the *Free Ride*.'

Kieran yanked hard on the zipper of his uniform, grateful that the quartermaster sergeant on Enoc who'd given him a new personal shielding device had also agreed to replace the jumpsuits he'd lost in Ilbb's orbit. Smoothing out the fabric, he whirled around to face his friend. 'If you are insinuating that I should focus on my career, then don't worry. I know that GLEA is my future. But I won't need to get married to climb through the ranks. Unlike you.'

Pina sucked in a breath. Kieran felt the guilt like a punch to the gut.

'I'm sorry,' he murmured. 'That was thoughtless of me.'

'Yes, but it wasn't wrong,' Pina said.

'Pina...'

'If I was any good at my job, I'd have saved that girl,' Pina continued, his face tight with pain. His energy was laced with it too. 'And I'd have earned my former rank with hard work, like Sies did for hers. She deserves to be in charge of this outpost—no, a temple on a more densely populated world. Jon and I rushed into marriage, both of us lured in by the promise of major. I see that now. We should not have been promoted that fast. Oh God. What good am I, Kieran? How did I ever think I could help you?'

Kieran shook his head repeatedly. 'No, no, you *have* helped me, Pina. By convincing Yetz to assign me to the *Free Ride*. I've learned that I can use my visions to help people. And meeting General Sins showed me that if I obtain a higher rank and gain enough popularity, then I can make people listen to me. I can change things. I can change GLEA.'

'You are making progress,' Pina told him, sounding pleased. 'So I haven't been shouting into the wind.'

'You're not a terrible mentor, you know. It's just that I'm a terrible listener.'

Pina chuckled and clapped Kieran on the shoulder. 'That's kind of you to say so! I may even pretend it's true. Come on. Time to report in. You've kept your superiors waiting long enough.'

NINETEEN

'Have you ever heard of the Desine stalking someone who isn't one of his followers?' Ami asked.

She and Ralcha had taken a booth in the corner, one that did not have a clear view of the bar. Ami was grateful that Tends hadn't come by to take their orders. The bartender had clearly guessed that she'd wanted some privacy this morning (it was indeed morning by Old Earth time, despite the seemingly eternal twilight outside).

Ralcha had arrived early, when Kieran was still sleeping. Ami had ordered Avurn to look after him while she dealt with the Yabul chief, but when she was heading over to the bar meet Ralcha, she'd spotted Avurn sneaking off to his unit beside Xan and Jensa's. If he wasn't working at the bar, then he was tinkering with something that might even be worse than a reverse-engineered chip.

Ami had glowered at Avurn—until he'd had the decency to inform her that Kieran's colleague had come to get him.

Ralcha's eyebrows shot up in response to Ami's question. 'Ami, the Desine has reasons for all the things he does. Just as we mortals do. Some of his reasons, I suspect, are no less personal than ours.

But no, I cannot imagine him being interested in someone who does not worship him.'

Ami worried the inside of her cheek between her teeth. 'Even if that someone can create a huge sandstorm out of nowhere and kill a whole bunch of people?'

'This has happened?' Ralcha demanded, leaning forward, his golden eyes intense.

My poker face isn't as good as it used to be, huh, Ami reflected. 'Yes. There were casualties. But this friend of mine doesn't have your brand of powers. Well, that's what they say. I'm kind of dubious. I'm starting to think they didn't just grab a sandstorm that happened to be conveniently nearby.'

Ralcha relaxed back against the torn vinyl seat, rubbing a thumb underneath his chin. 'I do not blame you for being dubious. The Magic is not inherited, as such. Any children born beneath the Desine's eyes, in his domain, have the Magic bestowed upon them. There are many who leave the deserts and become City Dwellers— or they may choose to move to another sub-level god's domain. Their children do not receive our god's blessing or his powers.'

'He never knew his parents,' Ami murmured. 'So it's possible then, that he was born on a world controlled by the Desine. Oh gods.' She slapped a hand over her mouth. Thinking out loud wasn't going to do her any favours.

'Possible,' Ralcha agreed, a frown creasing his features. 'But the Desine looks after all his people, especially those he gifts with the Magic. They must be trained or they can lose control and become dangerous. By the sounds of it, this friend of yours is extremely powerful. Even I cannot move a sandstorm, much less create one.'

'So why didn't the Desine do anything before the sandstorm? Why didn't he make sure my friend received that training? Unless he didn't know about my friend until recently...'

Ralcha jerked upright on the other side of the booth. 'No! He knows his people. He looks after and guides us all.'

'Ralcha, I'm just saying—'

'No, Ami, listen!' Ralcha said urgently.

A battered lasgun, easily as long as Avurn was tall, hit the table. Denton pulled a stool over to the booth and plonked himself on it. He ignored Ralcha completely and turned to Ami. 'This sand flea bothering you?'

Ami gritted her teeth. *Stark. Sober and steady on his feet—he must have done the night patrol alone.* 'Denton. Back off. This man is my business partner. And my friend.'

'Doesn't look like a friend to me,' Denton sneered. 'He looks like a troublemaker.'

'Denton! Drag your corpse over to Petria, since she's the one who actually wants it. I hear Allen finally kicked you off his couch last night.' Ami smiled briefly. 'Should I call Tends over and see if they know why? Or maybe we should ask Avurn. I thought I saw him whispering into Allen's ear last night...'

Denton's face reddened. He grabbed his lasgun, strapped it back onto the belt running diagonally across his torso, and shot away from the booth as though it had burst into flames. But then he swooped back around for another pass, shaking a finger in her face. 'That little shit of a kid isn't here to blackmail me right now. You watch out.'

Ami had long suspected Avurn's involvement in Denton's decision to leave her alone after that regrettable night, but she found that she appreciated his interference more than it annoyed her.

She shook her head. 'No, *you* watch out, Denton. Ralcha here has the ability to bury you underneath a pile of sand. He's far more dangerous than a drunkard who constantly forgets to charge his weapon. Also, what do you think Xan will do once he hears what you've been saying about his brother-in-law? He's your only friend left. You can't afford to lose him.'

'Fuck you!' Denton threw at her as he stalked off.

'Sorry, Ralcha,' Ami said, grimacing. 'Where were we?'

Ralcha's gaze grew unfocused instead of following Denton over to the bar. 'I was no one. I was an outcast. No longer acknowledged as the chief's son. I thought the Desine did not know of me. But he came to me, encouraged me to fight and take back control of my tribe, to save my people—and those other tribes who fell prey to the usurper.'

'So he didn't actually help you or stick his neck out for you at all?'

'He did help me.' Ralcha smiled. 'He assumed his human form and protected me as a bodyguard would. He also gave me the confidence to unite this planet's tribes, so that we could confront and unseat the usurper. I did not know who he was at first, how blessed I was, but he revealed himself to me afterwards. I do not think he meant to. He seemed...lonely. Anyway, he said that everyone under his protection, everyone gifted with his powers, is known to him. There is no one that could hide his people from him.'

'Except maybe the Creator God...' Ami trailed off, her heart slamming against her ribs. 'Ralcha, could a chip—you know, the GLEA tech—dampen someone's desert-based powers? The Chippers threaten to kick out anyone who shows signs of the Magic, but I've never heard of that happening. Maybe it's because Chippers with the Magic can't access those powers. The chips could be nullifying them, right? It could even be hiding those beings from the Desine!'

Ralcha looked aghast. 'Ami, what are you suggesting? A *Chipper* has the Magic?'

'He said he followed a cord in his mind and someone answered him...' Ami shivered. 'Oh gods. It wasn't his chip that killed them. It was the powers he was born with.'

She stood abruptly and turned to go, didn't even plan to say farewell—but a hand grasped her wrist, stopping her.

Ami scowled down at Ralcha.

She wasn't in the habit of letting someone push her around, even a friend. She'd had enough of that as a child.

'Who is it, Ami?' Ralcha pressed. 'He needs to be taught to use his powers safely. If what you say is true and this person, this Chipper, has killed others, then what is stopping him doing it again?'

Ami snatched her arm away, unbalancing herself in the process and hitting a nearby table. She fought to keep her voice low. 'Me. He has me.'

Ralcha's face softened. 'You can't do this alone, Ami.'

'Look, I don't—' Ami cut herself off when she felt the air heat up around them. This wasn't a climate control malfunction (that was the one thing Tends did maintain in their bar). This was much worse. Ami didn't have a chip, but even she knew she was standing in the presence of something angry, turbulent, and sufficiently god-like.

A sandy figure rose from the floor.

'What the stark!?' Tends exclaimed, swiftly dropping behind the bar.

'Oh shit, I am not staying around here long enough for the Desine to skin me,' Ami said and ran for the exit.

'YOU HAVE CONDUCTED YOURSSSELF ADMIRABLY,' Major Nexis Yetz declared. 'And have done wondersss for our galactic image, by ressscuing ssslaves on Enoc—and you did thisss in front of sssome of our mossst generousss donorsss. Very good work.'

Kieran nodded along with his superior's words, trying not to show his impatience.

Everyone looked expectantly at First Lieutenant Sies Ryn. She scowled, then slowly, reluctantly bowed her head. 'I had my doubts, but Private Krendasta's unusual methods have garnered adequate results.'

'That is the equivalent of raucous applause from her,' Pina noted, a hand over his mouth to shield his smile.

'While Krendasta's achievements in this one matter should be commended,' Ryn continued, her voice rising in pitch, 'you should not be condoning and adopting his insolence, Lieutenant.'

Pina met her gaze squarely. 'Really. I think insolence becomes him. And change is the lifeblood of the Agency, Lieutenant. If General Sins hadn't changed things when he was elected, the Agency would still be ignoring those unable to defend themselves and unable to pay for assistance—before him, we only helped those who could afford sizeable donations.' Pina paused, looking thoughtful. 'Who knows, Kieran could one day become Head General himself and change things further.'

Ryn simmered in her chair, but made no further comments.

Kieran flipped a grin at Pina. They didn't always get along or agree with each other, but Kieran knew his Lentarian brother had his back.

Yetz snapped zir arms several times in short succession, in an apparent attempt to cross them. 'A pity you showed no sssuch dedication to your dutiesss before, Krendasssta. With thisss new drive to succcceed, you would have had no trouble finding yoursssself a like-minded spoussse within the Agencccy. You ssseem too busy to ssseek one now. But that is no longer the problem it onccce was.'

Kieran coughed. 'Excuse me? I mean, sir, I'm only twenty-five. I have plenty of time to earn an enlisted rank—or a position in officer training—without resorting to marriage.'

'For centuriesss, the Agencccy's growth has been ssstymied by the ssslow paccce at which itsss agentsss forge meaningful connectionsss,' Yetz said. Kieran found himself surrounded by nodding heads, though curiously Ryn's was not among them. 'Thanksss to the new developmentsss, it will be much easier to match pairs and groupingsss who are more sssuited to each other. Not all unionsss have been succcccessful before now. Lieutenant Pina-Sssai can attessst to that.'

Kieran frowned. 'New developments?'

'The update currently being downloaded into our chipsss,' Yetz said.

Kieran's fingers rose to his temple.

Ryn spoke up, her eyes lasering in on Major Yetz. 'An invasive update that is unfair to those who wish to truly earn their ranks. *Some* agents do not need to reproduce in order to exemplify themselves.'

'What is going on?' Kieran murmured aside to Pina.

'I wish I knew,' Pina answered. 'Can someone please explain?'

Ryn leapt out of her chair, fists clenched. Her energy roiled with anger so potent it scalded Kieran's senses. 'This *update* means that the chip will monitor your desires, what you find attractive in the genders and species you prefer. Then you will be matched with someone inside the Agency. Can you guess why?'

Kieran had already guessed, but he dared not answer. Even Yetz was too nervous to interrupt zir inferior, if Kieran was reading zir features correctly.

'They now *expect* us to breed,' Ryn said distastefully. 'The new mandate from above. If we marry outside of the Agency or refuse to breed when ordered to, we will be stripped of our chips and thrown out of the temples and outposts we call home.'

Kieran stopped breathing for several seconds. *Oh God.*

'Why was I not told before now?' Pina demanded.

'You no longer possessss a rank that givesss you the benefit of knowing these thingsss in advanccce,' Yetz told him. 'Not sssince your unsssuitable pairing ended in divorccce. You can now look forward to a more compatible partner, with the choiccce made for you.'

'Compatible!' Ryn spat. 'And who decides what's compatible?'

Major Yetz extracted one of zir arms from the nest of limbs on zir chest and indicated Ryn's chair. 'Sssit, Lieutenant.'

'Your love of your rank is blinding you, Major!' Ryn snarled. 'You don't understand how dangerous this is for the Agency's future.'

Yetz watched her steadily. Zir silence was so heavy it seemed to press down on Ryn's shoulders. She dutifully slid into her chair, allowing Yetz to focus back on Kieran. 'Don't worry. You will not need to plan a wedding jussst yet. The timing dependsss on the feedback the ssservers reccceive from your chip and how quickly the sssystem can find a partner who matches your preferencesss.'

'I...' Kieran forced a smile that cracked his lips, dry from the *Free Ride*'s faulty climate control system. 'I am definitely going to worry about it. Sooner rather than later.'

Then he turned and fled, closely followed by Pina.

Once he was outside, in the long shadows shed by the buildings that stood between him and the low-lying suns, Kieran snapped, 'Stark it! Is that all I'm worth to them? Breeding stock! Never mind about saving lives!' He kicked up clumps of sand, knowing it made him look petulant but not particularly caring. The fine particles shot away from his boots like geysers. 'And if the chip discovers someone with attributes I find attractive, wouldn't I be better off with them instead of the closest match they can find inside the Agency?'

Pina stared into the dim horizon. 'Maybe I would have had a better marriage if a more suitable husband had been chosen for me.'

'Pina, don't you dare,' Kieran said. 'Don't you dare buy into this nonsense.'

'Why are you so quick to dismiss it?' Pina asked, glancing aside at Kieran. Pina's cheeks hollowed. 'Oh. I can guess what's going on here. Captain N'uni. You're thinking about her, aren't you? You shouldn't.'

'Why? Because the chip will record what I like about her and transmit it to some programmer back on Gerasnin? Make them find a suitable match even faster? Force me to get married next week?'

'There is that,' Pina said quietly. 'And because it is no longer possible for you to start anything with her. I know you'd like to—do not insult my intelligence by denying it. But attraction is as far as you can go there without jeopardising your place inside the Agency.'

Kieran snorted. 'My place? I still don't have a rank to speak of! But don't worry, Pina. I won't be able to start anything. Kind of hard to do that when I know GLEA is monitoring my "feedback" the entire time I'm on the *Free Ride*. Really kills the mood, don't you think?' His gaze wandered to the bar. There were several lifesigns there, Ami's among them.

'Kieran, the Agency needs to ensure that all of its agents have the proper upbringing,' Pina told him.

'Over three quarters of agents enter GLEA after the age of eighteen—or their species' equivalent of adulthood,' Kieran pointed out. 'I don't see how we can control *their* upbringing.'

Pina clasped his hands together in front of him, but Kieran saw that they were shaking. 'The Agency seems to have decided that it prefers to raise its own members and I think I know why. Our superiors are keeping it quiet, but I have heard that a lot of agents are leaving because they disagree with this or that issue and they don't feel they owe GLEA anything, not even the benefit of the doubt.'

A dark laugh snaked out of Kieran. 'I see—they prefer their

agents to be brainwashed into blindly accepting how things are done. Stark it, I thought the Head General was a decent man. He deceived me. Or perhaps he isn't popular enough to make the right changes anymore. He doesn't want to upset too many people and lose his position.'

'Kieran—' Pina began.

'No, don't even try to convince me,' Kieran said. 'I was raised by GLEA. I'm not their best product. Maybe it's not such a bad thing if we seek partners outside the Agency. Lieutenant Ryn is right—this is bad for GLEA's future. We will only lose more agents.'

Pina's grey eyes were dull and lifeless. 'We have to obey our superiors. It's better for the galaxy, for the people we protect, if we heed their orders.'

'Is it?' Kieran mused. 'We should just trust that our superiors know what is best for us? When no one ever dares to tell them they're wrong? And this is *wrong*, Pina. You are still not recovered from your previous marriage. Entering into another union for the wrong reasons will only hurt you more! I won't let you do that to yourself!'

Pina shrank, hunching over until his head nearly dropped below the line of his shoulders.

'I could really use a drink,' he muttered.

Kieran knew he shouldn't oblige him, given Pina's history, but the moaning winds were beginning to sound out syllables, words, and threats. The whispers were going to drive him mad if he stayed sober. And the Desine's intentions were far worse.

Kieran nodded towards the bar. 'Have you ever tried a Minty Madness, Pina?'

They had barely reached the door of the building when Ami exploded from within. She stopped dead, her face pale. 'Kieran, he's here. He's in there right now.'

'Who's here?' Pina asked, confused.

Kieran wavered. His chip was still non-functional, his blazing hangover a testament to that, but he didn't need it to feel the presence of the desert god in the bar, a dark pit threatening to swallow the entire town. Ami's hand slid into his and within nanoseconds they were running for her ship, fingers intertwined. She slapped her earpiece with the heel of her other hand, calling for Avurn who appeared almost instantly, though Kieran didn't see where the boy had sprung from.

'My sister is not going to like the fact that I left without bidding her farewell!' Avurn shouted, but he was grinning.

'Are those coin-chips falling out of your pockets?' Ami demanded. 'Do they belong to Jensa or Tends!?'

Avurn swore colourfully in response.

Kieran had his boots on the ramp by the time Pina caught up to him and snagged his arm, tearing him away from Ami who kept going. Pina had to bend over to fit underneath the vessel's protruding bridge.

'What is happening?' Pina asked. 'Let me help.'

Kieran jerked back a pace. 'You can't help me, Pina. Not with this.'

'If you won't accept my help, then please ask our god for guidance. He is always with us, even if we can't hear him—send your distress to the Creator and he will answer, in his own way—'

Kieran planted his hands on Pina's chest and shoved him off the ramp, which groaned reluctantly as it began to rise. He shouted down at Pina, 'The Creator God should have answered me when I needed him that day on Fintaz. It's his fault I attracted the attention of another! I can't escape—he always finds me!'

'Kieran, what are you talking about?' Pina called.

The ramp clanged shut between them.

TWENTY

Ami steepled her fingers beneath her chin and tried to remain calm.

Despite being consigned to the communications console again, Avurn was sporting a broad smile, though Ami couldn't tell if this was due to the fact that they were no longer planetside or because he could now roll up the sleeves of his dark jumpsuit as he went about the ship. Ami was well aware that she should have been more suspicious when he'd started wearing long sleeves a year ago. There was always a method to his madness. Unfortunately.

Ami had learned not to look at the pulsing red lines marring the skin around his chip for too long, especially after Kieran had studied Avurn's arm and suggested that the boy was doing irreversible damage to his body.

Ami slapped the side of her chair, impatience getting the better of her. 'So we've heard nothing from the Trading Post since the Captain Jackson tip?'

'Complete silence,' Avurn confirmed, turning in his chair to face her. 'And I will point out that our sources were already becoming more reticent with their tips, a trend that began after our enter-taining jaunt on Enoc.'

'Since we drew too much attention to ourselves,' Ami added sourly.

Kieran was standing closer to the viewport than usual, his arms clasped behind him, his gaze lost to the stars. But clearly part of him was still present because he asked, 'Do you think Pendergast published something about our activities in her e-paper?'

'No,' Avurn said, tapping his fingers together and activating his palm-based techpad. 'I subscribed to her reports years ago and I've seen nothing about us yet. Which is quite out of character for her—and a pity, by the way. It would really help build my galactic profile, if I was featured in *The Pendergast e-Post*. Unfortunately, someone at the Harem had a vidcam on them. They followed us down to the landing pad and had a decent enough zoom on their lens to see the serial number on the hull. The *Free Ride* is publicly registered on the Galactic Database. That's not the worst of it—the vidcam also recorded our faces and mediaists wasted no time in Webcasting that footage. So I'm afraid you're right, Ami, about us drawing too much attention. It will severely hamper our missions in future and I am not sure how to deal with this complication.'

Avurn fell silent, his expression mildly constipated. Admitting that must have hurt.

'Shit,' Ami said. 'Now everyone thinks we're raiding clients on their homeworlds instead of simply hijacking the ships of the middlebeings. We're starked.'

'Isn't that a good thing?' Kieran asked. 'The usual buyers may be less likely to purchase slaves if they're concerned about being targeted. It should decrease demand and thus supply. Fewer beings will be kidnapped and trafficked.'

Ami smiled wryly. 'In a perfect galaxy? Sure. But that's not how it works in *our* galaxy—and we're only three people, crewing one small ship with a shields that is dodgy on the best of days. We can't do much to affect supply. We might have just pissed everyone off.'

'The Trading Post allows slavers to dock, but those trades are banned from taking place on the space station,' Avurn said, stroking his chin. Ami wondered if he would keep performing that gesture once he actually grew a beard. 'The Post's administrators claim to be neutral on the issue. But our source on the admin board, the one who checks the manifests for us—they were once trafficked themselves and have strong feelings about slavery. *They* should have sent something, at least.'

Ami rubbed her itching eyes; the *Free Ride*'s climate control system was definitely getting dryer. 'Messages sent between Web relays can be intercepted. Pirates might be trawling through them to guess where we'll go next, maybe even planning to ambush us. Our sources at the Post have probably gone quiet for our safety as much as their own.'

'We rely on those tips,' Avurn said. 'We can't save anyone if we're aimlessly roaming through space.'

'I know, Av.' Ami sank further back in her chair, considering her options. Then she sighed. 'We'll head for the Trading Post, see if we can't get any tips in person.'

She fiddled with the manual controls, her stomach clenching. Rescuing trafficked beings had been a lot easier when no one took note of her vessel. When no one recognised her. How much longer would Ami be able to operate? How many people would suffer and never be saved because she'd exposed herself on Enoc?

Ami looked up when she heard Avurn ask, 'Kieran, can you teach me how to create forcefields using your method? I am already capable of erecting shields that are larger than what any Chipper can manage, but I...am not always successful at establishing them.'

Clearly, Kieran was in the mood for a useful distraction, as opposed to moping like Ami was tempted to do, because he indulged Avurn. 'It takes practice. And patience. The universe's energy is in a constant state of flux. You need to conduct enough *stable* energy to generate and sustain your forcefields, instead of throwing them out recklessly and hoping for the best. It can take several seconds to create a serviceable shield and that's a long time in certain situations. Which is why agents also use personal shielding devices, to cover that gap. It's also common practice to have a forcefield ready, no matter how small, before entering a hostile environment. We rarely go after a criminal alone—safety in numbers is a large part of our success—and we try not to harm our quarry, aiming to incapacitate them instead. A good forcefield can replace a fatal lasbolt.'

Avurn brightened. 'I see. There would be some benefits to keeping your assailant alive. You can immobilise them inside a forcefield and interrogate them!'

Ami was sure the glare she threw in her crewmate's direction could have scraped the old lasbolt scoring off the hull of her ship. Her mood soured further when she saw that Kieran was nodding in agreement. He offered her a small, apologetic smile. 'I'd rather he immobilised people instead of the alternative.'

Well, there was that. Give the kid some nonlethal tools and make him less likely to kill people—or maybe give him just enough knowledge to make him even more dangerous.

'Fine,' Ami said. 'It could come in handy.'

'Do you think I could create a forcefield big enough to move an asteroid?' Avurn asked Kieran. Ami knew exactly what was on his mind—in order to reach the Trading Post, they had to fly through a fairly thick asteroid belt. It involved a lot of concentration, sweating, *and* swearing. Avurn had always crewed the weapons console for that trip. She could understand the appeal of being able to shift any obstacles out of the way with the wave of a hand.

Kieran shrugged. 'I don't know, Avurn. It depends on how

much you've boosted your chip's power levels. I certainly couldn't do it on my own. With more Chippers—*agents*—on board, it might be possible to create a combined forcefield of that size.'

'Would the two of us manage it?' Avurn pelted at him.

There was a minute twitch at the corner of Kieran's lips. 'Maybe. I would need to teach you how to create a link with me first. I don't even know if our chips will complement each other, given what you've done to yours.'

Avurn was not deterred. 'Perhaps we should have a lesson in linking now?'

While Ami selected the Trading Post's coordinates in her ship's navigation system, her crewmates sat cross-legged on the floor in front of the viewport, eyes closed and shoulders slack. Kieran instructed Avurn to focus on his energy, to get used to how Kieran felt to him.

Avurn jerked. 'Whoa. You're...buzzing.'

'So are you,' Kieran told him with a laugh. 'I've always thought of it as static or interference—most agents don't encounter it. Try to match my *buzzing*, if you can. Once we're at the same frequency, we'll be able to link our chips.'

Ami had a feeling this was going to take a while. She couldn't just sit there and watch them—aside from not wanting to bore herself into a stupor, she did have things to do. Then again, this gave her the perfect opportunity to admire the way Kieran's jumpsuit clung to certain parts of him, the fabric delightfully taut now that he'd straightened his spine.

Kieran's eyes snapped open and his gaze locked onto hers.

The flush on her cheeks was probably obvious, but Ami didn't see a reason to look away. There was no use hiding her desire. He had already sensed it in her energy—she could tell by that smile.

And then his smile abruptly died.

His eyes closed again.

Well, that was...interesting. But this wasn't the time to ask him about it.

Ami turned her attention to her ship's sensors, in the unlikely but not impossible event that a wandering planet or comet or whatever else had distorted the gravity along this particular path through leapspace.

'ALRIGHT, OUT WITH IT,' Ami ordered. 'The leapdrive is locked in and Avurn's on watch. Us adults have some time to talk. Something's clearly bothering you and I'm all yours until midnight.'

Kieran was poised in the doorway of his quarters, a hand on the zipper of his jumpsuit. He was clearly about to have a quick rinse in the communal shower down the corridor, a wise move given the state he'd ended up in the night before. Ami stowed the temptation to ask if she could join him. She couldn't remember what he looked like naked, because she'd been highly strung at the time, but she could recall the intimacy of being in his arms—and how much of a relief it was to finally feel safe, accepted, and *understood*.

'Ami, I can't,' he said.

She crossed her arms. 'Can't talk? Can't adult? What?'

Kieran reached up for his temple. His fingers ghosted over the chip and then his face twisted, a mixture of revulsion and longing.

'What is it?' Ami asked softly, moving forward.

Kieran immediately took two steps back. Ami froze; there was no misinterpreting *that*.

He didn't want her anywhere near him.

'Kieran?' she tried again.

'I need to tell you what's happened,' he said. 'You deserve to know.'

Ami stood very still, barely even breathing, while he told her about his chip's new update. About his fears for the future of the Agency. About how there was no future for *them*. When his voice eventually failed him, he sat down heavily on the bed and she drifted until she was just inside the door, hands on her hips so she wouldn't do something stupid like touch him, comfort him, love him...

Ami reined that thought in quickly. *What the stark is wrong with you, Ami? You've known him for five nanoseconds!*

'Is it going to affect Avurn's chip, this update?' she asked.

Kieran pursed his lips. 'I don't think so. We couldn't establish a link with each other earlier. He's probably on the wrong frequency and so he won't receive any updates.'

'Do you have to create a link, or can you just skip to teaching him how to do stuff?' Ami began to sway from side to side, unable to pace because of how confined his quarters were, but still needing to exercise out some of her agitation.

'It's easier to lead by example,' Kieran explained. 'If he can sense how I use the chip, then he can replicate it.'

'I guess we'll have to dodge the asteroids the old-fashioned way,' she said.

Kieran nodded.

'There's something else we need to talk about,' Ami continued. His blue eyes narrowed and grew wary. 'No, it's not about...' She trailed off, wishing she could wrap herself up in his arms again.

His smile was slow, wistful as he waited her out.

Ami took a small step towards him, then another when he didn't tell her to stop. 'I met up with a friend of mine, a Desine worshipper who has their Magic. While we were talking, I started thinking... maybe you *do* have desert-based powers, but they're repressed by your chip. Which is why no one ever picked up on it. And it seems like you need to be in a pretty bad situation for them to make an appearance.'

Kieran frowned down at his knees. 'No. I'd know. The agent who assessed me as a baby before the chip went in would have noticed, surely, if I had this "Magic".'

'Do you know who that was?' Ami asked. 'Do you know the names of your parents, at least?'

'No. I've never looked at my file. I've never needed to.'

Ami studied the bulging skin hiding the chip in his temple. Short of cutting it out, there was no way to test her theory. Kieran wanted to stay with the Agency badly enough that he was putting a stop to the *thing* between them. So in it would stay.

'I bet Av made a copy of your file,' Ami said. 'If not, he can access it again pretty quickly.'

Kieran raised his eyebrows, effectively smoothing out the lines that had been webbing across his brow. 'I'm not sure how I feel about that. He shouldn't be hacking the Agency's records, but nor should our servers be that vulnerable.'

'No firewall can stop Avurn. He's really keen on collecting data about everyone and everything. In case he needs to blackmail someone and we're nowhere near a Web relay, I guess?' Ami shrugged. 'He once downloaded the receipts from every sale Numeni Corp ever made. And they shut down *years* ago. Anyway, it might be worth taking a longer look at your file—Av and I can do it if you don't want to.'

'Alright,' Kieran said softly.

A small concession, not a complete victory.

'Here's a thought,' Ami said. 'If you don't have the Magic, then why is the Desine showing an interest in you?'

He looked troubled. 'The sub-level gods are closer to the Creator God than we are. Perhaps in GLEA's attempts to reach our god, we have somehow reached his divine children instead. That's how I caught the Desine's attention and, apparently, invoked his wrath.'

'Yeah, but has any Chipper done that before now?' Ami demanded. 'Before you?'

'I don't know,' he whispered.

She left him alone after that, even though she suspected he'd avail himself of the Minty Madnesses that he was keeping in plain view beside the bed. Ami had accepted Tends' delivery back on Ilbb herself, so it wasn't like Kieran could have hidden the fact that he'd bought them. She should have told him that he needed to ask his captain if it was okay to bring booze aboard, but all Ami did was order him to rest. She wouldn't need him for tomorrow's run through the asteroid belt anyway. She and Avurn had done that countless times before.

Ami leaned against Kieran's closed door and released a hiss of air.

You didn't realise how badly you wanted him until he was out of your reach, she thought, annoyed.

TWENTY-ONE

Kieran killed a few minutes in the ship's communal shower cell, weathering the frigid water the malfunctioning system spat down on him, then retreated to his cabin. He lay down on his bed, the wafer-thin sheet reluctantly settling over him, and closed his eyes. Sleep did not arrive, leaving him at the mercy of his turbulent thoughts.

Was Ami right? Did he have the desert-based Magic?

It made more sense than he wanted it to. But in the end, it didn't matter. So long as he heard the voices, so long as the Desine pursued him, he was in danger of losing control of whatever powers he had at his command.

Oh God. Was that a whisper or his imagination? What if the Desine could somehow find him out here, in the darkness between the stars?

Kieran reached into the case of Minty Madnesses and opened a bottle. The first of many.

KIERAN'S FEET felt numb and almost foreign, but he managed to avoid tripping as he entered the bridge of the *Free Ride*. He knew this was a dream instead of reality, because the viewport showed him the impossible: thousands of planets, all crowded into one small, warped pocket of space. Each world had a voice and shouted at him, ceaselessly demanding, never negotiating.

Kieran stood there, helpless, as he watched the galaxy descend into war and chaos. Purple lines streamed across the stars—his fellow agents, Kieran realised—trying to glue it all together. But those lines were shedding people, individual dots sprayed across the inky void, and they spoke to him in a barely discernible cacophony, revealing why they were abandoning the Agency. Some left to marry a being of their choosing, some left because they never wanted children, some left because they had killed to maintain peace and felt conflicted—and others left because they wanted to join individual planets and causes.

GLEA fractured and so too did the universe.

I can't leave, Kieran thought, staring at the disarray filling the viewport. *They need me. They all need me to stay where I am. Only I know what's coming. Creator God, this is what you want, isn't it? For me to fix GLEA, so we can prevent the galaxy from falling apart?*

Chiding laughter tinkled over him. It heralded a presence deeper than the deepest chasm, a presence that would outlast the stars. The Creator God. *Do you presume to know the grand design better than the one who devised it? You do not control this universe, child. It is mine still.*

Kieran clenched his fists at his sides. He couldn't feel the nails digging into his skin, but he knew they must be. 'Why didn't you come to me when I needed you?'

Because you did not need me.

'Yes, I starking did! And I need you now!' Kieran roared. He belatedly realised that he was arguing with his god, his Creator, and bowed his head.

It is not me you require, the Creator God told him.

Another presence arrived, infusing the bridge with warmth, strength, and determination. The woman who would stand between Kieran and a god, if she needed to.

Ami smiled at him. 'You're not alone. You never will be.'

His frustration melted away almost instantly, even though he knew she wasn't really here, wasn't really sitting in the captain's chair, wasn't really watching him with green eyes that shone with unfettered love. Kieran returned his gaze to the viewport and saw that the stars had been replaced by complete darkness. Oblivion. Ami had said she dreamed about being stranded in oblivion and he'd sensed the fear in her energy when she'd mentioned it.

But this Ami was no longer afraid. She had conquered oblivion. For him.

Do I need her? Is that what you mean? Kieran wondered.

No answer. The Creator God had deserted him yet again.

Kieran blinked once, then Ami was gone and the bridge was full to the brim with agents. All of them wearing purple. All of them with judgement written over their faces.

'You must forget her,' they chanted. 'You must marry one of us.'

'But I need her! Our god practically said so!'

'Did he? Really? In a vision?' They threw back their heads and laughed as one. 'Kieran Krendasta does not see visions. We will not listen to Kieran Krendasta.'

Kieran peeled open his eyes, hissed in pain against the pervasive strip lighting, then tried to swallow the grit that had lodged itself beneath his tongue—and failed. He bolted down the corridor to the communal toilet and barely made it there before the contents of his stomach rebelled and hurtled out of him.

His skin slick with sweat, Kieran curled up on the cold floor and shook with suppressed sobs.

———

AMI WAS SLUMPED in her chair, listlessly kicking the air with her legs and wishing she had the concentration to read even a paragraph from the latest issue of her favourite adventure zine. She glanced over at Avurn. He was frowning down at the screen on his palm, his fingers curling over the words on his skin without touching any of them.

'Anything useful in Kieran's file?' Ami asked.

'No,' Avurn replied. 'Whoever created it in the first place never bothered to include any data about how he came to be in GLEA's Orphanage Division. Since there was no point in wasting any more of my time on it, I decided to try linking up with Kieran's chip from here, to see if distance improved the interference. When that theory did not pan out, I began scouring the Chipper server for anything that might assist us.'

Ami visualised the Minty Madnesses Kieran was keeping stashed in his quarters. 'He's probably drunk. I wouldn't expect his chip to work right now.'

'That is highly unprofessional.'

'He's...self-medicating,' Ami said. 'You would be too if you were in his jumpsuit.'

'Don't make excuses for him, Ami.'

Ouch. That's exactly what she'd been doing. The alcohol was useful in keeping the voices at bay for Kieran while they were planetside, but he had no cause to be imbibing now.

Silence fell across the bridge. Ami had long ago deactivated the beeping sounds her consoles should be making (they were on the same system as those starking alarms), but she found herself missing the background noise, if only to have some kind of distraction. Kieran could have provided that for her—if he wasn't doing his best to blast himself into unconsciousness.

'Ha!' Avurn said.

Ami smothered the yawn. 'You connected to his chip?'

'What? No.' Avurn held up his hand and wiggled his fingers, making the lines of text dance over his skin. 'It occurred to me that I should broaden my search. Instead of perusing the Agency's laughably incomplete files, I entered Kieran's name into the Galactic Database. Fortunately, there's only one of him in the galaxy.'

Ami straightened and whipped out her own techpad, opening the file as soon as Avurn had flicked it her way. Her eyes pored over the words. 'His birth was registered on Yalsa 5. That planet is half desert—literally half, since they decided on a rigid hemispherical boundary when they terraformed it a couple of decades ago. Most of Yalsa 5's tribes have moved into Atsa City, but...Av, this file doesn't list his parents.'

'How astute of you to notice,' Avurn said with a smirk that would have induced homicidal tendencies in most beings. 'His father was never listed. His mother was at some point, but her identity has been scrubbed off the Galactic Database, so Kieran's file is no longer linked to hers.'

'You can tell the difference between scrubbed and never listed?'

Avurn tutted. 'Do you really need to ask? After I scrubbed your ID for you?'

Ami knew that rolling her eyes wasn't going to improve his opinion of her intelligence. It was hard to stop herself doing it, however. 'So maybe his mother was a struggling single parent? Someone who might hand her son over to the Chippers?'

'Or his father *was* around, but was never entered into the Galactic Database to begin with and had no ID to link to.'

Ami frowned. 'That still happens?'

'Oh yes,' Avurn assured her. 'We have encountered a few of these beings in our time.'

'Av, do you check *everyone* we run into?'

He gave her an incredulous stare. 'It would be foolish not to. Anyway, the last one we came across was that Micadei fellow.'

Ami pinched the bridge of her nose. There was a puzzle laid out before her, one that she was slowly, painstakingly finding the pieces for, but she had no idea what the final image was meant to look like.

'Is he worth this much trouble?' Avurn asked.

Ami dropped her hand and glared at her crewmate.

Avurn spread his arms in a defensive gesture, presumably to convince her that he was only trying to help, although all it did was draw Ami's attention to the throbbing patch of skin that housed his chip.

'You can't save everyone, Ami,' he told her.

He wasn't wrong. But she wasn't going to give up just because it seemed impossible.

TWENTY-TWO

Vibrant streaks of light tore across the viewport as Avurn swirled his fingers over the sensor pad on the weapons console, shredding the obstacles in front of them. While the asteroids were dangerous all on their own, even worse were the shipwrecks with their knotted cables and jagged metal bones that could snag any vessel that came too close. Ami had told Kieran that she knew most of these wrecks by sight, if not by name. She'd also said that she expected to find many more crowding the area since her last visit.

The *Free Ride* ploughed through fragments and flames, heading ever onwards through the dense clouds of debris shielding the Trading Post from view. Everything here orbited an unusual gravity well; at its heart, a pocket of space that was empty but for the artificial safe haven they were seeking.

'It's a pattern, all patterns can be learned,' Avurn muttered as he worked away at the console. 'Even seemingly unpredictable patterns. Stark! That was a close one.'

Kieran winced and turned sharply from the spectacle. 'God, that hurts.'

'If you hadn't just spent two nights reliving your glory days in Carton City, you might be able to handle it,' Ami said from her chair, her lips a grim line and her eyes locked onto the viewport. The *Free Ride*'s manual controls remained tight in her grip. 'I take it your chip is still fritzing?'

'Yes.' Kieran wished he could sound more remorseful.

Ami didn't even flick a look his way. 'Well, it's not like you could have done much to help us with the asteroids anyway. You don't have Av's experience with the lascannon. But if we get jumped at the Post and you can't block a single lasbolt? That's when I get an apology out of you. Now sit down and strap in. Things could get rough.'

Kieran headed for the communications console, offering no argument. She hadn't said anything that he disagreed with.

He had almost made it to the chair when the corners of his mind ripped inwards—and suddenly he was no longer on the bridge. He was floating in space behind the *Free Ride*, watching a brilliant red streak shoot past him. A comet? No, a high-powered blast from a lascannon slamming into the ship's hull and puncturing it, adding the *Free Ride* to the countless dead bulks in this unofficial starship graveyard. If they somehow avoided the first blast, the two following it would finish the job.

Kieran blinked. He was on the bridge again.

They weren't dead yet, but what he'd seen in his vision was not far enough in the future for his liking. He turned and strode back towards the captain's chair. 'We're about to come under attack from another vessel. Do you trust me?'

Ami didn't say a word. She thrust the ship's steering rods into his hands and Kieran immediately gave them a shove. The ship shot downwards (or at least the direction that appeared to be 'downwards' from the bridge) into a section of the asteroid belt that Avurn hadn't yet cleared—and nor did he have the time to clear it now.

The blast tore through the space above them, blistering some wrecks and obliterating others.

'Stark!' Avurn shouted. 'Should I prioritise power to the shields?'

'No!' Ami said. 'Divert nothing from the lascannon. Our shields are shit against that kind of firepower. The lascannon will last a lot longer—and we'll need it to cut a path out of here!'

Avurn's face twisted into a snarl. 'Your funeral, Captain!'

The *Free Ride* shuddered underneath a constant shower of debris. Most of it bounced away harmlessly, but a significant chunk of rock arced towards them and scored a direct hit on the viewport, causing a crack to wend its way up the centre of the plexiglass.

'*OUR* FUNERAL!' Avurn shrieked. 'The shield's out!'

Less powerful lasbolts started strafing the unprotected hull. Ami yanked the steering rods out Kieran's grip and sent her ship through a series of evasive spirals. The vessel chasing the *Free Ride* might have been recharging its lascannon or perhaps the turret was running too hot (aftermarket mods were notoriously unreliable), but even smaller bolts could destroy a ship if they were constant enough.

'Any more visions?' Ami asked breathlessly.

Kieran shook his head.

'Then get strapped in and contact the Trading Post!' she shouted.

Kieran lunged across the deck and practically fell into the chair at the communications console. For several heart-stuttering seconds, he felt himself rise out of the chair after the artificial gravity briefly cut out. He punched the console. Once the safety straps had finished whining and were fully engaged, he said, 'What should I say? We're coming in hot? Don't shoot us, shoot the ones chasing us?'

'All of the above!' Ami barked. 'Fighting isn't allowed this close to the station so they should help us out!'

Kieran opened a public communications link and tried hailing the Trading Post. He received only static in response. *What now? Should he bother praying to the Creator God? Could he do anything except sit here and let death come to him?*

The ship juked wildly to one side and his hand slammed down hard against the console, his wrist aching in protest.

'Av, how did you miss a chunk of rock that big!?' Ami snapped.

'I didn't—it was twice that size earlier!' Avurn said indignantly.

Another impact on the hull. Not so bad this time, but the damage was clearly cumulative.

The strip lighting overhead went dark so abruptly Kieran wondered if he was about to have another vision. But he didn't need to see the future to know that he was headed for a galaxy of hurt. The panel concealing the fire extinguisher, hastily repaired after their trip to Bagaran but clearly not secured well enough to last through a violent encounter, rocketed across the bridge.

Its destination? His head.

Kieran threw up a hand, trying to generate a forcefield before the small projectile reached him. His chip responded sluggishly, then cut out.

The panel struck a glancing blow and bounced onto the floor.

He plunged into darkness.

AMI LEANED over the storage locker that Avurn had appropriated as his desk in the cramped hold of the *Free Ride*. 'Can you fix it, Av?'

'Not sure,' Avurn replied, tiny tools pinched between his fingers as he fiddled with Kieran's chip, which was lit up brilliantly beneath a halo of magnified plexiglass. Ami suspected that ordinarily the Chipper tech would be a seamless, silver disc. Right now it was in four jagged pieces, its innards spewed across Avurn's so-called desk.

Avurn squinted at the chip and frowned. 'I'm hoping I can at least figure out why he gets those visions and I don't. Mine's a better model. It is incredibly unfair that he has visions by accident and I don't by design...'

Straightening up and resting her hands on her lower back, Ami released a groan. She tilted her head from side to side, but this action only added more aches to the ones she's collected during her frantic attempt to reach the Trading Post. Their pursuers had backed off the moment the *Free Ride* had come within range of the space station's lascannons.

Ami knew that she should visit the infirmary, in case it was whiplash creeping up her spine instead of tension-related stiffness. Kieran was down there already, blissfully passed out and enjoying the extensive treatment afforded to an agent of GLEA. The drugs that eased a concussion in mere hours were too pricey for most beings—Kieran's stay in the infirmary would no doubt replace the Post's yearly donation to the Agency.

But the medical professionals hadn't known what to do with the broken chip, its edges so sharp it had punctured his skin. The nearest Chipper outpost was on Ilbb and Ami suspected they didn't have the facilities to deal with this.

'Creator God,' Ami said, addressing the ceiling, 'Av's trying to help out one of your agents. Might be a good time to overlook his general skeeviness and work a miracle.'

'He has overlooked me most times, except for that one incident when he—ah, shit!' Avurn shook his finger. 'Touching that wasn't a good idea. Back to the tools. I am not some starking amateur...'

Ami blinked. 'What the stark.'

'Unfortunately, most of your offensive vocabulary has been absorbed by my brain.'

'No, I don't care about that. Well, I do but—Av, what incident are you talking about? Did you...did you hear the Creator God?'

Avurn rearranged his tools on the desk and sighed deeply. 'I have indeed heard him. When I first inserted the chip, he told me that if I really wanted keep it then I would have to use my powers to help people. As a form a recompense, I suppose. I nodded and made the usual platitudes until he left. He was a heavy, immense pressure on my mind. Very uncomfortable.'

'Wow,' Ami said. She wondered why the Creator God had spoken to Avurn instead of Kieran, who had served his god as an agent of GLEA for his entire life. She really couldn't blame Kieran for his recent crisis of faith.

'Yes, wow,' Avurn grumbled as he selected a pair of tweezers. 'I initially accompanied you on your runs to avoid my sister, but I now do so for another, more important reason.'

'So you're...atoning?' Ami asked warily.

'Who said anything about atoning? I figure that if I save enough people to satisfy the Creator God, then I can use the chip for my intended purposes. Ami, do you have nothing better to do? I can't work effectively if you keep hovering.'

Ami left him to it. There was no point trying to continue the conversation and she'd rather not distract him. If there was anyone outside of GLEA who was capable of fixing their tech, it was the ten-year-old boy with a penchant for murder, mayhem, and deception—stark, he'd lied to the most powerful god in the galaxy! Avurn never did anything by halves, huh.

Laughing, Ami walked down the boarding ramp and into the hanger the Trading Post had assigned to the *Free Ride* on this occasion.

'Yeah, so far laughter has been everyone's reaction to the state of your vessel,' a nearby mechanic noted.

Ami stopped dead, clamped her hands to her hips, and spun around to face the mechanic. 'How dare you. How dare you breathe the same air as me, let alone use that air to insult the *Free Ride*?'

'Hello, Ami,' Jets said, grinning.

Jets was sixteen and her dark coppery features were enhanced by the long scar that slashed its way from her temple to her chin, a souvenir of an altercation on her homeworld. Ami didn't doubt that story. Jets came from Yalsa 5, a planet made infamous by its gangs— even if they weren't as violent as they had been in the past, some of them occasionally grew bored with the peaceful status quo and rebelled.

'Hey, Jets,' Ami responded. 'Still avoiding your parents, I see.'

Jets sighed and rubbed her greasy hands on her khaki overalls, which were already so stained Ami couldn't tell if any new splotches had just been added. The less said about the shirt underneath—it might have been white and untorn at some point—the better.

'I'm good at fixing starships,' Jets said. 'I can strip an engine the size of yours and have it running again in under a day. I'm that fast. But I'm no good at politics and I hate lasguns. Mum and Dad are the ones who deal with that shit. They don't listen. They can't seem to get it into their thick skulls that I'm nothing like them.'

Jets was practically royalty. Her father was Governor Bock Atsason, ruler of Yalsa 5, and her mother was Subofficer Ala, the overseer of the Maria clan, one of the most respected gangs in Atsa City.

'I get what you mean,' Ami said with feeling.

'What, you also have some sob story about your *fantastic* parents practically forcing you to become the next great leader of an entire starking world?' Jets joked, absently scratching her head and sketching oily lines over her closely shaved scalp.

Ami shrugged. 'Don't we all?'

'Whatever,' Jets said, then smirked. 'I take it you're finally going to call in your marker? For smuggling me off Yalsa 5 and out of my parents' grasp and all that?'

Ami smiled apologetically. 'Yeah. I can't afford to pay for these repairs. Figured you could foot the bill this time.'

'Sure, fine,' Jets said and smothered a yawn into her shoulder (after briefly considering her grimy hands). 'Best thing I ever did, getting Avurn to shunt a chunk of my parents' money over to an account based on Enoc. The interest alone gives me a pretty solid slush fund. Listen, Ami, the *Ride* is in safe hands. My crew knows what they're doing. You get yourself checked out, okay? You look rubbish.'

Ami nodded, heading for the passageway at the end of the hangar, but then she quickly swung back around. 'Oh! I need you to do one more thing.'

'Yeah, what's that?'

Ami hesitated. 'Can you look into a person for me? He was born on Yalsa 5 about twenty-five years ago. The name is Kieran Krendasta. There's not much on the Galactic Database about his origins, but I figured you could put the word out. You've got connections.'

'My parents'll notice if I send any messages to Atsa City,' Jets pointed out. 'They'll trace them back here and find me. Not cool.'

'Talk to Av—he can mask your Web account.'

But Jets remained unmoved. She even threw in another yawn for good measure.

'Please, Jets. I'll...' Ami sighed. 'I'll owe you a ride somewhere.'

Jets perked up immediately. 'Got yourself a deal! Now shoo. Give us some time to work our magic. You're going to need a tight ship.'

'Why's that?' Ami asked, starting to walk away again.

'The rulers of Rochaccia put out separate bounties on your head,' Jets called after her. 'They both want you dead, no bonus for live delivery. Shooting you would set most beings up for life! Why else would someone risk coming after you so close to the Trading Post? You better watch out, Ami. Recent images of you and the *Ride* are circulating the Web.'

Ami's head ached fiercely.

She should have known that changing her name wouldn't keep her hidden forever. As for her parents suddenly deciding they didn't need her alive anymore...that was a very unsettling development. She didn't want to think about it too much.

Luckily, she knew exactly where to find her favourite distraction.

TWENTY-THREE

Something was very, very wrong.

Kieran woke inside a blazing white room that reeked of chemicals designed to smother other pungent scents. If this hadn't clued him in about his location, the continuous beeps and the rasp of a medical gown against the side of his bed would have been sufficient. He stared blearily up at the Jezlo doctor who was enquiring after his health, her tentacles weaving to and fro.

'I'm fine,' Kieran said curtly when the questions began repeating on a loop. He had a feeling the doctor wasn't going to be satisfied with those two words, however, and braced himself for an intensive check-up.

But then Ami breezed in and jerked her head at the door. 'Out, Doctor. I'll deliver the bad news. It'll sound better coming from me.'

'Bad news?' Kieran echoed.

Once the doctor had skittered out of sight, Ami approached the bed. Her lips were crooked and she managed to straighten them after a few attempts, but the worry in her eyes lingered like the shadows in an Ilbban twilight. She snagged one of his hands in hers and guided it up to his head, where a bandage clung.

'You really should lay off the booze when we're in space,' she said.

Kieran smiled ruefully. 'I see that now. How badly did I injure myself?'

He tapped the bandage with two fingers.

Oh God.

Kieran pressed further into his temple. The pain did not deter him. He stabbed and stabbed, desperately trying to—

'Kieran! Stop! The synthglue hasn't set. You'll reopen the wound.' Ami's hands clamped down on his wrists, pinning his arms to his sides. Kieran writhed for countless seconds, frantic and mindless, but he stilled when her chin dug into his shoulder and her lips touched his ear. 'Kieran. I'm here. I'm here and I'm not going anywhere.'

'My chip,' he said hoarsely.

Ami drew back, cupping his face in her hands, her thumbs tracing his jaw. 'It broke. Badly enough to cut through skin.'

'I need it back—I need it now!'

'Av's fixing it,' Ami said.

'I need my chip,' Kieran insisted, his cheeks heating up when he realised how infantile he sounded. 'I need it, Ami. Without it, I'm not...I'm not...'

'Not a Chipper?' Ami finished.

He closed his eyes and nodded.

'Kieran, the only clothes you own are purple jumpsuits,' she said, her voice as gentle and soothing as waves lapping against a shore. 'This fetching white gown you're wearing is *temporary*. I'm pretty sure the Chippers won't kick you out for a freak accident, because they want you to raise snotty little agents for them. If Av can't fix the chip, then we'll just get you another one, okay? I'll fly you to Gerasnin myself.'

'I've worn it since I was a baby,' Kieran whispered. 'I feel like I've lost a limb.'

Dousing himself in alcohol and rendering his chip inert had been so incredibly stupid. And now he'd lost access to his powers entirely. He wished he could hurl every single Minty Madness in existence into a sun. He could do nothing. *Nothing*. He could not keep the galaxy in one piece, he could not help Ami, he could not teach Avurn...

His breaths came in short, sharp gasps. He was lost, cast adrift from everything he'd ever—no, he wasn't lost. He was grounded inside an embrace, a cocoon of safety that would never abandon him. Ami.

The panic subsided. He sagged, boneless.

When Kieran managed to peel apart his eyelids, he realised that he and Ami were chest to chest, her knees braced either side of him on the bed. The weight and warmth of her body soothed every tense muscle and every ragged nerve. His hands, no longer restrained, were at her waist and Kieran couldn't stop himself caressing her through her shirt. Ami wriggled her hips against his, a wicked gleam in her eyes. He didn't know who moved first—she bent down, he lifted his head—but their mouths connected in a fierce kiss that sent a jolt straight through him.

She licked her lips when she pulled away.

'Ami, I...' he murmured. With his chip gone and incapable of tracking his desires, the temptation to space his loyalty to GLEA and keep kissing her was almost overwhelming.

'Distracted?' she asked, grinning.

He nodded emphatically.

'Good.' Ami slid off him and readjusted the rumpled sheet covering his body. 'Now listen. Avurn is fixing your chip.' She held up a hand to forestall any comment. 'If there's anyone who can manage it out here, it's him. You know it. I know it. Painful as it is to admit.'

Kieran rolled to the side, wanting to maintain eye contact with her. 'You do realise he'll use this opportunity to see if there's something in my chip he can replicate to get my visions?'

'He would do that, huh.' Ami rubbed her forehead. 'Look, I don't want him having visions of the future, but...he's my crew and my responsibility. I'll do whatever I can to keep him out of prison and out of GLEA's temples.'

'Do you make a habit of trying to protect every single being in the galaxy?' Kieran asked with a gentle laugh.

Ami's answering smile was bitter, fragile. 'Funny. Avurn made a point of telling me that I can't save everyone. Well, someone has to pick up the slack. The Chippers take a starking long time to send out their agents when shit starts hitting the turbines.'

Kieran couldn't disagree with her. The Agency had been known to spend an entire week deciding if a threat required any consideration, much less their full attention. Their resources were not exhaustive and they could not assist everyone, which was why Head General Zareth Sins worked with some of the sub-level gods. Kieran had briefly considered informing Sins about the Desine's unusual interest in him—but that was before the Head General had introduced the new mandate and shown that he was more concerned with getting re-elected than in doing the right thing.

Kieran's trust in Sins had gone from burgeoning to non-existent.

'Do you believe that Avurn can fix my chip?' Kieran asked.

Ami grimaced. 'Not sure. We might have to make do without it until we get our butts over to Gerasnin. Or Enoc, maybe—those temples are a lot closer. But even that trip might be too dangerous for us. We have some pretty big problems right now.'

'How big?'

'So big the people who need our help are actually safer with the slavers,' Ami said gloomily. 'Things were already pretty starking bad when people knew that it was Captain Ami N'uni of the *Free Ride* rescuing slaves. But then someone in the Harem grabbed an image of my face, my parents realised it was me putting a dent in their profits, and now they are *pissed*. As in, giant-bounty-pissed. Everyone's gunning for us. Tell me, Kieran, are you a decent enough shot with your lasgun that you won't need the chip?'

'I hope so, but again...we might have to make do,' Kieran said.

They spoke some more after that, mostly about her ship's ongoing repairs—or so he assumed. He knew his lips were moving, saw hers doing the same, but their voices became distorted, as though they were talking over a communications link filled with static. His body felt weightless, like he was floating above the bed, and when he looked down at his hands, his useless hands, for a moment he saw himself flinging stars through space. A vision? No. His chip was gone.

This was nothing but a delusion.

Dizzy, Kieran dropped his head back onto the pillow and fought the urge to throw up.

AMI KEPT a persistent grip on Kieran's arm as she led him back towards her assigned hangar. She nodded at those she passed in the corridors who looked vaguely familiar, but they kept their eyes either on the metallic floor or her not-so-shiny boots. Ami was certain that at least one or two of them would have usually waved—before she'd ignored all common sense and gone planetside, exposing herself to the galaxy.

Lives had been saved, yes. But now she might not be able to save any more.

'Ouch,' Kieran said, smiling.

Ami looked down. One of her nails had punctured the sleeve of his jumpsuit. She quickly retracted her fingers. 'Sorry. I'm really tense. We've docked, announced our arrival, and we still haven't received any tips. Our contacts are avoiding us. So's just about everyone else here, it seems. That's not a good sign.'

'How do you usually pay for tips?' Kieran asked, his palm grazing the small of her back. The sparks his touch generated coalesced there before radiating out to each and every nerve ending. She shivered.

'Money, rides, favours,' Ami answered, when she was sure her voice would remain steady. 'But even all the coin-chips in the Post couldn't get us out of this mess.'

'Is the bounty really that sizeable?'

'*Bounties*. Plural. My parents have *very* deep pockets and they know exactly where to advertise this kind of thing. Just about anyone with a ship and a lasgun will be after us.' Ami gritted her teeth. 'We need to get gone. And fast.'

Kieran nodded. She watched his eyes slide to the right, as though he was trying to get a look at the small plaster that was affixed to his temple in place of the more cumbersome bandage he'd been wearing in the infirmary. It would be a lot harder for him than it was for her to pretend that the plaster was concealing his chip, not his lack of one. The doctors had given him extra synthglue for when he managed to reinsert the tech; Ami had needed to grab the tube of gel while Kieran had stared at a wall, his face entirely blank.

'Will bounty hunters know to find you on Ilbb?' he asked.

'Yep. It's registered as the *Free Ride*'s homeport and that's public info. Looks like we'll have to stash ourselves someplace even more obscure for a while.'

'I think I might enjoy obscure,' Kieran murmured—right before he pulled her into a nearby alcove.

Ami embraced the shadows as eagerly as she embraced Kieran, hoping the large pylons set into the wall were adequately hiding them from prying eyes. His lips skirted hers, like a whispered promise. Impatient, she hooked her arms over his shoulders, yanking him down into a searing kiss that completely obliterated her senses. All she knew was *him*. Kieran's hands fell to her hips and he twisted her slightly, backing her up against one of their pylons.

The jerk in her navel told Ami she would definitely enjoy whatever he had planned.

But she flattened her hands against his chest and gave him a gentle push instead of succumbing. 'Kieran. I can't be your anchor. I'm not strong enough.' It hurt to admit that. Gods, it hurt. 'And I don't want to chase this *thing* with you if I'm just going to have to take my hands off you the moment you get a working chip.'

'I'm sorry,' Kieran said softly. 'I know this isn't fair to you.'

'It's not fair to you either, Kieran. Are you sure GLEA still deserves your loyalty?'

'There's a great conflict coming. I've seen it in a vision. The Agency can't afford to lose me. I need to help them keep the galaxy in one piece.'

Ami blew out a breath. 'Didn't need a vision to know a shitstorm was coming. It's only a matter of time before planets start having a go at each other. There's no single governing body in this galaxy—there's *thousands*. We won't get along and play nice forever.'

'The lack of a central government has always caused the Agency great difficulty,' Kieran agreed. 'There are times when we must appease one planet without offending another when a criminal has broken a law on both worlds.' He grimaced, perhaps remembering a particular incident in the past. 'Our founders hoped that the galaxy would remain united under the Creator God, as we were when humans first left Old Earth and met his other mortal children. But our combined populations expanded so much and so far that everyone became isolated, made unique and contradictory laws, needed more gods to care for them—gods they understandably worship instead of the Creator God. The galaxy is poised to fracture.'

Ami tried not to give him an incredulous look, but she failed. 'So you're staying with the Chippers, letting them force you into marriage and parenthood, in some last-ditch attempt to throw synth-strips on a much bigger problem.'

'Ami...'

'*Kieran,*' she returned, squaring her shoulders. 'You can't hold thousands of planets together by yourself. No one can. And let's not pretend GLEA will be much help when this conflict does happen. So you have a vision about some war involving an entire system? Too bad, GLEA won't listen to you.'

He flinched and recoiled, as though she'd struck him.

'Kieran?' Ami queried.

His grimace lingered and grew. Then he hesitantly explained the vision he'd had while the *Free Ride* had been in leapspace.

We will not listen to Kieran Krendasta, Ami mused. Why not just say 'we won't listen to you'? Maybe it wasn't important—maybe visions had more formal language or something. But still. She turned it over in her mind and nearly lost track of their conversation.

'I can't leave GLEA,' Kieran protested. 'If I don't have the chip, I won't be able to help anyone and I won't have any visions. Right now, I'm powerless. Useless.'

'You're not useless *or* powerless,' Ami said. 'Because if I'm right, then you've got a whole other set of powers to draw on.'

Kieran's face went rigid and Ami immediately regretted bringing it up. Creating a sandstorm accidentally was bad enough.

Being able to do it on command and with greater force because the chip was no longer hampering him?

Yikes. No wonder he looked terrified.

Kieran shook his head repeatedly. 'There's nothing. I would have felt something by now.'

'Have you tried?' she asked.

'No,' he admitted. 'And you're wrong, Ami.'

Ami raised her eyebrows and leaned against one of the pylons, crossing her arms. 'About what? I've said more than a couple of things you're inevitably going to take issue with, Kieran.'

'You are more than strong enough,' he said and his eyes glazed over, a vacant smile stealing across his face.

'Did you just have a vision?' she demanded.

'No!' Kieran retreated further from her, his expression guilty as stark. But she wasn't going to push it. Not now, not when he was teetering on the edge. 'Ami, you survived what your parents did to you. Your painful past hasn't kept you from saving lives. Your retrieval missions must remind you constantly about what happened on Rochaccia. And yet you keep on doing it. For those who can't escape on their own. Ami, *you are strong*.'

Ami knew she should have left the alcove then and there, but she found herself drawing him back into a passionate embrace, her lips seeking his. The groan in his throat sent heat racing down her abdomen to settle between her thighs. Gods, she wanted him. Needed him.

Kissing him in the shadows couldn't possibly lead to any regrets, right?

Ami decided she could hate herself later.

TWENTY-FOUR

Kieran followed Ami up the boarding ramp and towards the hold of her vessel, keeping his head down. He hadn't been honest with her. He *had* seen something—had seen her lying beside him in countless moments, nothing between them, not even sheets. And he had also seen her standing in front of a turbulent, sandy figure, with her hands defiantly set on her hips, in no way intimidated by the god she was confronting. Ami was so strong and he envied her for it, envied that she, without a chip, could have so much power.

Kieran swallowed. *It can't have been a vision. It's wishful thinking, to see her in my future. To see anything at all.*

'What is *she* doing here?' Ami demanded, drawing up short at the entrance to the hold.

Kieran stepped around her to get a better look. Sitting beside Avurn in one of the kitchenette's fold-down seats was a teenage mechanic—and leaning against the wall near them was Grace Pendergast, e-paper reporter. Kieran opened his mouth but he wasn't sure what he'd intended to say, because a surge of awareness hit him and wiped the words clean from his thoughts.

Kieran froze and so too did Avurn. The buzzing sensation that frustrated Kieran whenever he attempted to link with someone was entirely absent. And this link snapped into place inside a nanosecond, creating a much deeper connection than he'd ever experienced before. Avurn's mind was laid bare to him—the boy felt calm and in control, though there was some seepage of exasperation over Ami's 'yell first, clarify later' attitude.

Kieran leaned heavily against the doorway.

Ami was right, he thought. But this wasn't the Magic, as she'd suspected—he seemed to be touching his usual powers without a chip. They also seemed more potent. *Potent enough to hold a sandstorm inside a forcefield.*

Kieran sensed wordless agreement from Avurn. The boy wasted no time in diving into the well of Kieran's power, testing it out for himself. While Avurn hadn't initially shown any outward signs of the link forming between them, what he had found inside Kieran must have taken him completely off guard.

'Oh shit,' Avurn whispered.

'"Oh shit" is right!' Ami said, marching forward. She grabbed Avurn's shoulders, but didn't quite yank him out of his chair. 'Av! You let an e-paper reporter onto my ship!? Have you lost your starking mind?'

Kieran narrowed his eyes, hoping the link conveyed his desire to keep his powers secret (at least for now). Avurn nodded sharply before transferring his gaze back to Ami. She scowled, reminding the boy that she was his captain, not Kieran, and there was no point in looking for help elsewhere.

Ami let go of Avurn, stepped back, drew a stabilising breath—and then moved onto the teenager. 'Jets. No bullshit. What is going on?'

'Ami, cool it,' Jets replied. 'You told me to look into this "Kieran Krendasta" for you. So I did.'

Ami's cheek twitched. 'Sorry, Kieran. I asked Jets to do this before I went to get you from the infirmary. We hit a dead end with your file and she has contacts on the world where you were born.'

Kieran's gut gave an uncomfortable lurch. He didn't like the thought of strangers digging into his background, but he understood. Ami wanted to help him. And if he was honest, he needed that help, especially since he now knew that his powers were not reliant on the chip.

'Thank you,' he said quietly.

'Stark, I'm glad you said that,' Ami muttered. 'I felt like a real shit there for a nanosecond. But what I really want to know is how Pendergast relates to any of this.'

Jets slapped her knees impatiently. 'If you'd just let me starking finish! My contact back home couldn't scrounge up much. Av and I were spitballing some other info paths we could try, but then suddenly someone is dinging us from the docking ramp—Grace Fucking Pendergast! And it's awfully convenient that she showed up when she did...'

'I'll say,' Ami said darkly.

Avurn nodded. 'I agree, it is suspicious, but I was intrigued. Especially since there is no evidence of Pendergast boarding this station at all. The Trading Post considers any unregistered visitors to be here illegally and the administrators would be *very* interested to know where to find one such being.'

Grace Pendergast was seemingly unbothered by the obvious threat.

Kieran watched her closely, but her face proved to be as unreadable as her energy. Micadei had said she knew everything. That Kieran should ask her. Ask her what, exactly?

'I really don't have the patience for sneaky reporters right now,' Ami said. 'Get off my ship, Ms Pendergast. I'm a shit shot, but my hold isn't that big. I'll eventually hit you.'

Kieran moved forward, drawing in line with Ami. Her eyes scored across him: a warning and a question. He indicated their unwelcome visitor with a slight tip of his head. 'Ms Pendergast clearly has her own reasons for being here, but that doesn't mean we can't gain something from her presence. Your usual contacts at the Trading Post are not speaking to you. I'd hazard that a reporter has a greater selection of sources to choose from.'

'Stark, I should have thought of that angle,' Avurn mused, looking impressed.

Grace straightened away from the wall and crossed her arms. This new stance made her look even more formidable. 'It's a good angle. Even I can respect that, as a reporter. You will not be getting any tips out of your contacts here at the Post. No one wants to risk their skin or their hide *that* much. I would find some of those tips for you myself if I thought it would do any good, but you are in no position to rescue anyone. There are hundreds of bounty hunters on your trail. You can evade them for a time, but the best will track you down eventually.'

'Clearly, Ms Pendergast agrees with my assessment of the situation,' Avurn said.

'Oh, does she?' Ami asked wryly.

The boy smoothed out the sleeves his jumpsuit, paying special attention to the section of fabric that hid his chip. 'We cannot keep targeting the symptoms of this disease. We must attack the source.'

'AKA the slavers who set those bounties,' Jets added.

'Avurn and Jets want us to head to Rochaccia,' Kieran said, the link with Avurn confirming his guess.

Avurn beamed. 'Exactly. We could put an end to Rochaccia's contribution to the galactic slave trade, which is not inconsiderable. No bounty hunter will work for a client who can't pay them the promised fee. And if we do manage to take out this wyvern nest, then no one will want to tangle with us ever again. Now, Rochaccia is protected by a blockade, but we have a way in. You, Ami. You're the daughter of Rochaccia's rulers, the heir to both the Roch and Accia factions.'

'Wow, Ami!' Jets blurted. 'Just wow. I thought *my* parents were bad. Yours are a whole other hold of gargantua. No wonder you kept smirking to yourself whenever I went on about mine!'

'So you *were* born Unify Naiman, not Ami N'uni,' Grace said.

'You knew who I was on Enoc,' Ami accused, clenching her fists. 'You knew the moment you clapped eyes on me.'

The e-paper reporter did not deny it. 'I wasn't going to expose you, Captain. Your anonymity and your safety are more important to me than any accolades I would receive for writing a story about you. And to be clear, my interest is not in you, but in Kieran Krendasta.'

'Oh yay, that makes me trust you *way* more,' Ami said. 'Av, I'm not going back to Rochaccia. Forget it.'

'Do we have any other options at this point?' Avurn asked.

Ami rubbed her temples. 'My parents want me dead and they won't pay any extra coin-chips to the bounty hunters who deliver me still breathing. You really think they're going to let me through the blockade?'

'Yes,' Avurn answered, his eyes wide and eager. 'From what you've said over the years, I can surmise that they would enjoy watching you grovel for forgiveness a lot more than being presented with your corpse. And you are the only heir they are legally allowed, unless they can agree on another one—which is unlikely, given their turbulent history. You just have to remind them of this fact.'

Kieran was already shaking his head. 'Even if Ami can convince her parents to meet with her, I don't see how we can do anything about the situation on Rochaccia.'

'We could assassinate both rulers,' Avurn suggested.

'My parents would love it if I tried to kill them,' Jets said gloomily.

Ami glowered at Avurn and Jets. 'No way! That's not how we do things. I will not take any more lives. *Especially* when I'm in my right mind. I refuse.'

'I know that's not your thing and I totes get it,' Jets assured her. 'Even I don't like the thought of nixing anyone, which is why I'm the biggest embarrassment on Yalsa 5. I was supposed to be the next Governor or Clan Leader or some shit—and here I am, hiding out at the Trading Post. Getting grease on my heads instead of blood. Mum and Dad are *so* proud of me for bailing on the future they picked out for me.'

Grace flashed a startled look at Jets, though Kieran couldn't tell if she felt genuine surprise or if she was just performing it. 'You're Governor Bock Atsason's daughter? Interesting.'

'Interesting? More like a big starking hassle.' Jets rolled her eyes. 'Look, Rochaccia has the biggest fleet in this spur. Even my parents don't have the firepower to match that. But okay, let's assume we manage to get planetside—we'd need some kind of divine intervention, I reckon—and then what? How do we plan on dealing with Taylar and Neffron Naiman if we're not gonna nix them?'

'Rapture,' Avurn replied. 'We dose them with their own product, make them smile while they tell everyone that slavery is henceforth outlawed on Rochaccia. Beautifully poetic, given how they use Rapture to control their victims.'

'*No*,' Ami growled. 'No Rapture. I told you. Not even my worst enemy.'

Kieran cleared his throat. 'An agent of GLEA must uphold the laws of a planet's governing body. I am not currently able to take Taylar and Neffron Naiman into custody. They've broken none of the laws they created for themselves.'

'The Agency is restricted by its code of conduct,' Grace spoke up, her words clipped and hard. 'There is no arguing with your Head General on that matter. Believe me, I've tried. I am not so cautious or hamstrung. If I followed every planet's laws, I would not have been able to save as many lives as I have. I use my e-paper to deal with people like Captain N'uni parents. I can turn the entire galaxy against them.'

'Ami, she should come with us,' Avurn said. 'Her skill set may prove useful.'

Ami straightened and lifted her chin, but this clearly failed to intimidate Grace, who was quite a bit taller than her. 'That's probably what she was angling for all along, to be invited on board. Seems like you're getting a lot out of this, Ms Pendergast. A big story about Unify Naiman returning to her homeworld, perhaps to depose her parents and take control of Rochaccia! Your sponsors will throw coin-chips at you to be mentioned alongside that kind of scoop. And you get to stay close to Kieran, whom you seem to like following around—I'm not even going to pretend that's not creepy. What do *we* get out of this?'

'I get answers,' Kieran murmured. 'I believe she has some of them.'

Ami's shoulders sagged. 'Yeah. We do need those. But...are you sure about this, Kieran? You weren't too keen on getting answers before now. And is this the way you want to do it? Letting a reporter set the agenda?'

'It doesn't seem like Avurn and Jets have had much luck,' Kieran said. He wished they didn't have an audience, so he could tell Ami that his powers hadn't been lost along with his chip. If he could find out why he was like this, find someone who knew how to help him...

Jets ran a hand over her grease-streaked scalp. 'Yeah, I can wear that failure because it fits so well. But I'll still take that ride you promised me, Ami. The *Free Ride* will be ready to go in a few hours and I won't need that long to get my shit together. My boss might be a little snarky about me quitting on such short notice, but hey. He shoulda paid me more.'

Avurn looked—and felt—decidedly annoyed about his inability to find anything substantial.

'I need to know more about who I am,' Kieran said.

Grace looked away from him, her gaze settling on a bulkhead. 'I've spent a year waiting for this moment. And yet I'm still not sure if it's safe for you to know what I do.'

'He's not safe as it is!' Ami snapped.

'For stark's sake,' Jets said. 'Just give them a crumb or something, Pendergast. To prove you've got the goods. You can hand said goods over later.'

The reporter pursed her lips, her expression distant. She could have been weighing up her choices, but Kieran had a feeling that something else was going on. Finally, Grace nodded. 'Very well. I can give Private Krendasta a "crumb" that won't immediately endanger him, since he will not have the full story. Krendasta, I have an image of your parents on their wedding day.'

'What? How!?' Avurn exclaimed. 'Jets and I scoured the Galactic Database. We found nothing like that. No images or recordings whatsoever. The best Jets' informant could give us was confirmation that a Krendasta family had lived on her homeworld at some stage.'

Grace raised one eyebrow, as though disappointed in the boy. 'On Yalsa 5, it is not unusual for people to have two names: their birth name and their gang name.'

'Yep,' Jets confirmed. 'But my name works as both. Ain't I lucky?'

'Private Krendasta's parents used their gang names for the cere-mony,' Grace continued. 'Therefore, their names are listed as Bolt and Dancer.'

Jets' eyes saucered. 'No shit. No shit!'

'Do those names have any importance?' Avurn asked.

'They're, like, legends on my homeworld!' Jets cried.

Grace drew a techpad out of the pouch on her belt. 'I can send you the image right now, Krendasta. I realise it is not enough to sate your curiosity, but I am treading a very fine line here. More knowledge will bring you more attention. Much of that that will be unwanted. Some of it will even be dangerous, for you and everyone who travels with you.'

'Yeah, well, we'll take our chances,' Ami said. 'Send the image through. *Now.*'

Once his own techpad had received an unread message from Grace Pendergast, Kieran turned and left the hold without a word.

He found himself standing alone on the bridge and for a long while he simply stared at the blotchy stains on the hanger wall visible through the repaired viewport. Inhaling deeply, he opened Grace's message and downloaded the image. His breath caught inside his lungs.

His parents were clearly leaving the location of their wedding ceremony, hand in hand, smile for smile. His father was tall and had tied his long blond hair into a slick ponytail that, due to the static nature of the image, would always hover above his shoulder. His eyes were startlingly blue—the same eyes Kieran saw whenever he looked into a mirror. The woman beside his father...she was shorter, slighter. Despite the delicate white dress she wore, there was an edge of danger to her. Or perhaps the distressed leather boots on her feet were giving him the wrong impression.

Kieran lowered the techpad when he heard footsteps on the bridge. 'Ami.'

She hugged him from behind, her chin digging into his shoulder as she looked down at the image. Kieran smiled and closed his eyes. Her presence at his back kept him from spiralling into thoughts that would only hurt and hinder.

'Do you think Pendergast can help us with the Desine?' Ami asked.

'I'm not sure,' Kieran answered slowly. 'She has information I want, I won't deny that. But there is no point in waiting for her to drip-feed me each morsel when we have more important things to do. Let's deal with Rochaccia. Then we'll ask her if there's a reason the Desine is stalking me. Frankly, Ami, I don't care about parents I don't remember. I don't need them. I...I need you.'

Ami drew away from him, her energy tangled, her face shadowed with pain. He knew she wanted more than kisses in an alcove. But she wouldn't pursue anything with him, not while he was dedicated to GLEA. Kieran's stomach hollowed out.

'Okay,' Ami said. 'Should we let Pendergast tag along?'

'Having an e-reporter on board isn't a bad idea.'

'Oh, how's that?'

'Her reports are widely read,' Kieran explained. 'It might work to our advantage if she gives a firsthand account of the atrocities committed by those engaged in the slave trade. Pendergast can influence billions of beings—perhaps she can convince enough of them to do something. GLEA can't put an end to slavery alone. And neither can you, Ami. The more help we have, the better.'

'We'd have help, huh?' Ami sighed dramatically. 'But I thought saving everyone was my job!'

Kieran laughed. 'It's about time you delegated some of your work.'

'Ha! Never.' She playfully elbowed him in the side. 'Alright, I'll go tell the e-paper reporter she can stick around. But I'm not averse to sticking her in a lifepod and stranding her in a system without a Web relay.'

Kieran waited until Ami had left before poring over the image of his parents once more. He didn't need them. He didn't.

But the yearning would not cease.

TWENTY-FIVE

The bridge felt crowded, even with only two extra people on board, and Ami found she lacked the patience to deal with an audience. Avurn was more than happy to take the captain's chair in her place and was busily making small, frequent course corrections, possibly an attempt to impress the resident e-paper reporter. He had made no secret of his desire to build his 'galactic profile', a phrase that Jets had been mercilessly taunting him about ever since he'd unwisely used it within her earshot.

Wow. They'd only been in leapspace for twelve hours and Ami already wanted to space everyone in sight.

Ami's new passengers had been given bedrolls to use in the hold, though so far only Grace had gone down there to do 'some work'—or whatever *that* meant. Maybe she was writing a dramatic account of life aboard the *Free Ride*, highlighting the incident where Jets had spilled coffein in the corridor outside the bridge. Avurn had slid through the ensuing puddle on his way back from the communal toilet, mere seconds before Jets had returned from the hold with something to mop up the mess.

The 'indignity' of his butt hitting the floor had caused Avurn to forget his so-called galactic profile in an instant. He and Jets had spent half an hour tossing increasingly lewd insults at each other, the great Grace Pendergast witnessing it all.

Ami sank onto the bed in her quarters and sighed.

Blessed silence.

Then her door screeched open and Kieran appeared, his own brand of silence as heavy and oppressive as the sludge on Ranta. He simply stood there, looking pained. Ami waited for him to leave, to step back those extra few micrometres to clear the door's sensor so it would shut again. She didn't know if she wanted him to stay or piss off.

'Do you think Jets will be able to convince her father to help us?' Kieran asked before she could decide.

Oh right, that was part of the plan they'd collectively concocted last night before leaving the Post. Ami had just wanted to sleep, but *nooo*. Everyone else had decided they'd wanted to figure shit out right then and there, not during the four whole days they'd spend in leapspace.

Now she'd have to spend those four days wondering if she was insane to go ahead with this flimsy plan. Since it was pointless trying to convince her parents to make slavery illegal, they were going to do something slightly less impossible. As in, lock up Rochaccia's rulers, take over the entire planet, and install a new governing body.

Yeah, they were starked, weren't they?

Ami attempted a shrug. Her tense shoulders ached in protest. 'Don't know. It's unlikely that Governor Bock Atsason will want to risk his fleet against my parents'. The governor runs a terraforming company, a very profitable one, but it doesn't pull the same amount of coin-chips that the slave trade does. Hence, a more modest fleet.

Though I did hear a rumour about Yalsa 5 putting in an order for Behemoth-class starships...'

'Someone still makes those?' Kieran asked, startled.

'Yeah, Istastellar Shipyards, they're owned by Ista Israr...' Ami kept talking, hoping he was focusing on her words instead of her energy, in case it contained something that might give her intentions away.

Right, it was now or never. She had to know.

Ami ripped the lasgun off her belt and hurled it at him. Kieran's hands were raised in an instant, fingers slightly curled over his palms. The weapon hovered in the air between them. Ami smirked, grabbed the lasgun, and clipped it back onto her belt, flush with vindication.

'I knew it,' she said. 'Those forcefields form a lot faster now, huh.'

Kieran lowered his arms to his sides, having the decency to look chagrined. 'I couldn't exactly mention it in front of our guests. I'm sorry. I should have found the time to tell you.'

'You and Avurn were a little obvious,' Ami told him. 'Might want to work on that. I had to put on a big performance about being shitted off with Av—okay, maybe it wasn't a *complete* performance.' She snorted. 'Anyway, I'll tell our guests that you and Av are getting some winks while I'm on watch, so you two can sneak off for a bit and practice linking your powers. I'll make it an order if I have to. We might need a forcefield as big as this ship and if that's at all possible...please. Get it done.'

Kieran took a step forward. The door whined as it unstuck from the frame but it shut seamlessly, leaving the two of them alone. In complete privacy.

They stared at each other, several paces still between them. Ami knew she wasn't going to be able to resist closing that gap so she didn't even try. She jumped off the bed and wrapped her arms around him. He surrendered to her without protest, the stiffness in his body easing as he matched his exhales to hers.

Ami pillowed her head against his shoulder. This—this was dangerous. She couldn't get used to it. He was GLEA's. He wasn't hers.

'Well, this explains a few things,' she said.

'It does?' Kieran asked.

'The visions don't come with the chip, that's obvious by how your superiors reacted when you mentioned them,' Ami said, leaning back to meet his eyes. 'Your powers are something you have naturally, hence'—she waved at the plaster on his temple—'why you still have them. I know telekinesis isn't a part of Chief Ralcha's skill set, even if he can make sand dance a bit, but that doesn't mean we can rule out the Magic completely.'

Kieran shook his head. 'I've never heard of anyone having a Chipper's powers and the desert-based Magic at the same time.'

'Could be the rest of them keep a low profile,' Ami suggested. 'And unlike you, they haven't had chips interfering with their powers since birth. I could ask our onboard reporter. If anyone would know…'

'She'll guess why we're asking, she's not a fool,' Kieran warned. 'We don't want her to know what I can do.'

'She might already know,' Ami said, lips pursed. 'I have a feeling she's been chasing you for a while.'

'We can't take that risk.'

He was right. If Grace suspected…well, a suspicion wasn't a fact. She had no proof. Maybe this was the real reason the e-paper reporter hadn't published anything about Kieran yet. Grace might talk a good game about protecting her sources, but Ami couldn't trust someone who was deliberately withholding information that could help Kieran.

Ami idly noted that her fingers were fiddling with the zipper of his jumpsuit, but she couldn't seem to stop herself doing it. 'Kieran, the Desine wanted you to ditch the chip. We need to prepare for what's going to happen next. You've been able to fight him off so far, but the loss of your chip might have changed things. For the worse.'

'I kept wondering why he wanted it gone...' Kieran trailed off, his brow creasing. 'You think it will be easier for him control me now. That I won't be able to stop him using me to kill people.'

'Creator God trumps sub-level god,' Ami said, beginning to pace, grateful that her quarters were large enough for her to take six steps from wall to wall. It gave her something to do that didn't involve touching him. 'Okay. So if your powers aren't desert based and are from a higher authority instead, then maybe you can find some way to block the Desine. And stop him coming after you.'

A shudder passed through Kieran's frame and it took all of Ami's willpower not to go back to him, to kiss away the lines radiating out from the corners of his taut lips. In the vastness of space, while his chip wasn't working, with GLEA unable to spy on him...it was tempting to give in. But she couldn't. Because being dumped the moment they landed near a temple with a spare chip wasn't going to do her self-esteem any favours. Never mind what it'd do to her already bruised heart.

'I don't think it's possible to block a god,' Kieran said.

Ami's boots hit the wall again and she turned around. 'Rochaccia's surface has a fair amount of desert. He will find you there, Kieran. And that's going to really stark things up for us when we're in the middle of taking down my parents.'

'I can't keep running from him,' Kieran said softly. 'Especially since Ilbb is your homeport...no. No more running. I won't do it. Not anymore.'

'I guess you'd better find a way to block a god then,' Ami remarked.

Kieran looked down at his hands, closing his fingers over his palms. 'I don't even know where to start.'

'Yeah, but you better start,' Ami said. 'If I have to confront my parents and deal with their shit, then you better do your part and handle whatever's on your end.'

'And if I fail?'

Ami rubbed her forehead. She didn't have a headache, more like a...mindache.

'I'll just do what I usually do,' she declared. 'Aim my ship's giant lascannon at the Desine and tell him to fuck off. Or else. I haven't heard anything about the gods being able to survive a direct blast to the face. That has to scare him off, right? Get him to take human form—I've heard they can do that—and let's see what happens.'

Kieran's chuckle was weak, but it still managed to warm her from head to toe.

TWENTY-SIX

Kieran had never imagined that four days in leapspace could feel like an eternity.

Four days of sitting awkwardly in Avurn's cramped quarters, merging and growing their forcefields until his head began to ache. Four days of dodging Jets' keen, probing questions about his life with GLEA. Four days of encountering Ami in every nook and cranny of the *Free Ride*, knowing he shouldn't stand so close to her, shouldn't offer something he couldn't give her. Sometimes...sometimes Kieran was sure he caught more than desire and frustration from Ami, almost as if he was snatching a word or two, here and there. But that couldn't be right. It wasn't possible to read someone's thoughts.

The only person who managed to avoid Kieran for a decent stretch of time was Grace Pendergast. She seemed determined not to engage with him. But she watched him constantly, paying close attention to the plaster on his temple. Had she realised that there was no chip beneath it?

Maybe Ami was right. Maybe the reporter *did* know what he could do.

He had another, more immediate problem to contend with, however. He and Avurn were still unable to create a forcefield larger than the boy's quarters. Kieran's doubts often clogged their link. Avurn rightly took him to task whenever it happened, but Kieran couldn't stop himself wondering. How long would their shield last if the rest of the ship was blown to bits? Could a forcefield even hold any oxygen?

Yalsa 5 swelled in the viewport. Kieran didn't need to be told that this world had been terraformed at some point in its past—two straight lines ran between its magnetic poles, neatly dividing the planet into distinct hemispheres: one an immense sandy desert, the other covered in lush green rainforests.

Kieran braced his hands on the safety railing that ran behind the captain's chair, his knuckles whitening as Ami took them closer to the planet. Jets and Avurn were occupying the bridge's other two seats, leaving Grace no other option but to stand beside him. She gave no signs that this made her uncomfortable, or that she felt any guilt about withholding secrets she surely had no right to keep. Kieran hoped that indifferent mask of hers was concealing at least *some* inner turmoil.

Jets kicked the communications console, clearly agitated. 'Why are parents such starkers sometimes?'

'Let me know when you figure out the answer to that one,' Ami said with a snort.

From what little Jets had said about her father since they'd left the Trading Post, the governor didn't seem like a cruel man, just a little too uncompromising. He no doubt believed he knew what was best for his daughter. Kieran couldn't remember his own parents, even if he now knew what they looked like. Was this kind of friction normal between a child and their father?

Lascannon blasts streaked over the top of the *Free Ride* just before they made orbit.

'That was close enough to set off the alarms,' Avurn announced. 'If they were enabled. But of course they are not, thanks to the wisdom of our esteemed captain. Fortunately, those blasts skimmed our shield only. A difficult set of shots, made by a competent gunner. Prepare yourselves for a very different type of opening salvo.'

'Attention vessel registered as *Free Ride*,' a gravelly voice intoned after Jets slapped the sensor pad on the console in front of her, accepting the incoming verbal-only link. 'You have entered space governed by Yalsa 5. Please state your intentions.'

Jets vacated her chair and shook herself out. 'Take over for me, Av. And make sure our side of the link has visual output. They need to see me.'

She waited for him to seat himself at the communications console, then adopted a loose stance that favoured one hip and threw on a severe expression that could have shattered n'radian. She didn't so much as speak to the planet looming before her as she did challenge it. 'You tell my starking father, Governor Bock Atsason, that if he wants me back under his thumb he'd better not fucking me blow me up.' Jets sliced a hand across her throat. 'Cut it, Avurn. Let them stew.'

Avurn complied. The commanding presence Jets had wielded was gone in an instant. Her shoulders slumped and she released a long, drawn-out 'whewww'.

'I hate doing that,' she said. 'It's exhausting.'

'But it's a persona that could allow you to rule a planet,' Avurn pointed out.

'Oh yeah, like that's worth the misery of forcing myself to be someone I'm not!'

Grace cleared her throat, finally breaking her silence. 'The governor will not be interested in doing anything other than retrieving his daughter. It is very unlikely that he will agree to take on Rochaccia's fleet...but he might do so if his reputation for always repaying his debts is at stake. We should mention Kieran's name.'

Kieran glanced at her. 'Why?'

'Everything Bock has...' Grace lifted one finger and singled out the gleaming settlement on the planet below. Even the orange semi-spherical shield smothering Atsa City couldn't dull its shine. 'He owes all of it to your parents. Peace after centuries of chaos and destruction, the steep incline of economic growth, an enviable place on the galactic stage—this was handed to him on a platter, thanks to Bolt and Dancer. They stepped aside as rulers and insti-tuted a democratic system, which the current governor benefits from.'

Jets nodded emphatically. 'True! All of it way true. Bolt and Dancer put a stop to the intergang warfare *waaaay* before I was born. Dad could never have done what they did. Gotta be honest with you though, the whole system is due for a crash. Our galactic neighbours on Yalsa 3 keep sending new gangers over to start shit. Things are really tense in Atsa right now.'

'Why did my parents leave this world?' Kieran asked Grace.

'That's a question for another time,' she said evenly.

Of course it is, Kieran thought.

'I'm about to accept an incoming visual link,' Avurn warned everyone. 'Please adopt whatever persona you deem suitable for conversing with a planetary leader.'

A bar of light swiped across the viewport once the link was established. Governor Bock Atsason stood in what was presumably his office, the spires of his city visible through the large window behind him. Sporting a razor-sharp suit with its sleeves rolled up to reveal his sprawling tattoos, the governor carried no obvious weapon, but his stance suggested that he was a weapon himself.

The generous silver streaks in his hair did nothing to soften his image.

'Where the fuck have you been, Jets?' he demanded. 'I ought to blow you out of the sky for daring to show up again after you bailed on us. Your mother's off-world at the moment, so don't be thinkin' she'll save you.'

'Are you kidding?' Jets exclaimed. 'You're the softie. I'm not afraid of you.'

Ami pitched her voice low. 'Jets. Please. We need his help.'

'This the captain who smuggled you off-world?' Bock asked, throwing a scowl at the vidcam on his end. It was clear he meant to aim it at Ami.

Jets crossed her arms and her chin shot up, a clear visual of the determination Kieran could sense in her energy. 'Yep! She's the heir of both rulers of Rochaccia, 'cept she's planning on taking them out. Something I'll never do to your worthless hide—mostly because you're not into slavery. We need your ships so we can go attack Rochaccia's fleet, by the way.'

Bock's face went as still as stone. He asked softly, dangerously, 'Why would I launch my fleet against a significantly better one? And without provocation?'

Ami remained casually draped over the captain's chair as she mustered an easy smile, perfectly crafted, her anxiety obvious to no one except Kieran. 'Governor, you would only need to provide a distraction for my parents' ships while we go planetside. Once my boots are on Rochaccian soil, I should be able to take command and order a ceasefire.'

'The only reason you're still alive is because my daughter's on your ship,' Bock said. 'Once she's off that junker—and you better get a docking port ready—you'll get yourself out of this system and never come back. I won't shoot at you if you don't stick around. Very generous of me, ain't it?'

Kieran knew there would be no better time to speak up. 'There is a reason why you should assist us.'

'A starking Chipper?' Bock laughed. 'You expect me to help you out after you lot messed with this planet a while back?'

Kieran winced. It seemed that Governor Atsason still wasn't appeased after over two decades of apologies and playing nice—not that Kieran could blame him. Rogue members of GLEA stationed on Yalsa 5 had participated in unlawful conflicts and while those agents had been expelled, this hadn't erased what they'd done.

Kieran spread his arms, hoping he did not appear too beseeching. 'My name is Kieran Krendasta. You owe my parents, Bolt and Dancer, a significant debt. I'm here to collect.'

Bock's face lost all colour.

'Holy Creator shit,' he breathed.

Panic began radiating off him in waves and Kieran glanced at Avurn, who nodded discreetly. The boy was feeling it too, courtesy of their link. Kieran's chest spasmed. If he was this strong, if he could sense someone's energy from orbit...then it wouldn't be long before the voices reached him up here.

'No,' Bock said decisively. 'I won't go down that alley. Give me my daughter and fuck off. Believe me, fucking off is for your own protection. That you knew to use your identity against me means you're dangerously close to tripping everyone's sensors. Drop it, Chipper. Before this goes too far.'

Ami's eyes found Kieran's. He heard the words as if she'd spoken them, but her mouth remained sealed. *Do you want me to chase this?*

Had he read her thoughts?

Kieran shook his head, both to himself and in response to Ami's questioning gaze. Bock was already too belligerent and would not give Kieran any answers, even if he had them.

'I won't be waiting at the docking port unless you agree to help them!' Jets was saying, her hands stuck fast to her hips and her voice beginning to waver. 'At least consider it, Dad. Please. I'll make it worth your while.'

'That mean you'll stop pouting and carrying on like a spoiled brat?' Bock demanded.

'Oh, you don't want me to *carry on*?' Jets scoffed. 'Fine. I can get real succinct. I'll sneak into your bedroom tonight and press my lasgun against your temple. That worked last time, didn't it? And what about the time I clocked you so bad you got laid up with concussion? Maybe I can knock you out enough times that your brain turns to shit and you agree to anything I say.'

Bock sighed. 'Jets. You'n me both know you hate violence. I won't make you resort to that, alright? While I'd love to get in on this action and see what I can get out of it, it's too dangerous. Roch and Accia ain't pushovers. Even if we survive an encounter with that combined fleet of theirs, they'll come after us—I reckon they'd even throw coin-chips at our friends over on Yalsa 3 and we'd soon have a fucking war on our hands.'

'Okay, what if we neutralise the fleet for you?' Ami asked.

Kieran was amazed that she could maintain the appearance of being calm and in control, even when their plan was falling apart at the first step.

'After we do that and get planetside,' Ami went on, ignoring Bock's sceptical snort, 'we'll be up against two separate armies. We don't have the bodies or weapons for that. I would really appreciate it if your fleet conducted orbital strikes on key targets—you won't even have to face any of Roch's or Accia's starships. And as a bonus, once Rochaccia is under new management, Yalsa 5 will be first in line for any trade agreements.'

Kieran knitted his eyebrows together. She made it sound convincing. But he could hear her voice in his mind saying something entirely different. *Oh stark, how am I supposed to do this? I can't take out an entire fleet with one lascannon and a shitty shield. I'd rather take my chances going up against the Desine.*

He really was reading her thoughts, wasn't he? What else could he find if he pried deep enough?

Perturbed, Kieran turned back to the viewport.

Bock's gaze grew distant for a few moments, then he nodded. 'Alright. After—and only after—you folks nix that blockade, I'll show up and dish out some orbital bombardment. Because I reckon I do owe your parents, Chipper. Even if other folks see it differently.' There was a flash of pity in those pale eyes, gone almost as quickly as it had come. 'Just how much do you actually know?'

'Not much,' Kieran admitted.

'And yet you decided to use your crumbs of knowledge against me anyway.' Bock grinned broadly. 'I'm almost impressed by your unstable mix of stupidity and confidence. You remind me of the kid I used to be. Jets, get your arse to that docking port. You're comin' home.'

'Fine,' the teenager snapped. 'But if you don't hold up your end of your deal with Captain N'uni, then I'm fucking *gone.*'

Another bar of light swept across the viewport, leaving them staring at the two-toned planet instead of Bock's face. Jets sagged. She looked drained, like a cloth that had been wrung repeatedly until every last drop of defiance was gone.

'You better take out that fleet fast or he's not coming,' Jets said.

'I wonder how our esteemed captain will handle that particular obstacle,' Avurn remarked.

Ami looked at Kieran, her expression wavering between beseeching and horrified. He could see that her initial reluctance to go to Rochaccia had become a growing hunger. She didn't want to face her parents, but if there was a chance that she could put a stop to all the pain and suffering they continued to cause...

'We'll find a way,' Kieran assured her.

'I do not share your optimism,' Avurn said. 'Yalsa 5's fleet was our best option to make it past the blockade. Unless you want to try to talk your way through instead? You seemed to think that wasn't going to work. We cannot hope a solution into existence.'

'Hey now, you're the one who wanted to go after the source of the disease, not the symptoms,' Ami reminded him. She tilted her head to the side, now addressing Grace. 'Speaking of sources. Someone like you must have informants on Rochaccia. You know, people who can put us in touch with an underground resistance or something like that.'

Grace's lip twisted. 'I have no sources there. No one does. Any mediaists and e-paper reporters who tangle with Rochaccia find themselves with two large bounties on their heads.'

'Can anyone actually form an underground resistance if they're shot up with Rapture?' Avurn wondered.

'Perhaps we can help them form that resistance,' Kieran said.

Avurn chortled. 'We're good, Kieran, but not that good. Don't misunderstand me—I still want to try to end Rochaccia's reign over the slave trade in this region of space, but things are more difficult than we bargained for. At least we have the famous Grace Pendergast with us. Her report on our ill-advised adventure will do wonders for my galactic profile. If I survive, that is.'

Ami covered her face with her hands and groaned.

TWENTY-SEVEN

The whispers found Kieran while Grace was walking Jets down to the docking port.

Ami had told the reporter to accompany the teenager under the guise of ensuring that Jets actually left the ship; Jets had received a much quieter order to make the transfer last as long as possible. Kieran had seen the wink Jets had thrown at Ami as she'd left the bridge. The teenager intended to deliver. So for the moment, the *Free Ride*'s crew had the bridge to themselves.

Ami dropped heavily into her chair. 'Okay, we're down a starship fleet. We need a workable plan for getting around that blockade. *Fast.* Or your galactic profile is never going to be a thing, Av.'

'You must convince your parents to let you through,' Avurn supplied.

'Not happening,' Ami said. 'Kieran? Any ideas?'

Avurn's lip curled. 'Don't bother looking to him for help, Ami. Kieran has other things on his mind. Talking to your parents is our next best option. Unfortunately.'

Kieran was vaguely aware of Jets' lifesign departing the *Free*

Ride, though this was quickly shunted to the bottom of his priorities when the whispers grew louder. He forced himself to look away from the vast hemisphere of sand stretching across the viewport. Had the voices been inside his mind since he'd arrived, subtly building in strength until now?

Ami left her chair and moved towards the railing, emerald eyes filled with concern. 'What's wrong?'

Kieran drew a shuddering breath. Images of the recent past played over his vision, temporarily blinding him. The desert god coming after him on Enoc, the sandstorm on Fintaz: events heralded by the whispers that he could no longer run from. He fixed his gaze on the floor. 'My ability to read the energy of others is a lot stronger without the chip. I can sense the people on the planet's surface— possibly even further, if I tried. I think that's why I can hear...things all the way out here.'

'Shit,' she said. 'I can't take you to Rochaccia. Or anywhere, really.'

Her mind said something else. *Gods, I need him with me. There's no way I can do this without him, but I can't endanger him like this...I can't...*

Kieran basked in the warmth of her lifesign, strengthened by the growing feelings she had for him despite her best efforts. She wouldn't make him go with her to Rochaccia and he was grateful for that. He'd been trying to ignore her thoughts, since it felt like an intrusion, but he'd rather have her voice inside his head instead of the desert god's.

'You need me with you, Ami,' Kieran argued. 'I'll...I'll find a way to block him. I have to do it. *Somehow.*'

'I have a suggestion,' Avurn piped up from his chair.

'You can't possibly have a suggestion for this,' Ami gritted out. 'You don't even know what's going on here.'

Avurn rolled his eyes. 'Please. I was just treated to a short version of the story over the link. Thank you for having those well-timed flashbacks, Kieran. Anyway, my suggestion is not radical, merely an adaptation of what Kieran can already do.'

Kieran shrugged helplessly when Ami shot him a look. He wasn't aware of a link ever functioning like that before, but it wasn't impossible that he'd inadvertently Webcast his problems to the boy. He would need to be a lot more careful in future.

'You will create a shield'—Avurn held up his hands, replicating the gesture he used to project forcefields—'but inside your own mind. You manage, for the most part, to put a stopper on your emotions inside our link. Surely it cannot be that different.'

'Kieran's probably not stoppering that stuff on purpose, though,' Ami told him.

'Imagine what he could do if he tried!' Avurn said. 'If he can pull a sandstorm down on his assailants by accident...'

Darkness edged Ami's words. 'I will do everything in my power to make sure Kieran is never forced into a situation like that ever again. If he is, then so help the person who did it to him. Because I'm going after them.'

Kieran fought to keep his hands seated on the safety railing. What he really wanted to do was pull her into his arms and kiss her.

'Ugh, Kieran, focus,' Avurn pleaded, wrinkling his nose.

Kieran bowed his head. 'Sorry. I'll give it a go, but I have serious doubts about a mental shield working like a physical forcefield. And you do realise that I'm trying to hide myself from a god?'

'I thought we agreed that the Creator God's powers trump a sub-level god's?' Ami said.

'I'm not sure we agreed,' Kieran replied with a tight smile.

Avurn rubbed two knuckles beneath his chin, looking thoughtful. 'It isn't a completely laughable conclusion. We won't know if it's true until the Desine shows up, however. That requires you getting his attention, since he clearly hasn't received the invitation yet.'

'I'll lock the bridge door,' Ami said. 'We don't want Pendergast seeing this.'

It was now or never. Kieran closed his eyes and cast his awareness towards Yalsa 5. His ability to sense the universe's energy had been average at best when he'd worn a chip, but now he could scour an entire planet. The lifesigns on Yalsa 5 came with a deluge of thoughts, too many for him to focus on, and all of them were as complex as a star. He might never understand some of these minds. And there were other things down there. Most beings could not feel or hear them. But he could.

Kieran breathed slowly, forcing his fear deep down inside him. Then he turned the volume up on the whispers.

We are here! We are here for you! they cried.

Something tightened in his gut, as though someone had knotted a rope around his intestines. Kieran jerked and nearly fell. His hands continued to scrabble uselessly at the railing even after he forced his eyelids apart.

There wasn't time to steady himself. The Desine had arrived.

'Kieran!' Ami called, clearly panicked.

A vortex of sand was sweeping across the bridge, headed directly for Kieran. He acknowledged the support he could feel flowing from Avurn in the link, then warned the boy not to interfere. Avurn was tempted to try, to make himself famous as the mortal who had trounced a god. But the Desine would shred him.

Kieran wasn't sure that *he* would survive this encounter. The Desine's presence was probing his consciousness, trying to find a way in.

Kieran bit into his lip and felt it give, tasting blood.

You have thrown off your shackles, noted the Desine.

Kieran's fingers drifted to his temple, grazing the plaster that covered his mostly healed wound. His chip was still gone. It had cut him off from his more potent powers, helping him to remain hidden for more than two decades—but it could not have kept him hidden from the Desine forever.

'Yes, I have,' Kieran agreed. 'Which means I now have enough power to banish you.'

A disbelieving laugh, as dry as a desert wind. *You think you can overpower me?*

Wordlessly, Kieran raised his hands as if to physically ward off the god, but the forcefield he was creating remained inside his mind.

As small as a seed to start with, but once planted it grew and kept growing, until the shield had expanded to encase every single thought, emotion, sensation. He wasn't safe. Not yet. The surface was flimsy, weak. Easy to puncture. The Desine's energy hadn't yet lost that triumphant twist and the vortex was slowing, solidifying, forming a sandy torso and limbs.

Kieran smiled grimly and dug deeper into the well of his power.

No! the god cried.

It was Kieran's turn to laugh. 'I won't have to listen to you anymore. Not when I'm done blocking you.'

Kieran tasted the Desine's panic, revelled in it—and then he slammed back against a bulkhead when the god stole through the link he had formed with Avurn, forcibly shoving the boy aside. Avurn cried out. Kieran staggered, his head throbbing and his joints aching, but Ami was already beside Avurn's crumpled form. Her eyes met Kieran's.

Finish this, she mouthed.

Kieran straightened, facing off against the gritty, shifting figure that continued to advance on him. Why was the Desine so angry? What had Kieran done to offend him? Perhaps it was nothing, simply that he had dared to exist with powers that no mortal should have. He had never intended to step outside the shadow of the gods.

Kieran hardened his voice, just as he'd hardened the shield

inside his mind. 'With the powers of the Creator God, I cast you out.'

He had expected a strong reaction but not...not this. The Desine's anguished scream filled every corner of the bridge. The climate control system wheezed and groaned, struggling to adjust to the heat spilling into the ship. Then Kieran's hands were yanked forward, weighed down by sand that filled every crevice, grinding against every bump.

You can't deny this! hissed the Desine. *You have my power too. Don't turn your back on it! On me!*

Kieran shook his hands, the sand cupped inside them surprisingly soft and gentle when he had expected it to be coarse and cruel, but the granules were stuck fast. And the voices, the voices that he was trying so hard to stifle—they called to him, begging him to command them. Suddenly, Kieran knew the exact number of grains on the planet below him. It was a mind-boggling number, but he knew it, and he knew he could order the sand to shape a storm that would spread across the sky, ripping skin from bone—

This was what he'd felt that day on Fintaz. A heady rush, a desperate aching hunger that needed satisfying, an undeniable force that could pulverise any obstacle that dared to stand in his way.

Kieran shied from what the sands offered him, afraid.

You will need my power if you wish to complete your task! threatened the Desine.

'I already have enough power—I don't need this!' Kieran shouted. 'I cast you out!'

He threw a second layer over the shield inside his mind, hammering it into place with the dual force of desperation and determination. He caught one last glimpse of the Desine—a tortured, insubstantial whirlwind—and then the bridge fell silent, the air cool and stagnant once more. Kieran's gut finally stopped squirming. He sank to his knees, exhausted.

Avurn reached for him again, so Kieran hollowed out a tunnel through the shield, allowing the boy in.

'Impressive,' Avurn said as he studied Kieran's handiwork. 'If I didn't have this access point, I would not have been able to feel anything from you. I will need to use a shield similar to this one when I am in the vicinity of other Chippers, to hide my ability to link with them.'

Ami slapped her earpiece, looking irritated. The communicator had been squawking for several minutes, Kieran realised, though he hadn't registered it until just then. Grace wanted to know what was happening on the bridge. Ami threw on a smile and answered her, tossing out various lies—a million a minute by the sounds of things. She killed the link before Grace could call her out on any of it.

'Stark, how did she get my communicator details?' Ami grumbled.

Avurn slid back into the chair at the weapons console. 'You have about ten seconds before our resident reporter starts banging on the door. That lie about the fritzing regulator was a good one, Ami, though Jets would have been most unimpressed to hear it. Since she was the one who fixed that particular component.'

'Kieran?' Ami questioned, leaning over the railing towards him.

He closed his eyes briefly, fighting the shivers that were gathering at the nape of his neck. 'I could feel the Magic, Ami. And I could feel the deserts down there. This...' He touched his chest. 'This isn't just the Creator God's work.'

'You can keep using your usual powers instead of the Magic, right?'

'I hope so,' Kieran murmured.

'The important thing is...' Ami gestured towards the viewport. 'You can now touch down on Rochaccia without the Desine finding you. And if there are consequences to ignoring your desert powers? Fine. We'll handle those. But *after* we deal with my parents.'

Her mouth was pressed into a firm, uncompromising line. The galaxy wouldn't dare to disagree with Captain Ami N'uni and neither would he. Kieran tried to resist the urge to kiss her, knowing he shouldn't, but her sigh touched his lips and then he was lost to her. Ami cupped his jaw with both hands and breathed strength back into him.

'Spare us,' Avurn grumbled. 'This convoluted dance between you two is impairing everyone's ability to function on this ship.'

Kieran pressed his forehead against Ami's. He couldn't find the right words to express himself, wishing they had a link so he could share his feelings directly with her.

But she nodded, as though she'd somehow heard him.

'I'm unlocking the bridge door,' Avurn warned them.

Ami hurled herself away from the railing, neatly landing in her chair. A yawning gap now stretched between her and Kieran. He wavered, but only for a few nanoseconds, and managed to stand straight before Grace Pendergast entered the bridge.

'I take it we're not about to disintegrate in orbit,' Grace said.

'Nope,' Ami replied.

The reporter lifted one eyebrow. 'Or about to be boarded by an uninvited guest.'

An awkward, lingering silence followed this.

Ami cleared her throat. 'No one's here if they're not invited, you can bet on that. And we can rescind your invitation any starking time we want to.'

'Noted,' Grace said. 'Would you mind telling me how you intend to reach the surface of Rochaccia? I believe your Plan A was to get Yalsa 5's fleet to distract, if not destroy, the ships forming the blockade, but that won't be happening now.'

'Plan B is me,' Ami said. 'I ask nicely. My parents let us through.'

'Failing that, Plan C is you,' Avurn told the reporter. 'Ami's parents might be more inclined to allow the great Grace Pendergast to go planetside than the daughter they've slapped two separate bounties on. Anyone with a galactic profile, no matter how small, wants the chance to impress someone as respected and clever as you.'

Kieran hid his smile when Ami sighed in exasperation. 'Av. Knock it off. Don't you and Kieran have...*stuff* to do?'

Kieran and Avurn traded nods. They both headed towards the doorway, ignoring the reporter's shrewd eyes. With only a handful of days to go before the *Free Ride* reached Rochaccia, their combined shield needed extensive and exhaustive work. The upcoming trip through leapspace wouldn't feel quite so long, Kieran was sure.

'And Plan D?' Grace prompted.

Ami didn't even hesitate. 'Plan D is Kieran and Avurn. That's if they can climb this steep learning curve of theirs. But I think they can manage it. Especially after the...regulator issue we just put to bed. Now sit down and don't ask any more questions. Or else.'

Avurn waited until he and Kieran had left the bridge before he mused, 'Blocking a god—that's only a fraction of what you can do, isn't it.' Envy tainted his every word.

'You wouldn't want to have a god chasing you,' Kieran said.

'Depends on the benefits.'

'They don't outweigh the drawbacks, trust me.'

Avurn slowed and turned towards Kieran, his expression hooded. 'I know what you think of me. I can see it in the link. But there is a lot I could do—could have done—with abilities like yours. My parents and my sister need not have...Kieran, if I was in your position, I would make it my mission to lose the fear of something that is as much a part of me as a limb. You fear your powers, you deny them—which means you'll never have control over them. And that is dangerous. Especially for those around you.'

Kieran bowed his head. He couldn't argue with that.

'Now, we can't afford to waste time,' Avurn said, clapping his hands together. 'We need to expand our admittedly dismal shield. Show me what you did to strengthen your mental one and I believe we may stand a chance of protecting this entire ship.'

Kieran followed Avurn down the corridor, chagrined to realise just how badly he'd misjudged the boy.

TWENTY-EIGHT

Ami watched Kieran pace end to end in her quarters from her comfy nest of pillows, smiling lazily whenever she got a good view of his backside. She knew she should have been sleeping and shoring up her strength, since they were due to arrive at Rochaccia within hours, but that was impossible with Kieran so close. He'd said he wanted to talk. Ami had let him in—and definitely not because his jumpsuit was slightly unzipped.

Kieran abruptly stopped pacing, his cheeks tight. 'I don't want Avurn to fix my chip.'

'He's not that fond of fiddling with it anyway,' Ami said wryly, thinking of the chip sitting on Avurn's desk in the hold. Her crew-mate hadn't touched it in days. 'It won't give him what he wants. He can't replicate your powers with tech.'

'Not that he would admit to it out loud.' Kieran dropped onto the end of the bed, barely giving Ami enough time to retract her feet. 'The chip is no longer useful to me. I would be unable to hide myself from the Desine with those minimal abilities—or create the shield we would need to protect your ship. As for the Magic…I intend to ignore it for as long as possible, but Avurn has rightly pointed out that this may not protect the people I care about. Avurn is much wiser than he looks.'

'He *wants* you to think that, Kieran. Don't forget it.'

Ami plonked her feet onto Kieran's lap and raised an eyebrow when he stared at her socks—her toes were poking through the holes in the ends. His lips thinned and a chuckle reluctantly escaped him.

It took mere nanoseconds for his face to grow serious again. 'My own personal reasons aside, I…I *feel* that people would suffer if I remained "shackled". My powers are needed. *I* am needed.'

'Does that frighten you?' she asked.

'Of course it does.' His frown deepened. 'But the Creator God gave these powers to me, so I must use them. It's my duty to fix the Agency and thus stop the galaxy fracturing.'

'But you can't do that—GLEA won't listen to Kieran Krendasta, remember?' she said, recalling the vision he'd told her about. 'They don't even listen to you now. Why would the Creator God put you in such a shitty position?'

'I don't know. But we'll figure it out.' He glanced sideways at her. 'Or at least, you'll figure it out. I'm adrift without you.'

Ami grinned. And her stupid, foolish heart leapt.

Kieran rubbed his hand over his jaw and paused when the skin of his palm rasped, apparently surprised that he'd forgotten to shave. Ami admired the dusting of bristles on his face—it gave him a very rugged and decidedly unChipper-like look. She wondered if he would ever agree to hang up the purple jumpsuit and wear something casual. And tight. Possibly black.

'I shouldn't use you to put tomorrow out of my mind,' she muttered.

'But?' he prompted.

'I could really use a few minutes of amnesia right now.'

Kieran traced indistinct patterns across the tops of her toes, an innocent caress that had no place sending bolts coursing up her thighs. He said nothing, gave her no encouragement. Ami sighed, disappointed, when he withdrew and stood from the bed. But then his fingers found the zipper of his jumpsuit.

'I'm happy to just keep talking, if you like,' Ami croaked.

A smile flitted along his lips.

'I'm an excellent liar, by the way,' Ami said. 'I'm having an off day, is all. An off week. An off month, an off year...'

Her clothes fell to the floor and she ran for the ensuite. He beat her there by a nanosecond. Laughing uproariously, they tumbled into the shower cell together. It took precious seconds for Ami to find the door sensor, even more seconds for the panel to close—that definitely took too long, the system needed an overhaul—and then they were standing beneath the spray, taking each other in with hungry eyes. Ami waited for him to make the first move. If this was a terrible mistake, then by the gods he was going to take half the blame.

Kieran wound his arms around her waist, pulling her in close, his lips whisking away the moisture that had gathered along her neck. Ami moaned softly and sank into him, her fingers following the lines that eager droplets were drawing for her. Kieran hissed when her hand settled low on his hip. Ami shifted, trying to nudge her knee up his thigh—

Her foot slid wildly and her body made a fleshy slap against the wall.

'Ugh, that could have been sexier,' Ami muttered. 'The anti-slip pads are worn out.'

Kieran chuckled. 'Give me a moment.'

The water immediately stopped hitting her skin, but she could still hear it fizzing through the holes in the ceiling and gurgling away beneath her toes. Ami looked up, startled. He still had one hand on her hip while the other was aimed at the ceiling, this particular forcefield made visible by the cascades erupting around its edges.

Ami pursed her lips. 'Drop your arm. But keep the shield up.'

'That's not how it...' Kieran trailed off, then shrugged. 'No harm in trying.'

He planted both of his hands at the small of her back.

The forcefield held.

'I'd hoped this was the case,' Ami said. 'Chippers need to focus energy through their hands before they can get a forcefield going, don't they. It's a little obvious when they're doing it. Obvious enough to invite a lasbolt before the forcefield's ready!'

Kieran was now gazing at her with an intensity that might have actually caused steam to rise from her skin, if that wasn't happening already. The hot water scoring down around them was thanks to a quick fix from Jets, who'd had no tolerance for the cold showers that had intermittently plagued the *Free Ride* for months.

'You find it hard to switch off your thoughts,' Kieran said softly. 'Your past. Your fears. The things you're too afraid to hope for. They all haunt you. So you constantly put yourself in danger and make flippant comments to block out the noise.'

'Your powers extend to reading minds now, huh?' Ami teased.

'Yes, I believe so. I...I didn't want this ability, but it seems to be another gift from the Creator God.'

She groaned. 'Okay. I apologise in advance for any flashbacks I have of this steamy shower moment of ours in future. Because I *will* get them.'

Kieran slid his fingers beneath her chin and lifted her lips into a brief kiss. He smiled as he released her. 'I don't need mind-reading abilities to know you'll be reliving this, because I will be having the exact same problem. And I don't need to use my powers to know who you are, Ami. I *know* you.'

'I know you too,' she murmured. 'I'm the only one who does.'

His next kiss was longer, deeper, like a solemn vow he couldn't voice. Ami shivered, but then he dropped his shield and the hot water splashed back down on her. If she was honest, there had been parts of her that weren't entirely dry before that happened.

Kieran's touch drifted and roamed, slowly exploring her body. Ami didn't have his patience. Her hands slid down his thighs and then back up again. A soft noise escaped his throat, but he made no move to stop her as she skirted her fingers maddeningly close to his hard length before retracting them. She did this several times, relishing how tense he felt beneath her, a great and terrifying power waiting to be released. An impatient hiss parted his lips.

Ami's smile was wicked when she finally cupped him.

Kieran surged forward and pinned her against the wall, his kisses hot and desperate and all consuming. She kept her strokes firm and slow, even when he bucked impatiently against her, even when he pleaded her with his eyes. Ami's hand stilled. She waited.

Then, just as she'd hoped, he unleashed himself.

With a growl, Kieran bit into her shoulder and fisted his hand over her breast, the roughness of his actions sending a thrill shooting through her and wresting every iota of coherence from her in an instant. She didn't need to be in control, not anymore. Not with Kieran. Not when she could be lost inside this strangely synchronised dance of limbs and hands and teeth and tongues. He knew exactly what she wanted. Her body and her mind were laid bare to him.

'Should we be doing this?' Ami rasped as his fingers drew lines of pleasure up her folds and around her throbbing bundle of nerves.

'Ami,' he said lowly. 'You're not the only one trying to forget something.'

Oh. Right. That's how she'd ended up in this position.

Ami slapped a sensor on the wall. Brisk air replaced the hot water in an instant. She stepped back, putting as much space between them as she could, knowing it would never be enough. He was the perfect portrait of patience and sincerity, even with his cock hard and singling her out for attention. It would have been easier to turn him down if he'd been angry.

'What I want isn't possible,' Ami said. 'Because I want all of you. Forever. Not just this one time when you don't have GLEA spying on you.'

'I'm never wearing a chip again,' Kieran vowed.

Ami stared at him, disbelieving, until his gaze flinched away from hers. 'Right, so GLEA won't get at all suspicious that your chip isn't feeding them any details about what you find attractive in a partner. Maybe they won't even bother to check if the chip is working, just pair you up with some random agent. What will you do when that happens? You say the Agency needs you for this big conflict that's coming, so you can help them stitch the galaxy back together. They don't listen to you now—imagine how they'll react when they find out you're sneaking away from your designated spouse to see *me*. And don't think I'll stand by and smile while you make vows to someone else. I won't share you. Not like that.'

His expression fell. His eyes filled with shadows.

'Sorry,' Kieran murmured, moving forward to kiss her forehead. Because, stark him, he knew she'd wanted him to do that, knew she would draw comfort from the gesture.

The laugh spilled out of her. 'You bought me a few minutes of amnesia. That's all I needed.'

She really *was* having an off year with that lying thing, huh.

And oh yeah, he could read her mind now.

'Only if you want me to,' Kieran told her. 'I'm getting better at turning it off.'

'Might be a good idea to work on that, especially if you don't want to keep seeing those flashbacks I mentioned...and it'd be a shame if you saw what else I want to do to you.'

Ami grinned as she left the shower cell, his pained groan following her.

TWENTY-NINE

Over a hundred armoured bulks filled the void between them and Rochaccia, all studded with wickedly sharp spikes that looked like they could puncture the *Free Ride*'s shield and hull in one go. Ami didn't bother trying to count the lascannon mounts. It was pointless. They were so high powered even a handful of them could destroy her. This was the fleet belonging to Neffron Naiman, ruler of Roch —and her father. On the other side of the planet, the blockade was maintained by the small, gnat-like ships belonging to her mother.

The Roch and Accia factions would fight to death about almost everything else, but the blockade guarding them against extraplanetary threats was the one responsibility they could agree to share equally. Too bad their respective rulers had never managed to do that with their own daughter.

Ami stood before the viewport, her shoulders so rigid they ached. She was wearing the best shirt she'd managed to dig out of her closet. No stains, no tears, no offensive odours. She'd even pressed the wrinkles out of the fabric—okay, she'd had some help from Grace, who had experience with laundry systems. The reporter had commented that her professional appearance was her armour, especially in the face of certain death. Ami had managed not to scoff.

But if Grace really had survived all those dangerous events she wrote about in her insanely popular e-paper...well, maybe looking sharp wasn't such a bad idea.

Situated behind the safety railing, Grace was poring over something on her techpad. Occasionally her eyes would lift, her fingers still moving at a frantic pace while she watched things unfold before her. Either Grace was going to score another scoop and throw the *Free Ride*'s crew onto the galactic stage—or they were all about to end up very, very dead.

'How are you going to spin this?' Ami asked Grace, genuinely curious. 'The prodigal heir returns to her homeworld, intent on dismantling her parents' dynasty and throwing a planet into chaos in a vain attempt to save a million lost souls?'

Grace lowered the techpad into its pouch on her slim black belt, which had to be sturdier than it looked. 'I do compose preliminary drafts to save time, I will admit. But no, I'm not writing this story yet —I was scheduling a message for my wife and daughter, in case they're not able to...in case,' she finished guardedly.

'In case they're not able to what?' Ami demanded.

'I misspoke.'

Ami knew she wasn't imagining Grace's discomfort, because Kieran glanced up from the weapons console, eyebrows bunching together. Ami waited for him to detect something untoward in the reporter's thoughts, but he merely looked perplexed. He'd told Ami that her and Avurn's minds were a lot more open than Grace's. Was that because Kieran knew them better—or because Grace knew how to evade people who could read minds?

Ami shook her head. There wasn't time for conjecture.

Grace could keep her secrets—for now.

'Someone is attempting to create a public link with us,' Avurn announced from the communications console. 'Shall I let them?'

'You shall,' Ami echoed, trying not to smile.

'Captain Ami N'uni of the *Free Ride*, you have been identified as an enemy of Roch,' a terse voice said. 'Prepare to be destroyed.'

'A warm welcome, as expected,' Ami commented.

She nodded at Avurn. He tapped the sensor pad on his console, enabling visual output, but the being on the other end of the link didn't respond in kind. The *Free Ride*'s viewport continued to show the blockade and the star-scoured, ridge-marked world behind it. Some planets looked beautiful from space. Rochaccia was a dirty brown ball—if it wasn't so dry or round, it could easily be mistaken for a piece of shit (in Ami's opinion).

Ami cleared her throat, straightened, and adopted a voice that she hoped sounded more stern than performative. 'I was born Unify Naiman, which makes me the heir to Roch and Accia, and I demand an audience with the leader of either faction. Happy to talk to whoever wants to listen. Dad. Mum. Anybody at all.'

Nothing happened.

Avurn thumbed the link off. 'There's a jamming tower close to the planet's equator, making it impossible for anyone down there to connect to the Web. No messages, written or otherwise, can get through. It seems that one faction, namely Roch, is responsible for this. Neffron must be using a closed system, sustained by local relays, in lieu of the Web. That's an assumption, obviously, but I wouldn't trust *my* planetside forces without any oversight, if I was in his position.'

'Huh,' Ami said. 'Doesn't really change how we'll be approaching this, though. My mother still has ships on the other side of the planet and they can easily find a Web signal—but I'm not really expecting her to fly to my rescue anyway.'

'Incoming visual link,' Avurn announced.

Ami's stomach lurched as the viewport swiped to reveal a brightly lit bridge, the glaring chrome design a distracting backdrop to the man standing directly in the centre of the room. An olive-green uniform with a severe cut. A stocky head set onto a stocky neck, all supported by an even stockier body. Aside from the colour of their eyes, Ami didn't think they had much in common. Her father had accused her of being difficult—mostly because she resembled her mother, no matter how many times he ordered her not to. Never mind that she couldn't do a starking thing about her genetic makeup.

As far as Ami was concerned, the only thing of value she'd ever got from her mother was the *Free Ride*. And she'd needed to steal that.

'Sweet little Uni,' Neffron crooned. He might look and sound as genial as a grandfather—not that Ami would know, since she'd never met hers—but that wrinkled face and those soft tones hid a shipload of cruelty. 'Why have you put your hair up? It's more beautiful when you wear it out. And it looks less like your mother's that way.'

Ami swallowed bile and forced herself not to retch. 'Hello, Neffron. It's been a while. I no longer wear the name I was given at birth and you will instead address me as Ami N'uni, captain of the *Free Ride*. The way your crew did already. If they can do it, then so can you. Right. I hear your clients haven't been receiving their shipments lately. And now you want me dead, which I have to say is an extreme reaction. Could have tried grounding me and sending me to bed without dinner, you know. But wait, that's the kind of punishment your ex-wife liked to use. Can't do that. Better get the laswhip out.'

'You targeted Roch's exports on purpose,' he snarled. 'You barely touched Accia's!'

'Noticed that, did you.' Ami wasn't about to admit that *she* hadn't. She waved carelessly at each person arrayed on the bridge around her. 'I had help, by the way. Let me introduce you to Grace Pendergast, e-paper reporter. Kieran Krendasta, Chipper. Avurn Singh, ah, tech expert.' Avurn sat up straight, as though pleased with that fancy label. Ami hid her amusement and pressed on, 'This is the tiny crew that managed to put such a large dent in your exports. No fleet or army required.'

Neffron Naiman rubbed his chapped lips together, causing them to rasp loudly over the communications link. 'Did your mother put you up to this?'

'Nope,' Ami said. 'This was all my idea. I knew exactly how to get under your skin.'

'What is your endgame?' he demanded. 'Did you think that endangering my profit margins—and turning up in one of *her* ships—would convince me to spare you? If you die, then Taylar and I will simply choose another heir. I'm sure even we could agree on someone, so long as they aren't you!'

Ami seriously doubted it, but she wasn't going to argue. 'Would you have hesitated to kill me if I'd come back simpering? Don't lie, Dad. This whole conversation is you hesitating.'

Neffron tipped his nose forward, the better to look down on her. He knew exactly how that looked when his image was magnified, as it was now. 'At least you seem to have inherited some of my acumen. So why do I get to have you? You know that whichever surviving ruler has the heir benefits from their inheritance. Unless, perhaps, you are planning to take over my faction *now*, too impatient to wait for me to die of natural causes...'

'A little paranoid, huh,' Ami remarked.

'I'd hate to think, sweet little Ami,' he said, his eyes narrowing, 'that you chose to side with me solely because I happened to answer you first.'

Ami shrugged. 'Well, that and you owning the largest chunk of the fleet.'

He roared with laughter, spittle spraying the vidcam on his end and covering the viewport of the *Free Ride* like a smattering of rain. Ami waited him out, a patient smile sketched across her brittle lips. Her father's mirth faded as his eyes darted to the side, in the direction of her weapons console.

'Why did you bring *that* with you?' Neffron demanded.

Ami tipped her head towards Kieran. 'Oh, him? The Chipper? You mean, someone who can remind the Agency that we have a legitimate government with laws they should be upholding for us? The Chippers might talk a good game about looking after everyone, but they tend to avoid places like Rochaccia. Sudden staffing issues and other various excuses...all of that can be resolved. And maybe your authority can suddenly take precedence over Taylar's.'

'Why would he arrange that for us? For coin-chips? You promised him my coin-chips?'

'*Our* coin-chips, Dad,' Ami said pleasantly. 'I also have the galaxy's most famous e-paper reporter on my side. She can't be bought with money, so I had to get creative there.'

Neffron seemed to be mulling over her words. Then he nodded sharply. 'Alright. You've impressed me and earned yourself a longer reprieve. My heir, you may proceed through the blockade—do not deviate from the path I give you—and head towards my headquarters. You do recall where they are, don't you?'

'Slap-bang in the middle of the big desert in the northern hemisphere, got it,' Ami said, hazarding a quick look at Kieran.

He nodded slightly. His mental shield was still holding.

'See you soon, Dad,' Ami finished and threw a sarcastic wave at the vidcam affixed above her viewport.

'Lose that insolence before you land,' Neffron ordered.

His face vanished the instant the communications link was cut and his extensive sea of vessels began to part before the *Free Ride*, forming a narrow gauntlet. The spikes on those ships didn't seem to be extendable, but they were still a little too close for comfort.

Ami swallowed. 'I trust that guy about as much as I trust myself to hit a stationary object with a lasgun. Which is…not very. Kieran, Av—two heads are better than one. Can you get this little side project of yours to work?'

'We'll *make* it work,' Avurn said.

Kieran grimaced, but didn't object.

Ami didn't miss the sharp eyes of Grace Pendergast flitting between the three of them. The reporter would definitely notice if Kieran and Avurn projected a shield around the whole vessel, something a group of Chippers couldn't do on the best of days, let alone one misfit and one supposedly powerless boy.

'Pendergast, get into the hold,' Ami ordered.

'I'm staying on the bridge this time,' Grace said calmly. 'I need to witness these events personally, so I can report on them more accurately.'

'I can't let you write a report on this. Not this specific thing.'

Grace folded her arms together, seemingly unfazed. 'Whatever secrets you feel you have to hide, Captain, I can assure you they would already be in one of my reports if I had any intention of revealing them.'

Ami wasn't sure why, but she believed the reporter. Still…

'Kieran,' she murmured. 'Are there any problems with keeping her on the bridge?'

His blue eyes glazed over in an instant, the vision apparently arriving as soon as he'd reached for it. Ami fought the urge to go to him. He didn't look like he needed her to pull him out of it, not now, perhaps never again. That caused an unwelcome ache in her chest. She knew she had no right to feel so hurt about it.

Kieran blinked and shrugged. 'I don't think it matters either way.'

'I cannot risk expo—' Avurn cut himself off, scowling, when Ami shook her head.

The plaster on Kieran's temple was beginning to peel and it was pretty starking obvious he should have ripped it off by now. Grace hadn't said anything, but she'd definitely noticed. She might have even guessed that the chip was missing.

Ami tapped two fingers against her own temple, a meaningful gesture that the reporter wouldn't fail to understand. 'She already knows what we're about to do.'

Grace's smile was small, but it spoke volumes.

'The reporter stays,' Ami declared. She dropped back into the captain's chair, her hands fumbling for a few seconds before she managed to get a firm grip on the manual controls. 'Kieran, Avurn— I need you to project an extra shield around this ship. Our current one might not hold.'

'You're certain that your father won't extend safe passage to you?' Grace asked.

Ami laughed darkly. 'I've cost him a shipload of money. He wants me gone. It's stupid that he thinks he and Mum can choose another heir, since by law they both have to agree. Which they never do...but I can't make him see that. He won't listen to me. He never has.'

'We will be attacked the moment we enter the gauntlet,' Kieran confirmed.

'Don't suppose you saw any further than that,' Ami said with a grin that only continued to widen when Kieran answered in the negative. 'Oh well. Two minutes until we're heading in. You better have that shield up by then.'

SITTING cross-legged in front of Avurn, Kieran tried not to let his mind wander. Avurn would, quite rightly, take him to task for not focusing when lives were at stake.

But how could he concentrate when Grace was watching?

Ami trusted her; Avurn didn't. Kieran wasn't sure what to think, since in his most recent vision he had seen the reporter standing above and slightly to the side of him, perched on a higher branch of the same tree. The symbolism of this was archaic, but not so archaic that it wasn't lost on him. Grace didn't just know about his family— she *was* his family.

But she had done very little to help him. If their connection meant nothing to her, then it also meant nothing to him. As far as Kieran was concerned, Pina-Sai was the only family he had.

'What are you waiting for?' Avurn demanded.

Kieran shook out his limbs and forced himself to relax. It was so easy to do this now. So easy to think a forcefield into existence. Avurn was already encased inside one of his own, his energy spiked with annoyance, because he'd had to use his hands to create it.

Kieran gave him a tight nod. It was time.

They melded their forcefields together with them at its core, one unified power source. Breathing deeply, Kieran began to expand the shield. He faltered for a moment, wondering if he should even be trying to do something that was so impossible, but then Avurn moved in and shored him up at his foundations.

Kieran's eyes began to itch, heralding a vision he had not reached for. He blinked and caught a glimpse of the man the boy would become. Sometime in the future, those black jumpsuits and surly scowls would be replaced by formal wear and the patient impassiveness of a leader. Avurn would favour a beard when he was older—and he would use the powers at his command to help others, those he was sworn to protect.

Kieran swiftly dismissed the vision, to stop any of it creeping through the link to Avurn. But he was unable to kill the smile it inspired.

'You do realise that this shield of ours has to grow two hundred-fold before we get shot at?' Avurn muttered.

'I know. But I can move fast—faster than I need to.'

'Are you saying I can't keep up?'

'I'm saying I'll race on ahead and you can strengthen my groundwork.'

A short laugh escaped Avurn. 'I will miss this, when I have a much larger galactic profile and am surrounded by sycophants. It's nice to work with someone who is my equal.'

'Hey!' Ami interjected. 'I know you didn't just suggest that I was your inferior.'

Neither Kieran or Avurn responded, both of them now completely devoted to their task. The bridge and its distractions faded away, leaving nothing between them and the starry void.

Kieran hesitated. Something was scratching at his mind from a distance—the Desine hadn't given up, would never give up. If Kieran lost control and inadvertently broke the barrier that kept him safe from the god...

Don't worry—I will maintain your personal shield. Avurn's voice was disembodied, mental only, but no less appreciated. *Focus on the one around this ship instead. Focus.*

But I can't make the shield strong enough on my own, Kieran argued.

That's not true, Kieran, and I believe you know it.

Ami doesn't see the real you, does she?

Avurn abruptly withdrew from Kieran and veiled his side of the link, trying to obfuscate how he really felt about the people in his life.

Do not let someone else determine and control your image, Kieran told him, the words coming from somewhere deep inside his gut. *There is so much more to you than a desire for power. You don't need to keep playing up to it.*

Oh, but I do, Avurn responded. *My parents were exactly what they appeared to be. They looked like prey and died because of it. It is too dangerous to be anything but a lie.*

Kieran knew that one day his young friend would think otherwise.

But this was clearly not that day.

Avurn's energy blazed with purpose as his shield shrank and solidified, containing Kieran's mind, giving Kieran the opportunity to expand his own forcefield outwards.

Kieran pushed and kept pushing, until he felt something nearly snap inside him. The shield wobbled at first, sloppy and reluctant, but it dutifully encased the *Free Ride*. It was still too weak—Avurn made sure Kieran knew this, knew that a handful of lasbolts could penetrate the surface—so Kieran reached out, seeking more of the universe's energy. And he found it.

The stars themselves answered his call and pumped raw power back at Kieran, filling him to the brim. They sang his name, these ancient celestial giants, and they were more than willing to give him anything he deigned to ask of them.

Avurn sounded equal parts envious and intrigued. *Drawing energy from the stars...Kieran, I know of no one who can do this.*

Av, I need you to concentrate, Kieran said.

I have you covered, the boy shot back. *Now do your part.*

'We're ready,' Kieran said out loud. 'Both of us. The shield will hold.'

Ami's voice sounded so far away, but her words were sharp enough to penetrate the fog that clouded his senses. 'Okay. I'm going to run the gauntlet. Gods help us.'

'I don't think we need their help,' Grace commented.

Kieran hoped she was right.

THIRTY

Taylar Naiman watched as her daughter began to make planetfall.

Her ex-husband had paid pirates to secure the planet's fleet mere nanoseconds after they'd made their divorce official, so Taylar had needed to borrow and steal her ships for a time (not too long, fortunately, since her Rapture factories were always productive and profitable). She'd grabbed anything vaguely spaceworthy and the *Free Ride* had barely qualified back then. To her knowledge, it was still a sluggish, underpowered death trap.

And that foolish girl had just taken it into Neffron's gauntlet.

A sea of lascannons glowed red around the stolen ship, seemingly more numerous than all the stars pricking space. Neffron's ships took aim—and fired. Blast after blast struck the *Free Ride*, gnawing deeper into the shield with each passing nanosecond.

There was no attempt to retreat. The *Free Ride* swerved and banked, avoiding only a fraction of the brilliant, persistent death that poured towards it. The shield wouldn't last half a minute at this rate. Someone was firing the ship's primary weapon in response, but either they were a poor shot or they were not used to the program loaded into the console. Not that a single lascannon could have saved that wreck anyway.

Taylar, standing with her hands clasped behind her, was blissfully unaware that her daughter often assumed the same stance. This knowledge would not have pleased her.

Inferior stock should not have a throwback to its progenitor.

'Madness,' an awed voice murmured behind Taylar.

'Remember your place and hold your tongue, Lius,' Taylar cautioned her slave. If he hadn't devised her ship's cloaking device, several times more efficient than the generic ones for sale, she would have shot him through the eye for his impudence. He could still form his own opinions and speak for himself. That was dangerous. Unfortunately, his mind performed better he wasn't under the influence of the injections. But so far he had not taken advantage of his privileged position. Perhaps it was loyalty?

The *Free Ride*'s shield failed with a spectacular flash of light.

Taylar's smile showed teeth.

But the ship survived. Not only that, the next slew of lascannon blasts bounced away, striking and shredding the shields of the nearest vessels in the gauntlet. One of Neffron's ships even exploded. So. That girl wasn't as witless as she seemed.

'A secondary shield?' Taylar mused, but this time Lius waited for permission to speak. An improvement. 'Tell me what is happening here.'

His frowns were always a prelude to something interesting. He did not disappoint her. 'I've seen this before. Back on my homeworld, when the Chippers came to put a slumlord out of business. They created a shield that protected the six of them. It was about the size of a hovercar. But...there is only one Chipper aboard the *Free Ride*. Lifesigns on the vessel number four and all of those were accounted for over the public communications link.'

'Can a single Chipper do this?' Taylar wondered. 'Answer me.'

'I don't know. It's possible, but very unlikely.'

'Most interesting,' Taylar said.

Somehow, *somehow*, that handsome Chipper had erected a forcefield large enough to protect an entire starship. And somehow Unify had recruited him. How had that pitiful girl done such a thing? No matter. Even a Chipper could be bought, for the right price. If not, there were other ways to make him capitulate.

'How much longer will the Chipper's shield hold?' Taylar asked.

Lius offered her a shrug, a gesture that he knew she disliked. Perhaps she would need to inject him, like the others. A shame. No one else in her collection had his skills. Or perhaps she would wait until he did it again.

'Before today, I'd have said a few minutes,' he said at last. 'But this Chipper is clearly stronger than the others I've seen.'

Taylar wet her lips. She really wanted that Chipper, but if she failed to obtain him the e-paper reporter was not a bad consolation prize. She'd heard of Grace Pendergast. It was a rare being in the galaxy who had not! Pendergast had sources everywhere. To have such a being in her collection, to be able to locate and steal ship-ments of slaves from her rivals...Taylar could not pass up this opportunity.

Unify Naiman was superfluous. Taylar would not need her once Neffron was dead; any heir would be acceptable at that point and he wouldn't be able to stop her choosing another.

Only *living* rulers could have any say in that decision. A small but significant loophole—and a very recent one too. Having discov-ered that their daughter was the starship captain targeting their exports, they had agreed to a parley that was just long enough for them to write it into law.

'Let's save the silly girl from herself,' Taylar declared and turned to the rest of her fine crew, made even more fine by their inability to refuse her commands or cover their goosepimpled chests with shirts. 'Fire on Neffron's flagship. Take out his engines. His ego would never allow him to entertain the notion that my weapons systems are now superior to his. He's always been a man who prizes quantity over quality, especially when it comes to his ships.' Her tongue slid lazily along her top row of teeth. 'And once he opens a link and starts squawking about it, I'll inform him that we will destroy his ship unless he lets Unify through to Accia. He'd escape in a lifepod, naturally, but the loss would still sting.'

'And what then?' Lius asked.

'Then we shall address your disobedience,' Taylar told him.

VIVID CRIMSON SPLATTERS covered the enlarged forcefield, throwing an angry tint over Ami and her crew. Somewhere behind them, the large lascannon that had been the *Free Ride*'s pride and joy was floating aimlessly off into space, along with the boarding ramp and parts of the hold. Ami was relieved that she hadn't insisted on sending Grace down there. Vacuum had rapidly filled the living quarters and the automated systems had responded by sealing off the bridge, making it the only habitable section of the ship.

Inadvertently killing the galaxy's beloved champion of the truth wouldn't have been a good look for Ami—and it wouldn't have done any favours for Avurn's galactic profile either.

'Neffron's ships are converging, possibly in an attempt to crush us,' Grace said from the weapons console. She leaned back in the chair, arms crossed, unable to do any more. She seemed oddly at ease, as though they hadn't just lost access to the lifepods.

'Shit, *shit!*' Ami cursed.

She gripped the unresponsive manual controls even tighter,

refusing to let them snap back into the armrest, refusing to accept that she was now a passenger on her own ship.

'Kieran can't take much more of this!' Avurn informed Ami, between stints of his own colourful swearing. 'And I'm not confident about his ability to stave off those spikes. Ow! Fuck! It starking hurts to do it, but I'm maintaining his mental defences. That *friend* of ours is going to find him if I have to shunt any energy into Kieran's shipwide shield.'

Ami felt her knuckles tighten. Should she pray—and if so, who to?

She might have actually picked a god and done just that, if her father's flagship hadn't suddenly come under fire.

Precise strafing took out Neffron's shields, then sliced across his engines the instant they became vulnerable. One or two shots even scored his viewport. The speed at which his flagship was rendered inert hinted at an intimate knowledge of exactly where to hurt him.

Within seconds, the hundreds of lascannons targeting the *Free Ride* stilled and Neffron's gauntlet went ominously dark around them. The eternal silence of space slinked across the bridge—that is, until Avurn stumbled over to the communications console and accepted the incoming link.

That trilling voice was painfully familiar. 'Unify! How lovely to see *youuu.*'

Ami ignored the woman displayed on her viewport and instead watched Kieran, who was flat on his back. After Kieran nodded slightly at her, indicating—well, hopefully confirming—that he was alright, Ami rose to her feet, clasped her hands behind her, and forced a smile. 'Hello, Mother. I take it you are to thank for Neffron backing off. He won't underestimate you next time, but I'm sure you don't need the warning.'

Taylar Naiman reminded Ami of a blade: thin and trim, her brunette hair terminating in perfectly straight lines on either side of her jaw, her mouth possessing a tongue sharper than the teeth surrounding it. Taylar's pale features and modest, long-sleeved dress made her an obvious contrast to the shirtless bronzed men she had on the bridge with her. Ami sucked back the next few words she wanted to lob at the viewport. She couldn't blast Taylar for her use of slaves now, not if the woman was actually coming to her rescue.

Neffron's ships slowly began to part. In the centre of this widening chasm, a much smaller ship appeared, its hull slick and silver, its prow studded with the deceptively small lascannons that had caused Neffron to capitulate.

Taylar cleared her throat in an exaggerated fashion, no doubt expecting her daughter to offer more gratitude or perhaps some kind of apology. Ami did not indulge her.

Avurn whistled appreciatively. 'That cloaking device...few beings could build something that advanced and even fewer could afford it.'

Taylar tossed her head and preened.

'Yeah, nice ship,' Ami muttered.

'Isn't it just?' Taylar said, waving a hand in front of her face. Ami wasn't sure if she was fanning herself because her brilliant ship made her all hot and bothered, or if it was meant to be a dismissive gesture. 'Darling, your father and I both know you are not here to resume your role as heir apparent. You clearly have your own agenda.'

Ami's mouth went dry. 'Then why are we having this conversation? You can take me out easily enough. I've lost my lascannon and my secondary shield may or may not be functional, so what gives?'

'You have something I want,' Taylar said.

'Oh? What's that?' Ami asked, aiming for flippant, though the fingers she had curled around her manual controls began to tremble.

Taylar simply smiled, waiting for Ami to connect the dots. Ami glanced at Grace who offered nothing, then at Avurn who seemed to have an idea but clearly wasn't going to interject—and finally she looked at Kieran. He was now sitting up, but his dazed expression and mussed hair suggested that he'd fallen one too many times on his climb back to lucidity.

He didn't say anything. He didn't need to. He was in Ami's head and she could hear him loud and clear.

Even with his immense powers, he thought her stronger than him.

Ami wasn't used to that. No one had considered her strong or powerful when she was younger. Not even herself. The memories of standing by helplessly while her parents 'dealt with' the slaves in their factories for not meeting increasingly strict quotas still twisted her stomach. She had failed more than once to hide the horror and sympathy she felt.

Taylar and Neffron had used Rapture to put a smile on her face and she hadn't been able to stop them. A faulty dose had enabled her to escape. She'd always thought she had luck to thank for that. But maybe luck wasn't the only reason she had made it out of there.

Whatever. If she hadn't been strong enough then, she certainly was now. And her parents were way less scary than a desert god.

Ami dropped her useless manual controls, then slapped and rubbed her hands together, as though dusting them off. 'Well, I'm down to negotiate, but I'm not doing it up here. You want something of mine? Let's discuss it over dinner. You're hosting.'

She watched Taylar closely, saw the slight tick on that smooth cheek, saw the flash of anger in those glittering eyes. But Taylar did not argue.

Whatever she was after, she wanted it *badly*.

Taylar performed another of her venomous smiles. 'Alright, darling. I'll throw a tractor beam over your unfortunate vessel and tow it down to a landing pad at my palace. Then you will be told how you can help me.'

'Help? I said "negotiate", so you'd better have something *I* want.' Ami sliced her finger through the air and Avurn swiftly cut the communications link. Ami allowed a smile of her own, a much more genuine one. 'That will upset her, not getting the last word.'

'What do you think she wants?' Grace asked. 'I doubt I will be of any use to her. I cannot be bribed or persuaded to write a report that favours one side over another. I remain objective when covering situations like these.'

Avurn chortled. 'Objective? You always side with someone. But you like to conceal your opinion with clever language, using words that evoke sympathy or loathing.'

'Words are my greatest weapon,' Grace said, which wasn't a denial.

Shaking her head, Ami moved towards Kieran and made sure she halted a full pace away from him. She wanted to get down on the floor and check him over, but that wouldn't be wise. Not when she might fail to stop herself touching him. Kissing him. Loving him. Shit! *Shit!* She did love him. But he appeared to be preoccupied, so maybe...gods, let him not have heard any of that.

'What do you think my mother's after?' Ami asked him.

Kieran's frown was as distant as his mind seemed to be. 'Taylar...I sensed her interest in me. And my abilities.'

'Was the forcefield really that obvious?' Ami wondered.

'No one could have failed to notice *that*,' Avurn said, practically vibrating with excitement. 'I have never seen anything like it, not even in Webcasts covering significant Chipper operations.'

Grace pursed her lips. 'That's a problem.'

'How?' Avurn demanded. 'Kieran being so powerful that it gives our enemies pause does not seem like a problem to me.'

'That doesn't mean he's invincible, Av,' Ami said tightly. 'Kieran has limits. But the real issue here is my mother is now expecting

Kieran to be as strong as several Chippers and she'll have measures in place to counter that.'

'What sort of measures?' Kieran asked.

Ami sighed and rubbed her forehead. 'I don't know. A lot of lasguns pointed at you. At us. Something even worse, maybe.'

'But we now know that my forcefields can withstand an entire fleet of starships,' Kieran said.

'How long would your shield have lasted if Neffron had kept blasting, though?' Ami asked. 'Be honest with me, Kieran. I know you're powerful...' *Powerful enough to block a god,* she added silently. 'But we nearly blew up back there. And Taylar has always been good at the slow, insidious attack. We'll need to be careful. She's dangerous.'

Avurn clucked his tongue. 'Yes, I suppose you're correct. All eyes will be on Kieran. Alright. It falls to me to be our secret weapon. I will do my best to play the part of a helpless child in front of Taylar. It is a difficult role, but I'm sure I'll succeed.'

Avurn met Grace's firm gaze with his own, seemingly daring her to disagree and tell him he wasn't a suitable 'secret weapon' because of his age.

'My daughter is younger than you,' Grace said mildly. 'She is already a force to be reckoned with.'

'I doubt she could do what I can,' Avurn sniffed.

Grace laughed and said nothing, which clearly irked him.

'No killing,' Ami reminded Avurn.

He visibly clenched his teeth, but his voice remained steady. 'I know the price of acting in haste. And it is too high for me.'

'A very mature outlook,' Grace noted. 'Any loss of life is a terrible outcome.'

Ami snorted. 'No, he means that I will ground him on Ilbb if he disobeys my standing orders again.'

Avurn's face darkened and he stood from the communications

console. 'Fuck you, Captain! Tends sees me. Kieran sees me. You don't and you won't even try.'

He stormed towards the door, then stopped dead when it refused to budge. Annoyance crossed his features. Avurn, unable to escape into the vacuum-filled corridor, instead chose to loom in the corner like a noxious fog. Kieran soon followed him and began to speak softly to the boy, making Ami wonder what Kieran saw in him that she couldn't.

Ami's gut twisted. She couldn't allow the sensation to manifest into guilt.

'Something funny, Pendergast?' Ami demanded. She suspected she'd regret her sharp tone later, when her ship wasn't in the grip of a tractor beam belonging to her mother.

Grace kept smiling. 'I was just thinking that Avurn Singh would fit in with my family far better than my nephew ever could.'

'Are we talking about Micadei?' Ami asked.

Grace fell silent.

Ami stalked her way over to the weapons console. Though Grace remained seated, she was acutely aware that the reporter would be much taller than her if they were both on their feet. Ami glanced at Kieran and Avurn, then pitched her voice low. 'Whatever secrets you're hiding up those pressed sleeves of yours, you might want to consider handing them over sooner rather than later. I'm doing my best to support Kieran, but he needs a lot more than I can give him. Don't you care about him at all?'

'The more I say, the more dangerous his situation becomes.'

'He's already in danger!' Ami snapped. 'Do you have any idea what's stalking him? He needs help—now.'

She definitely didn't imagine Grace's eyes widening in alarm.

'Who is stalking him?' Grace asked. 'Specifically.'

Not what. *Who.*

Ami recalled the sandy figure that had invaded her bridge and shuddered. Yeah, not an experience she wanted to repeat any time soon. Irritation pricked at her scalp when Grace relaxed into the chair and released a long, low breath. As if the reporter knew what she was thinking. Which wasn't impossible, really.

'Then there's still time,' Grace said.

'Time for what, exactly?'

Grace arched an eyebrow. 'Not for this discussion. We're currently dropping into the atmosphere, unless I'm mistaken.'

'We're not done here,' Ami warned her.

When Grace didn't respond, Ami backed away and headed for her own chair, even though she couldn't do anything from there. The *Free Ride* was no longer under her control and she was fast losing her grip on her crew. Haranguing an uncooperative Grace Pendergast would only make this more obvious to everyone on the bridge.

Ami's main, burning question remained unasked.

Judging by the concerned look Grace suddenly flashed her, Ami had a feeling she knew what the answer was. Which raised another burning question.

If Kieran's family knew about him, then why the stark weren't they helping him?

THIRTY-ONE

Ami paced while a set of collapsible stairs was affixed to the emergency docking port near the bridge, a replacement for the boarding ramp that was floating somewhere above Rochaccia, destined to be chewed up by the atmosphere—and the less said about the landing gear the better. Having to be propped up on scaffolding supplied by Taylar's ground crew was necessary, but it grated on her.

Stark! Why couldn't she stop her heart racing or stop grinding her teeth? Why did Taylar still have this much power over her?

'These things take time, Ami,' Kieran murmured beside her.

Avurn and Grace were salvaging what they could from the living quarters. Ami had said yes to spare clothes and no to everything else, though Avurn had quietly interjected that he needed to retrieve Kieran's chip so he could reassemble and reinsert it later. The old plaster that had concealed the tech's absence had fallen off and Avurn had replaced it with another one, but not without warning Kieran that it might draw unwanted attention.

'Oh, sure,' Ami said darkly. 'Time. My whole life, more like it.'

'I suspect that's how long my past will haunt me as well.'

Ami wasn't sure who needed the embrace more: her or Kieran. She allowed herself to enjoy his steady warmth, his breaths playing over her ear, his fingers riding her hips. She could imagine for a moment that he wasn't what he was, that she could keep tightening her arms around him and never let go. Kieran jerked away from her nanoseconds before she heard the approaching footfalls. Ami quickly put two large paces between them.

Avurn's little smirk when he rounded the corner—not to mention Grace suddenly being fascinated by a nearby bulkhead—told her just how well that ruse had worked.

Ami slapped the sensor pad on the wall. Nothing happened, so she tried again and again—until finally, success. The emergency docking port groaned as it opened for the first and last time. Ami tried not to look back at her broken ship as she strode out into daylight, her crew of three at her heels.

She faltered halfway down the stairs. They'd been towed to the highest landing pad available, the better to view Taylar's domain. The palace crowning the much lower platform beneath them was constructed from a glittering black rock imported from another world, the walls made up of shards instead of bricks, and it was so completely at odds with its surroundings that it looked like it had been dropped haphazardly from space. The telltale glimmer of orange in the sky revealed that the palace and its surroundings were under the protection of an anti-bombardment shield.

Sprawling into the distance were ragged canyons filled with pockets of greenery and twinkling lascannon mounts. The nearest ridge hid an impressive waterfall, thundering ever downwards and sending up a spray that coated Ami's skin. The air was hot, thick, and wet. She wished the wind had blown the droplets in a different direction. Being this close to the waterfall was not refreshing.

Waiting for them on the landing pad were at least fifty shirtless men, all of them aiming their lasguns at Kieran. Ami stiffened.

'We expected this,' Kieran reminded her.

'They're not expecting me, though,' Avurn said, a gleam in his eyes. 'Are we deposing your mother before or after dinner?'

Ami's teeth trapped a hiss of air. 'After. We might as well try asking Taylar to help us take out my father. If she says no, then we'll switch to a more *powerful* method of persuasion. Or maybe I'll just aim a lasgun at her face. She's never been one for personal shielding devices—Taylar's always said that if someone gets that close, you deserve what they do to you. Let's prove her right.'

'I approve of this plan,' Avurn declared.

'Don't need your approval, Av, but thanks all the same,' Ami said. Her grin felt like it was cracking apart the skin on her cheeks.

'Are you going to go over and greet her?' Grace asked.

Ami shook her head, still grinning. 'No. That's what she wants: me to make the first move, to prove I'll play nice and dance to her tune.'

Grace nodded slowly. 'You want to meet her on your own terms.'

'Do you think she will have fewer guards at dinner?' Kieran wondered. 'In case powerful persuasion is required.'

'Maybe,' Ami said. 'But don't ditch your lasgun or your shielding device just yet.'

A tall, slim figure blew through the ranks of men waiting in front of the stairs, causing them to bow violently away from her like trees caught in a gust of cyclonic wind. Tilting her head so that the platinum band threaded through her hair caught the sunlight, Taylar spread her arms and threw on a radiant smile. 'Unify! My little darling. Won't you come and hug your mother?'

'Depends,' Ami shot back. 'Are you going to get your guards to point those lasguns someplace else?'

Taylar tsked, setting her hands on her hips. 'And allow you to capture me, as is your desire? Your Chipper is more powerful than average. Even I can see that! I also know you, darling—you're stupid enough to believe that one man can lock me up and give you Accia on a silver platter.'

'I've no intention of locking you up in a cell.' The tremulous laugh escaped Ami before she could stop it. 'Yet. I need you on my side if I have any hope of ending Neffron's reign.'

Taylar's eyes narrowed slightly. 'Honesty does not suit you any better than the lying tongue you possessed in your childhood. We will speak of this later. Come. I need to show you the arrangements I have made for your stay.'

Ami looked over her shoulder at her crew. Grace widened her eyes slightly, indicating that she had something to say, but it seemed she wasn't going to interrupt. Maybe because Grace knew it would have weakened Ami's image if someone spoke for her. Or maybe because the reporter was meant to observe only, instead of altering the events that would make it into her e-paper.

Ami suspected Grace did a lot more 'altering' than she was supposed to.

'Grace!' Ami said. 'Do your thing.'

Grace slid past Ami, seemingly unfazed as fifty lasgun butts followed her. She stopped at the base of the stairs, then took the time to leisurely cross her arms. 'I have multiple reports scheduled to be released upon my untimely demise, or in the case that I am unable to stop them going out. No one from this vessel will be harmed during our stay here—unless you want the galaxy to side with your ex-husband against you, that is. I think you will find that I can convince even your most loyal clients to go to Neffron instead. It is as simple as casting doubt on the quality of the Rapture being manufactured in your factories.'

Taylar glowered. 'There is no need for threats.'

'And there is no need for this many guards in your welcoming party!' Ami called down.

Taylar's lips reared back from her teeth, though she didn't quite manage a smile. 'Holster your lasguns, slaves—but keep a hand on them at all times.' Once her guards had obeyed, Taylar appraised Ami. 'My, what desperate lengths you've gone to in order to prove you're not a little girl anymore.'

Ami shrugged carelessly. 'No worse than the lengths you've gone to in order to pretend that people like you. Laswhips. Drugs. Starvation. Manipulation. Pathetic, really. But you can't just ask nicely, can you? No one wants to do you any favours. So you force your dolls to play-act and you've even started to believe that they actually want to be near you.'

Ami had never seen her mother's cheeks turn that brilliant shade of red before. And she relished the fact that she was the one who had ruffled the impervious Taylar Naiman.

She descended the stairs to stand beside Grace, distantly aware of Kieran and Avurn following her. For a moment, Ami allowed herself the fantasy that the sight of the armed men withdrawing to create an unobstructed path on the landing pad was a sign that the entire planet would soon give way to her.

THE QUARTERS ALLOCATED to Ami were grand and full of voluminous silks that shone beneath a spray of lights. She was reminded strongly of the Enocian Harem as she paced from room to room to yet another room. There were no connecting doors between the guest suites and so she was divided from Kieran, Avurn, and Grace by several walls and a string of guards (still armed and still shirtless, which Ami found tasteless and cruel, especially given how cold the climate-controlled rooms were).

After her brief self-guided tour of her suite—she had tried not to admire the massive marble spa bath—Ami stepped outside. The guards didn't so much as glance at her. But Ami's skin burned with awareness, as though someone was watching her every move. She looked up and saw the vidcams mounted along the ceiling, almost as numerous as the guards lining the corridor. She had just enough time to count the first twenty when the guards suddenly became animated and began herding her towards her destination.

Ami forced herself to keep walking. She'd play along. For now.

She wasn't surprised to discover that Taylar's dining hall had lost none of its extravagance. The transparent ceiling afforded a view of the stars spread across the velvet night sky. Seemingly arranged to reflect this, the black satin cloth on the table was liberally scattered with diamonds. When Ami was younger, she had enjoyed this fancy addition, because it had felt like she was eating off the stars. This time she saw it for the waste that it was.

Ami nodded at each member of her crew, more to reassure herself that they were there than to give them any signal. They sat in matching high-backed chairs, their positions denoted by the names lasered into the dark wood—Taylar must have done that immediately after they'd exchanged introductions. A shame, really. The furniture was antique, purportedly from Londinum (built when the industrial world still had anything resembling a tree), and would now fetch much less on the open market. The casual vandalism was yet another status symbol.

There was a chair bearing the name 'Unify', but Ami took the time to pull out her lasgun and score the lettering.

Avurn raised an eyebrow at her. Ami raised both of hers in response.

Eventually, Taylar floated in through the arched doorway, having been poured into a periwinkle dress that accentuated every line and crevice. Her eyes lingered on Kieran a little too long, much to Ami's discomfort, and then she coasted into her throne—there was no better word for it. Her intricately wrought, gilt chair took up half of the opposite side of the table. The cylindrical cushions that covered most of the crimson padding were a nice touch. And a nice way of saying 'this chair is for one butt only'.

Hot on Taylar's heels, servers filed in and deposited appetisers on the table. While these slaves lacked the heavy lasguns the guards kept strung across their bare torsos, they all shared the same blank expressions. A trickle of unease filtered through Ami's guts. She watched the servers closely as they left, but none of them broke out into the sloppy smiles that were the hallmark of beings under the influence of Rapture.

Did Taylar no longer use the drug? Were her slaves free to act as they chose?

Ami knew she wasn't in a position to judge these people; she'd had a similar checked-out look to her during her teenage years. She might have dreamed about escaping, but it had never seemed possible and she'd given up on making plans to do so. Even before her parents had started dosing her with Rapture, she had been too sore and hungry from her punishments, and too fixated on survival, to do anything else.

There could be many reasons why these men didn't try to overwhelm their captor.

'Your negotiation skills are somewhat lacking, my darling,' Taylar said, her smile stretching her lips unnaturally, until it appeared as though she was wearing an ill-fitting rubber mask. 'It's obvious that you mean to do away with me once I have helped you depose your father. You might consider sweetening the pot. Giving me something of value. But we both know you can't pay me anything near the amount I'd need to retire, since I require the comforts of a planet like Enoc, so perhaps you should just accept that Rochaccia will retain one ruler. Surely I am a better alternative than Neffron the Warmonger.'

Taylar had always considered herself superior to her ex-husband, because she didn't wreak such obvious destruction. Neffron often lent his forces out to warlords and rebel leaders on other planets. He had no compunctions about who he dealt with. If his ships and personnel completely decimated the opposite side, leaving no one alive, then his clients were happy—and happy clients always returned to do more business.

But there wasn't anything superior, in Ami's mind, about Taylar sticking to 'mere' drugs and slaves for her income.

Ami inhaled deeply. She wanted to lean into Kieran who was sitting to her right, to steady herself, but her mother would have seen her do it—and guessed how much Kieran meant to her. Ami didn't want to know what Taylar would do with that information. So she lifted her chin instead, reaching for the strength that Kieran was so sure she possessed.

And she found it.

Ami visualised herself hammering steel along her spine and tightening every vertebra, until she was impervious to anything that might be thrown at her. *Even a sandstorm.*

She saw the corners of Kieran's lips lift. Oh, he'd heard that alright.

'I'm well aware that I'll need your assistance, my darling mother,' Ami said through her teeth. 'I think you'll even agree to give it, since you hate Dad so much. You hate that your part of the fleet is laughably small compared to his. A sneaky cloaking device and a handful of advanced lascannons on your flagship won't change that. Dad didn't capitulate in orbit because you were *superior* in any way —he wants to see what your plan is, why you let me live, and if he can benefit from it himself. And anyway, if you could have nixed your rival by now, you'd have done it. Maybe it's *you* who needs help.'

Soft tinkling laughter from Grace on Ami's left.

Taylar's mouth snapped into a frown that barely left any lines on her smooth features.

'I'm not your game piece or your plaything,' Ami went on. 'Not anymore. And I've seen beings that are a lot scarier than you. By comparison...you're an insect.'

Annoyingly, her mother recovered within seconds. 'You certainly have an unusual view of our relationship, darling.'

Avurn chortled. Blatantly ignoring the warning in Ami's gaze, he said, 'I did not have a conventional upbringing myself, but even I know that you are not the best mother the galaxy can provide. Are you quite finished? Or do you intend to keep on throwing this elaborate tantrum?'

Taylar's eyes lasered in on the boy. 'You are not what you appear to be.'

Ami glanced at the crook of Avurn's elbow, but it remained concealed by his black jumpsuit. Avurn suddenly seemed to realise what he'd done; he had blown his cover as an ordinary boy. He bowed his head, contrite. Hopefully, Ami could deflect any further attention from him.

'He's a member of my crew,' Ami said. 'And my crew answers to me alone.'

'Even the Chipper?' Taylar asked, pursing her lips.

Ami performed a casual shrug and settled into her chair. Its rigid lines were not very comfortable, but she made it look like they were. 'His loyalty wasn't that expensive. Chipper pay is pretty shit, you know, but don't think you can poach him off me. I know things about his past that he doesn't care to see in any Webcasts. So if you want the use of him and his powers, you'll need to cut a deal with me.'

Taylar reared her head back and laughed. 'Unify, darling! You do me proud for once in your life. Such boldness. Attempting to take over a planet with only an e-paper reporter, a Chipper, and a child—no one could conceive of such a thing.'

'That's probably why she'll succeed,' Grace remarked.

Taylar shrugged, unbothered, and threw a sultry wink at the guard to her right. His eyes remained fixed on the archway opposite him. No reaction whatsoever.

'I know why you're really here, darling,' Taylar told Ami. 'You want to release all of the slaves on Rochaccia. Well, I am certainly prepared to help you achieve that goal. And I'll even depart the planet once you've taken over, if that's what my daughter so desires.'

Ami leaned forward, frowning at her mother. 'What could possibly motivate you to give up your money, your power, and your unpaid workforce? Basically, everything you love?'

'I want your Chipper,' Taylar said.

Silence filled the room, interrupted only by gentle clinking as a slave held the neck of a wine bottle against Ami's glass.

Ami dared not look aside at Kieran.

Taylar's smile was back in full force, so wide it revealed the jagged tooth that had been repaired with a gold filling. 'That is my price, darling. You give me your Chipper. One single life in exchange for the million I possess now and the millions I might have possessed in the future.'

'He's not mine to give,' Ami snarled and stood, slapping away her glass. It hit the rim of her plate and then bounced, the crimson liquid spilling towards Kieran. He curled his fingers, his forcefield catching the wine before it dripped off the edge of the table.

Ami could feel the heat flooding her cheeks, but she didn't back down.

'What my captain means is—' Avurn broke off, evidently startled by the crack in his voice. Frowning, he spoke slower and more cautiously, as though afraid it would happen again, 'Sentient beings are not owned by anyone and we cannot lay claim to them. Even one life in slavery is not acceptable to us.'

Ami flicked him a grateful glance. The boy tipped his head towards Taylar, reminding Ami that this was her moment, not his. She focused back on her mother, fists seated on the table in front of her, those decorative diamonds stabbing into her knuckles.

Taylar lifted her own glass and drained it. She sedately set it down again.

She knows, Ami thought, fear curdling in her stomach. *She knows how I feel about him. Stark it, Ami, she was testing you and you fell for it. Kieran is the prize, but hurting me is a bonus.*

Taylar slicked her tongue across her teeth. 'He would certainly be able to protect me, no matter where I choose to retire, if he can project shields as big as a ship. I would not need all these slaves, would I? And if any of my stock wishes to remain in my service, that's up to them. You'd all stay with me, even if you could have your freedom, wouldn't you? You agree! Now!'

'Yes, Mistress,' all twenty guards in the room murmured.

The hairs on the back of Ami's neck stood on end. 'Kieran, can you sense anything unusual? Are they...are they all there?'

Kieran's eyebrows knotted together. 'They're not feeling anything.'

Avurn abruptly jerked and revulsion spasmed across his face. He pushed his chair away from the table, as though to escape whatever he'd sensed with his own chip. Mercifully, Taylar either didn't notice or care about his reaction.

'What have you done to them?' Ami demanded.

Taylar patted a serviette against her lips. 'This is my final offer: Rochaccia for your Chipper. Please do consider it.'

The wyvern wasn't going to answer her, Ami knew.

Kieran shrugged when she looked meaningfully at him. So

either her mother wasn't conveniently thinking about her current method of subjugation, or Kieran couldn't get a read on her at all. Stark.

Ami drew a long breath and buried all of her frustration and anger into a pit in her stomach. It wouldn't help anyone if she lost her cool again—worse, Taylar would take it to mean that she had won this round. And she wouldn't be wrong.

'I will consider it,' Ami said steadily. 'But that discussion can wait. Right now, what we should be talking about is how we're going to wrest power away from Neffron. There's no point promising you anything if we can't even get the job done.'

Ami paused. Waited. Hoped that her mother might show some sign of weakness.

Taylar's expression remained seamlessly saccharine. A giggle trilled out of her lips. 'That's an excellent attempt at stalling, darling. Clever. Very clever. I'll indulge you, just this once. But I think we could all use a good meal and a good night's rest before we decide how we're going to defeat your father.'

Ami sat back down. She might have assumed a defeated hunch if she hadn't looked aside at Kieran and caught his small smile.

She *had* rattled Taylar.

Grinning, Ami picked up her fork and twirled it. 'Alright. But don't keep me waiting too long, my darling mother. Or I might start to think you're more useful locked up inside a cell.'

Taylar's cheek twitched.

THIRTY-TWO

Taylar did some stalling of her own after that sumptuous feast, refusing to meet with Ami and presumably taking her meals elsewhere. She hadn't reappeared in the dining hall for two whole days. Kieran hadn't minded all that much, since it had given Avurn the time he needed to reinsert the non-functioning chip. Even though the device no longer served a purpose, it still gave Kieran a measure of comfort.

If Taylar assumed the freshly glued wound on his temple meant that he'd been tampering with his chip to make himself more powerful, then he would not disabuse her of the notion.

Ami had told Kieran that her mother's silent treatment wasn't unusual, having been on the receiving end of it as a child. She'd added wryly, 'At least she's letting us out to eat and socialise. I didn't get that much when I was a kid. Wait, where's our errant reporter? Is she playing hide and seek with Taylar or something? I've barely seen either of them.'

After sitting through yet another meal with only Kieran and Avurn for company, Ami was pacing in the antechamber of her assigned suite, preoccupied with the thought that her crew no longer looked unified. A weakness that Taylar would happily exploit.

Kieran was reluctant to deliver the bad news, but Ami had to know. So he told her.

Grace's lifesign was frequently near Taylar's—and this had been going on ever since their first night on Rochaccia. Ami's response to this was mental only and not particularly complimentary towards Grace. Kieran wondered why it didn't bother him that some of their conversation was being conducted telepathically. He was even able to project some of his own thoughts into Ami's mind, somewhere he always felt welcome. She would never erect a wall to keep him out—not like Grace apparently had.

'Taylar won't go up against Neffron,' Ami said, turning around at the archway that fed into the grand master bedroom. 'Why would she bother? She's got us right where she wants us and I'll never be able to leave again and I'm stuck and I...'

'Breathe,' Kieran murmured.

Ami stopped dead and quirked an eyebrow at him. *Fine. I'll shut up. But I can inunclate your head with thoughts and keep breathing at the same time! Stop me now, if you can!*

Kieran fought the grin, but failed.

Then he remembered that they had company. Avurn waved away Kieran's apologies about accidentally excluding him. The boy wasn't annoyed with his crewmates, just exasperated about their situation.

'Taylar isn't indulging in mind games to entertain herself,' Avurn said. 'She's avoiding us because she lacks the necessary fire-power and bodies to take on Neffron.'

He raised his hand and swiped each finger along his thumb, not activating his hidden tech but making his meaning clear: he'd been using his idle time to hack into Taylar's files. While the Web was not available on Rochaccia, Taylar used a local system inside the palace to connect her devices and communicate with her people. The system was public and not at all hidden. Even Kieran did not need Avurn's skills to access it.

'Roch and Accia rely on mercenaries for the bulk of their armies,' Avurn continued. 'Taylar's funds are dismally low and all it would take is a simple pay rise for Neffron to persuade her soldiers to defect to his side. As soon as she takes any serious action against him, he will try that tactic. And he will win. That's why she is stalling. She does not wish to reveal how meagre her war chest really is—or how *inferior* she is as a ruler. She's very big on separating everything into "inferior" and "superior". Her files are even ordered that way. It's an incredibly inefficient system.'

'Yep, that sounds like Taylar alright,' Ami muttered.

Avurn had so far failed to locate any mercenaries in the palace, which meant that every man who wielded a lasgun in Taylar's residence was a slave. Kieran wondered how that might work against them. If Taylar's guards were as dull and lacklustre as they appeared to be, then they would not fare well if Neffron's soldiers attacked the palace. He sent his concerns to Ami in a burst of words and images.

She twisted her bottom lip around her teeth. *It's not Rapture. What is it? Gods, what's to stop her using it against us?*

She released a frustrated hiss of air—then noisily sucked it back in when Grace dropped from the ceiling. Both of Grace's legs, real and prosthetic, were arranged expertly beneath her as she landed. She stood to her full height and slapped her pants, sending eddies of dust scurrying away from her.

'You should have sensed me approaching,' she scolded Kieran and Avurn.

Kieran passed his grimace onto his young crewmate, who looked similarly chagrined. Kieran had been aware of various lifesigns moving above him, but that was to be expected in a building that had multiple levels. It hadn't occurred to him to be suspicious of the air ducts. And it should have, since Avurn had used similar ones to infiltrate the Enocian Harem.

'You were up there?' Ami sounded suspicious.

'Yes,' Grace answered. 'I was.'

'You don't look dirty enough. Taylar always waits too long to get those ducts cleaned. It's an *inferior* task, even for her slaves.'

Kieran tentatively tried probing Grace's mind again, but all he could see was—flames?

Grace shrugged. 'I've always chosen clothes designed to repel dirt. I find myself in precarious situations quite often, you see. I had to use this method to reach you since Taylar is under the impression that I have transferred my loyalty to her.'

'Very prudent,' Avurn remarked, 'announcing that where any spy tech could hear you. I was only able to locate and disable the devices hooked up to Taylar's local network. She could have a few stashed in here that require manual access.'

A secretive smile stole across the e-paper reporter's face. 'I think you will find that even those are no longer functional.'

Avurn hmpfed, clearly dubious, so Grace sent him a file from her techpad. His palm out and his skin-based screen displaying the location of the devices she had mentioned, Avurn immediately went to check on them.

His burgeoning frown continued to grow. 'They are all indeed fried. Strangely enough.'

Flames, Kieran mused.

'Don't ask, I don't have the time to explain,' Grace said.

'No time?' Ami remarked. 'We're not doing much else here, just twiddling our thumbs.'

Grace eyed Ami for a moment, then laughed. 'If I was a god, I would be very afraid of you. How fortunate for me that I am not.'

'Yeah, lucky you. So are you going to be forthcoming?'

'No, not right now,' Grace said, though at least she looked regretful. 'It would only be a distraction. A potentially fatal one at that. Anyway, I offered to conduct interviews with Taylar in her office. She was quite keen to accept after I disparaged you and said I did not consider myself part of your crew.'

'The files you just gave me, they aren't static so—' Avurn began, then fell silent. His expression became pinched.

Grace nodded and slid her techpad back into its pouch on her belt. 'As Avurn no doubt noticed, there was no real-time data about the position of Taylar's forces on the system readily available in her palace. She keeps—or rather, kept—that information on a separate console hooked up to a *second* system, which hosts an impressive fleet of surveillance drones. I convinced Taylar to connect this console to her palace's main system as well, without any security, since it's important for me to have all the details if I'm to give her the best write-up possible. She promised to do this a few minutes ago. You should now be able to remotely access the console, Avurn.'

Avurn's scowl was reluctantly impressed. *She can't be that good. She can't be that convincing. No one can. But perhaps she can teach me how to manipulate...* He gave Kieran an unrepentant look. *If you're going to spy on my thoughts, stop being so judgemental. And stop being so obvious when you react to those aforementioned thoughts!*

Kieran retreated, wondering what had given him away. A physical tell of some kind? He needed to know how to stop this happening in a room full of his fellow agents—especially if they asked why his chip wasn't sending any data to the servers on Gerasnin.

'So that means...' Ami pursed her lips. 'We know exactly where all of Taylar's mercs and ships are at any given time.'

'She also has Neffron's forces closely monitored,' Grace added. 'With coordinates accurate to five human paces.'

'We could feed that info to Jets and her father,' Ami said slowly. 'For their orbital bombardment. We'd be able to take out Neffron's army without even picking up a lasgun. If we had Yalsa 5's fleet on standby and clear space above Rochaccia, that is. And we'd need to take out Neffron's jamming tower first.'

Kieran watched Avurn's face twist. He reached for the boy in the link, but Avurn shut his side down and spitted Ami with a venomous glare. 'So when *you* condone killing it is acceptable. If I dare to do the same, I'm on some slippery slope or I'm about to take over the galaxy for unspecified, nefarious purposes!'

Ami pinched the bridge of her nose. 'Av, once we deal with tower you can do a planetwide Webcast. Give all those mercs a chance to surrender. And if there's anyone hit with Rapture listening, we can say something to make them leave the targeted areas.'

'But people will still die,' Avurn said as he advanced on her, his dark eyes flashing. 'You cannot deny it, Ami. Your father isn't foolish with his investments, he pays his mercenaries well—enough that they will fight to the bitter end. They will die for those coin-chips. Do you understand this?'

'Av…if it means we can save an entire planet…'

'Don't,' Avurn cut in. 'Don't even try to defend yourself, Ami. I will not listen to anything you say if you won't live by your own words. Hypocrite!'

Avurn turned on his heel and stormed from the suite. Ami started to follow him but Kieran held out an arm, barring the exit until the door slid shut again. 'Let him go. He understands what we need to do. He won't hesitate to follow your orders when it really matters.'

'He's right, though,' Ami moaned, dropping onto a luxurious divan that was so large Kieran doubted it had entered the suite through the door. 'I made it my personal mission to avoid even the loss of one life—I always, *always* go on about this to Av—and suddenly I'm justifying the deaths of the thousands of mercenaries standing in our way of liberating Rochaccia. Stark the consequences, Ami! Oh gods. I'm a terrible role model.'

Acutely aware of Grace's presence, Kieran kept his feet planted on the floor, though what he wanted to do was kneel before Ami instead, hands sliding up her thighs...no, that could not happen. It could *never* happen.

Kieran wrenched himself out of his imaginings, hoping that's all they were and not something more prescient. 'Ami, you can't refrain from returning fire when someone is trying to kill you. We all need to make sacrifices if we want to accomplish something on this scale.'

Her eyes were dark and her expression wistful. Stark, he'd accidentally shared those tantalising images with her.

'I just wish we didn't have to sacrifice...' Ami's sigh evaporated when she also took note of their witness. 'Grace, can I trust you to transmit the live data to Jets?'

'Once the Web is available down here, yes,' Grace responded. 'The jamming tower is on the ridge to the west of Neffron's compound, according to Taylar's information. We'll need to take control of it if we want to communicate with anyone beyond Rochaccia. But, Ami, this data will be of little use to Governor Atsason if he cannot bring his ships into orbit. The blockade is still our greatest obstacle.'

'Yeah, I don't need the reminder,' Ami said. 'Just get the message ready—and pray to whichever god you think will listen. But you know what, I'm feeling bizarrely positive about all this.'

'Any particular reason why?' Grace asked.

Ami grinned. 'Look what we managed to dig up inside two days. Imagine what else we can find if we keep at it. Maybe Neffron's ships all have the same self-destruct code—or maybe there's some other incredibly convenient gotcha we'll stumble across.'

Grace shook her head. 'Doubtful.'

'Yeah, no disagreements here.' Ami's good humour immediately faded. 'I don't know why I feel so confident that it'll all work out. Or maybe I just *need* it to.'

Kieran swallowed. He didn't want to invoke another vision, here and now, especially one about something so important—it would be hard to reassure Ami if all he saw was disaster. Ami looked at him, seeking comfort, but he had none to give her.

'I'm going to get some sleep,' was all he said before he left the room.

THIRTY-THREE

Kieran dropped his belt to the floor, sat on the edge of the bed, and stretched out his back until his shoulders twinged in protest. The gaudy rubies rimming the windows, the soft silksein sheets rustling beneath him—it was all courtesy of slave labour and he knew what it cost Ami to accept this comfort. But she'd do what she had to in order to put an end to Rochaccia's contribution to the galactic slave trade. There was one way to know if they would succeed. He hoped he didn't see another outcome.

Kieran closed his eyes and the vision came right on cue.

Rochaccia. Hanging in space. Dusty brown. Eminently unwelcoming. It looked the same as it had when they'd first entered the system. But instead of a blockade, a lone starship was in orbit around the planet.

'Closer,' he murmured. 'I need to get closer.'

He wiped his mind clean of any physical discomforts. As for his body—he didn't need that at all. A fleshy shell would only slow him down.

Breathing. He was distantly aware of his lungs performing this function.

That hardly seemed important anymore.

AMI WAS STANDING on the bridge of a ship that was much larger than the *Free Ride*, its gleaming hull bare of even a single smudge and protected by an unwavering shield. Her jaw was clenched, her hands locked into place behind her back. Rochaccia rotated ever onwards, free of its blockade and the dual yoke of Neffron and Taylar Naiman.

'So we do win,' Kieran said, moving to stand beside Ami.

'Depends on your definition of winning,' she replied.

Unease pooled in his gut. 'Does Taylar help us? Or does she betray us? Tell me, please. I need to know.'

Ami laughed gently. 'You should not be concerned about Taylar Naiman.'

'What does that mean?'

'There are greater challenges ahead of you, child.'

'You are not Ami,' Kieran accused.

She gave him an even stare. In her eyes, Kieran saw every star that had ever warmed and blazed and cooled, every soul that had ever been born and lived and died. The entire universe rotated around this eternal being.

'I need to know,' Kieran repeated.

'Do you?' the Creator God asked.

Kieran refused to look away. 'You owe me. For abandoning me on Fintaz.'

'Do I?'

He should have expected that response. A mortal like Governor Bock Atsason might acknowledge owing him something, but a god who counted time in aeons instead of years?

'Do we succeed in liberating Rochaccia?' Kieran pressed.

His companion rearranged Ami's lips into a chiding smile. 'The fate of a planet so often rests in the hands of one or two individuals. Stop trying to see the future of millions. Focus on fewer beings. At least for now, until your capacity to handle more increases. Do not voice the questions in your thoughts, for I will give you no answers —you are not ready for them.'

Ami exploded into wisps of light and the bridge melted away around Kieran, leaving him suspended in space. All by himself. Without Ami. She made all of this so much simpler and easier to bear.

He wasn't the only one who felt alone.

'Avurn,' Kieran murmured and his feet touched down on Rochaccia a nanosecond later.

Avurn was standing on the edge of a rocky cliff, his arms spread wide as he took in the field of destruction beneath him. Thousands of broken bodies littered the ground. He turned towards Kieran, a blood-red sunset crowning him.

'Stop me,' Avurn said in a monotone. 'Before I kill them all.'

'Don't,' Kieran pleaded.

Avurn shook his head sadly. 'I've been on this path since before we met. Ami was right to fear what I would become. She's always so starking right.'

Kieran reached for the boy's shoulders, but his hands never seemed to land where they needed to go. 'You're better than this, Av. Stronger than this. I've seen your future and this isn't it. You'll use your powers for the good of the galaxy.'

'I don't know how do that!' Avurn cried. 'I only know how to be my worst self!'

'I trust you, Av. You won't become the character you portray.' Kieran drew a breath. He couldn't remember ever saying or thinking these words, but they were strong and sure, as though he'd practiced this speech a hundred times before. 'You've made mistakes, but you're learning from them. You've come this far already. Let's see how far you can go.'

Avurn smiled, stars filling his eyes. 'And you, Kieran...you will go very far indeed.'

KIERAN BLINKED, snapping back to his body mere nanoseconds before the door to his suite slid open. Taylar sauntered through the antechamber and into the bedroom, flanked by two of her guards. As usual, her companions were wearing only trousers and weighty lasguns, their gazes and minds still disturbingly vacant. Taylar's thoughts, however, were clear.

Kieran stood swiftly. 'Taylar. I will not make any deals without my captain present.'

Taylar performed a pout that prominently displayed the smear of purple on her lips. 'Forget Unify, or whatever she calls herself these days. She found you first, but her offer is not the best one you will receive. We could achieve so much together, Private Krendasta. I do not know why you insist on shackling yourself to a starship captain, especially one who has no coin-chips and not a single iota of taste.'

Kieran reined in the anger that prickled along his skin like hot needles. It tempted him to do something foolish. He moved forward a pace, just one, but Taylar's guards found this reason enough to bring their lasguns to bear. Taylar smirked. Kieran glanced down and realised he'd left his belt, along with his lasgun and shielding device, on the floor beside the bed. He could defend himself regardless. But to so easily forget his gear after years of being careful to ensure he always had tech as a backup...he was becoming careless.

'You have to force your guards to stand beside you,' Kieran

commented. 'I won't bother to explain how true loyalty works. It's clear my words would be wasted on you.'

Taylar clapped her hands. Though her order was never verbalised, the guards immediately jerked into mechanical bows and swept back into the antechamber. The prearranged performance was meant to show him that she was powerful and brave without her guards, but Kieran saw through this, just as he saw through her next attempt to sway him. 'My darling Chipper, there will be no more slaves here once Roch and Accia are united and ruled by me—by us. I give you my word. And we can even conquer other planets and free *their* slaves as well!'

'GLEA would not allow me to take part in that,' Kieran told her in a measured tone.

'But they'll let you stand by and watch while a murder is being committed?' Taylar mused, tossing her hair out of her face as she moved to a different method of attack. 'I know Unify means to end my life, regardless of what I do for that ungrateful wretch. You should protect me from her!'

'I believe there is no law against murder on your world. I have no obligation to help you if Ami tries to kill you.'

'You Chippers are all the same!' Taylar hissed at him. 'Useless! More interested in following orders than in actually serving the galaxy.'

Kieran ground his teeth together. 'Death and imprisonment aren't the only options available to you, Taylar. You can choose to atone for your past actions, by helping us liberate Rochaccia.' He paused until she met his gaze again, so that he knew she was actually listening to him. 'I will ensure that your safety is a priority.'

'I can atone right now, if you'll let me,' Taylar said, circling him. She was close enough that he could feel the heat of her body. 'Just promise me you'll be mine. I will immediately release every single slave I own and leave this planet behind. With you.'

Kieran kept his eyes ahead, trying not to let his discomfort show. 'No. You can't offer me anything I'd want.'

'What has she got that I don't?' Taylar demanded, rearing back and stomping one of her leather sandals. 'She cannot be that good of a lay. I have far more experience.'

Her mind was bare to him, as were her insecurities.

He struck one of them. 'Is it experience, I wonder, if someone else does all the work.'

The skin around Taylar's eyes spasmed. 'You have spent too much time with that wyvern. I can hear her words on your tongue. You must taste foul.'

Kieran laughed. 'Ami does not think so.'

He saw the slap coming, thanks to a split-second thought that he'd nearly failed to intercept from her. Taylar's blow struck air instead of his cheek. Kieran's own hand had risen slightly too late to have created a forcefield with the aid of his chip, but she did not seem to notice this.

Taylar scowled, cradling her wrist against her chest. 'She's inferior! Why would you want her?'

Kieran stared at Taylar. How could anyone be this conceited, this deficient in character? 'Ami isn't inferior. She has confronted and overcome her past and is far more beautiful than the desperate, grasping tyrant I see before me. Ami...Ami respects my choice to remain with GLEA, even if it means being without me.'

'Smart enough to snare you, foolish enough to lose you over something so trivial.' Taylar sniffed and turned on her heel. 'I will make you mine, Chipper. You can't stop me.'

Taylar's guards mechanically clomped after her as she left the suite. The door in the antechamber snapped shut behind them. There was a brief hiss of air afterwards, which could have been a sign of the door's hydraulics failing. Kieran didn't doubt that Taylar had some maintenance issues, since most of her coin-chips went towards the war with Neffron. And if Avurn was right, she didn't have enough money for that as it was.

Kieran pressed his palm against the temple housing his useless chip. He winced. Taylay's energy was now a dark storm of emotions and her thoughts were chaotic, constantly knotting together and then rapidly unravelling. It made her incredibly difficult to read. He gave up trying to make sense of what he saw.

Kieran sank back onto his bed, even more weary than he'd been in her presence. He drew several more breaths, but the pressure inside his skull increased. His tongue seemed to be growing furrier with each passing moment.

Sedative gas, he realised. *This wasn't planned. She didn't think, she just…did it…*

His hands were heavy, flopping across his thighs like completely separate entities and refusing to move when he bid them. His body was no longer under his control. Panic did not arrive, though he suspected this was due to whatever was in his system.

Kieran heard the door in the antechamber open again and all he could do was lie there, trapped by the quagmire that the soft, cavernous bed had become. He stared up at Taylar as she bent over him, a hyponeedle clenched in her fist. Her smile was concealed by the protective mask she was wearing, but he could feel it, and he could almost taste her smugness as she pressed the tip of the hyponeedle against his neck. It nicked his skin. That was all it took. She had wanted him and now she had him.

Kieran fell inside himself, desperate to escape the *thing* that was marching through his veins.

He raced ahead of it, running towards the shield around his mind, the one that kept a god at bay. The Desine could not reach him in there. If it was that strong, then surely it should offer him sanctuary from mortal threats. He staggered, losing speed as the invader gained on him, his pulse erratic as he took that final step—

THIRTY-FOUR

Avurn knew it would be unwise to tell Ami that he was enjoying the long, luxurious nights of sleep his hovercar-sized bed was giving him, so he was already preparing fresh criticisms of the provided accommodation when he left his suite.

Tapping his middle finger and thumb together, Avurn called onto his palm the live data he'd been studying since the previous night—after he'd made that awfully childish retreat from Ami's presence. Hmm. He really had to work on how he responded to situations like that. It wouldn't help his galactic profile if he gained a reputation for being petulant.

Anyway, he was hoping to use this information about Taylar's and Neffron's forces to construct a workable strategy, something that minimised the loss of life.

Not that Ami would appreciate my efforts, he thought sourly.

Grace was still in her suite by the look—and feel—of things. Her lifesign never seemed to dim, even in the middle of Rochaccia's fifteen hours of darkness.

Did she ever sleep? Avurn wondered if it was possible to forgo sleep in his future, since time spent on nothing was time wasted, though he doubted that would make him a reliable partner for Kieran. He knew that alcohol hampered a chip's functionality, therefore exhaustion might have a similar effect. That was something to ask Kieran about. It was also worth noting that Kieran had yet to test if alcohol hampered his chipless powers...

Avurn meandered into the dining hall, anticipating the steaming buffet that was spread across the table every morning. His nostrils flared, flooded with the tempting scent of sizzling muskoxen bathed in radush syrup (the only acceptable pairing, naturally), but he made sure to complete a quick scan of the room for threats before indulging.

Ami had arrived earlier and was hunched over in a chair, avoiding any eye contact with the servers and guards. He did not blame her—their faces and minds were like blank techpads, completely devoid of data, which meant there would be no warning if they suddenly decided to attack.

Disturbing. He'd never encountered anything like it.

He seated himself beside Ami, unsurprised to find that the names of her crew had been blasted off the back of all the chairs. There were also scorch marks on the table, burned through the velvet cloth, which he might have blamed completely on Ami—if not for the fact that some of the damage was caused by blasts too large to have been emitted from Ami's lasgun. Both women seemed to be communicating via destruction in lieu of words.

'Sleep well?' Avurn enquired innocently.

Ami snorted.

Avurn grinned and reached across the table. He would start with the muskoxen and the mealworm pancakes, then try a spiky fruit that was poisonous unless it was pumped full of salt. He could get used to this kind of lifestyle, though he'd never say so out loud. Ami would accuse him of wanting to get there the quick and dirty way, by exploiting others. So far his morning had been quite relaxing and he had no intention of ruining it.

Avurn.

He stiffened. It had been a year since he'd last heard it, but he knew that voice, recognised that threatening undercurrent.

Avurn.

'I am listening,' Avurn murmured.

Ami gave him a strange look. He ignored her.

He is not himself. Help your mentor.

Kieran entered the room. His uniform was rumpled, his belt was missing—not a surprise, given his apparent inability to adhere to Chipper regulations—and his shaggy hair always refused to obey the laws of gravity, no matter what planet he was on. So he was the usual amount of dishevelled. Nothing to be alarmed about.

If the Creator God hadn't slid into Avurn's thoughts, that is.

Avurn skimmed the link that connected him to Kieran and felt... nothing. Nothing at all. The Chipper took the chair on the other side of Ami, his expression vacant instead of neutral.

Drugged. Not with Rapture, but something else. Something worse. Something that eroded a being's ability to think or feel at all.

Avurn stood, Ami's lasgun firm in his grip; it was far too easy to obtain the weapon, but he was never going to rebuke her because he preferred to have access to it. He didn't have to wait long. Taylar swanned into the room mere seconds later.

Avurn aimed the lasgun directly at her head. 'Tell me what you did to him. Now!'

'Av,' Ami said, also rising from the table. 'What's wrong?'

Taylar clasped her hands behind her back, a tainted smirk pulling at her cheeks.

Pure hatred flashed through Avurn, instantly raising his temperature. He breathed deeply, battling the memories from his childhood, those laser-sharp images of his parents' bodies hitting the floor, the eardrum-shattering sound of Jensa's screams as she was being taken from him, and—no. He had saved her. With Ami's help.

'Taylar dosed him with something,' Avurn told Ami. 'It's as if he's not even there. I cannot feel him.'

Ami seized Kieran's shoulder and shook it. 'Kieran?'

'This is a fair trade,' Kieran said lowly, haltingly. 'Me. In exchange for the freedom of a million other beings. I will serve Mistress Taylar. I am hers.'

Ami opened her mouth to say something, but her throat seemed to close up on her and she coughed instead.

Avurn winced when her pain and hopelessness hit his senses. He'd tolerated her and Kieran dancing around each other on the *Free Ride*, assuming it would eventually stop since Ami was not prone to making those kinds of attachments, but he hadn't been aware of the depth of Ami's feelings until just then.

Gods, he hoped he never felt this way about someone. It would be distracting. Fatally so, in situations like these.

'This is what you wanted, my darling,' Taylar said, smiling broadly. 'An end to my wicked ways. I can release all my slaves right now, if you wish, though it might be best if we don't do that until they have fought for us. They may hesitate too much otherwise. Once we have defeated Roch and freed Neffron's slaves—such a waste of inexpensive labour but I shall help you do it—my Chipper and I will leave this pathetic, dusty world.'

Ami's voice rose in pitch. 'This isn't Rapture. What is it?'

'Something new.' Taylar laughed and tossed her head. 'Have you really not noticed the way my men are acting? This does make you look rather stupid, darling.'

'Oh, I noticed. But I'm not so stupid that I'd mention it to you and provoke a demonstration like this!'

Ami and Taylar's argument grew louder, bouncing between condescending and furious. Avurn paid them no mind. The Creator

God should not be kept waiting—not when he could terminate Avurn's connection to the universe and its energy.

With a muttered curse, Avurn shoved away the chair Ami had vacated, making more space for himself. He knelt beside Kieran and stared into those distant blue eyes. No reaction. Not even a twitch. Avurn tapped the link—and once again heard a silence as endless as the vacuum of space.

Avurn scowled. 'I refuse to believe that you are not in there somewhere, Kieran. You can block a god. Surely you can overcome this.'

'What are you doing, boy?' Taylar demanded.

'Helping Kieran,' Ami snapped. 'Because that's what we're supposed to do—help our fellow beings, not subjugate them. You might say you'll put an end to slavery here, but you won't promise not to start it somewhere else. There are other worlds for you to set up shop on. You'll always need money and you can't think of a decent way to make it. Kieran will make all of that so much easier, which is why you're so set on taking him. You know, I used to get pissed off about a lot of shitty situations, especially since I had no power to do anything about them. But guess what? Nowadays when I'm pissed, I get *results*.'

'Stop the boy, shoot him!' Taylar shouted at the guards lining the walls.

'Av—!' Ami's cry was bitten off.

Avurn threw up a hand, his forcefield exploding out of his palm and expanding to form a protective barrier. The nearest guard hit the invisible shield face first. Blood gushed from his nostrils and he dropped to the floor like a puppet with its strings cut. The remaining guards followed him blindly, heedless of his fate. Still more of them spilled into the room from the corridor outside.

Too many. Far too many. Avurn wasn't prepared to waste that much energy repelling his assailants. He had work to do.

'Call off your guards!' Avurn said. 'Or I'll blast a forcefield right into your chest, Taylar, and I'm not as precious about life as your daughter is. I'll crush your heart!'

He held Taylar's eyes and let her see the darkness in his, the darkness he'd carried around inside himself for years, the darkness he excavated and used whenever it was most convenient. Taylar glanced away within nanoseconds and barked out a set of orders. The guards withdrew until they were all standing behind her. They did not approach again.

Avurn let his triumphant smirk break through. Briefly.

Time to appease the Creator God.

He grabbed Kieran's wrist, his nails marring the Chipper's pale skin with tiny crescents. *Kieran, stark you, I do not have enough training to divide my focus between reaching you and keeping the guards at bay. Taylar won't desist for long. I need you. Ami needs you.*

Kieran blinked. That simple gesture wouldn't have convinced anyone else, but it was the sign that Avurn had been looking for. He dug further. There—a feather of awareness. He would have preferred silence for this, but Ami and Taylar were shouting at each other again; Avurn suspected that Ami's intention was to distract her mother, to buy him time until Taylar called his bluff. It was working so far—no lasguns blatted at the air where his shield had been. No footsteps approached Kieran's chair.

Trusting Ami to watch his back, Avurn devoted himself to his task.

Kieran? he called. *I can feel you in there. Clever, using the shield you erected against the Desine to protect yourself. Very clever.*

It was my only option, Kieran replied. *I could not fight the substance Taylar injected me with, so I retreated into the last safe place I had left. I hoped you would find me, even if it required more finesse than you are used to.*

You're not a bad teacher, Kieran. I should be able to help you.

Avurn inhaled deeply, a hand cratered on Kieran's chest. He waited until he heard/felt/sensed Kieran's breathing match his, then tapped the mind at the other end of the link, a gentle knock on an intangible door. An invitation. The Chipper's presence unfurled, stretching outward. Avurn met him halfway and *pulled.* Kieran began to emerge—

—and met sudden resistance. The link went taut.

I tried this before, but I did not have the strength, Kieran said.

Avurn frowned. *This is no mere drug. It's as if there's an invading consciousness...stark! Nanobots!*

Incredulity warred with panic in Kieran's energy. *Bots? But they are prohibited. Everywhere. Just like clones. These are the only two laws that are shared by all inhabited worlds.*

Taylar is not the type of person to let galactic bans put a damper on her fun, Avurn noted.

This was so, so bad. All of the galaxy's sentient species had nearly been wiped out during the successive bot uprisings of millennia past, which was why bots were outlawed, even 'harmless' ones without artificial intelligence.

Avurn's teeth grazed his bottom lip. *I don't think I can give you what you need, Kieran. Draw on the stars, like you did in orbit.*

Kieran hesitated. He was still so afraid of what he could do. Avurn managed not to roll his eyes. He'd have given anything for even a skerrick of that immense, raw power, but Kieran wasn't him.

The Creator God imbued you with this power for a reason, Avurn said. *Just like he had a reason for letting me utilise this chip— I now suspect it's because he knew I would have to give you my assistance at some point.* He grimaced. *I do not like the idea of the Creator God using me this way, but it seems neither of us can escape his interference. Nor can we escape Ami's ire if we continue to delay this rescue attempt. Help me out here, Kieran.*

Kieran laughed out loud.

Avurn jerked, startled, then laughed as well.

Emboldened and purged of doubt, Kieran reached directly for the nearest star. The resulting surge was so intense it blinded Avurn, seared his senses, and sent him reeling. He found himself on the floor, staring up at a sea of lasguns wielded by blank-faced men. It would have been disappointing if Taylar hadn't called his bluff, especially since he was flat on his back.

The nanobots turned to dust as they were ejected from Kieran's pores, then scattered into the air, a fine spray that slowly dissipated. Kieran stood from his chair, arms out, gathering the universe's energy around him like a cloak.

He smiled.

A wave of pure light radiated out from his body, sweeping into every corner of the room and destroying every shadow that lingered there. Taylar and her guards fell about like debris in a storm, but Ami and Avurn remained safe and standing. Avurn would have said he'd never felt anything like it—if he hadn't recently been in the presence of the Creator God.

Stark, Avurn thought. *He is something else.*

After he'd helped Avurn to his feet, Kieran hesitated, his grip tightening on Avurn's arm. Avurn nodded and spoke inside the link, not wanting Ami to overhear him. *I would like that. You have my permission.*

The Chipper grinned and pulled him into a hug. *Thank you.*

I did very little, Avurn returned. *You brought yourself back. I just...convinced you that you could do it on your own.*

Kieran released him shortly afterwards, much to Avurn's relief. Avurn stepped back and looked over at Ami. She was holding her lasgun, having reappropriated it from him (Avurn had, admittedly, been distracted), the butt of the weapon tracking Taylar as she stood from the floor and advanced. Taylar's dazed guards began shambling forward as well. The transparent ceiling was offering them all a blazing blue sky today, a cheerful counterpoint to what was going on beneath it.

'Hold it right there,' Ami said with an uncharacteristic snarl. 'Give me one good reason why I shouldn't scorch my name into your chest.'

'Stop,' Taylar ordered.

Her guards went still so suddenly that Avurn wouldn't have been surprised to discover that they were bots themselves, not inhabited by millions of nano-sized versions instead. The tech was impressive. Once those bots got into someone's brain, their body became a puppet for the being they were programmed to obey.

Avurn was interested to see what Taylar would do now that her daughter had the upper hand. She'd start with a cutting remark, most likely, but Ami was more than capable of parrying any verbal blows—

Taylar ripped a lasgun out of the lax grip of a nearby guard. She fired several shots at Ami.

Avurn lifted his hand. But he was too late.

The lasbolts bounced away from Kieran's shield as the Chipper moved towards Ami, taking up a protective position beside her, his arms loose by his sides. Avurn discreetly began gathering the energy required for a forcefield of his own. He did not move his hands. Predictably, the would-be shield collapsed inside him, trapped and aimless.

There was no use sulking. Still, it was very tempting to do so.

'Are you going to kill her?' Avurn asked Ami, not bothering to filter the sarcasm out of his voice. 'Will your precious principles let you, I wonder? Such a fine line between self-preservation and revenge.'

'Av,' Kieran cautioned.

Ami tossed an impatient look at Avurn, but he could sense the uneasiness vibrating through her energy. 'I won't have to. Taylar has all her weapons keyed to recognise her biometrics. The blasts will only incapacitate her, not kill her. It's a great way to play dead. In case of situations like this, I guess. Kieran, if you please…?'

Kieran nodded and Taylar's lasgun flew into Ami's hand—well, the one wasn't already holding her own weapon. Both lasguns were steady in her grip.

'Shoot them, shoot them!' Taylar shouted at her guards.

Ami didn't hesitate. She pulled the trigger.

Taylar hit the floor and went still.

Her guards were firing as ordered, lighting up Kieran's shield with angry red dots that swarmed together into larger splatters of colour and light. But if Kieran was drawing on the stars, nothing would be able to get through. Avurn wondered how long he would last—celestial power was one thing, the ability to conduct it quite another.

'Ask your mistress for orders!' Ami barked at the guards. 'Ask her what you should do!'

Avurn opened his mouth to tell her this tactic probably wouldn't work, since it wasn't Rapture in their systems—but then the lasgun fire silenced and so did he.

The guards kept their hands on their weapons, their eyes remained fixed on distant, invisible horizons, and their chests were glistening with whatever oil Taylar had made them douse themselves in earlier. They waited. Simply waited. No order was forthcoming, which was apparently what they needed in order to act. Ami's gamble had paid off.

'How long until the drug's out of their systems, do you think?' Ami asked.

'It's not a drug,' Avurn informed her, his throat tightening—no, he wasn't upset, he had not shed tears for his parents and he would never do so for strangers. 'It's nanobots. I suspect they need to be removed entirely before we can free Taylar's guards. But how do we go about doing that? Any ideas?'

Ami looked at Taylar's crumpled form and then at Kieran, who shrugged helplessly. Avurn conceded that it would be difficult to read the mind of a woman who was now unconscious.

'They don't need to be removed,' an unexpected voice answered. 'The bots will degrade in a matter of hours.'

Grace Pendergast appeared between the two columns framing the entrance to the dining hall, patently unsurprised to find Taylar on the floor with a forest of silent guards surrounding her. Grace continued, 'There are files on Taylar's console that go into detail about the bots. She purchased the blueprints from a disgraced programmer who desperately needed the coin-chips—their starship was destroyed with them on board several months ago and it's highly likely that Taylar was involved. Fortunately, the bots break down in organic systems about six hours after insertion. The programmer did not solve this problem, either due to time constraints or as a deliberate safety precaution. No one wants a bot uprising in this century.'

Avurn swallowed his chagrin. He had been too busy looking at other files...and he had not bothered to look into how Taylar controlled her guards, despite how obvious it was that Rapture wasn't involved, because he'd deemed it irrelevant to their plans. Something to investigate after Neffron and Taylar had been dealt with.

An amateurish oversight.

'Wait, she must have billions of these bot things in storage,' Ami said, face pale. 'Just waiting to be inserted.'

Grace shook her head. 'She was running low on the coin-chips and raw materials required to manufacture them.'

Avurn allowed an exhale of relief. There were many things he would do, many products he would deal in, but bots were several steps too far. He made a mental note to locate and securely destroy the blueprints as soon as possible.

'I suggest we move Taylar into her panic room,' Grace said. 'It was designed to keep people out, but I reprogrammed the lock mechanism—thanks to a friend's hacking software. Taylar will be quite comfortable in there. It has a private bathroom and a fully stocked kitchenette.'

'I'll do it, I'll move her,' a guard announced, appearing in the doorway behind Grace. He smiled nervously, hands held up in a defensive gesture, and waited for Ami to lower her lasgun before speaking again. 'I'm Lius. She stopped putting the bots into me, said she needed me functional so I could build her cloaking device and pilot her flagship.'

Avurn and Kieran exchanged glances. Neither of them sensed anything that indicated Lius was lying.

'Do it,' Ami said after Kieran nodded at her.

Watching Lius carry Taylar's limp body away, Grace remarked, 'Neffron will not be this easy to defeat.'

Ami sighed and moved back to the table, then sank into one of the chairs. Kieran and Grace soon joined her. Around them, the guards continued to stand, eerily still and silent, an army seemingly carved from stone. Ami tried to get them to sit down, but they ignored her. The nanobots ensured that they accepted Taylar's orders only. Ami's cheeks tightened.

Avurn made himself comfortable on Taylar's throne and opened his palm. He began a quick study of the relevant files once he'd snatched them from Taylar's server, to see if he could override the programming and deactivate the bots sooner.

'I'm not making any plans regarding my father until I eat something,' Ami said.

Avurn silently agreed. They could afford to waste some time, since he'd just discovered that the bots weren't connected to either of the local systems. He couldn't do anything to them. Stark. He hated being this useless.

He gazed down at buffet spread before him. Shrugging, he deactivated the tech in his palm and reached for a fork instead. The rest of their meals would not be this sumptuous, since the slaves would refuse to serve them once they were free. Avurn hoped they'd still cook something, perhaps some basic fare—he paused, the fork perched on his bottom lip.

'Av?' Kieran asked.

Avurn flushed. Kieran could read minds—how foolish was he to think such a thing near him?

'I wish you hadn't heard that,' Avurn said.

'You are not your thoughts, Av,' Kieran told him gently. 'It's what you do that matters. Your actions have a greater impact than the words you'd never say out loud.'

Avurn tapped his tongue against the roof of his mouth. The ensuing clicks were very satisfying for some reason. 'Do *you* have any thoughts that should never be voiced?'

'Yes,' Kieran murmured, his eyes resting on Ami.

Ah. Yes. Kieran's thoughts were more likely to cause trouble. And soon. Especially if—*once* they returned to Ilbb. Avurn tuned back into Ami and Grace's conversation, pleased to discover that he hadn't missed much.

'How do we get Taylar's people to overthrow Neffron for us?' Ami was saying. 'I'm assuming you have some experience with that sort of thing—I mean, you've witnessed a few insurrections, haven't you? Any ideas?'

Grace crossed her arms. 'I report the news. I don't create it.'

'I don't believe you,' Avurn declared. 'You might be renowned for being the galaxy's champion of the truth, but I can read between the lines, Ms Pendergast. I know that planets like New Dunedin, Butisl, and Frossi didn't miraculously free themselves of their rulers while you just happened to be there. Help us. Or you'll die here along with us.'

The reporter wasn't fazed. 'Those are not the only options available to me. But I promise you this—you'll have whatever assistance I can give you.'

'Thank the gods for that,' Ami muttered. 'I have no idea what I'm doing.'

Truer words have never been spoken, Avurn mused.

But when she was standing on the bridge of a ship that was hers, she commanded a presence that could shatter n'radian. It was this that had caused so many pirates and slavers to capitulate, not the lascannon the *Free Ride* had once possessed.

Not that Avurn would ever admit to admiring Ami, especially when he was still pissed off with her.

THIRTY-FIVE

'I won't make you fight Neffron with us,' Ami announced.

At least a thousand men were assembled on Taylar's largest landing pad, which featured a curved vidscreen that permanently displayed the waterfall hidden behind the ridge. To Ami's knowledge, Taylar had never travelled the short distance to clap her eyes on the waterfall in person. Easier—and safer—to view it from here, no doubt.

The crowd in front of Ami represented a fraction of Taylar's victims, with at least a million more spread across the hemisphere in various factories and outposts, but every man who'd been freed was listening to Ami, thanks to the mangled chrome box attached to her shirt. Part communicator, part amplifying device, it had been cobbled together by Goss Kwon, the former guard who had handed it to her. Ami wasn't sure how reliable the tech was. Unlike Lius, Taylar's old favourite, Goss hadn't avoided being injected with nanobots. He'd only had a few hours to put the device together.

'Behind me are a number of ships that used to belong to Taylar.' Ami waved vaguely over her shoulder. 'They're yours now.'

Avurn had groaned when she'd suggested this earlier, because she wouldn't exclude the vessel with the cloaking device. It would have made a handy replacement for the *Free Ride*—especially since it was more advanced than the other ships on offer.

But Ami would be starked before she ever used something that her mother considered 'superior'.

'You can leave and make lives for yourselves,' Ami continued. 'Although, I'd suggest you wait until my father's fleet is dealt with before attempting to run that blockade. I don't know how he heard about Taylar's downfall, but he pounced on her ships in orbit the nanosecond we locked her up. The reinforced catacombs beneath this rock shelf should be safe enough if you want to wait the action out. They were built to last a bombardment. A short one, anyway.'

The catacombs had been equipped with power and running water back when Ami was a teenager, probably because Taylar had realised the shield protecting her headquarters wouldn't last more than a day if Neffron had a good go at it. Interestingly, there was a new feature down there that Ami hadn't seen before: a tunnel plunging deep into the rock, wide enough to fit a modest cargo ship. Grace wasn't sure what purpose that served, but the reporter had promised to look into it.

Ami took a moment to reassess her audience. Some of them rubbing their eyes; others were wavering on their feet. The nanobots decayed in a matter of hours, but the grogginess seemed to last a lot longer.

Was now the right time to be launching all of this at them?

Slowly, they began to nod. Then came the enquiries about food and coin-chips. Ami didn't see a problem supplying them with these things, given that they had nothing but the clothes on their backs (figuratively speaking, since most of them didn't even have that). Taylar's treasury might have dwindled too low to fund her side of the war, but it wasn't exactly bare. Her food stores were also very healthy.

Ami waved Grace over to deal with these questions. The reporter had a much better idea about what was on hand than she did. Taylar had kept a detailed inventory and boredom had chased Ami away from those files, but Grace had enthusiastically combed through them.

Ami cast an eye towards the palace, wondering how Kieran and Avurn were getting on. They were moving through the rooms and clearing out anyone who was still in need of rescue. A few of Taylar's victims had been stowed away in tight spaces, a punishment for those who looked too inferior. Taylar deserved a far worse cell than that comfy panic room of hers.

But at least she couldn't anyone. Not anymore.

'You're not even going to try to convince us to fight, Captain?' Goss Kwon asked, also wearing a wonky amplifying device. He had constructed that one for himself and Ami was starting to wonder why he'd wanted his voice to be heard by a million people. 'We can do some serious damage with the arsenal that wyvern kept stashed in her palace. Since her mercs pissed off to Neffron's side as soon as you took her down, we won't have any problem grabbing that gear for ourselves.'

Yeah, they'd lost Taylar's army and every single starship inside an hour. Ami knew she shouldn't have been surprised, but stark! Neffron had moved a lot faster than she'd expected him to.

She had already turned off her own amplifying device and stepped down from the loading crate she'd used to make herself seen by the crowd, but that hadn't stopped Goss approaching and engaging with her. He had told Ami that he'd been sold into slavery for political reasons, which made him interesting. Or dangerous. Or both.

His face was so rough and uncompromising it wouldn't have

looked out of place in one the nearby canyons. 'You assumed we'd happily hide in this starking rock, doing fuck all instead of seizing the chance to free those enslaved by Neffron. Don't insult us, Captain N'uni. And don't you dare presume to decide this planet's fate. We deserve a say in that, more so than you—some of us have been here a lot longer than you ever were.'

Ami thumbed the power switch on the device clinging to her shirt, turning it back on. 'It doesn't seem right, asking for more after how much was taken from you. I won't do it.'

'You need us,' Goss said flatly. 'We're doomed if we don't fight with you. Forget hiding—that shield won't last very long and those catacombs won't protect us once Neffron's army comes after us on the ground. I don't need a fancy intelligence network to tell me he's getting ready to come after us, because he knows this side of the planet is ripe for the taking. He has thousands of mercs—tens of thousands, actually, now that he has Taylar's. But we outnumber them.'

Ami was very conscious of the fact that the eyes and ears of the crowd hadn't left her, though a few of them were still throwing questions at Grace—*distracting* Grace, Ami realised.

Get the out-of-her-depth starship captain away from the seasoned reporter...

'Okay, fine,' Ami said, climbing back onto the crate and clumsily interrupting Grace. 'Goss here has a good point. I do need you. I don't exactly have an army and I'm well aware that you aren't one. I promise you that I will do everything I can to get you off this rock and back to your lives. But it'll be easier if you help me.'

'You're their starking daughter!' someone shouted.

Tough crowd. But Ami was ready. She'd unknowingly spent a lifetime preparing for this moment.

Ami turned away from that sea of accusing faces and reached for the hem of her shirt. She lifted it in one swift motion, exposing the scars on her back. They didn't gasp or make any dramatic pronouncements, so Ami's only companion was a mournful, howling wind. It felt hot and arid, swept up from the desert on the other side of the anti-bombardment shield—the same vast desert that Neffron had chosen for his headquarters, despite there being better, further locations to wage war from. But he wasn't the only danger lurking out there.

Ami held her breath, but she heard nothing untoward and no sandy figures suddenly appeared—not that she could do a starking thing if the Desine chose to attack.

She faced her silent audience. None of them flinched away from her gaze.

'Neffron punished me whenever I refused to use the laswhip on anyone,' Ami said. 'Guess he thought me taking those strokes instead was poetic or some shit. Taylar preferred to starve me. My parents didn't stop there—they found a way to make me hurt people. Rapture. But that drug is nowhere near as awful as what you got hit with. I know I can't compare my experiences with yours.'

'That's right, princess, you can't!' someone in the crowd hollered. 'You up and left when you could and not a nanosecond sooner. You abandoned us!'

Ami swallowed and tried again. 'I was a teenager. Could barely look after myself. Now I'm older, not exactly wiser—but definitely more capable of fighting back. Do you know what I've been doing for the past few years? Chasing slavers and pirates and hijacking their ships with an outdated, if powerful, lascannon. I recently got myself some extra crew members, but before they showed up I only had a kid as my companion. Together, we saved hundreds of lives. But that's all we could manage.'

She opened her arms, as if to encompass her audience and the hundreds more who remained inside the palace, some of them no doubt hoping to get a crack at the person responsible for their current situation. Ami wasn't too worried about them succeeding. Taylar was being kept in a panic room they knew nothing about, steadfastly watched over by Lius, who had offered his help before Ami had even realised she'd needed someone to stand outside Taylar's makeshift cell.

Ami had dithered over letting Lius guard Taylar, because without the nanobots he'd had the mental capacity and the time to plot his revenge. But Kieran had sensed no such desire in him. Lius was seemingly content to taunt Taylar about her reversal of fortunes.

'My crew and I took out Taylar,' Ami declared. 'Now we have to take out the other main player. And that's Neffron. I can't do it alone. I need help.' Ami straightened and clasped her hands behind her back. 'I need you. I need every single one of you on my side or this won't work.'

'Can you guarantee our safety?' Goss asked, though his smile told her there was no malice behind the question. He wanted her to put it all on the table for them.

Ami shook her head. 'No. But I can't guarantee your safety once you take one of these ships up into space either. Whether or not you stick around, I'll get my tech person to wipe your records from the Galactic Database. I also know someone who can create fake IDs. You'll get a fresh start. If that's what you want.'

'Do you have a plan?' was Goss' next attack.

The wry laugh escaped Ami before she could stop it. She had a feeling they were expecting the answer she had for them.

'Not yet,' she admitted. 'But right now, I'd say we've earned ourselves a small reprieve. Taylar can't eat all that food herself, can she? And it'll go bad if we don't do something about it...'

The crowd cheered. Goss bowed his head and said no more, but he was still smiling. Ami chose to translate that as approval.

Those who had been forced to cook for Taylar as part of their duties offered to produce a liberation feast; no one refused them, unsurprisingly. What was surprising were how many people were willing to go after Neffron—all but a handful of men volunteered. Ami watched her new-found army, Goss among them, trickle away back towards the palace. Her shoulders slumped. Stark.

Grace's lips were pursed.

'What?' Ami challenged. 'You don't think we can come up with some way of knocking my father off his perch?'

'Difficult, but not impossible—given time.' Grace hesitated. 'Time we may not have. No. I was thinking that some images are incredibly powerful. What you did just then, showing them all that you're one of them...it was inspiring.'

'"Inspiring" doesn't win wars,' Ami said.

Grace waved her techpad. It came perilously close to flying from her fingers. 'You have the potential to do so much more than win mere wars. I have spent years reporting on slavery in text form, but it changed nothing and convinced no one to take on slavers and pirates the way you did. And you just swayed a thousand men by baring your back—possibly even a million of them, since we don't yet know how those in the factories and outposts responded.'

'You've based your entire career on never using images in your reports,' Ami pointed out. 'To protect your sources.'

'And somehow I succeeded,' Grace said, her gaze distant. 'Billions of beings read my reports and, despite their inability to verify what I wrote, call me their champion of the truth. I value their trust. Unfortunately, my notoriety encouraged others to copy me. There are thousands of e-paper reporters now and the galaxy has started to believe their every word—but many of my colleagues are being paid off by slavers, even agreeing to be *sponsored* by them. If you would permit me...' Grace trailed off, seeming to gather herself. Then she made her request. 'I'd like to take an image of your back. To use in my report.'

Ami winced. She'd had no trouble showing her scars to Kieran, because he knew her in ways that no one else did—and that was before you factored in the mind-reading thing. As for Goss and the others, she'd had to earn their respect and prove she wasn't some pampered princess.

But baring her back and exposing her past to the whole starking galaxy?

That was something else entirely.

'Alright, sure,' Ami said, not realising she'd made her decision until the words left her mouth. 'I'll also talk to Goss and the others and see if they'll agree to give you something for your e-paper. Although, you might want to consider changing careers and becoming a mediaist, because their testimonies will be more compelling in a Webcast—you really should holster the techpad and whip out a vidcam.'

'I do have some experience with vidcams,' Grace said, sliding her techpad into its padded pouch on her belt. 'Thank you. I know it won't be easy for you and I will avoid showing your face, if you prefer.'

'Isn't this going to be dangerous for you, Grace? Other slavers might feel threatened and think they're next on your exposé list. They'll come after you.'

Grace laughed shortly. 'They're welcome to try. This isn't my first controversial report, Ami. I have certain protections in place.' She patted the pouch. 'On another note, I can't find anything in Taylar's files about the tunnel in the rock beneath us and when I asked her, she said she would only speak to you about it. No one else.'

'She won't tell me anything until I agree to release her,' Ami grumbled. 'And that's not happening.'

'Perhaps Kieran could...' Grace caught herself in time.

Ami let rip. 'Could what? Read her mind? That's impossible,

isn't it? I seem to notice you picking up on some stray thoughts yourself, so why don't *you* do it?'

'I can't read minds, Ami,' Grace said evenly.

'I guess a reporter wouldn't like using that kind of crutch when she can be clever and figure shit out on her own, huh?'

Grace glanced away, cheeks tightening.

Oh yeah. Ami knew she'd hit a sore spot. But she had no patience or sympathy for this so-called champion of the truth.

'It's obvious to me,' Ami continued, 'that Kieran wouldn't be suffering quite so much if his family had bothered to be there for him.' She turned away from Grace and began marching back towards the palace. 'It's a good thing he's got me. Anyway, I don't need him for this. I can handle Taylar all on my own.'

She hoped her voice had sounded a lot steadier than she felt.

THIRTY-SIX

Ami called her crew to a meeting in the private conference room adjoining Taylar's office sometime in the afternoon, while the rest of the palace's residents were sleeping off their festivities. Kieran knew he was the last to arrive before he made it through the door, having sensed three familiar lifesigns behind it. They'd started the meeting without him.

Ami's welcoming smile caused something to unfurl inside his chest.

'So now we know why this palace is sitting on top of a tunnel,' Ami continued, as though his arrival hadn't fazed her in the slightest. He knew better. 'Taylar had it bored so she could sneak her people behind Neffron's border—it's connected to an underground road system which runs for, I shit you not, three thousand klicks. And that's not all. Grace poked around a bit and managed to find forty subterranean transports stowed in the catacombs beneath us.' Ami laughed darkly. 'There's a couple of reasons why no one else knew about them. Firstly, there's nothing on Taylar's consoles to indicate that they exist at all. Secondly, she always killed those who managed to return from missions in Neffron's territory. She didn't want anyone knowing her little secret.'

'That must have wasted a lot of time and resources,' Avurn noted. When Ami shot him a frown, he added stiffly, 'The loss of life is, of course, unconscionable.'

Ami repeated his words under her breath. Avurn remained outwardly unmoved, but on the inside he was coiling his frustration and anger into a bomb that could go off at any moment.

Kieran rested a hand on his shoulder. Avurn relaxed, but only slightly.

Grace slid her techpad across the table in the centre of room; the glossy vidscreen that formed the surface immediately lit up when her device connected to it. A map of chaotic tunnels appeared on the large display, a glaring contrast to the smooth chrome edging that arced around the circular table, marred only by an artistic spray of diamonds. Grace's fingers travelled through the air, the lines directly beneath them glowing as she explained the full extent of the tunnel system. She had found these schematics on the console of one of the subterranean vehicles.

Avurn leaned over, his eyes saucering. 'Incredible. Taylar might have made some horrendously inept decisions, but this is the perfect set-up for guerrilla activity. Hit-and-run tactics might just work for us. We can attack Neffron and then disappear back into the tunnels via their concealed entrances.'

Kieran watched Ami closely. She had her arms wrapped around her torso, her thoughts shadowed and fragmented.

'What did you trade for this information?' he asked.

Ami shook her head from side to side, as though trying to wrench herself out of a stupor. 'Taylar wanted me to hug her. I'm not sure what she expected, maybe for me to get overtaken by feelings I've never had for her...'

Ami looked meaningfully at Kieran, her mind filling with the memories that she entrusted to him alone. The panic room. Taylar, adorned in her fine clothes and jewellery. She stood a little less tall now, though she was no less dangerous.

Ami stood rigidly before Taylar and, grimacing, allowed the ensuing hug. When she tried to step back, Taylar seized her tight with arms that squeezed her like a serpent. Weeping prettily, Taylar exclaimed, 'Don't you want this? Isn't this what you've always wanted? A loving mother! I can be that for you, if you'll let me!'

Kieran kept his feet still, despite the overwhelming urge to give Ami a more tender embrace than the one she had most recently received. She gave him a small nod, letting him know that she appreciated him keeping his distance.

She could handle this kind of thing on her own.

But I've got nothing against you coming to my rescue when I ask for it, Ami added.

Always, Kieran promised.

Avurn shrugged off the hand Kieran had left on his shoulder and gave him a pointed look. *Pay attention*. 'These vehicles will allow us to get into position beneath key parts of Neffron's defences. If we plant enough explosives in the right spot, we could destroy his headquarters and possibly even hobble his ability to launch a counterattack.'

Ami gnawed on her bottom lip for a moment. 'It would depend on how structurally sound the tunnels are, where they run, and the condition of the roads inside them. We'd need to get out *fast*.'

'These machines aren't high tech,' Grace supplied. 'Most of Taylar's profits went towards funding her mercenaries, her nanobots, and her own indulgences. They're also not currently capable of connecting to any type of system, local or otherwise— another reason we initially couldn't find them.'

'So they cannot be driven and destroyed remotely,' Avurn said, his nose so low it was almost grazing the schematics on the vidscreen. 'We'll need to crew them.'

'Do we?' Ami frowned. 'I know Taylar's always had mines in her arsenal, but if they're as old and outdated as I suspect they are, then there's a chance the timers won't work or they'll detonate early. It's too dangerous to use crews. We'll hook the vehicles up to Taylar's local system.'

'It will take too long to outfit them for that purpose,' Avurn said. 'Weeks, perhaps. And that's if the tech is on hand. Which I highly doubt.'

'Stark,' Ami muttered.

Avurn sighed deeply. 'I agree. We'll have to set the mines ourselves and then effect an escape. Like you, I am not comfortable with endangering beings who've only just had their freedom restored to them. If Kieran and I alone could do it in their place... but two people cannot do it quickly enough.'

'Like me?' Ami echoed, then snorted. 'No way. You're nothing like me and thank the gods for that.'

Kieran didn't need the benefit of the link to know this was the wrong thing to say to the boy, even though Ami had meant it as a self-deprecating joke. Avurn's brow creased and his mouth oscillated for several seconds before he turned and marched out.

When Kieran mentally reached for Avurn, the response was bitter and resentful. *I refuse to stay where I am not wanted.*

I can relay everything that goes on in here, Kieran offered.

Don't bother, Avurn snapped back at him. *It is clear Ami only sees me as she always has—a megalomaniac without morals. I will never be able to convince her otherwise.*

'Ami...' Kieran hesitated.

'What, don't tell me he's actually upset?' Ami shook her head. 'It's all a big performance. I won't buy into this *galactic image* he's trying so hard to build.'

'I have a very personal connection with Avurn,' Kieran said. 'His feelings are far more complex than you give him credit for. You have seen him make questionable choices, but he is growing, becoming something else. You can't keep branding him as a—well, a megalomaniac. Maybe that will happen, if we don't guide him properly, but he's still a child.'

Ami stared at him for several long moments, her lips warring together. Eventually, she looked away and said, 'I don't have time to fix this right now. Grace, can you tell me how many timed mines Taylar actually has in her stash?'

'Yes,' Grace answered. 'I've seen them listed in her inventory. We have enough to cover the most important targets.' She indicated specific locations on the schematics. 'Using a small group of volunteers for this mission will limit casualties in case of discovery or in case the mines are faulty.'

Ami rubbed her temples. 'We have forty vehicles to crew. They each need a driver, someone to set the mines, armed guards to cover their backs if Neffron's mercs start gunning for them...that's not a small group. I don't want to lose anyone. Not a single being. Kieran, any foresight on the matter? And by foresight, I mean visions of the future. If you're having trouble, then maybe Grace can help?'

Kieran wasn't surprised or bothered that she'd brazenly mentioned his abilities in front of Grace. Ami had been trying to wear the reporter down for days—and he was interested to see if she would succeed on this occasion.

Grace looked resigned. 'I don't know how to help Kieran with...that.'

'Is that all you're going to say about it?' Ami demanded.

'Yes,' Grace said quietly. 'For now, anyway.'

Kieran closed his eyes and cast his mind adrift. Like the countless stars filling the dark void of space, there were too many visions out there for him to know which one he needed. But when he narrowed his focus to his future only, the choice became easy. He saw himself and Ami standing outside the palace, struggling to stand as a wall of wind slammed into them. Ami's clothes were rumpled. His body was tight with tension. A great sense of loss was palpable, so thick even the wind couldn't force it to disperse, and there were deep shadows in Ami's beautiful green eyes. They couldn't do this alone. They needed help.

The vision flickered and died.

Kieran opened his eyes, perturbed. 'I...I don't think faulty mines are what we should be worried about.'

'Okay, so what *should* we be worried about?' Ami asked.

'I don't know,' Kieran said, sighing.

Ami tipped her head from side to side, stretching out her neck. 'I guess it was greedy of me, expecting you to provide me with the outcome of every decision I'll ever make. But we've got the bare bones of a plan, right? I should go talk to Goss and the others. Ugh. No, first I'm going to hit the gym upstairs. I need to work off some of my anxiety or they'll pick up on it and rip me to shreds. That or just refuse to listen.'

Not my preferred method of exercise, she was thinking dourly as she left. *Oh gods, Ami. He can hear you, remember!*

Kieran was tempted to join her, because he had let his mandatory strength training lapse somewhat in the past year, but he knew she was trying to distract herself, trying to banish salacious thoughts. She needed the distance. Stark, he needed the distance too. Kieran nodded at Grace and also departed, heading for the catacombs. He could drive and pilot most machines, but he wanted to check the controls of the subterranean vehicles.

He paused when he felt his link with Avurn wobble and fray. Then Avurn's frustration swept through their connection and took up residence inside his skull, throbbing like a vengeful headache. Kieran put on a burst of speed, rounded the corner, hurtled into

Avurn's suite—and found the boy sitting in the middle of the floor of the antechamber.

'Av?' Kieran asked.

His cheeks flushed and his whole body trembling, Avurn flung a desperate look up at Kieran. 'I can't create a forcefield without my hands. I can't! I keep trying and I—'

Kieran knelt beside him. 'It's alright. No one will think any less of you for needing to use your hands. Chippers have been doing it this way for centuries.'

'Can you tell me, honestly, if I'll ever be able to keep my hands down?'

Kieran nodded and carefully scanned his companion. He saw that though Avurn was indeed powerful, his ability to manipulate the universe's energy was dependent on the chip in the crook of his arm. The tech limited him; the Creator God could limit him further still. He would never be able to create forcefields the way Kieran did.

'I knew it,' Avurn said before Kieran could tell him any of this. 'I knew it! Stupid of me, to think I could ever match your power. But I can't stop wanting it. I want it so much.'

'Why?' Kieran asked.

Avurn's eyes glistened. 'Because then Ami might treat me with the same respect she gives you.'

'You have other skills, Av.'

Avurn's eyes rolled up towards the ceiling and then back down again. 'Really. Are they the type of skills that will make Ami see me in a completely different light? Prove to her that I can finally be trusted? I cannot suddenly become the perfect being she expects to see.'

'You could try telling her how you feel,' Kieran suggested. 'But do it *before* you explode, when you are able to express yourself properly and in a less reactive manner.'

'She will not listen. She has already established in her mind what I am and I...' Avurn scowled. 'I am tired of making small changes that she will never notice. Why should I bother trying to better myself?'

'I'll talk to Ami about this, if it will help,' Kieran said.

'Is there time for that, I wonder?' Avurn mused.

'I'm not sure. But we are about to do something very dangerous and my visions aren't specific about the outcome. We should say what we need to say now, while we still can. Just in case.'

'I believe there are certain things you need to say to Ami,' Avurn told him, his energy brightening as he distracted himself with Kieran's problems instead of dwelling on his own. 'Things that could not be said before, when you possessed a functional chip.'

'Ami knows that the chip isn't what makes me a Chipper,' Kieran said calmly. 'Av, if I want to save the galaxy, I can't be anything else. I can't *belong* to anyone else. The Agency is my home and I'm not going to let it fracture. They need me.'

Avurn gave him a sardonic smile. 'How will you save a single soul, let alone the entire galaxy, if GLEA kicks you out for refusing to marry and breed for them? Don't lie, Kieran. I know you'll refuse.'

'That won't happen. They won't kick me out. I'll gain enough support and clout inside the Agency that they'll have to listen to me when I tell them to end this short-sighted mandate. They *will* listen to Kieran Krendasta. They will.'

'Stop being so naïve, Kieran.'

Kieran retreated from Avurn's presence, painfully aware that he was avoiding an argument that he had no hope of winning.

THIRTY-SEVEN

Ami lifted her head from the cushioned edge of the spa when she heard the door to her suite swipe open. She had a pretty good idea who it was, even before he flashed a greeting into her mind.

'Need some amnesia, huh?' she called out. 'This isn't exactly a shower, but I think it'll do under the circumstances.'

His laugh was gentle, but it still managed to strike a spot somewhere behind her navel. Ami watched with half-lidded eyes as Kieran shed his uniform, doffed his belt, and hopped into the spa. She didn't stop him. Didn't protest. It would be cowardly to use exhaustion as an excuse. But her body *did* ache from that ill-advised trip to her mother's gym (trying to match Taylar's personal bests had been a mistake) and her head was spasming from three hours of mental sparring with Goss Kwon.

It hadn't helped that said sparring had occurred in front of hundreds more men than last time and in the catacombs, where the acoustics turned the slightest whisper into a nail scraping at her skull. Compounding the issue, she and Goss had been wearing his amplifying tech again and their voices had boomed backwards and forwards.

Goss seemed to be angling for a leadership position. She had no intention of getting in his way—and she had a feeling he could easily eliminate her if he wanted to.

He and his people had chosen to set up camp in the catacombs, which were rough, gloomy, and hardly private. But Goss had said they felt more comfortable bunking down there instead of in the sumptuous palace, where the doors to their quarters could be locked from the outside.

'How did the meeting go?' Kieran asked, effortlessly finding a comfortable position that allowed him to maintain as much distance between them as possible. The spa would not have fit inside the bridge of the late and great *Free Ride*, so it was a decent amount of distance. The subsiding suds, however, did a poor job of hiding Kieran in all his glory.

Ami tried to avert her eyes. Completely and utterly failed.

She smiled ruefully. 'Actually, the meeting went pretty well. Practically everyone wanted to volunteer to crew those deathtraps.'

'The mines will take out a significant portion of Neffron's defences, if all goes to plan,' Kieran commented. 'It does improve our odds of capturing his headquarters—and perhaps even Neffron himself.'

'Yeah, and it's the only plan any of us have got,' Ami said. 'Gods, we're so cosmically starked. Anyway, that's tomorrow's problem. Right now, I just want to relax and pretend that all this'—she released a hand from the surface of the water, throwing out a spray of droplets that never reached him—'is something I bought and earned, not something my awful mother got from exploiting her victims.'

Kieran's eyes grew darker as he lowered them from hers. And he kept lowering them.

Ami was well aware that her cheeks were reddening and knew she couldn't blame the temperature of the water. She threw him a challenging look. But he did nothing, drew no closer. He lounged against his side of the spa, seemingly content to stay there. Muttering under her breath, Ami bobbed over to a diamond-studded net full of small bottles and retrieved more scented oils, tossing them about with wild abandon until the suds grew mountainous again, hiding what needed to be hidden.

Ami sighed as her shoulders slid back beneath the water. This was as close to what even the Creator God might consider perfection.

Well, there was one thing that would make it completely perfect…

'I'd be lying if I said I wasn't terrified,' Ami admitted, stopping to clamp down hard on a yawn. Her jaw ached indignantly. 'And I won't lie and say I'm not trying to figure out how to turn this into a "we might horribly die tomorrow so let's do that thing we probably shouldn't do" speech.'

'Ami…' he said lowly.

'Or you could just read my thoughts,' Ami suggested. 'Those images are a *lot* more succinct.'

His presence fled her mind then, creating an absence that left her shivering despite the hot water smothering her. He was afraid. It caused him to withdraw. Her fear did the opposite and always had. Always sent her seeking comfort where she really shouldn't, in places she'd regret finding herself later.

Ami forced a careless grin. 'Forget I mentioned it. Or at least pretend you've forgotten it, so this doesn't get any more awkward than it is already.'

'Ami…' Kieran closed his eyes briefly, a small shudder passing through him. 'I know my chip isn't working anymore, but…'

'You're worried about what it'll mean,' Ami mused while he floundered.

He stared at her.

'We can't *just* have sex,' Ami went on. 'Because neither of us wants to end it there. So if we actually do the deed, it'll mean you've abandoned your devotion to GLEA and your purpose. And I won't be the reason for that. I won't let you betray a part of yourself. The part that has to save the galaxy or something.'

A hiss of air escaped his lips. 'I didn't have the words to explain it, thank you.'

Ami's heart clenched when she saw the relief smoothing out the lines that had marred his features. This was for the best, she knew that. But she did wish he'd drift back into her thoughts. It should have been weird when he was inside her head. Somehow, it wasn't.

It was like...he belonged there.

'About Avurn,' she blurted, desperate to fill the silence.

Kieran sat up abruptly, the water level falling past his chest. So he'd meant to discuss Avurn with her, huh.

'I know I should give him the benefit of the doubt,' Ami continued. 'Like you do, especially since you can see him in a way that I can't. I guess I'll never understand him.'

Kieran smiled. 'To be fair, Avurn doesn't make it easy to understand him. Obfuscation is one of his defence mechanisms. But, Ami, you can't keep assigning him the same role, even it helps you to make sense of him. He plays up to it, when he feels he needs to. But eventually it will stop being a performance.'

Ami felt a grimace pull at the skin on her cheeks. 'I'm being a shit to him, aren't I? Av was right, you know—people will die because of my decisions, no matter what I do. There's no way to avoid it. Going after my father is going to cost us dearly. And Neffron gets to live, because I want to capture him and hold him accountable for what he's done. He doesn't deserve that courtesy. Maybe I should go against my principles and shoot him.'

'That's not who you are,' Kieran told her gently. 'I won't let you betray a part of *yourself*, Ami. And not only that, the galaxy has to know that you didn't conquer a planet for selfish reasons, but to exact justice and cut off this arm of the slave trade. That's why having Grace with us is so important—we need her write the narrative.'

Ami snorted. 'It's a good thing I didn't make her get into the hold in orbit, huh. She's pretty useless otherwise. She could be helping you with your powers—or she could actually tell you what you need to know about your family, but *noooo*.'

'I'm sure she has her reasons,' Kieran said, but he didn't sound convinced.

'Right. Sure. There's definitely a reason for letting you wander around the galaxy, alone and confused and dangerous.'

'I'm not alone,' Kieran countered. 'I have you.'

Ami squirmed as his hungry gaze drowned her, consumed her, invited her in a way his words never would.

'Ouch!' she exclaimed.

'Are you alright?' Kieran asked.

'Neck cramps, shoulder cramps, back cramps—you name it,' Ami grumbled. 'Okay, that gym workout was a bad idea. Then there's the bonus stress of trying to liberate an entire planet! So yeah, I'm a little tense.'

Kieran made a circling motion with his hands. 'Turn around. I'll deal with it.'

Ami swallowed. Considered telling him to stark off. Knew she should say no instead of lighting this fuse. But she really was in pain.

Switching off her common sense as easily as she'd switched off the alarms on the *Free Ride*, Ami turned her back to him and crossed her arms on the edge of the spa. She was acutely aware of him closing in on her. Of the water lapping against her skin. Of his breaths kissing her neck.

His touch was gentle at first, but then he began to knead more deeply into her muscles, the intensifying pressure very, very welcome. Gods, that felt good. Her shoulders were the worst off; her lower back was a close contender. Kieran dealt with those and more. His fingers soothed every twinge that they uncovered.

Ami's eyes drifted shut—only to snap back open when one of his hands crept around to her stomach. But it didn't stop there. The hand went lower, to her thighs, which clenched reflexively as he worked on them.

She bit back the moan.

'Ami?' So much left unasked in that soft voice.

Ami didn't know how to answer him. He halted the massage and rested his hands on her abdomen, just firmly enough that she drifted back against his chest. Ami shivered as sparks erupted inside her, starting at her tightening nipples and then plunging into the folds that were already aching for him.

'Do you want me leave?' Kieran asked roughly.

'Gods, no,' Ami breathed. 'We're both adults, Kieran. We can keep this legit.'

It took a mere nanosecond for him to agree. 'Of course we can.'

How far could she push it? Push them both? They were balanced on the edge of a treacherous cliff and there was nothing below to break their fall.

Ami relinquished her hold on the side of the spa and flopped backwards, weightless and vulnerable, letting him steer her into the centre of the spa. His hands returned to her thighs and she held her breath, but his touch never went where she needed it the most. His thumbs dug into her flesh, massaging away the tension that had anchored there without her noticing.

'Relax,' Kieran told her.

Parts of her were relaxed, as ordered. Other parts...not so much.

His confident strokes mirrored the beating of her heart—or was it the other way around? She didn't care. A knot tightened and then abruptly released. Pleasure swelled in that one spot before radiating throughout her entire body. Ami gasped but he held her still, murmuring into her ear that he wasn't done with her, not yet.

Ami wriggled. His hardness pressing against her back wasn't uncomfortable, but it was prompting countless visuals of her spinning around and sliding down onto it.

'I hope you're not inside my head right now,' she remarked.

'I'm not,' he said. 'I've been getting better at withdrawing inside myself.'

'Yeah, I know. I was lightening the mood. Trying to, anyway. I can tell when you aren't in there. And when you are. I...I always know. In case you were curious, I'm not doing a very good job of finding innocent things to think about.'

He chuckled. 'I'm not surprised, given the situation. I have a feeling my imagination is no less *succinct* than yours.'

'Shut up and work on that knot you found about half a minute ago.'

Ami breathed deeply as his ministrations continued, neither fast nor slow, keeping her poised on the brink of indecision. But just like the bassline of some grungko song, she was throbbing for him with ever increasing intensity.

'Kieran...' she whispered. 'You need to stop. *Now.*'

He immediately revoked his touch, but she could still feel his handprints on her skin, a burning, lingering reminder despite the rapidly cooling water sloshing against her.

'We shouldn't let it get this far again.' Kieran paused. 'You're right about what it would mean, making love to you.'

Before she could regain her senses or say anything, he stood and vaulted over the rim of the spa, using one seamless motion to grab his jumpsuit and yank it over himself. The fabric deftly absorbed the water snaking over his body. He was mostly dry by the time he'd pulled on his boots and snapped his belt back into place.

Ami started to follow him, but then felt herself being lifted out of the water, droplets dripping away beneath her as Kieran used a forcefield to move her into his waiting arms. Ami leaned against his chest as he carried her into the next room. The bed was unmade and the sheets hadn't been washed since Taylar had been imprisoned, but Ami didn't plan on sticking around long enough to do the laundry.

Kieran laid her down gently and pulled the sheet over her body, the silksein lingering on her breasts like the caress of a lover. Ami trapped the sigh deep down inside her.

'What are you thinking?' he asked.

Ami snorted. *As if you need to ask me that.*

Still, he didn't pry. He waited her out. And that just made him even sexier, stark it. She managed a small smile that didn't hurt her cheeks as much as she'd expected it to. 'I'm thinking that the right decision is the one that will hurt me the most.'

'I'm sorry,' Kieran murmured.

'Do you think we can keep working together?' she asked. 'I'm not made of n'radian, Kieran. I might exhibit sudden and unexpected strength when it comes to facing off against slavers and my own tortured past, but I'm weak as far as you're concerned.'

He leaned away from her, but didn't leave the edge of the bed. 'We'll make it work. Even if I have to bring Pina-Sai on board to chaperone us.'

Ami shook so hard with laughter that the silksein sheets rippled around her.

'That'll kill the mood, alright,' she said, once she'd calmed down.

'Okay, sure. We can give it a go. But I'm worried this'll end in tears anyway. Or worse, a fiery explosion.'

He grinned. 'Which option do you prefer?'

'The fiery explosion, obviously! But, Kieran...' Ami sat up, the sheet gliding down her torso. He inhaled sharply but didn't look away. 'The moment one of us slips up? You're off my ship.' She frowned. 'If I actually manage to get myself ship after all this is over and done with. Whatever. Look, I don't want you touching me anymore. At all. Because it's obvious that neither of us can be trusted to keep things legit.'

'Noted,' Kieran said.

Ami rubbed her forehead. Her hand didn't quite drop in time to catch the yawn before it peeled out of her. And he kept watching her, still sitting there, not moving a single micrometre. He didn't want to leave her side and he wasn't going to until she showed him the door.

Oh well, someone had to be the adult here.

But she never got the chance to kick him out of the room.

THIRTY-EIGHT

'Kieran, I don't want to order you to go, but—'

He threw himself on top of her. Ami collapsed back onto the bed, struggling against his weight and preparing a piece of her mind —until she felt and heard the explosion. Jagged shards of Taylar's palace fell and shattered around them. The tremors chasing the initial blast were violent enough to take out a nearby wall.

Kieran fisted his hands into the pillows either side of Ami's head and lifted his body from hers. Debris skittered across the shield he'd erected above his back.

'Shit!' Ami exclaimed. 'What the stark was that?'

Kieran frowned. 'No idea. I didn't get much warning before the ceiling came down. I was afraid I wouldn't get a forcefield over you in time.'

His shield expanded, throwing every obstacle in its path out of the way. Kieran left the bed and moved to stand beneath the archway leading to the suite's antechamber, unfazed as more sections of the ceiling splintered apart and bounced away from the invisible barrier protecting him.

Ami rolled off the side of the bed and wrestled with the ruined dresser she'd stashed her spare clothes in. The wooden furniture had cratered beneath an impressive chunk of marble moulding. She sat back on her haunches, irritated and defeated, then grabbed the tired pile of clothes she'd been wearing all day and threw them on. She didn't dare check the underarms of her shirt. The jeans took some manoeuvring since her hands wouldn't quit trembling, but at least the boots didn't require her to fiddle with any complicated fastenings.

The next explosion sent her tumbling back towards the bed. Ami thought she'd managed to recover her footing, then realised she was hovering at a sharp angle, courtesy of a forcefield. Nodding her thanks to Kieran, she rightened herself. He vanished into the corridor before she could reach the archway.

Right. Now would be a good time to leave.

Ami left her lasgun on the floor—it was twisted and mangled, more likely to take off her fingers than take out anyone coming at her—and hurried after Kieran.

Without needing to discuss it, they both ran towards the main exit and burst outside, but they would never be able to reach their destination. The bridge connecting the tiered landing pads to the palace had become a blackened, twisted mess and Ami stood on the serrated edge of what remained, her fists knocking against her hips. A wide chasm yawned before her. The ships she had promised to those who'd wanted to leave Rochaccia—all gone. Even the smaller, higher landing pads hadn't been spared.

'It looks like Taylar's mines were set and detonated inside her own palace,' Kieran said in a low voice. 'I believe the catacombs were also targeted.'

'Oh gods,' Ami said, her eyes shooting downwards, as though she could see the destruction inside the rock beneath their feet. 'Someone betrayed us. I'll bet this *someone* also told Neffron the moment we'd taken Taylar down, which enabled him to grab her fleet and her mercs before we could. Stark, I was so stupid for not looking into how he did that! I just assumed he knew I'd do something to Taylar and had been waiting around for me to give him that opening. Stupid!' She spun towards Kieran. 'How many...how many of our people survived?'

His expression grew vacant as he scanned for lifesigns. It didn't take long for a grimace to appear.

'How many?' she repeated.

'Ami...'

'HOW MANY!'

'About a quarter of them,' Kieran said. 'I don't think all the mines in the catacombs went off as planned. And those who remain elsewhere, in the factories and outposts scattered across Taylar's territory, are still alive. For now.'

Ami wished she'd told Goss and the others to stay in the palace instead of the catacombs. Not that they would have listened to her—they'd had a good reason for sleeping down there.

Her vision swam. She thought the tears might come at last, but they didn't. She hated herself for being unable to properly grieve for the people who had lost their lives because of her. They'd have had a chance if she hadn't persuaded them to stay. They might have been able to escape the blockade ringing the planet. Maybe.

She didn't ask if Kieran had felt the lifesigns winking out, one by one, ten by ten—or in a single, horrific moment. She didn't want to know. And it was obvious that she and Kieran were still in danger. The dark sky was filling with lights, too big and bright to be mistaken for stars. Neffron's ships were descending. With a start, Ami realised that the anti-bombardment shield had vanished, either switched off or sabotaged. There was nothing to stop those ships wreaking further destruction on Taylar's headquarters.

'Avurn! Grace!' Kieran said suddenly and his head jerked, back towards the palace. He bolted in that direction. She followed.

Ami had always figured she was more of a sprinter than a marathon runner, but she was out of breath by the time they reached the entrance. Kieran skidded to a stop and looked over his shoulder, waiting for her to catch up.

'Unless your new personal shielding device is better than your old one, you'd better keep a forcefield up,' Ami told him and drew closer as he complied, so he wouldn't need to make it too large. 'That traitor might still be in here somewhere. There's no point finding Av and Grace if we're only going to lead danger right to them.'

The palace was eerily silent as they moved through it.

They checked the suites in the main corridor first—all empty. Then they tried the conference room attached to Taylar's office. Debris littered the floor; dust covered everything else. There was no sign of a fight or any smears of blood, but Kieran wavered in the doorway, eyelids flickering rapidly.

His lips formed a grim line. 'Lius, the one who didn't usually have nanobots injected into him—he contacted Neffron as soon as he was freed, revealing the state of Taylar's ships and offering to sabotage us. Neffron was more than happy to pay him for his services. Avurn and I sensed Lius' dislike of Taylar and assumed that meant he was on our side. Obviously, we were wrong. He deactivated the palace's shield, right here in this very room. Avurn and Grace walked in on him doing it, so Lius used his lasgun to stun Av and forced Grace to carry him outside. A small shuttle was waiting for them on the nearest landing pad.'

Icicles needled their way through Ami's guts. 'You can see into the past?'

'Yes. Maybe. I don't have another explanation for what I just saw. But a vision of the past doesn't help me! Why couldn't...why couldn't I see this coming?' Kieran cried, agonised. 'Why didn't I hear Avurn call for help in the link? I shouldn't have let myself get so distracted—and I should have looked deeper inside Lius' head before I trusted him. But I didn't! I was so afraid of going too far, seeing too much. This is my fault, Ami. Not yours.'

The floor bounced beneath them, heralding more explosions—except this time they came from outside the palace and bloomed so brilliantly that they turned night into day. Nope, not timed mines. These were targeted shots from heavy lascannons that could rip an armoured starship apart inside a minute. A planet-bound building without a shield was easy prey.

Ami swallowed. Her tongue rasped across the parched roof of her mouth. 'I think I know what happens next.'

Right on cue, Neffron's voice boomed through the corridors, causing more dust to stream down around them. Ami jumped as a beam dislodged from the ceiling and fell with enough force that it would have made her see stars—if Kieran's shield hadn't blocked and deflected it.

'Sweet little Ami, if you are in there...' Neffron's ensuing bark of laughter did its best to shatter what remained of the palace's foundations. He was using amplifying tech. 'I suggest you come out and face me. We have much to discuss, you and I.'

'He has Avurn,' Kieran said softly. 'I do not know where Grace is and I don't want to make assumptions, but I can't feel her lifesign nearby—or anywhere on this planet, in fact.'

Ami saw her own anxiety reflected in his eyes. 'Is Avurn able to free himself?'

'He's not responding in the link.'

Ami worried her lips together. Her father had started a fairly generous countdown—after announcing that he had multiple lascannons homed in on the lifesigns that his ship's sensors had picked up inside the palace. Blatant overkill, in Ami's opinion, since the building was already groaning ominously around them. They were starked—unless she managed to form some sort of plan.

Ami snapped her fingers. 'Taylar. We'll get her out of the panic room and trade her for Avurn.'

She ran down the corridor, only to freeze when she saw that her mother's panic room wasn't just inaccessible—it was non-existent. Ami stared at the gaping hole in the wall, nothing between her and the screaming wind. Taylar Naiman was dead. The woman who had tormented her constantly, throughout her childhood and in her memories as an adult, was gone for good.

Ami expected to feel something about her mother's death—grief, relief, shock—but there was only panic swelling inside her chest. Frankly, this wasn't that much of a setback. Neffron might have just blasted Taylar instead of trading Avurn for her anyway.

'Shit, okay,' Ami said. 'Can you look into the future for me?'

'What is it you're hoping I'll see?' Kieran asked.

'I don't know. A plan that doesn't fail? If not...well, at least we'll be prepared for the worst outcome.'

Kieran nodded and his eyes immediately lost focus. Ami doubted he heard Neffron issuing a final warning for them to come out and face the inevitable. She waited, dancing on the balls of her feet, for Kieran to come back to her.

Kieran blinked.

'I...' He visibly gritted his teeth. 'I don't see us winning this one, Ami. Not alone. We need...we need help.'

Ami turned and sprinted back towards the ruined bridge. Kieran matched her frantic pace. Neffron's countdown was getting worryingly low.

'What aren't you saying?' Ami asked, panting as she dropped into a jog.

'The Desine,' he said simply.

'Stark, that might actually be worse than our current options.'

Kieran's steps faltered. 'Ami, if I have to make a deal with the desert god in order to free Avurn...'

'Don't,' she said and slid her fingers through his, unable to stop herself. It had only been a few minutes since she'd decided that they shouldn't touch each other ever again—but if they were going to die, then it didn't really matter, did it? 'Don't even suggest it, Kieran. I would sacrifice a lot for Av, don't get me wrong, but we fought so hard to keep you safe from the Desine.' Ami tightened her grip. 'We'll figure something out. I'm sure we will.'

'Can I kiss you?' Kieran murmured. He didn't have to add 'one last time'. His meaning was clear.

'Yes,' Ami breathed. 'Gods, yes. But make it fast.'

Her lips still tingling from his bruising kiss, Ami stepped out into the glare shed by the spotlights on her father's ships. Kieran remained at her side. Close enough to touch. Close enough to feel the heat of his body and draw comfort from it.

A platform was hanging from Neffron's flagship, bordered by two mounted lascannons that could turn Ami and Kieran into a cloud of blood with a single shot. There on the platform was Neffron, grinning triumphantly, and at his feet was the crumpled form of a boy. Lius, adorned in gleaming n'radian armour clearly given to him by Neffron, knelt down and positioned a hyponeedle mere micrometres from Avurn's neck. The threat was obvious.

Ami stood very still, refusing to let her father have the satisfaction of seeing any outward sign of her rapidly multiplying fear. The platform dropped lower and lower, into the gap where the walkway used to be, then drifted towards the ruined palace. Neffron's fingers brushed the circular amplifying device sitting on the pressed collar of his shirt, but he didn't adjust the volume despite them now being close enough to read each other's expressions.

'Ami! Sweet little Ami!' he bellowed. 'Were you ignoring me? Did I raise my own daughter to be this disrespectful? Perhaps I need to discipline you again! Mind you, the laswhip never managed to correct your behaviour, did it? It's a good thing I brought lascannons instead.'

'Stark,' Ami hissed. 'How long will this shield of yours last, Kieran?'

'I managed to protect the *Free Ride* for several minutes before I ran into trouble,' Kieran said quietly. 'This shield isn't nearly as large. And I can draw on the stars to make it last longer, but doing so will exhaust me to the point of passing out. Even if I could protect us indefinitely, Neffron might inject Avurn anyway, out of spite—it's Rapture in that hyponeedle, not nanobots, but I do not want to risk it.'

'Can you throw a forcefield over Avurn?'

'In order to do that, I think I would need to sacrifice the shield hiding me from the Desine. Avurn isn't in a position to maintain it for me.'

'Well, better listen to what that starker wants then,' Ami said and waved at the platform.

Neffron's smile was cold and cruel. 'No doubt you wish to beg for my forgiveness. Here, this will make it easier.'

He hurled something towards her. It bounced on the concrete instead of shattering, then skidded towards Ami's boots. She bent down and retrieved the spare amplifying device, deliberately taking her time as she attached it to her own shirt. Having stalled as long as she could, she finally said, 'What do you want, Neffron? Just remember—you need me alive. I'm your heir.'

'Why would I need you?' Neffron demanded. 'Taylar is no longer with us, judging by a lack of lifesigns beyond the sorry pair I see before me. Perhaps you thought to use that old law to protect you—alas, it will not. I am not surprised you didn't bother to check if it had been amended before fumbling your way over here. Yes, Rochaccia's rulers must agree on an heir. But a ruler must be *alive* in order to make any objections and Taylar can no longer impede me. A single vote now triumphs.'

'Shit,' Ami said, then belatedly clapped a hand over her mouth.

Neffron's mocking laughter rocketed right through her bones. 'So you see, sweet little Ami, you have no other pieces to use in this game you unwisely chose to play with me. Your e-paper reporter friend is dead, so you cannot have her write something that turns the galaxy against me or persuades my clients to go elsewhere. I would have made her see things from my perspective, anyway. All it would have taken was a touch of Rapture, perhaps even a few lashes from the laswhip. As for your purple-clad companion...'

Kieran's hands were linked behind his back and his feet were positioned evenly beneath his shoulders. Ami had seen this stance reflected enough times in her viewport to recognise where it came from. Catching Ami's gaze, Kieran glanced down at himself and smiled briefly.

'...his powers are impressive, it's true,' Neffron continued, then gestured down at Avurn. 'But I need someone younger, someone more malleable. Lius here informed me of the boy's abilities—and how he had to rescue that weak excuse of a Chipper from Taylar. Why would I pass up the better option? He'll be an excellent heir. *And* he can double as a bodyguard!'

Ami cleared her throat. 'He can't protect you, Neffron. Avurn doesn't have the maturity or the training to use his powers properly. He's just a kid.' *Forgive me, Av. Hopefully you're still out cold or I'll never hear the end of this.*

But that's exactly what he was, wasn't he? Just a kid. And she had judged Avurn as she would an adult, thinking the worst of him and never giving him a chance to prove otherwise.

'Enough of this idle chitchat,' Neffron said. 'I have better things to do with my time. But I will allow you to say some last words, if you have any.'

Ami opened her mouth, but nothing emerged. Her skull was full of empty space.

All she could do was stand there, once again beaten by the man whose voice had always done more damage to her than his laswhip ever had.

THIRTY-NINE

The situation was beyond desperate.

Starships blanketed the sky above Ami and Kieran. Countless lascannons on those countless vessels were glowing hot, ready to blast them into oblivion. On the platform, Avurn remained limp and prone. Kieran felt nothing active at the boy's end of the link. His lifesign indicated that he still breathed, but that was it.

'Don't you dare hurt him!' Ami shouted at her father.

Neffron made a swift, cutting gesture across his throat. Lius jabbed Avurn with the hyponeedle. Kieran fixed a glare on Neffron and peeled his lips apart, exposing his clenched teeth. Even without the drug, Avurn would have been vulnerable to exploitation, especially when handed an entire world. Now he would be lost to them entirely—unless he'd managed to erect a mental shield, as Kieran had done. But the boy was unconscious.

'He's my heir now,' Neffron declared. He pointed at Ami. 'She is of no use to me. Kill her.'

A barrage of lascannon fire surged down on them, none of the blasts indistinguishable from each other as they merged into a constant swarm that smothered Kieran's shield and drowned them both in harsh red light. The wind battered him with blows that felt almost solid but Kieran kept his arms loose by his sides, forcing himself to breathe deeply and evenly. He had to make the shield last as long as possible.

'Gods, all the things I wish I'd done,' Ami whispered.

'Me too,' he said with feeling.

Kieran was well aware that his body would fail before his powers ever did. That wasn't his main concern. Even if they somehow survived this, he had no idea how to proceed, how to rescue Avurn, or how to deal with Neffron.

'We need a plan,' Ami murmured. 'And I've got nothing. I'm useless.'

Kieran's shield warped alarmingly when one of Neffron's ships fired an object larger and more devastating than a simple lascannon blast. A rocket-based missile, it had to be. Missiles were expensive, because they were disposable and coveted for their ability to reduce entire settlements to dust. Lascannons were deadly enough. But for the impatient buyer, they were much too slow.

Several more missiles follow the first, each extracting a flinch from Kieran that he felt right down to his gut. The ground beneath him shook and heaved. Still, the forcefield held.

'We need to retreat before we can make a plan,' he gritted out.

Ami's laugh was strained, incredulous. 'How do you suggest we do that? Ask them to stop firing long enough for us to escape?'

'I'm not going to ask *them* for anything.'

'Kieran, you can't. You can't! You can't do this to yourself.'

Kieran cupped Ami's face in his hands and leaned into her. She met him halfway, her kiss as desperate as his own. Her fingers tugged on the zipper of his jumpsuit, a promise of something more, something they might never get the chance to enjoy. The missiles striking Kieran's shield had started taking small bites out of it—and those bites were fast becoming chunks.

When they drew apart, Kieran looked into her eyes, seeing the tears she couldn't shed. 'Ami, I don't care what he does to me. I'd do anything to keep you safe.'

'Kieran...'

His thumb slid across her bottom lip. 'Ami, I...'

He'd never experienced this strong surge inside his chest before. Never found someone whose heart matched the beat of his own. Never felt a connection like the one that had formed between them —an unbreakable, flexible chain that moved to allow growth on both sides. Words seemed inadequate to convey any of this. So he shared his mind with her instead.

Ami gasped, took everything he gave her—and gave him everything in return.

Buoyed by her steady, unyielding support, Kieran closed his eyes, discarded the physical sensations that might have served as fatal distractions, and sank within himself. His mind took him to a barren plain of sand, the horizon smeared by dust in all directions. Visualising an astral body for himself, he spread his arms and called, 'Desine! I'm here.'

A sudden gale surged around him and scoured his face, furious, vindictive, and so blistering hot it could have emanated from an explosion. That meant the sub-level god had heard him, at least. But he needed a response. And he needed it *now*.

Kieran bowed his head. 'Please help me.'

You cast me out, the Desine hissed. The sand around Kieran began to ripple and roil like the surface of a restless ocean. *Just as so many others have before you.*

Kieran's jaw tightened, but he maintained his submissive posture.

'I know what I did,' he said. 'But can you blame me? After

what...what happened on Fintaz, I was afraid. Of myself. Of my powers. And of you. But I have not come to you so we can discuss our grievances. I am asking you to help me save Ami.'

Why would I help you?

Kieran drew a breath and exhaled, but he failed to expunge the trepidation that had taken root inside him. 'Because I will serve you. I will renounce GLEA and my god and worship you alone.'

A laugh, underscored by a baleful wind. *I accept that price, for I know how steep it is to you. But why are you sacrificing everything for this woman?*

'I love her.'

She will abandon you.

'Only if I asked her to do it! Please. *Please.*' Kieran blinked; his lips felt raw, as though they were grating against a rough surface. Concrete? He realised his body had fallen over and Ami was shouting in his ear, ordering him to come back to her.

His shield was failing.

He straightened and prepared to say more, to plead until he was hoarse, but then realised he didn't need to. He felt a change in the wind; it glided gently through his hair, almost like a tender gesture.

You will learn to use my powers, the Desine said. *And do as I bid you.*

'Anything,' Kieran promised.

Very well.

Kieran attempted to sit up when he returned to his body, but Ami firmly held him down. His shield was now so low and flat that it was close to crushing them. He did not panic. He simply turned his head to the side and watched the sand roar out of the deep chasm between Neffron's platform and the remnants of Taylar's palace, rising and rising until it crested into an immense wave, blotting out the ships and the starry sky beyond them.

Ami's eyes widened. Kieran gripped her hands in his.

The wave fell. But before it hit, before it could smother them, Kieran felt his body completely dissolve. Ami shouted his name. Sand trickled from the fingers she tried to touch him with. If he'd still possessed a mouth, he would have screamed.

He was the sand. He was the desert. And he was rapidly losing his very being, just as he'd lost the flesh and blood that housed it.

Stay calm! the Desine told him. *I am here now. I'm here for you.*

Kieran tried to hold onto the arms that roped around him, but he fell into darkness.

SHADOWS FOLLOWED her as she paced her prison, cold and alone, trapped in an eternal void that was so much worse than walls and chains.

There was no escape. Oblivion had no beginning—and no end.

The screams tore from her throat.

Her usual nightmare was abruptly cut short. Ami woke with a gasp and sat up, her blood pounding in her ears.

A blanket slithered down her torso, exposing her bare skin to the cool, dry air. Cursing, Ami grabbed the blanket and pulled it back over herself. The cave enclosing her was gouged into beige, gritty rock, the type that should have been made by innumerable grains of sand being packed together over millennia. But Ami had a feeling this structure was a lot younger than that. And created by a sole sentient being.

The perfectly square hole in the ceiling served as a skylight, allowing Ami to case out her surroundings. Her gaze roamed along the seamless walls of the cave before sweeping across the wavy, unstable ground. No weapons. No food. Not a single stitch of clothing. Aside from the blanket, she had nothing to work with. Nothing to wield against a god.

Okay, there was a pool of water up against one side of the cave, but it was barely deep enough to wash her hands in and definitely couldn't be used to drown someone.

Beside her, Kieran lay supine on the sand, his eyes gyrating frantically beneath his eyelids. His lips parted to emit a strangled sound. Warm relief coursed through Ami, replacing the lingering chill her nightmare had left behind. Good. He was in one piece. She couldn't quite remember why she'd been worried about him not being...whole.

Awkwardly pinning the blanket under her armpits, Ami knelt and grasped his shoulders, giving them a shake. 'Kieran!'

He shot upright, nearly ramming into her in the process. 'Ami! Where—where are we?'

'I don't know,' she answered, pressing her forehead against his, ignoring the tingling in her lips that demanded she apply pressure to them as well. 'What's the last thing you remember?'

Kieran clenched fistfuls of the blanket, causing it to drop to a perilous position on Ami's torso. 'I...I lost my body. Oh God, I turned into *sand*.'

Disjointed images dripped through Ami's mind like the beads of sweat escaping his brow. She shook her head, but the memories didn't surface, not completely. She remembered the fear, though. The fear that she had lost him at the exact moment she knew she could never let him go.

'The shield was failing,' she said slowly, her words gathering momentum as her voice steadied. 'Everything went dark, like the oblivion I dream about sometimes. I think I fell unconscious. Or maybe I pushed myself there. Things were *bad*. I don't mean to sound ungrateful, but I can't say I'm a huge fan of the Desine's method of transportation—and don't ask me what he did with our clothes, because I have no idea.'

Kieran glanced down at himself then up at her, a smile dancing over his lips.

Ami barked out a laugh. 'Really? The desert god teleports us, imprisons us, steals our clothes—and you're thinking about sex?'

'I'm thinking about a lot of things, actually,' Kieran said, relaxing his grip on the blanket. Ami did not pull it back up. 'Like how glad I am that you're here, because there's no one else I'd rather be trapped inside a rock with.'

'Yeah, okay. That's your story and you're sticking to it, huh. But you should know that you're not the only one thinking about *a lot of things.*'

His smile became increasingly unrepentant.

The air between them shifted as a gentle waft of wind stole its way through the skylight-esque hole in the rock. When the breeze touched his face, Kieran sighed deeply and titled his head to the side, as though a great weight had been lifted from his shoulders. Ami watched him closely. Something was strange about this situation and it wasn't just the cave...it was him. *He* was different. He wasn't the Chipper she had met.

'Kieran?' she asked softly. 'What did you do?'

'I offered to serve and worship the Desine. I didn't expect...' His throat bobbed as he swallowed. 'I didn't expect to feel...'

'What did you feel?'

'He was happy,' Kieran murmured. 'Elated. After waiting for so long. And it was as if...' He blinked. 'He embraced me.'

Ami waited him out for a short while, until she was sure he wasn't going to say any more.

'None of this makes sense,' she said. 'Nothing Ralcha told me matches up to my experiences with the Desine so far. I have no idea how to get us out of this mess. I'm also really thirsty, but I know how to deal with that at least.'

Ami stood and kicked the blanket away from her feet. Kieran's gaze followed her as she moved to the edge of the cave, ducking to avoid grazing her head on the strangely smooth ceiling as it sloped downwards. She sat back on her heels beside the pool of water and cupped some of it up to her mouth, drinking deeply.

Her thirst quenched, Ami wiped the back of her hand over her mouth and said, 'As far as prison cells go, this is a pretty good one. I definitely can't fit through that hole. Stark. How long do you think the Desine intends on keeping us here?'

Gods. Avurn. The longer her crewmate remained in Neffron's clutches, the less of a chance she had at rescuing him. Could she ask the Desine for help? Would the desert god even care that an innocent boy's life was at stake?

The unflappable façade she'd spent years building and perfecting began to disintegrate.

No! Kieran needs me to keep my shit together. I've been through worse. I've been through so much worse. Haven't I? Stark! I can't, I can't fall apart now...

The shivers were threatening to consume Ami when Kieran's warmth suddenly surrounded her. She let herself go limp as Kieran braced her against his chest, her legs nestled between his. Kieran said nothing. Just held her. Let her feel his presence without intruding on her thoughts. He was also shivering, she realised, but their combined discomfort eased as they drew strength from each other.

'We need to save Av,' she said.

Kieran rested his chin on her shoulder. 'You may have to do it without me. I can ask the Desine to release you, but I'm not sure he will let me go now...now that I've agreed to be his.'

Ami snorted. That sudden injection of righteous indignation on Kieran's behalf did wonders for scouring the rest of the fear and uncertainty from her head. 'Nonsense. Ralcha, the Yabul chief back on Ilbb, gets to do whatever he wants. He has a family. He has friends. He watches lasball tournaments on the Web—I'm pretty sure he does, anyway—and chases Xan and Denton back to Carton City in the same day. I've never heard of a single Desine worshipper being locked up inside a starking rock.'

'Have any of them refused to worship the one who gave them their powers?' Kieran asked.

'I'd be surprised if some hadn't,' Ami said. 'I've run into hundreds of former desert folk who've migrated to cities in the domains of other gods and they all had the Magic. Plenty of beings move around the galaxy—us humans in particular, you can't tie us down to one planet. Or one climate. And we're allowed to choose who we worship. The Creator God made sure of that. Free will, Kieran. You're good.'

Kieran sounded resigned. 'I don't think it's that simple. I can't undo what I've done. For all my powers...I am *powerless*.'

'Kieran...' Ami trailed off.

'Yes, Ami?'

She pointed. 'Look.'

Inside the cave, the sand was tossing and turning, agitated and restless. Ami held her breath, waiting, but no one came, no simmering entity appeared. She twisted around slightly and looked up into Kieran's pale, defeated face.

'It's me,' he said in a broken whisper. 'I'm doing that. I can feel it.'

'With your chipless powers?' she asked.

He bit his lip. 'No, it's...it's the Magic. Oh God, Ami. I promised the Desine anything. *Anything*. What if he wants me to hurt people? These powers are dangerous! And the things I can do with them...'

The sand shifted beneath Ami, evoking a tickling sensation at first, but then its movements became sensuous. Targeted. An intimate exploration of her body. Ami instinctively arched her back as soft grains began to creep up from her toes. Kieran's mind, so close to her own, revealed the delight that this use of his powers gave him.

He could cause pleasure instead of pain.

Ami slid her hands over his, which were anchored on her thighs. 'Kieran. Are you able to lock up these powers behind that shield in your head?'

'I don't think I want to,' he admitted.

She forced the groan back down her throat, but it was too late. He'd felt her fingers tighten on his own. He'd seen the desire building inside her.

It should have been embarrassing to be turned on by the touch of *sand*.

But it wasn't. Because it was his touch.

The sand caressed her calves, then her knees, moving its way up her body, working in tandem with his hands; he curved one around her hip and the other cupped her breast, a thumb teasing her pebbled nipple. His kiss on her shoulder, chaste and gentle though it was, completely eroded her last shred of resistance.

'Should I stop?' he asked lowly, the sand and his fingers stilling.

This time the groan escaped. 'Kieran...'

'Should I stop?' he repeated.

'Gods, no,' she said, then laughed breathlessly. 'I'd just prefer this to happen in a less cramped section of our prison. If you don't mind.'

His chuckle rolled over her, a deep, unhurried sound that raked heat across her skin. Ami took his hand and led him back over to the blanket. She lay down, palms flat against her stomach as he stood above her, darkness claiming his eyes and transforming their bright blue into something chasmic.

She wondered what he was thinking. So she asked.

He smiled as he lowered himself beside her. 'I was just thinking...that the desert god will never possess as much of me as you do.'

FORTY

Kieran paused, savouring the bright spark that his words had evoked in Ami's energy. His desire for her was reaching painful levels, stoked further by memories of their stolen moments together. He forced himself to go slow, ignoring the temptation to place his hands anywhere but her face as he leaned in and kissed her. Her lips parted, an invitation for more, and he basked in the long, luxurious caresses that followed.

'Gods, I need you inside me,' Ami moaned.

Kieran knew she meant something more than merely physical. She wanted him back inside her mind. He went there willingly.

Her kisses quickly became feverish, consuming. Kieran met her with equal enthusiasm, fully unrestrained for the first time in his life. He was no longer a Chipper. He was a man who had pledged himself to another god, a man who had abandoned his purpose and the galaxy, a man whom even Lieutenant Pina-Sai would not find the patience for, nor the forgiveness. But now no one could order Kieran to marry a stranger and raise a stranger's children.

Kieran separated his lips from Ami's to study her beautiful features.

If he said the words, he would be admitting defeat, admitting that he was divorced from the path he had chosen.

'I love you,' he murmured.

Ami's eyes glistened. She smeared a hand over them and stared in surprise at the dampness on her palm. 'Kieran...I know what you had to do to save me, what you had to sacrifice. I'm not worth that.'

'I've made my choice, Ami,' Kieran said. He leaned forward and nestled his face into the gap between her breasts, lapping up the sweat that had gathered there, drawing a soft gasp from her. 'I've lost nearly everything. Please...I don't want to lose you too.'

Ami's fingers slid through his hair. Kieran shuddered as she stroked his scalp, an area he had never considered erogenous before now. He remained still as she worked away at a knot, glad he no longer needed to observe the regulations that governed a human agent's appearance—including how much hair they could grow. He would always keep it at this length. So she could touch him like this.

When he looked up at her again, there was a single tear wending its way down her face.

'I would never have made you leave GLEA,' she murmured. 'Or made you renounce the Creator God and your purpose. So help me, I will find a way for you to save the galaxy without them.'

'I know you will.' He believed her, utterly and completely.

Ami pulled him into a brief, chaste kiss. She drew back again, smiling even as more tears began to fall. 'I love you. But you already knew that.'

'I still cherish hearing it,' Kieran said quietly.

Kieran glanced around the cave when he heard the voices, the ever-present whispers, and realised they belonged to the endless sands. And they were not naturally violent, just extremely sensitive to his thoughts and feelings. On Fintaz, they had come to his aid and he'd unknowingly wielded them, his fury feeding the ensuing storm. This time, he was aware of the sands awaiting his next commands. He would need to be more careful in the future. He knew that. But right now…

He kissed his way down Ami's throat, intent on claiming a breast and lathering it with attention. The saltiness of her skin was addictive. He needed to lick and savour every micrometre of her, especially between her legs, where his fingers found her hot and wet for him. Ami wriggled and laughed, telling him to give her a moment so she could get herself ready. He withdrew, grinning.

The tears were gone. Her eyes sparkled with light and love.

She hooked her hands onto his shoulders, raised one eyebrow, then rolled him off the blanket and onto his back. When the shifting sands touched his bare skin, exhilaration raced through Kieran like an electrical current. Smirking, Ami lifted one finger, dabbed it with her tongue, made sure he was watching, and then raked it across his nipple. Kieran gasped and jerked. God! She'd barely started to touch him.

'You're mine,' she said.

'Yes,' he whispered. 'Yours. Forever. And I would love to taste you, Ami. Please.'

Distantly, Kieran was aware of water dripping somewhere in the cave, of the sand murmuring its approval all around them, of his heartbeat rising to a crescendo in his ears, as Ami positioned her moist folds above his mouth. His breathing quickened. His need to pleasure her was as desperate as his need to plunge inside her.

He couldn't remember a time when he had been gripped with such fervour. The few times he'd slept with someone had been due to curiosity or so he could relieve himself. He'd never known he could feel this way—happy, excited, and *free*. He was hers and she was his. Nothing stood between them.

His body ached to be as entwined with her as his soul already was.

'Can't really think of a reason to deny you,' Ami said with a short laugh and lowered herself into his intimate kiss.

AMI BRACED a hand against the ground, her other fingers buried in his hair as he delved between her thighs. The firm, steady glides of his tongue along the edges of her sex had her panting in seconds. He definitely knew what he was doing. She managed not to beg him to lick the knot of nerves that ached for his attention, but he heard her mental pleas, dutifully obeyed, and then drove her closer to her peak with patient precision.

When she slipped forward, her shattered focus causing her to lose balance, his tongue found her entrance and speared up inside it. The ensuing hot stab of pleasure multiplied into intense bolts that rocketed out in every direction. Her entire body shook.

'Ohhh!' Ami cried out. 'Kieran, I...*oh*...'

Somehow, she managed to crawl off Kieran, despite her trembling legs. She looked aside at him, at the moisture glistening on his lips, at the adoration in his eyes—and then her gaze roamed down his chest and taut abdomen, lingering on the telltale sign of his desire for her.

She kissed him, pleased and incredibly turned on by the taste of herself in his mouth. His response was deep, devoted, unhurried. If he hadn't shared his thoughts with her, if she couldn't feel his hardness against her thigh, she would have thought that he was content to merely hold her. Ami slid her fingers along his jaw, her heart so full it was practically bursting.

But her heart had nothing to do with what she said next. 'I've got the pregnancy implant. All in working order. Figured I should mention it before I sit on your cock.'

Kieran's hips jolted beneath her. 'God!'

'Should we be doing this now?' she asked, rocking back onto her haunches. 'I mean, yeah, we're stuck in a cave and we're both naked, but surely there's a better time for it.'

'Ami, please...' He tenderly lifted stray strands of her hair away from her face. 'I don't know if the Desine will allow us to be together again and I don't want to waste the only chance we might have. I want you. I want this.'

Ami marvelled that so many tears could leak from her eyes after so many years of drought. She blinked rapidly, dispelling the moisture, and vowed to have a stern word or two with the Desine when he inevitably showed up. This wasn't going to be the last time she and Kieran saw each other. She would make sure of that.

But right now, she was going to bathe him with her love.

Ami moved her kisses down his body, excited by the keening, desperate sounds that left his lips in response. Kieran writhed beneath her when she deliberately avoided his shaft, swiping her tongue across patches of his abdomen and inner thighs, never quite arriving at the destination he was clearly hoping she'd reach. She slid one finger beneath his balls, teasing the sensitive skin there and wrenching a breathy exclamation from him. It might have been her name.

Thrilled by how much power she had over him, Ami wrapped her hand around his cock and drew the pulsing head between her lips.

Kieran's head dropped back against the sand. A low groan left him as she encased him with her mouth, her tongue playing along the bottom of his shaft and her fingers skating upwards to flick one of his nipples. He fisted the sand either side of him, his hips rising, his breaths short and sharp. His desperate thoughts crashed into hers. He'd do anything, *anything*, to be inside her.

Ami slowly, teasingly released him, her eyes seeking his. He nodded.

She slid down his hard length, her hand circling him and sliding ahead of her wet heat. When they were fully joined, they stayed still for several long seconds, their breaths mingling and their faces anointed in dusky light. Ami closed her eyes, a wave of dizziness descending on her. This wasn't just sex. This was an everlasting union.

She heard a gentle sighing, as though they were enclosed by trees shifting in a breeze, and looked around the cave. The sand was vibrating urgently now. Clouds of it rose into the air, reflecting the restlessness of the man who controlled it. Ami shivered when the sand danced over her body and through her wild, unbound hair, her skin tingling as his powers explored her.

Kieran rested his hands on her hips, his blue eyes shining. 'That's me, Ami. That's me touching you.'

'I know. And it feels *amazing*.'

Time to wipe that smug grin off his face. She tightened her inner walls around him and his nails dug into her flesh, hard enough to leave dents. He mouthed her name.

Oh yes. He was definitely hers.

Ami clenched again. The ensuing sensations that rippled through her made her squirm, the movement eliciting a sharp spasm from his shaft. *That* felt even better. Ami eased her weight forward onto her hands, grinding her fingers into the sand either side of his head, and kissed him deeply. He thrust his tongue into her mouth, a delicious reminder of what he'd done to her earlier.

He was thinking about it, too. His mind was consumed with the memory of how she'd tasted, how he'd drowned in her.

'Maybe I'll let you do it again,' Ami murmured. 'If you're good.'

'I'll be better than good,' he promised.

Smirking, she began to move at a slow pace, an exquisite torture for them both. It also allowed her to glance down his abdomen to watch his shaft reappear after each stroke, glistening with her arousal. Gods, that was hot. Ami bit her lip and groaned, distracted. This gave Kieran the opening he'd clearly been waiting for. He grabbed her backside with both hands and pulled her down on top of him, the hair on his chest grazing her nipples and sending shocks of pleasure straight down to her core.

His body shifted rhythmically beneath her, his muscles hardening and contracting. Ami rocked backwards and forwards in response, positioning her hips so that he hit that sweet spot inside her. Again and again and *again*.

She buried her face in his neck and anchored herself there. He smelled of sweat and sex—a devastating combination. Her throbbing folds gripped him even harder. Kieran groaned his appreciation and his pace quickened. The sand continued its sensual caress, targeting the areas of her body his hands couldn't reach.

She was at the mercy of his powers. Powers that were capable of immense destruction. Powers dedicated entirely to her pleasure. She was the only one he'd touched this way, the only one he would *ever* touch this way.

This was the thought that tipped her over the edge.

Ami arched her back and stared unseeingly at the ceiling of the cave, her orgasm swelling low in her core before it claimed every micrometre of her. Each deep thrust of him inside her prolonged it. The intense, unrelenting pleasure began to overwhelm her, threatening to send her tumbling into the darkness creeping in from the edges of her vision.

'Stay with me,' he pleaded and she could not deny him.

His hands rode her hips, guiding them, helping her match his frantic pace. Ami felt her folds give one last, desperate squeeze, so tight he could barely move. With a shout, he exploded, filling her with a burst of heat. The ground inside the cave erupted, there was a howl of wind—and then the sand fell, still and silent, its master sated.

Kieran went limp. Ami barely managed to remain upright for a few extra seconds before collapsing on top of him.

She lay there for a while, boneless and happy, enjoying the movement of his chest beneath her as he drew deep, even breaths. There were a lot of things she didn't want to think about just now. So she remained in that pleasant daze, warmed by her lover, relishing his lax smile when looked down at her. His fingers trailed along her arm, leaving delightful tingles in their wake.

His voice was soft, wistful. 'That was wonderful. I wish we could do it again.'

'Why can't we?' she demanded, sitting up.

'The Desine...'

'Only has your worship and your service,' Ami said, pinning her knees underneath her chin and winding her arms around her legs. 'And your desert-based powers...from what I've seen, I think you can leave this rock any starking time you want to.'

'I don't want to leave,' he said. 'I can't face the galaxy after I abandoned it.'

Ami emerged from the cocoon she'd made out of her limbs and grabbed his jaw, forcing him to meet her gaze. 'You didn't do that by choice, alright? You were pushed. So the galaxy is going to fall apart? We'll just have to glue it back together. Somehow. I'm sure Avurn will have a few ideas. And if the Desine won't help us—well, fuck him. We can do this on our own.'

Kieran's lips twitched. 'God, I love you.'

Ami glared at a nearby patch of sand, wondering if a certain sub-level god was eavesdropping on them. 'The Desine hasn't sent me away yet. That says something about our chances of staying together. But you know what? It's not up to him. I'm not going anywhere. He can't get rid of me.'

'No, he can't, though he will try,' Kieran murmured. Ami knew he was looking into the future. Whatever he saw made him smile. 'But you're more than a match for him.'

'You bet your butt I am,' Ami said.

After that, there was no more talking. She distracted him with heated kisses that drew him into a much longer, less desperate session of lovemaking. He let her take him beyond all rational thought, their fears and worries forgotten.

They lost themselves in each other.

FORTY-ONE

He wants to speak to you, the sand told him.

Kieran stirred. The dim light in the cave had taken hours to finally succumb to darkness, but now orange shadows danced over the ceiling and he could hear the crackle of flames, the sizzle of meat. He rolled onto his knees, pausing when he realised that the source of light was bouncing through a doorway that had seemingly grown up into the rocky wall. Outside, stars dotted the sky like pinpricks on black silksein, shimmering faintly, a distant promise of the power they could give him.

Ami slept on, the blanket tangled around her body. Kieran bent down and kissed her forehead. She was beautiful. Clever. Brave. And he had no idea what he'd done to deserve her.

Kieran dressed himself in the cloak he found folded nearby. He used a strip of fabric to tighten it around his body, missing the security of his uniform's zipper. Reluctantly, he left Ami's side and lingered in the doorway, inhaling and exhaling, overwhelmed.

Deserts terrified him, yes, but they were also entrancing. They called to him. And a part of him answered that call.

A similarly cloaked form sat there on the sand, waiting, deep brown cowl drawn over his features. The desert god. Kieran perched on the opposite side of the small fire, careful to keep his eyes trained on the meats roasting above the flames on a spit. He felt more than heard the wall close behind him, trapping Ami within the cave once more. He would have been anxious had the sand inside not told him that she was safely ensconced in her dreams.

Kieran realised he could actually *see* Ami. The information the sand gave him was more than mere words; it also contained images. Her arm lay across the empty space his body had occupied and a frown twisted her lips as she sensed his absence. He was tempted to return to her, to wake her and worship her in ways that no one else ever could.

Kieran blinked, clearing his vision.

'I envy you,' the Desine rasped.

Kieran tossed a few stray grains of sand into the fire. 'Why? I am burdened by these powers you gave me. I could kill thousands of innocent people with them.'

A chuckle slid out from beneath that cowl, dry and jaded. 'She doesn't know what you truly are, not yet. But she will. You are enjoying those blissful moments before she leaves you forever. I remember what that was like.'

Kieran swallowed. He didn't want to risk angering the god, but...there was a lonely gust of wind swirling beyond the nearest dune, full of misery and pain.

'You lost someone,' Kieran said.

The desert surged around him. Kieran threw up his cloak just in time to avoid being battered by spheres of sand. He lowered his arm and another wave of gritty projectiles came for him, but his swift hands-free shield effortlessly repelled them. The Desine's attack collapsed into a pile of sand in front of Kieran. When he looked back at the shrouded figure on the other side of the wavering fire, he felt *surprise* emanating from the god.

'You have a lot of my father's power,' the Desine noted. 'The chip was suppressing that as well. I should have guessed, given how easily you cast me out over Yalsa 5.'

Kieran pressed his lips together for a moment. 'Your father. The Creator God. Which god is actually responsible for me?'

'*You are mine.*' The venom infecting the god's tone struck Kieran like a lasbolt, but he did not allow himself to be cowed by it.

'I agreed to worship you, to serve you,' Kieran said. 'But I am not yours, not completely. I belong to Ami. I belong at her side.'

'Because you see her in those *visions* of yours,' mocked the god. 'That isn't destiny. It's entrapment. The Creator God only gives you the visions he wishes you to see. He's herding and prodding you into a pen, like a mindless beast.'

Kieran frowned. 'I don't need those visions to tell me how I feel about Ami.'

The Desine stabbed a stick into the flames, causing them to roar high into the air, turbulent and full of fury. 'Do you intend to keep defying me at every turn? Ignoring me and yet expecting me to stay your hand when you kill too many of the people you are trying to save?'

'No, I intend to learn how to use the Magic, so I can avoid relying on you,' Kieran replied. 'But right now, I don't have the time to master these powers.'

'You want to return to Rochaccia and save that boy,' the Desine said flatly. 'But how can you do that here, on Ilbb, with no starship to take you back?'

Kieran drew a startled breath and glanced up at the stars. Aside from Gerasnin, he hadn't stayed long enough on any world he'd visited to learn their night skies. He didn't recognise these constellations, so he couldn't be sure that he was on Ilbb or where exactly he was on the planet. Even if the Desine was telling him the truth, he could be hours or weeks away from the Agency's outpost—not an easy trek for a mortal. But it was an insignificant distance to a god who could seemingly move between worlds.

Kieran lifted his chin. 'I *will* return to Rochaccia. You'll take me there yourself and you'll even assist me in liberating it.'

'Why would I do that?'

'A large part of Rochaccia lies within your domain.'

'No one on Rochaccia worships me.' Bitterness tainted the Desine's voice. 'No desert there deserves its god.'

Ami would have wielded some clever, cutting response. Kieran struggled to do so himself. Instead, his temper got the better of him and he hammered a fist into his hand. 'Stark you! Rochaccia needs your help! That planet is a major source of slavery in this part of the galaxy—people are being torn from their families—'

'Just as my family was torn from me!' the Desine roared. A clump of sand rose and fell over the fire, dousing it. 'They should feel the same pain!'

Kieran fell silent.

It wasn't fear that had chased the retort from his mouth, but a sudden ache of unwanted sympathy. The agony in the god's energy was like a constant simmer, one that could steam away every drop of moisture from the deepest ocean in the galaxy.

The Desine carelessly waved a hand, his powers bailing the sand away from the smoking embers of the fire. 'I made you. I brought you here to teach you and care for you. I put you in a position to consummate your feelings for the woman you love, an act that should have driven the final wedge between you and the Chippers. Why do you still resist your fate? What more can I do?'

A plaintive note threaded its way through those last few words and Kieran felt the god's irritation give way to something else, something desperate...

He wants me on his side badly enough that I can negotiate.

Kieran knew this situation was unusual, given what Ami had told him about her friend on Ilbb, but he couldn't outright demand answers from a sub-level god. Not when he needed that god's help. And he definitely couldn't express how angry he was that the Desine thought he was in any way responsible for what had transpired between Kieran and Ami inside the cave.

'Accept that there is more to me than subservience,' Kieran finally said.

He dropped his chin, waiting for the next attack—a blow, a kick, or a swarm of sand. But nothing happened. And then he felt it, the hand gently nestled on the crown of his head, the fingers ruffling through his hair.

'You are more like me than you know,' the Desine said. 'I will help you. But do not forget the promise you made me.'

Kieran gritted his teeth and resisted the overwhelming urge to jerk away from the god's touch. 'Don't worry. I can't forget what I have done.'

<hr>

AMI MANAGED NOT to pelt Kieran with too many questions when he roused her later, holding out a set of folded clothes and a pair of boots. They were all new and fit her perfectly, although she wondered about the choice of colour—everything was in black. So too were the jeans and fitted shirt Kieran was wearing. Catching her look, he remarked that the Desine wasn't overly fond of his purple jumpsuit. Ami wasn't surprised.

'My clothes were probably too disgusting,' she said with a snort.

Kieran grimaced. 'It was a deliberate choice on the Desine's part to remove our clothes before he imprisoned us in here together. He seemed to think the outcome would keep me from ever returning to the Agency.'

There were two ways she could have responded to that. The first wouldn't be nearly as satisfying since the object of her ire wasn't present—and Ami supposed she was in a good enough mood to go with the second, less shouty one. 'Well, there you go. The Desine sees me as the most convenient obstacle standing between you and GLEA. Which means he has no intention of getting rid of me. We're stuck with each other now. How horrible.'

She kissed his smile as soon as it appeared.

Kieran led her out of the cave and into blazing daylight, revealing a sumptuous array of food and drink resting on top of a large embroidered rug. It seemed perverse, sitting there and enjoying a picnic while there were so many others suffering.

Kieran told her everything about his conversation with the Desine—and what he intended to do about the situation on Rochaccia. Ami nodded in all the right places and made sure to fill the holes in his plan with her own ideas, but now that she knew she was on Ilbb her mind kept fleeing across the desert, to the empty unit that belonged to Avurn. Jensa had no idea what had happened to her brother. The guilt gnawed at Ami's stomach.

Kieran took her hands into his and kissed her knuckles. He didn't need to say anything. Didn't have to reassure her. Knowing that he was hers, fully and completely, was all the comfort she needed.

'I've never heard of a sub-level god taking this much interest in one mortal before,' Ami said. 'Never mind agreeing to that mortal's demands. Or helping said mortal hook up in a cave. Wow, I really don't understand gods. Look, Kieran, there's too much we don't know about this situation. I don't trust the Desine. At all.'

Kieran looked troubled. 'I agree. But we need his help.'

'And he was cool with you deciding to bring the Chippers into this?' she asked.

'I didn't mention that part of my plan, no,' Kieran admitted. 'I have a feeling the Desine doesn't like GLEA or the Creator God overly much.'

That explained a lot, Ami thought. The animosity between the Desine's worshippers and those who followed the Creator God was legendary and millennia in the making, though no one could pinpoint when it had begun. It made sense if the conflict had stemmed from the gods themselves.

Ami shook her head. 'Stark. I'm not sure if this new ambitious side of you is going to get us both killed, but I love you all the more for it.'

'I wish we had more time here...' he murmured, eyes dancing.

Ami leaned forward and darted her lips over his. 'We'll have plenty of time for that later.'

He pulled her into his lap, holding her close to him as he stood from the sand. She laughed as he swung her around, flailing her legs and mock-scolding him for trying to seduce her when they had so much else to do. Kieran grinned, offering her a much deeper kiss. She took it, gave as good as she got, and sneaked a hand down to squeeze his backside. When her boots dipped into the sand once more, Ami wondered how it was that she felt so sure-footed, especially since she'd never had a serious relationship before.

'Ami...' Kieran hesitated. 'I don't know who I am anymore. But I do know who I want to be with.'

He let her see what he was about to do, what he was about to say, the commitment he was about to make to her. Oh gods. No.

Ami sealed her fingers over his lips. 'Kieran...stop right there. Don't ask that question. Not now. I don't want you to do it when we're in middle of this chaos, but when it's quiet again and we can plan our future together properly, okay?'

He smiled. 'I'd like that. I look forward to planning a future with you.' His eyes slid past her, to the endless dunes. 'Desine, we're ready!'

Before Ami could open her mouth and ask what they were ready *for*, a gust of wind drove her back into Kieran's arms. She could do nothing but watch helplessly as the sand rose into a funnel around them, a roaring vortex with two mortal beings at its epicentre.

But Kieran didn't look afraid. In fact, he seemed...almost eager.

Ami held on tight to Kieran and shook her head at how absurd this was, being carried across space by mere sand instead of a starship.

Within moments, they were back on Rochaccia.

FORTY-TWO

Ami dropped to the ground, slithering up alongside Kieran and dodging the largest rocks in her way. She reached the cliff and peered over the edge at the vast field of starships below. With their sharp spikes and interlocking plates of shining n'radian, they looked strikingly similar to reptilian animals lazing in the sun, waiting to pounce on unsuspecting prey. And this was only part of Neffron's fleet; these ships were undergoing regular maintenance and upgrades before rejoining the picket of death ringing the planet.

Kieran drew a deep breath. 'Desine. Guide me. Use me.'

Ami shivered as a dark shadow passed over her. The sky vanished as torrents of dust and sand combined to form a heavy, oppressive cloud that hung there for several long moments, an unmistakeable omen.

And then it fell.

The cloud flattened out into an immense, gritty sea that swallowed everything in its path, churning in a way that reminded Ami of a feeding frenzy she had witnessed in an ocean when she'd done a foodstuff run to New Sydney with Avurn. But that wasn't chum down there. It was Neffron's ground crew. Living, breathing beings.

'They are unharmed,' Kieran assured her. 'The Desine protected them from me. He ensured that the ships took the brunt of my powers instead. And he'll transport the crews of the other vessels before I...'

His eyes went skyward, distant and unfocused.

At first, nothing happened—but then she saw them. Ships streaking through the atmosphere, the air beneath them glowing white from the rough re-entry, each and every one of them yanked out of orbit by a single man. Some hulls broke apart in the atmosphere. The vessels that made it through ploughed into rock and sand, shattering on impact and then transforming into blazing craters. Ami winced. Neffron had always been fond of the more powerful, more volatile power cores.

She could hear shouts of alarm and confusion down below, from both the ground crew who had witnessed the storm and the starship crews who had suddenly found themselves standing on sand instead of coasting through space. They'd escaped with their lives. But there was no time for them to celebrate, because a new cloud had roared into the sky.

This wasn't meant to happen. With the ships either destroyed or disabled, Kieran and Ami were free to move on with the next phase of the plan.

Kieran didn't flinch. Didn't even seem to realise what he was doing.

Ami grabbed his arm. 'Kieran. Stop.'

His expression remained blank. '*They took so much from me. Make them pay.*'

The shouts had become screams, intensifying as the cloud descended. The desert would soon be stained with blood—well, those parts of it that weren't already covered in blistered wreckage.

It would have been easy to blame the Desine alone for the destruction. But Ami knew differently.

Neffron had forced Kieran to make a deal. And that deal had taken nearly everything from him.

Ami framed Kieran's face with her hands, pulling his unseeing gaze to hers. 'Kieran! Stop! Can't you sense those lifesigns disappearing?'

He blinked, again and again, more rapidly each time. Below them, the cloud broke apart and dispersed. The dust slowly settled. Ami squinted, trying to get a better look. Neffron's crews had fallen prostrate on the ground, no doubt begging for help from whichever god they served, perhaps even offering their allegiance to the Desine. Ami wondered what her father was thinking as he looked at the vidscreens inside his office and saw that his entire fleet had either been smothered or plucked out of space, like mere toys in the hands of a violent child.

'Thank you, Ami,' Kieran rasped. 'The Desine is supposed to be curtailing my powers, because I can't control them yet...but his own loss feels even more painful than mine. We were both consumed by vengeance.'

'I'm starting to wonder if you were actually less dangerous when you didn't have his so-called help,' Ami said dryly.

Kieran's shoulders sagged. 'I could have killed them all and I can't...I won't be responsible for that. Are you listening?' he demanded of the air. 'If you can't control yourself, I don't know how you expect *me* to.'

Ami knew he wasn't speaking to her; she'd expected to sit through a few one-sided conversations. But she didn't expect to hear the reply.

The Desine's mind-voice simmered with barely controlled anger. Rivers of sand scurried down the cliff face, as though afraid of its master. *Do remember, you have offered me your service and as such you owe me your respect. You have much to learn.*

'I suspect you have a lot to learn from me as well,' Kieran murmured.

The god had no response for that.

Ami hid the smirk and kissed Kieran, her lips lingering on his as they parted, her fingers grazing his jaw.

'Ask the Desine to send me to the catacombs,' Ami said as she stood, the wind tugging at her hastily pinned hair and ruffling her puffed sleeves. She took a moment to straighten the shirt. Sure, black silksein was not something she'd have chosen to wear, but at least the sub-level god had respected her usual style. 'I need to speak to Goss Kwon and the others. If the Desine wasn't lying about the survivors hiding out down there, that is.'

You could ask me yourself, Captain, the Desine said icily.

Ami gritted her teeth. 'Fine, but I won't repeat myself. You heard me.'

'Ami...' Kieran warned, though he was smiling.

'I'll also need you to teleport me back out of the catacombs,' Ami continued, keeping her eyes on the ground, not sure where she should rest them. 'Along with Goss and his people, once we're all ready. Oh, right. I should ask nicely, because that's totally something you're used to doing.'

'You shouldn't antagonise him,' Kieran said softly. 'He's a god.'

'And you can't protect me from him?' Ami asked, waving up at the sky. 'You've shielded us from lascannons mounted on starships, Kieran! Starships you just pulled out of space! You can block the Desine from your mind whenever you want. Which means your powers can hold up against a god's. Forgetting all that, he has no right to control you because he had a hand in creating you or whatever. And respect is earned. I learned that from my parents, not that it was their intention.' She spun around, flinging her ire in every direction. 'Look, Desine, you don't want to give Kieran a reason to fight you. He might actually win. So I think *you* are the one who should be worried about antagonising *us*!'

Laughter on the wind. Sand skittered and danced around them.

Kieran tensed, his gaze wary, but Ami knew the god wouldn't hurt her. He'd have done away with her by now if he could. But he wanted Kieran to keep serving him and Ami was the reason Kieran had agreed to do it at all.

Very well, the Desine said at last. *I will fulfill your requests.*

Ami held her breath as the vortex exploded into being around her, taking her away from the cliff—and the man she'd gladly slay every god in the galaxy for.

KIERAN PASSED through the swirling sand as easily as walking through a doorway, continuing to work his way along the ring of towers defending the ascent to Neffron's headquarters. He no longer felt fear when using this method of transportation, only impatience to learn how to do it without the god's help. Distantly, Kieran knew that this ability was not available to most mortals, but he found himself caring less and less that the Desine expected him to master it.

Kieran barely had to think at all to maintain his shield as it repelled the heavy fire from the mounted turrets he encountered. He destroyed the lascannons by sending back the blasts meant to kill him and then crushed the guards' lasguns with his powers, completely stripping them of their offensive capabilities.

Sometimes the Desine brought forth sandstorms that roared and twisted into the sky, threatening to shred those sheltering inside the towers, but the god always helped Kieran to minimise the loss of life. Neffron's soldiers were given a chance to surrender.

Kieran kept his relief and his gratitude to himself. The god did not deserve it.

He turned and walked through yet another wall of sand.

It took Kieran several seconds to realise that his next target was a power generator. Hidden behind an outcropping, it might have escaped mortal eyes, but not the Desine's. This generator was responsible for the substantial semi-spherical shield spread out across the rocky mountain range that housed Neffron's extensive headquarters, including the communications tower where Kieran could sense Neffron hiding, along with...Avurn.

Kieran stared up at the ridge. The pack of guards ringing the tower watched him carefully, their weapons drawn. But he was still out of range, so they didn't fire. They didn't advance on him either. Perhaps they had realised how insignificant they were compared to a mortal who wielded so much power that he could make even a god pause.

No. His powers were a tool, not a mark of superiority. And none of these people were insignificant. No one was. A single being could change the course of an entire planet's history.

Kieran stretched out his senses, bypassing the link and touching Avurn's mind directly, trying to see if the boy remained in there somewhere.

Deafening silence was his only answer.

Kieran pressed harder. Something stirred, then scurried away.

Av, he called.

The boy fled further from him. Frowning slightly, Kieran withdrew his mental probe. Though a part of Avurn's consciousness was shielded from the Rapture's influence, the boy had refused to communicate with him.

A problem to be dealt with later. Kieran shoved multiple surges of energy towards the shield generator, destroying it in an instant. He surveyed the damage, trying not to visualise broken bodies in the place of blackened machinery. Despite his best intentions, he had taken too many lives already and he knew he deserved every nauseous wave of guilt that assailed him. But he couldn't let his regrets keep him static. He would remain dangerous if he never improved.

The Desine had returned his communicator to him, so Kieran reached for it and had nearly thumbed it on when he remembered that Neffron was still jamming the Web. Kieran clenched his jaw. He wanted to check in with Ami and find out how she was doing.

A solid blast of wind knocked his hand away from his belt.

You do not need that device, the Desine told him. *Every grain of sand in this galaxy will obey you and show you what you need to see. You only need to ask it of them.*

I assume you're going to make me do that now, Kieran said, using his own mind-voice.

The Desine's response was curt, revealing his frustration with his student. *Yes. You must get used to wielding this ability. You will need to hear and heed every single being that exists inside my domain.*

Why?

You promised me anything. Now do it.

Kieran closed his eyes, retreating from his body, spreading his awareness across the planet's surface. The sand inside the catacombs beneath Taylar's ruined palace sprang to attention, giddy that he had called for them, frantically delivering everything he asked from them—and more. Kieran wavered. Too much. It was too much, too fast. He was going to lose his grasp on his powers, going to lose his shield, going to expose himself to the guards—

I will erect a shield if yours fails, the Desine assured him.

The heaviness on Kieran's shoulders lifted. He might not like the god, but the Desine would not abandon him—or send him away when he needed guidance. Not like the Creator God. Not like Pina-Sai.

Kieran had finally found the mentor he'd been searching for.

His shield stabilised. Kieran drew a deep breath, focusing on the images the sands were sending him. He saw a large, hollowed-out space from millions of angles, the only sizeable cavern that had escaped destruction. There was a trickle of water, a hiss of precious air, but every viable exit had been blocked off.

Ami stood beside Goss Kwon on a boulder, a crowd gathered on the uneven ground beneath them. Goss had immediately believed Ami when she'd told him about the state of Neffron's fleet and the towers surrounding his headquarters, most likely due to her dramatic entrance inside a vortex of sand. He had persuaded his followers to hear her out. Those who were reluctant to tolerate any involvement from Kieran, whom they knew only as a Chipper, were swayed by the idea of having the backing of the Desine.

GLEA had abandoned them to their fate, because slavery was legal on Rochaccia. They were useless and could not be trusted. But a god? Well, that was different.

They might just have a chance now.

Goss tapped his chin thoughtfully. 'One more thing, Ami. I need a vidcam, to record our victory—we must show the galaxy that we took Neffron as a prisoner without harming him in any way. Afterwards, we'll compile some footage of us establishing a governing body with new laws, so the Chippers will have no cause to come here and lock us up for breaking the old ones, which will no longer apply.'

'Just kill the fucker!' someone shouted from the shadows.

But Goss was shaking his head, much to Ami's obvious relief.

Despite the restless energy flooding the cavern, Kieran knew that the majority of the people trapped in there were ready to agree to anything Goss said to them. It was his quick thinking, by moving them further down in the catacombs to conceal their lifesigns during Neffron's attack, that had saved so many lives.

'No,' Goss said firmly. 'If we want to create a government that will be taken seriously on a galactic stage, by GLEA as well as any potential investors, we're gonna have to do it right. Neffron can't be executed.'

Ami eyed him. 'You've given this a lot of thought, haven't you? One would almost think you've been planning to take over and run a planet for a while.'

'It wouldn't be the first time I've tried,' Goss remarked.

'I wish I thought you were lying,' Ami told him.

Goss smiled briefly. 'My homeworld was in desperate need of a regime change. Many of the governor's policies were actively harming my people, so I staged a series of peaceful demonstrations. The governor did not approve. I would not have needed to act so rashly had she deigned to listen to me, but I was just a humble advisor on her payroll. Not only did I lose my position, she sold me. To make an example for anyone who was also tempted to...disagree.'

'That's a nice, totally unbiased story,' Ami mused.

The skin around Goss' eyes crinkled. 'It is, isn't it. Someone else —a relative of mine, would you believe—eventually deposed the governor, as I had hoped to do. My past failure aside, it is obvious that I'm the only one here who knows anything about running a planet—wouldn't you agree?'

Ami *hmm*ed, as though considering his words, then shook her head and laughed. 'You can't do any worse than my parents, Goss. You won't have to worry about GLEA not endorsing the legitimacy of your government, by the way. Once he's able, Kieran will contact his superiors and tell them to send over a few agents to advise you on some things. They'll also act as a deterrent to any opportunistic pirates and slavers who show up to take advantage of Rochaccia's upheaval. I wish I still had a ship, because dealing with those kinds of starkers used to be my favourite pastime.'

Kieran blinked away the images and sounds the sands had been sending him from the cavern and returned his attention to his surroundings. The nape of his neck prickled with danger. None of Neffron's soldiers had dared to approach or fire upon him, but the Desine's fury was causing the sand to roll into deadly waves. Kieran swiftly funnelled more energy into his shield.

You are bringing the Chippers into this? the Desine demanded. *This world lies within my domain. It's mine! They have no say in what happens here.*

Kieran glowered at the empty space beside him, imagining that the god's human form stood there. 'Listen to me, Desine. GLEA can help these people install a new government and connect them to galactic trade routes. You can't do that for them. But they'll remember who saved them when GLEA wouldn't, believe me. Many of them will worship you out of gratitude.'

As they should, the Desine hissed.

Kieran ignored him, mostly because he did not have the patience to continue the argument—and partly because he sensed that he'd already won. He studied the ruins of the shield generator, grimly satisfied. Neffron's headquarters were now exposed. It wouldn't be long until Rochaccia changed hands.

Before Kieran could send his awareness back to the catacombs, he heard Ami call out, the sands carrying her voice to him unbidden. 'Desine, could you please take us all to Kieran, if he's done.' A pause, the hint of a grin creeping into her words. 'And if you could grab us a vidcam, that'd be great. I'd really appreciate it. You're so helpful, thank you. Did I ask nicely enough?'

Kieran caught the flash of amusement before the Desine buried it. The god confirmed that he'd do as Ami had asked, sounding flat and uncaring.

But Kieran knew better. He wondered what other emotions the Desine had experienced.

The awe from those assembled in the cavern as they were encased inside a vortex of sand was palpable. They weren't frightened by this display of power. It told them that a god was indeed on their side.

Shards of the future flashed before Kieran's eyes. The Desine would become Rochaccia's patron god, but that would happen later —after Neffron was defeated, after Goss and his people transformed the world that had been their prison. There was still so much work to do, but Kieran's part in all this was done.

Smiling, he simply stood there and waited for the arrival of the woman he loved.

FORTY-THREE

'I guess it's my turn, huh?' Ami said. 'I'll head on up to the communications tower, find a way in, then somehow get Neffron to give up Avurn and drop the jamming field,' she rattled off, then indicated the tower on the ridge with a casual wave. She holstered her hand at her side before anyone could see the telltale tremors.

The lascannon turrets clinging to the squat base of the tower were smoking ruins, courtesy of Kieran, and Neffron's soldiers had thrown down their weapons and surrendered without protest. Ami suspected that witnessing a sandy tornado deposit a small army might have had something to do with that. Even if said army was made up of men wearing tatters and little else.

But Neffron was still inside the building. With Avurn.

It wasn't the most defensible position, though Ami suspected her father had chosen the tower because he'd known she would go after it. He wanted the confrontation. He *needed* it. Avurn was his last weapon remaining.

Goss patted the flashy new vidcam hovering over his shoulder.

'Once you succeed in your mission, you will then bring Neffron out unharmed, which I will capture on this.' His eyes went skyward. 'You said you were expecting an orbital bombardment from Yalsa 5's fleet? That'll convince any holdouts in Neffron's outposts and factories. And it can't hurt, having Yalsa 5 as allies.'

'They're not the worst ones you can have,' Ami remarked. 'Alright, give me a minute to consult with my crewmate and then I'll get this over and done with.'

'Of course, consult away,' Goss said—and winked.

Deciding it was best to pretend he hadn't done that, Ami turned away and strode over to Kieran, who was perched on a nearby outcropping. He stood out there, alone and alluringly aloof, but it wasn't the dark clothing or the brooding expression that set him apart.

Kieran radiated raw, intense power. Even the sand seemed to be keeping a respectful distance from his boots, withdrawing to the edges of the outcropping. Undeterred, Ami walked right up to Kieran. But she stopped herself before she got too close, momentarily afraid that she no longer recognised him. Then he looked at her and the familiar sparkle returned to his blue eyes in an instant.

'Av is my responsibility and I won't fail him again,' Ami said, her throat constricting when she swallowed. 'You said there's a part of him still in there somewhere. I might not have any powers, but I know I can reach him. I think. I hope.'

Kieran's cheeks tightened. 'I will be monitoring everything that happens inside the tower building. If you need my help, you won't even have to ask.'

'But you do have to wait until I actually ask,' she warned him.

Kieran smiled. 'I wouldn't dream of disobeying you, Captain N'uni.'

Ami tried to suppress the shiver his words evoked. And failed completely. She would have kissed him if a vidcam and a sizeable audience hadn't been nearby. Kieran was still technically a Chipper and she wanted him to have one last moment of glory to make his superiors proud, untainted by his involvement with an outsider. She knew it hadn't fully hit him yet. He needed time to properly mourn the part of himself that had belonged of GLEA.

But Kieran clearly had other things on his mind.

'I'm impatient for all of this to be over,' he said lowly. 'So I can ask you that question...'

'Let's hope it's soon and not some time next century,' Ami muttered.

He took a step forward, his gaze on her lips. Stark, it was tempting to give in. But she spun around and left him there, aiming for the tower. Her breath caught in her throat when she looked back at the crowd; they were waiting for her to succeed, so they could return to their families—or stay to wrangle Rochaccia into something else.

Ami steeled herself and evened out her strides.

Were there less dangerous ways to retrieve Avurn? Yes. Would Goss be respected as a leader on the galactic stage if a Chipper or a sub-level god took out Neffron for him? Not so much.

'Wait!' Goss called.

Ami stilled. One of Goss' people hurried up to her, holding out a lasgun. It was a much clunkier, heavier piece than she was used to and it would make her aim even more atrocious, but Neffron might simply shoot her if she confronted him while unarmed. Ami accepted the lasgun. Hiding any outward signs of her brief hesitation, she turned to the watchful crowd and raised the weapon above her head in a gesture of premature victory. The resulting explosion of cheers made her stand just that little bit straighter.

She hadn't proved herself worthy of their trust or respect, not yet, but she would.

Smiling grimly, Ami marched up towards the tower.

The building itself was small and insignificant compared to the colossal rod positioned on its flat roof—and even though Ami knew better, the tower was so tall it looked like it had poked a hole right through the planet's atmosphere and entered the vacuum of space. No Web signal would ever get past the jamming field being maintained by that monstrosity.

Ami reached for the sensor pad on the exterior wall more out of habit than anything else, since she was sure the entrance would be locked, but all three sets of doors immediately whooshed open. The chilly air trapped inside escaped, flaying her face and filling her lungs. This didn't make her pause. Instead, it *invigorated* her. Ami exhaled and stepped inside.

'That's far enough,' her father said when the last of the doors had slid shut, sealing out the desert heat and muting the noise of the crowd.

Ami dutifully remained where she was and took a moment to study her surroundings. The single-level building was open plan and filled with consoles, all of them staffed by empty seats. Neffron stood in the narrow central walkway. Both his hands were on Avurn's shoulders, the boy positioned directly in front of him like a shield. Not a particularly subtle threat.

Neffron had always favoured a rigid olive-green outfit, even requiring his soldiers and mercs to follow suit as a sign of their loyalty. Ami had never had a strong opinion about it. Before now, that is. She was disturbed to see Avurn clad in a smaller version of the uniform, the pants and shirt hastily hacked to fit his slighter size.

Avurn raised a lasgun and aimed it at Ami. His other hand was clenching and unclenching at his side, a far more troubling gesture. Ami watched him warily. A forcefield could do as much damage as a lasgun bolt—and he was more powerful than most Chippers.

Avurn's lips curled into the manic smile that only Rapture could produce.

'Walk towards me, Av,' Ami said.

His smile widened, showing teeth. Cold perspiration trickled down the back of Ami's neck. The drug would have rewarded him for obeying her. But he hadn't moved.

Neffron tutted and shook his head. 'Oh, sweet little Ami. My forces may have bowed to you—*for now*—but do you have the coin-chips to pay them? Or the spine to lead them? You don't even have the benefit of the defences I spent decades building and perfecting. You didn't spare a single starship! This planet will be invaded by someone else within a week, if that. And do you really think you did these people a favour by freeing them? They will be enslaved once more. By beings far more unsavoury than me, I can assure you.'

Ami gnawed on the inside of her cheek. It would take too long to bring the bulky lasgun to bear. She could use her hip to steady the weapon, but she wasn't sure that Avurn's reflexes were intact enough that he could shield himself from an inevitably off-course lasbolt. And she might be unlucky enough to kill Neffron instead of wounding him. Stark. Her plan was falling apart. If it had ever really been a plan to begin with.

She frowned when she felt Kieran's mind brush hers.

Wait, she told him.

'You've never had much of an imagination, Neffron,' Ami said firmly. 'You can't see any future that doesn't involve pain and suffering. I might not have your military prowess or Taylar's cunning, but I'm not so stupid that I'd leave Rochaccia completely vulnerable. And I'm not stupid enough to assume I can run this planet better than the people who are actually going to live here.' She grinned carelessly. 'Plus, we've got a sub-level god on our side. Anyone who attacks Rochaccia will risk pissing off the Desine. And who wants to do *that?*'

The creases on Neffron's forehead came and went so quickly Ami couldn't be sure that she'd seen them. But then his eyes flicked from side to side, betraying his anxiety. All around the room, vidscreens glowed, showing countless angles of his vast territory.

Neffron had seen what had happened to his towers and his starships. He'd watched the very desert turn against him.

His voice, however, remained smooth and unhurried. 'This boy will grow into a fine ruler. Perhaps not of this world, but another. We can always go elsewhere.'

'What good is this heir of yours'—Ami bladed her fingers together and jabbed them towards Avurn—'if you keep hitting him with Rapture? Some heir, if he's more interested in following orders and feeling good than in learning how to run a planet. You'll need him clean at some point, you know. But oops, he won't go along with your wishes once the drug's out of his system. So what's the point in keeping the kid?'

'Ah, but have you ever asked him about *his* wishes?' Neffron's smile was almost as terrifying as Avurn's. 'I did. Tell her, you little rascal.'

'This is what I want,' Avurn said cheerfully. 'A whole planet to rule over! You cannot give me that, Ami. Neffron can. I don't need Rapture to do his bidding. But it does feel good. So good.'

'No!' Ami ground her teeth together until they squeaked in protest. 'I refuse to let you turn into...into *this*.'

Avurn's head tilted to the side and hung there, as though it was suddenly too heavy for him to lift. 'I am not turning into anything. I have merely removed my disguise.'

'Clever, cold, and capable of hiding his true nature,' her father mused. 'He's perfect. And you delivered him straight to me. I am grateful, sweet little Ami, but not enough to spare your life. I will get the little rascal to do it, since he'll enjoy it so much. The Rapture will help with that, of course, but I think he'd be delighted to get rid of you anyway.'

'I'm sorry,' Ami told Avurn.

'Sorry?' her father repeated. 'Are you actually going to shoot through him to get at me? How unlike you, sweet little Ami. I'd be impressed...if I thought you could actually do it.'

Ami flicked an annoyance glance at Neffron. 'No, I've hurt Avurn too much already. You said you were grateful I brought him here? Give me a few minutes. Let me say my piece. If he wants to shoot me afterwards, I'll stand here and take it.'

'Very well,' Neffron said. 'But only because I think I will enjoy your pathetic attempt to sway him.'

Ami kept her eyes on Avurn. Neffron hadn't caused this rift, just exploited it. This wouldn't have been nearly so hard to fix if she'd done her starking job. Some captain she was. Some friend.

'Av, I'm sorry,' she began quietly. 'I was scared. I was so sure I was watching you follow in my parents' footsteps that I didn't see... you. I decided who you were going to be without even giving you a chance to show me otherwise. That was shitty of me, especially since you're too young to have your identity sorted. And you're so smart, so mature—I often forget that you still need so much support. You were only six when you lost your parents and had to save Jensa. I somehow thought you'd got through all of that unscathed, but it affects everything you do, doesn't it? You're too good at hiding how much pain you're in. So I'm sorry. I don't have a link with you, but I still should have realised what was happening.

'Just *look at me*, stark it!'

Avurn met her gaze. Ami's heartbeat faltered in hope, but the lasgun remained firm in his grip.

'Kill her,' Neffron said.

Avurn's lips twitched, just slightly. He didn't fire.

Ami took a step forward, her ears ringing as though she'd stood too close to a discharging lascannon. 'Av. You've got decades to figure out who you are. Don't let this starker force you into one box, force you to wear one label. So you want to rule a planet some day? Sure, you can do that, but you can also be a champion for the defenceless. You could save lives with law and order instead of lasguns and tyranny.'

'Kill her now!' Neffron thundered.

'Av,' Ami pleaded.

Her crewmate began to laugh and kept laughing, his head thrown back as his small frame succumbed to violent hysterics. Neffron also laughed, plainly delighted. Ami's stomach clenched. She couldn't fire the lasgun, not even to defend herself. She'd failed. And she shouldn't feel this reluctant to ask Kieran for help, but—

Avurn's amusement died in an instant. He contorted himself away from Neffron and fired, frying Neffron's kneecaps with two precise lasbolts. Neffron swore as he hit the floor, a hand sliding along his belt to the lasgun hanging there. But he never got the chance to wield it; Avurn whipped Neffron over the head with the weapon his captor had given him. It was a single, smooth motion. One that spoke of how easily the boy could have killed Neffron.

Avurn clambered up onto his feet and spat, scoring a direct hit on the pale, sweat-slicked face beneath him. Neffron's eyelids twitched, but he did not regain consciousness.

'Are you alright?' Ami asked. 'Speak freely. Tell me what you want to say.'

Avurn looked down at himself, seemingly startled when he realised that his chest was heaving. The lasgun dropped from his hand. His shoulders, hunched awkwardly, began to jerk, synchronised to the violent sobs that were escaping him. He slapped at the smile on his face. Kept slapping when it refused to budge.

Ami moved closer, desperate to stop him, but he shook his head at her.

'If I...if I hadn't seen how Kieran did it,' he croaked, 'I'd never have been able to shield a part of my mind from the Rapture's influence.' Avurn swiped at the tears trickling down his cheeks. 'I knew what Neffron was trying to do. He wanted to mould me into a younger version of himself and I...he told me to hurt people, Ami. I did as he asked. I inflicted pain. And I enjoyed it.'

Ami clasped her hands behind her back, resisting the urge to embrace him and whisper platitudes about how everything was going to be alright.

She still wasn't alright from what her parents had done to her.

'I once thought that the ends justified the means,' Avurn continued, his teeth digging into his bottom lip and drawing blood. 'But this is not how someone should obtain and cultivate power, this is not how it should be wielded. The people Neffron paraded before me...the people I used the laswhip on...they all wore my sister's face. I was hurting them. And I was hurting *her*.'

Avurn crumpled to the ground. Ami ditched the heavy lasgun and was beside him in moments, gathering him up into her arms. He didn't protest. Just hugged her back until the Rapture-enforced smile bled from his features, leaving something broken in its place.

'Why didn't you warn me?' Avurn asked weakly.

Ami tucked his head under her chin. 'I guess...I thought that since you knew about my past and knew who my parents were, you didn't need to be told how bad those *means* can be. This kind of power, absolute and unchecked, always comes at a cost. Someone has to pay and it's never the person in charge. You seem to know everything...but that doesn't mean you do. Can you forgive me, Av?'

'Only if you go to the nearest console and finish what you came here to do.'

Ami laughed and relinquished her hold on him. The walls were soundproofed and all she could hear was the soft hum of the nearby consoles, but Ami suspected that some celebrating was already going on outside. Kieran would have told Goss and the others about her success almost instantly.

Well, she hadn't quite succeeded *yet*.

Ami knocked out the planetwide Web jamming by tapping a single sensor. She quickly swiped a second sensor, opening a link to every communications device on the planet.

Ami drew a long breath, calling forth the steady voice that had made more than one pirate captain capitulate. 'I am Unify Naiman. Some of you may know of me, which means you know what position I hold. Once held. That's not important. This world, Rochaccia, is no longer under the control of Neffron and Taylar Naiman. It's ours now. Agents of GLEA will soon be dispatched to help us set up new governance and a new way of life here. If that interests you, let me know and I'll invite you to the proceedings we'll be holding at Neffron's old headquarters. Starting from tomorrow. But if you have problem with any of this…you've worn out your welcome. Leave. Or I'll tell my friends, who are currently on their way to this system in leapspace, to blast you from orbit. Give me your decision. *Now.*'

Immediately, she started receiving calls from all over the planet, from those who were willing to accept her terms. A handful of mercenaries refused, calling her supposed 'bluff'.

Smiling grimly, Ami used the console again. Only one communicator received her next call.

Jets responded with nanoseconds.

'Fucking finally! We were waiting behind the third planet in this system!' Jets crowed, while Ami stared at the console in surprise. 'That's the last time Dad'll ever agree to a bet to see which one of us shoots best. Must've forgotten to tell him I can hit inanimate objects just fine. Anyway, he gambled and lost. And since he hates owing anyone anything, he had no choice but to move the fleet out this way. Figured you'd need us nearby. So what d'you want us to blast?'

Ami spent the next few minutes sending Jets the locations of targets who had either told her to stark off or hadn't yet responded. Any that changed their minds would get back into contact with her, she was sure—and there had to be enough coin-chips in Neffron's treasury to convince some of the mercenaries to stick around. Rochaccia was going to need paid protection until they managed to train up their own forces.

Ami turned to Avurn, who was unsteadily climbing back onto his feet.

'So I guess I don't need to worry about you taking over the galaxy anymore,' she said, forcing her tone to remain light.

Avurn stared at her, his cheeks hollow—but there was a flicker of defiance in his eyes. 'I wouldn't say that. The only difference is that I now know it needs to be achieved in ways that do not harm other people or exploit them. And my subjects would be far less likely to depose me if they're happy with what I'm doing—do you not agree?'

'Oh, Av,' Ami murmured. She knew that shadow on his face was permanent; she saw a similar one in the mirror sometimes, on the days she couldn't mask it. 'Do you want me to contact Jensa and tell her what happened?'

Avurn shook his head. 'She will not understand. If I do wish to talk about it...I will come to you. Or Kieran. Preferably Kieran, if you don't mind.'

'Good enough for me.'

They stood there together, countless seconds passing them by, watching the vidsceens and witnessing the beginning of Rochaccia's next chapter.

A deadly rain of lascannon fire swept across the planet, taking out the installations that were staffed by beings who even now, in the face of imminent destruction, did not surrender. They were dying, while the man who had caused so much suffering lived and breathed, lying unharmed on the floor.

Neffron regained consciousness a few minutes later. With Avurn at her side, Ami marched her father out into searing daylight, where a vidcam recorded his downfall.

Soon everyone in the galaxy would know that Rochaccia was free.

FORTY-FOUR

The planet's fifteen-hour night had begun by the time Kieran returned to the communications tower. A rapid sunset had chased him there from Neffron's headquarters, an oblong fortress crowned with multiple beacons that blasted away every shadow and exposed every potential hiding place, effectively discouraging any sneak attacks. Daylight wasn't going to be leaving the mountaintop any time soon, regardless of the sun's position.

Kieran could have contacted the Agency from the fortress, since the jamming field was inactive, but its corridors were packed with people whose minds thrummed with joy and optimism. He couldn't bear to be around that kind of energy just now.

Ami and Avurn were still there, sitting in on preliminary discussions about Rochaccia's system of governance. The *Free Ride*'s former crew were honoured guests. Kieran hadn't taken Goss up on the invitation, though not because of how crowded Neffron's old 'war room' was (it had been hastily converted into a conference hall and was clearly too small for this purpose). Most of Goss' people had needed to find space on the floor. The luckiest of them had scored loading crates to use as seats.

Kieran knew his absence had been noted but it hadn't raised any real concern, mostly because Ami had declared that she had some task for him to do. Unchallenged, she'd walked him right to the exit of the building, ensuring that she maintained a careful distance from him even though no one had followed them through the corridors.

'There will never be a good time for this,' she had said softly. 'But you need to break it off with GLEA sooner rather than later. So do it now. Well, after you ask them to come here and help out. Two ships with one blast.'

And then she'd grabbed two fistfuls of his shirt and flattened herself against him, capturing his lips in a long, deep kiss that sparked uncountable visions of all the other kisses they would share.

He wanted that future with her. He wanted the laughter, the love, the lingering touches. It should have been compensation enough for what he had lost.

At least he wasn't currently being hounded by the Desine, which would not have helped his mood. The god had attempted to contact Kieran barely an hour after Rochaccia had been liberated, but hadn't managed anything beyond a cordial greeting for Ami before she'd gone off at him. Ami had demanded that the Desine leave Kieran alone for a few days, to let him rest and come to terms with what had happened. The Desine had agreed with surprisingly little argument.

Kieran sensed that this had less to do with Ami's formidable nature and more to do with the desert god trying to get on his good side. Seemingly, it wasn't enough that the Desine had obtained Kieran's lifelong service. For whatever reason, he also wanted Kieran to *like* him.

Kieran had no intention of ever giving him the satisfaction.

Resting his forehead against the curved chrome of the console he'd chosen for his task, Kieran spent almost a minute trying to dislodge the lump that had taken up residence at the back of his throat. Ami had bought him some time. But he still had to honour the deal he'd made with the Desine.

Kieran breathed a prayer that took both his curses and his apologies to the Creator God.

Then he placed a call to Gerasnin, the sparkling world where GLEA's headquarters were based. Kieran could no longer picture the white marble temple he'd grown up in, or the sapphire ocean that surrounded it. He now only saw deserts when he closed his eyes.

'This is Private Kieran Krendasta on Rochaccia—I need to speak with Head General Zareth Sins.' Kieran broke off when his voice hit a higher pitch than he was aiming for. It certainly didn't impress the being on the other end of the link, who insisted that he make his request through a ranked agent.

'I have a direct superior, but ze is not currently with me,' Kieran gritted out. 'Fine. Contact Major Nexis Yetz at the Ilbban outpost. *Yes*, I'll hold.'

Kieran kept his fist anchored on his thigh. His frustration swelled inside him, like a restless river determined to break its banks, and it refused to settle despite his attempts to control and slow his breathing. His gaze flew to the doors when he felt a violent blast of wind slam into the building. More gusts continued to batter the mountaintop, hungry, howling, hunting for whatever had dared to upset him. The sands begged Kieran to unleash them, to let them carry out his will.

God, it was so tempting to transform his anger into something more tangible, something capable of shredding—

'No,' Kieran murmured. 'Please stop this. I will learn how to control my powers, I promise, but I still need your help. Please. Don't let me hurt anyone.'

The brewing storm died instantly.

Kieran tensed, but the Desine said nothing and swiftly withdrew his presence.

The link to Gerasnin was silent for a long time. No on-hold music was playing, either because someone had forgotten to key up a track or because the Agency had been unable to fit licensed music into their most recent budget. Kieran mentally prepared himself for the next round of negotiation, but then—

'Krendasta,' said the distinct voice of Head General Zareth Sins.

Kieran stared at the console. 'Sir, I didn't expect to be put through to you so quickly. Or at all, if I'm honest.'

'You don't keep up with galactic news, do you?' Sins mused. 'I would not usually have approved of my agents travelling with a reporter, but Ms Pendergast is one of the few that paints us in a positive light. Not that we are always deserving of it. I know better than to assume you sought her out deliberately—Ms Pendergast has a habit of showing up when one least expects it.'

Grace...? Had she published a report about Rochaccia? Grace certainly wasn't the type to let a little thing like death get in her way and Kieran recalled her mentioning that she scheduled some of her work in case of her timely demise.

Kieran's fist dug deeper into his thigh, the physical pain doing nothing to alleviate his mental anguish. Grace had been a valuable link to his family and he felt that loss keenly. He supposed he could attempt to pry some answers out of her nephew, Micadei, but the Desine had already tried to kill him once. Kieran did not want to put him in any further danger.

Sins was clearly waiting for a response, so Kieran gave him a noncommittal one. 'You did say you understood about working with unorthodox allies, General.'

'Yes, I did,' Sins agreed. 'Anyway, I was expecting your call. And you're lucky I was stuck in a budget meeting, so I wasn't having too much fun to make time for you.' A laugh chased Sins' words. Kieran didn't need to hear it to know that the Head General was not upset with him. He could read a lot more from Zareth Sin's mind if he chose to and the distance didn't diminish his powers at all; the three weeks of leapspace that lay between them might as well have been three feet.

That scared Kieran, even though he knew that Sins wasn't aware of the intrusion. What if his powers accidentally touched someone who could sense him in return?

'I assisted Unify Naiman in her bid to take control of Rochaccia,' Kieran said, speaking slowly and refining his vowels in a way that accentuated his Gerasnin accent. As befitting an agent speaking to his superior. 'Both Neffron and Taylar Naiman have been deposed. Rather than install herself as ruler, Unify has ceded Rochaccia to those who were previously enslaved here. A new governing body will soon be instated and I strongly recommend that the Agency acknowledges it.'

Sins grew serious. 'Your actions could have seriously damaged the Agency's reputation—they still could, come to think of it. We do not seek to alter laws or governments; we support them. You took over an entire planet! Without informing any of your superiors beforehand, I might add.'

Kieran relaxed his fist so that he could tap the console, but it was a poor substitute for the sand his fingers ached to feel beneath them. 'It was an extension of the duties I was already performing. Unify Naiman is the birthname of Captain Ami N'uni, whose missions against the slave trade you agreed to fund. Admittedly, this was on a larger scale than either of us expected…sir, I'll just get to the point.'

'I'd appreciate that, Krendasta.'

'Ami—that is, Captain N'uni—was only able to convince some of the mercenaries to stay on and transfer their allegiance. Additionally, the planet currently lacks any other forms of defence, as its fleet was destroyed in the conflict. This puts Rochaccia in a tenuous position. Captain N'uni is of the opinion that the people here will be able to defend themselves eventually, but it will take time before this is possible. Sir, we need more agents on the ground.'

There was a lengthy pause. 'Our resources are stretched thin as it is, Krendasta.'

'Yes, I know,' Kieran said. 'But one day the people of Rochaccia will be able to afford to make donations to the Agency. And they're more likely to do that if they feel they owe us…owe GLEA something.'

Sins made a choking sound that concealed another laugh. 'We are not so mercenary, Kieran! All beings in this galaxy deserve our assistance, whether or not they are able to donate to our cause. But I cannot deny that your involvement in Rochaccia's liberation has resulted in mostly positive publicity for us—and yes, a sudden and significant increase in donations. So I'll accede to your request… Second Lieutenant Krendasta.'

Kieran's stomach twisted and his mouth flooded with bile—or was it the taste of guilt?

He needed to end this fantasy, right now. He needed to resign.

'Sir, I was never accepted for officer training, so technically I should be promoted to an enlisted rank,' Kieran managed to say. He was stalling. He hoped it wasn't obvious.

'Surely you'd have to agree, Krendasta,' Sins remarked, 'that severing an entire branch of the galactic slave trade and saving a million lives in the process is a more than adequate substitute for officer training? Besides which, the mediaists and reporters will ask us some rather awkward questions if you introduce yourself as *Private* Kieran Krendasta.' A deep sigh. 'And to be perfectly clear, you've earned it. I'm sorry you had to do something of this magnitude in order for your skills to be appreciated. I will send some agents from a nearby system—you'll outrank a couple of them now! —to assist Rochaccia's new government. Take your time there, Krendasta. Relax. Recharge. And when you are ready, you can return to Ilbb and start plotting your next planetary liberation. Lieutenant.'

'General,' Kieran responded

The communications link died, terminated on Sins' end.

I did it, Kieran realised. *I achieved a rank on my own merits. All I have to do is keep earning more ranks and gaining more popularity until I can convince the Agency to cease enacting divisive policies. I can keep GLEA—and the entire galaxy—in one piece.*

Oh God. I can't. I made a deal with the Desine and I must honour it.

Even if everyone will suffer because of what I've done.

Resting his elbows on the console, Kieran planted his head in his hands.

KIERAN SOUGHT AVURN LATER, when the lights inside the fortress were dimming, leaving the corridors shrouded in a soothing darkness that the glaringly bright exterior walls would never know.

Avurn had used the link to inform Kieran that he could be disturbed if needed, which Kieran took to mean that the boy wanted his company but wasn't quite comfortable asking for it. Kieran found Avurn hunched over on the bottom bed of the bunk they shared in a room that was so tight it rivalled a storage closet, avidly reading whatever was being displayed on his palm. It looked suspiciously like Grace Pendergast's work.

Kieran wondered how recent the report was and if it mentioned Rochaccia, but he stowed the desire to ask. He sat beside Avurn, unsure if he could do anything to ease the disquiet buzzing in the boy's energy.

'I misled Ami,' Avurn said, his fingers closing over his palm.

'About what?' Kieran asked.

Avurn's lips twisted into what could have been a grimace or a mirthless smile. 'She believes that I was unable to resist the Rapture until she came for me. Until she bared her soul and said all those things—which I did not fail to appreciate, by the way.'

'You wanted to stay under the drug's influence,' Kieran guessed.

'I lay there and let Neffron's traitor inject me,' Avurn said, staring at the bare concrete wall. 'How pathetic is that? I could have resisted—perhaps even escaped—and instead I *embraced* the artificial bliss the Rapture offered me.'

'Avurn, you don't—'

'I want to talk about it,' Avurn interrupted him. 'I *need* to talk about it.'

'Then I'm listening.'

Avurn exhaled deeply and leaned into him. Startled, Kieran wrapped an arm around the boy and cinched him closer. Avurn's body was tense, his limbs stiff enough to dig in and bruise, but Kieran did not shift in the slightest.

He would wait Avurn out, even if it took weeks, months, years.

But Avurn was ready.

'I thought...I thought there was no other path for me,' Avurn said haltingly. 'I wanted to save lives and I also wanted to find some way to prevent those lives being endangered in the first place, but I always starked it up, especially in Ami's eyes. It seemed that my destiny was to hurt people instead. So why should I not feel happy while I did it? Rapture blocks everything else. There's no pain or panic or guilt.'

'It's not your fault, what happened to Grace,' Kieran began.

Avurn's body shook with laughter. 'You think that's what sent me spiralling? No, she didn't die. She gave up on me, just like Ami did.'

Kieran opened his mouth, then closed it. He wanted Grace to be alive, desperately, but it wasn't possible.

'She isn't dead,' Avurn affirmed. 'Her latest report includes events that transpired only after she disappeared. Look, I'll show you. I'll show you everything.'

The link grew wide and warm between them. Kieran saw Avurn's recent past, not scrounged from some vision but freely given. He watched the boy lie there on the platform, pretending to be unconscious while Lius nicked his vein and filled him with Rapture. Avurn kept a piece of his mind shielded—not so he could be rescued, but so that he could slay Neffron and take over Rochaccia at a time of *his* choosing.

When Neffron handed him a lasgun, Avurn smiled and shot Lius (no traitor could ever truly be trusted, Neffron had explained). When Neffron handed him a laswhip, Avurn smiled and flayed the backs of the people brought before him. When Neffron demanded to know what he must do to keep the boy at his side without Rapture, Avurn told him the truth—that he would gladly be Neffron's heir if he could remain under the drug's influence.

Ami had always known this would be his fate. And that reporter, Grace Pendergast—she'd left him as soon as she was able, because Avurn was never going to be the hero of a report read by the entire galaxy. He was always meant to become the villain.

Feared, hated, and irredeemable.

Kieran cleared his throat. 'I'm sure Grace would have stayed if she could have...'

'I doubt it,' Avurn muttered. Detailed images from his memories washed over Kieran as the boy continued to talk. 'Lius took us by surprise in Taylar's conference room. Grace and I had disagreed on the best locations for the mines and we intended to go over the data again so we could settle the argument. But Lius was already in there. He hit me with a mild stun blast, which meant that I couldn't move or use my hands to create any forcefields. He was going to kill Grace right then and there—I was the one Neffron wanted—but since I could still speak, I convinced him to make Grace carry me.'

'Why didn't you call for me in the link?' Kieran asked. 'You had enough time to do it. And you shielded yourself from me, didn't you? So I wouldn't know that you were in trouble.'

Avurn's despair and embarrassment overwhelmed that same link. 'I wanted to save Grace by myself—and do it without killing Lius. To prove that I could. I wanted Ami to see that I wasn't the megalomaniac she thought I was.'

'That was dangerous,' Kieran told him. 'You had to have known that Neffron was about to arrive and he'd be bringing an armada with him. What would you have done then?'

'Yes, well, I wasn't thinking clearly,' Avurn said, gritting his teeth as though this admission had physically pained him. 'Anyway, the effects of the stun blast wore off before we reached Lius' shuttle. He no longer had any need for Grace and I knew he would shoot her if I didn't stop him. Yes, I should have used my powers. But I foolishly thought I could persuade Lius to our side —my arrogance blinded me. Grace knew I'd failed before I did. She told me not to worry about her, ran to the edge of the landing pad, and starking jumped! Lius was too gobsmacked to do anything, so I went after her and looked over the railing just in time to see...she disappeared inside a *fireball*, Kieran. And I felt no fear in her energy. She was happy. Happy to leave me there. Happy to let me become the monster I was always meant to be. I went quietly with Lius after that. Why should I resist the inevitable?'

'That...' Kieran trailed off.

'Doesn't make sense?' Avurn finished. 'Of course it doesn't. But I know what I saw.'

Kieran frowned for a moment, then said slowly, 'Grace had to leave on her own terms or she wouldn't have survived.'

Avurn exhaled. 'She knew I was a monster. Beyond saving.'

'*No,*' Kieran said, his voice rough. 'I didn't just make that deal with the Desine to save Ami. I did it so we could come back and save you too, Av. You are a member of Ami's crew and if you were an agent I'd choose you as my partner without hesitation. Because I know you would never make me regret it.'

Ami and Kieran had agreed not to keep Avurn in the dark about Kieran's association with the Desine, since it might disrupt their future missions. Avurn also deserved their trust and he would be justified in feeling angry when he discovered what they were hiding from him—because he would figure it out on his own, Kieran had no doubts about that. Avurn had been intrigued by Kieran's situation and clearly wanted to ask more questions, but he'd managed to restrain himself. For the time being, anyway.

Kieran swallowed. 'You're not a monster, Av. No more than I am. You know what I did on Fintaz. And Ami was under Rapture for years while she did her parents' bidding. Are you saying she's a monster?'

Avurn muttered something that might have been 'no, I'd rather she didn't strand me on Ilbb'. Kieran hid the smile. That sounded like the Avurn he knew.

'But how do I live with what I've done?' Avurn asked quietly.

Kieran drew back so that he could meet Avurn's gaze. 'You will find some way to live with it, because there's no other option. And it hurts. God, it hurts. I've vowed to spend the rest of my life atoning for the people I've killed. I'd like to pretend it won't happen again, but I know that in order to save lives I may have to take some. I'll atone for those too.'

'Am I supposed to keep a tally?' Avurn demanded. 'I'd have to start with Julius, then Jackson and her mercs. Scum of the galaxy, but I still ended their lives.'

Kieran shook his head. 'No. No tally. Just make sure that you learn from these situations so you can prevent them in future—which might not always be possible, I'll admit. You have made some mistakes, Av, but your intentions were good.'

There was a dark edge to Avurn's words. 'Ah, the arrogance, to believe that our intentions can absolve us. Although...I think you might actually have the authority to absolve me. The very stars sing your name, Kieran. I can't reach them. Not like you can. So if this is your pardon, I'll take it.'

'I'm just a mortal, I can't pardon you, that power belongs to the Creator God...' Kieran silenced, belatedly realising that Avurn had changed the topic of conversation on purpose.

'Well, if he offers and you don't want that power, can I have it?' Avurn asked, deadpan.

Kieran laughed and grabbed Avurn back into a hug, playfully scruffing up his hair. He could see that a part of Avurn wished he was the innocent child he appeared to be, so he could cast off his responsibilities and have someone look after him for a change. Jensa treated Avurn like an adult, because he had rescued her and continued to watch out for her, even after her marriage to Xan. But Avurn had needed something else from his sister.

'That was incredibly undignified,' Avurn said when Kieran released him.

Kieran knew this meant that Avurn had exceeded his tolerance for socialising and quietly left. He was glad that Avurn had felt comfortable enough to open up to him.

An ache spread throughout Kieran's chest as he roamed the shadow-strewn corridors of the fortress. He so badly wanted to open up to Pina-Sai, like he had in the past. But if Kieran wasn't an agent, if he served another god, if they no longer had a common purpose to bind them together...

Would they still be brothers?

FORTY-FIVE

Ami's techpad emitted a small beep.

Relieved to have an excuse to look away from the jumbled lines filling the tabletop vidscreen in front of her, Ami didn't bother to conceal her movements as she slid the techpad out of her jeans pocket. The device was slightly too slick and shiny for her tastes, but Ami had lost her old one and she'd had to grab whatever she could find in the fortress. She squinted at the screen and frowned.

There was a message waiting for her. From Grace Pendergast.

That wyvern, Ami thought savagely. *The nerve, to contact me after abandoning Av...*

Kieran had filled her in on what had happened to Grace late last night. Right before that other conversation they'd had. The one with a lot less talking and a lot more of something else. Sure, it smarted that Avurn had confided in Kieran instead, but Ami knew she had a long way to go before she earned back her young crew-mate's trust.

Hmm. Come to think of it, Kieran had twice distracted her before she could ask him how his resignation had been received by the Head General. He must have seen the question in her thoughts on both occasions. Not that she'd minded the...*distraction.*

Ami sighed. He was so used to struggling with everything on his own. She needed to remind him that he wasn't alone anymore.

Chaotic echoes bounced around the conference hall as voices rose and tempers flared. The cold, grey walls of Neffron's 'war room' had previously been decorated with elaborate tapestries depicting him standing on the backs of his subjects. Unsurprisingly, the walls were now bare and so every whisper sounded like a shout.

Jets was on her feet, with her hands on her hips, demanding that Governor Bock Atsason (who cut a fine figure in that white suit of his, Ami had to admit) remove a clause from the proposed trading deal that allowed Yalsa 5 to take recompense by force if Rochaccia was unable to meet its obligations within six Old Earth months. Rochaccia's economy might not be stable for years, so he shouldn't expect a quick return on his investment. And why the stark was her father so set on pissing off allies they might need? Especially allies who felt beholden to them and might one day be in a position to help them deal with certain enemies...

Of course, Goss Kwon sided with Jets, the vocal agreement of his hand-picked advisors adding to the din. Bock's expression soured. Jets smirked at him. Ami wondered if Jets was just trying to piss her father off or if she actually knew what she was doing.

The Chippers stayed out of the argument; they'd already said their piece earlier when making suggestions about Rochaccia's security forces and the wording of some laws. It had taken them four days to show up, arriving behind the bevy of mediaists and e-paper reporters who were camped out in every spare room in the fortress, including storage closets.

One reporter was conspicuously missing.

Ami drew a breath and read the message Grace had sent her.

Captain Ami N'uni,
We all have a part to play in the grand design and I have
learned that there is no escaping this duty. Others in my
chosen family do not understand why I am so willing to
accept my fate. But I know that in order to protect the ones I
love, I must embrace the role I was given.
I hope you will embrace yours. Because Kieran needs you.
There is a great conflict coming and you are his best chance
at surviving it with both his body and mind intact.
Grace Pendergast

Ami lowered her techpad and growled under her breath.

Still as vague and useless as ever. Grace hadn't added any reports to her e-paper in days and had not refuted the claims that she had perished on Rochaccia. How was Ami supposed to get answers out of her now? If Grace wanted to stay 'dead', she definitely wasn't going to show up anywhere that Ami could find her.

'Ami?' Avurn asked. 'Do you need the meds? I haven't been able to source them yet and I was certain I had more time to do so.'

He was sitting on a loading crate beside her, boosted up by a couple of cushions that he'd either found or bartered for. So far Avurn hadn't contributed anything to the proceedings, but Ami knew it was only a matter of time before he did.

'No, I won't need the meds until next week,' Ami replied. 'I'm worried about Kieran. One of the higher-ranked agents that just showed up wanted to see him privately and I can't help but wonder if they're putting pressure on him to sign back up again. What if they manage to convince him?'

'Doubtful,' Avurn said with a soft laugh. 'We have something they do not.'

He raised his eyebrows at her, his meaning clear. Then he flipped his grin over at the Chippers, who were standing against the wall on the opposite side of the room. Not all of them had come to the conference hall today, presumably because they didn't see a need—or perhaps the others were currently ganging up on Kieran.

They didn't fail to notice Ami and Avurn looking at them.

'Goss!' Ami blurted out, hoping she could pretend that she was more interested in political minutiae instead of the Chippers. 'I understand that your government's decisions will not be made by one or two people, but everyone.'

'That's right, it's a democracy,' Goss agreed. 'We might have a leader and advisors, all of them elected by the people, but everyone has a voice. For example, Inz here has ten years of experience on a mixed crop-livestock farm so she's our advisor on agricultural matters.'

He indicated the woman beside him, one of Neffron's former soldiers. She'd originally signed up to escape a bad situation on her homeworld and had been quite happy to change sides. The loss of a steady income hadn't fazed Inz. She'd been looking for a more rewarding career and apparently this was it.

Ami shuddered. No, thanks.

'But she's *one* voice,' Goss went on. 'She will give us her informed advice and we can all choose what to do with it.'

Bock snorted but carefully maintained the smooth, cultured accent that he wielded whenever a vidcam was in the vicinity. 'Well, isn't that a grand, lofty ideal. You do realise that letting your people vote on every minor issue with their techpads is going to slow everything down? What about emergencies? If you can't respond to threats in a timely manner, you'll all end up dead. This is why we only have one person in charge on Yalsa 5.'

'Dad, this ain't your planet,' Jets snapped at him. 'So shut the fuck up. I like Goss' idea. I know how I'd vote on your stupid idea to prohibit the importation of heavy artillery...'

'The Alcazaar have been importing those on behalf of Yalsa 3's spies!' Bock exploded.

'They'll just smuggle them in! We should at least get the tax off the imports, Dad. All you have to do is make sure you buy better lascannons for your own clan. Stark. It's that easy, you know.'

Bock leaned back in his chair, throwing a chortle in Goss' direction. 'If your voting system stops annoying little upstarts bickering with you at the worst possible moment, then it can't be all that bad, can it? Now, here's a proposition for you. I've got a terraforming company and it strikes me that you could use some more fertile soil, with edible crops engineered to grow fast...'

Ami smothered the yawn and wondered if anyone would be offended if she fell asleep.

She jerked, startled, when Avurn abruptly stood on his loading crate, forcing his way into a spirited debate by suggesting that every Rochaccian be given the same amount of food and coin-chips, regardless of their contribution to society. Bock complained that people needed to earn their way or they'd get lazy. Undeterred, Avurn kept talking, a bright spark in his eyes—something Ami had never seen before. He argued that people needed time to recover from their injuries, to look after their families, or to retrain for another job when their old one became redundant.

Avurn paused, let the silence build for a few seconds, and then struck the final blow. 'You are less likely to lose your workforce to other worlds if you promise them they'll never starve because of hardships beyond their control.'

Goss nodded slowly. Jets' approval came in the form of a decidedly more enthusiastic whoop. Avurn sat back down on his loading crate, his grin wide and victorious.

Ami would be lying if she said she hadn't asked Kieran to check his visions for anything pertaining to Rochaccia. While he'd warned her that he couldn't focus on an entire planet's future ('Yet,' he'd added), he had managed to glean some of Goss Kwon's fate and had seen nothing terrible there. Goss would stay on this world for the rest of his life.

Rochaccia is in good hands, Ami decided, her eyes watering as she tried to hold back another yawn. It wrenched her jaw open seconds later, despite her best efforts.

'Tired?' Avurn asked. 'I don't suppose that has anything to do with Kieran disappearing from his bunk last night.'

Ami smiled briefly. 'No, I'm not...*that* tired. Just bored. I'm glad I can leave whenever I want to and not stick around for all the hard stuff.'

'Oh yes, this really isn't your arena, is it? However...' Avurn wrinkled his nose. 'We would have to procure a vessel first, Ami. Or do you think there is a piece of the *Free Ride* that might still be spaceworthy?'

Ami winced. Whatever had been left of the *Free Ride* after running Neffron's blockade might have had some value as spare parts—if Neffron hadn't blown it up along with the landing pads during his attack on Taylar's palace.

They were grounded indefinitely.

Ami slumped, face falling into her hands. No one paid her any mind. They were all too busy trying to decide if Neffron should be imprisoned on Rochaccia or Gerasnin. Technically, the Chippers had no cause to hold him in their cells, since any laws forbidding slavery couldn't be backdated to his rule. But they were worried about the treatment he'd receive on Rochaccia (as well they should be).

She roused herself nearly an hour later and looked at her techpad again. Grace's words hadn't changed, but that accompanying thrill of foreboding was new.

Kieran? Ami called. There was no response.

She hadn't seen Kieran since the early hours of that morning.

She'd had a blissfully dreamless sleep, his presence in her room an effective deterrent against any nightmares about dark, endless oblivion. Waking up inside his arms, his lips on her forehead...she wanted all of her days to start this exact same way.

He had made love to her one more time before he'd left. There had been a tension in his shoulders when she'd run her hands over them, but Ami had forgotten to ask him about it—or maybe he'd made sure that she forgot. She had enjoyed the slide of his slick skin against hers as he thrust slowly, carefully inside her, evoking a deep swell of pleasure that lasted so long and was so intense that Ami had thought she might actually pass out.

Afterwards, Ami had watched from the bed, laughing helplessly, as Kieran attempted to find where she'd thrown his clothes the previous night. He had swooped by for one last kiss while he was still fastening his jeans.

She kind of missed the jumpsuit—it had given Kieran a sexy, purposeful stride.

Ami wondered what he was going to wear to the party that was being held later on in the evening. For that matter, what was *she* going to wear?

Ami wasn't surprised that the Chippers had laid down the coinchips for the costs involved in the celebration. They were keen to maintain the image of being useful, of being worthy of the money their loyal supporters threw at them. One of their agents had saved an entire planet! The mediaists were equally keen to cover the event for their billions of viewers. Everyone loved a good party, no matter their species.

Ami smiled. The entire galaxy would be watching. And everyone would see that she and Kieran were together. They would no longer need to hide what they felt for each other.

So why was he hiding from her now?

FORTY-SIX

Kieran stood on the roof of the communications building, his back flush against the thick base of the tower and his grim expression aimed at the horizon.

Earlier, he had answered the summons to meet with the highest-ranked agent sent to Rochaccia, hoping it would be easier to deliver his resignation to someone he had no existing rapport with. But the colonel had interrupted Kieran before he could even offer her a customary greeting. She was so enthusiastic in her praise of him, so eager to tell him that his actions had inspired her to remain with the Agency, despite her previous doubts. And then she'd given him a new uniform, the gold stroke over the right shoulder denoting a rank he could never have.

Kieran sighed and rubbed his temples. He froze when his thumb hit the chip hidden beneath his skin. Once, it had meant everything to him. Now it was a useless, broken piece of tech. He dropped both of his hands to his belt, anchoring them there, and watched the sky for any sign that one of Rochaccia's famously fast sunsets was about to descend on the mountaintop.

Kieran could sense the Desine nearby. Waiting. Always waiting.

But the god was not content to wait for much longer.

'I suspect this isn't a good time,' a wry voice said behind him. 'But I don't think there will ever be a good time for this conversation.'

Kieran turned—and had to blink twice, to make sure he wasn't seeing things. Standing there, her arms crossed and her stance unbowed despite the large shadow thrown down by the communications tower, was Grace Pendergast.

'I was wondering when you'd show up,' Kieran said. 'You're too late, by the way. Nothing you can tell me will change what happened or what I did. Though I'll probably always wonder if you could have given me an option that didn't involve throwing myself on the mercy of the desert god. I'm in his debt and in his service for the rest of my life. I'll have to leave GLEA.'

'He can't make you do that,' Grace said, her brow creasing. 'What has he told you?'

Kieran glared at her, his patience completely eroded. 'Are you ever going to explain any of this to me? Or will I have to read about it in your e-paper?'

Grace glanced down at the pouch on her belt, guilt spiking in her energy. But it didn't take her too long to recover.

'Oh, I'd never put anything about this into my e-paper,' she assured him. 'I am not sure what I'm expected to do with all the information I've had the privilege to uncover, but it seems that for now my purpose is to collect it. Kieran, I risked your life when I showed you what your parents look like. Most of the sub-level gods can read minds and if the wrong one happened to see that image of them in your head...'

Kieran tried—and failed—to keep that same image from

appearing in his thoughts now. He didn't like the cold fear prickling at the nape of his neck. He preferred the heat of his anger.

Grace shrugged helplessly. 'But I...I had to give you something. You deserved that much. I thought I was forbidden from saying more and I'm sorry it took me so long to realise that I'd already received permission, so to speak. Why else would the Creator God have sent me to you? Frankly, I don't think your ignorance will protect you from our family. Not anymore.'

'Our family?' Kieran repeated. 'Who are they?'

'You'd have figured it out soon enough,' Grace said, casting a furtive look across the roof, as if she too could sense the Desine's presence. 'My wife is the goddess of fire, which makes me your aunt. Micadei is the son of the rainforest god—and he's your cousin. I'm sure you can put the rest of the pieces together.'

Kieran's stomach twisted. He didn't want to put it together. He couldn't—*wouldn't*—put it together. She was lying. She was delusional. Anything else would break him.

You should not be here! the Desine's voice thundered.

Kieran spun around and began to circle Grace with his back to her, his palms raised and offered to the air in an attempt to placate the Desine. He didn't know which direction the attack would come from, but he could sense how imminent it was.

'Tell him, Desine!' Grace shouted. 'He should hear it from you! Or are you afraid he'll realise that you have no power over him?'

Thick cords of sand climbed onto the roof and weaved into a mound that grew and grew, until it formed a dune that was almost half the size of the tower. It loomed there above them, twisting and trembling. A threat—or a sign that the one who had created it was rethinking his actions? Kieran doubted it. He kept very still, waiting. He didn't have to wait for long.

The dune surged towards them.

Kieran slapped his thighs; the mound toppled backwards, away from him, throwing a river of sand across the concrete roof. The dune rebuilt itself within seconds, roaring and roiling, ready for vengeance. The next attack was faster, harder, and the sands cried out an apology when Kieran failed to wrest control of them away from their god. He winced. This battle was unwinnable—unless he used his chipless powers. The forcefield Kieran called forth burst out of his chest like a blast from a lascannon, then arced back around both him and Grace.

The bulk of the dune shattered against his shield. But the Desine wasn't done. The ensuing cloud of grainy particles whisked through the invisible barrier as though it was passing through a sieve.

Kieran spat sand. He heard Grace coughing behind him and flicked a look over his shoulder. Her brown eyes were hard and her voice even harder. 'You don't owe him anything. Not your worship, not your service—we all possess free will, mortal or otherwise—and certainly not your respect or your love. He's done nothing to prove himself worthy of it!'

Stand aside! the Desine ordered.

Kieran gritted his teeth. 'No.'

I won't ask again!

'You didn't ask, you demanded—and anyway, I still refuse,' Kieran said. His shield continued to take a battering; the Desine hadn't let up. 'I don't care who you are or what you can do to me. I won't let you hurt anyone. I'd die to stop you.'

'Is this the kind of relationship you want with him, Desine?' Grace called. 'Kieran will never love you if keep trying to control him!'

'Grace—' Kieran broke off, gasping as a cosmic force struck his shield, nearly puncturing it. Above them, the sky darkened as a sandstorm swirled into existence. The Desine was using all of his powers in tandem and that meant Kieran would have to do the same in order to counter him. He had no confidence that he'd succeed.

'Get out of here, Grace!' he cried. 'I can't hold him off for much longer.'

'Are you dense or in denial?' Grace demanded of Kieran. 'No mortal can hold him off *at all*. No mortal can cast him out like you did over Yalsa 5. You are his—'

Knowing will put him in danger!

Grace recrossed her arms, defiantly staring up into the storm as it began to descend, swallowing the immense tower as it went. 'That ship has taken off and hit orbit, Desine! He's already in danger—he was in danger from the very moment he discovered his powers. You need to protect and guide him. But if you keep pushing, if you keep treating him like this, then you'll lose him all over again. Is that what you want?'

Will you tell me how to look after my own domain next, Pendergast? the god snarled.

'No, but I can track down your wife and tell her what you did— what you're *still* doing to Kieran!'

Menace was strung through each and every syllable. *You should have kept out of this.*

The storm roared and plunged to the ground in an instant, engulfing them in a dusty gloom. Kieran split his mind in two, maintaining his shield and frantically trying to command the sand, but the Desine was stronger and had more experience. The stars...he needed the power of the stars. They answered the instant Kieran called upon them, but in his panic he drew too much, too fast. Pain lashed through his skull. Zigzags of light scored across his vision. His forcefield exploded into useless wisps of energy.

Kieran cried out and fell to his knees. Grace hit the ground behind him.

'Stop!' Kieran drew a breath, one that tore down his throat like starship fuel. His voice became a croak. 'You're hurting me. *Father.*'

The storm died.

Kieran scrambled towards Grace, trying to shield her with his body. He had nothing else left. But she was already on her haunches, dusting herself off, seemingly unperturbed. Shaking with a toxic mixture of emotions, Kieran pivoted on his knees and then rose to his full height, confronting the humanoid figure that now stood mere paces from him.

The Desine was wearing his usual cloak, but the hood had fallen away from his face and the mane of blond hair framing it. Kieran immediately recognised his father from the image Grace had given him back at the Trading Post.

The Desine took a step forward. 'Kieran...'

'Don't!' Kieran snapped. 'Don't come near me.'

Fury sparked inside the Desine's chasmic blue eyes. The thick layer of sand on the roof swarmed, rising into the air like a cloud of angrily buzzing insects. Kieran looked back at Grace, unable to voice the apology. He couldn't protect her. The stars were still there, but he might destroy himself if he attempted to use them again so soon. If she left now, she would be safe.

Grace nodded tightly. 'I understand. I'll go. You can contact me anytime—Ami has my details. Kieran, don't you dare let him use his past and his pain as an excuse for what he's done. He owes you an apology, a real one. You don't need to forgive him, but you do need his help. Finara, I'm ready!'

She burst into flames. Kieran blinked—and then every trace of his aunt was gone. *She wasn't kidding about being married to the goddess of fire.*

He turned towards the god who had dared to take on the form of a man.

'My son...' The Desine held out a hand; it hovered between

them, an unwanted and unwelcome gesture.

'You have no starking right to call me that,' Kieran said flatly. 'No father should do this to his son. At least, I don't think so. I wouldn't know. I've spent my life without one.'

'It's not my fault, you were stolen from me—'

'So you tried to steal me away from everything and everyone I ever loved?' Kieran demanded.

His turmoil stirred up a tunnel of sand that sprang from the roof and spun around them, mere moments away from forming yet another storm. The Desine closed his hand into a fist and the vortex flattened.

'I wanted to protect you,' the Desine said.

'Seems like I need protecting from you,' Kieran replied. He sensed a flicker in the god's energy: the desire to come closer. 'No! Stay where you are!'

'Please...' The Desine visibly restrained himself. 'Please...what can I do to keep you?'

'Keep me,' Kieran echoed, frowning. 'You can't have me. I'm Ami's. And I'm GLEA's. I'm definitely not yours.'

He turned his back on the Desine and stormed his way over to the edge of the roof. His hands were shaking so badly they were nearly of no use to him, but Kieran managed to climb down the ladder set onto the side of the building.

He could feel Avurn tapping on their link, trying to find out what was going on. Kieran effortlessly blocked him.

'You can't be with her,' the Desine called from the roof.

Kieran's steps faltered. 'GLEA doesn't need to know about Ami. Not yet. There's still time to fix things. Stark, I'll even get myself elected as Head General if I have to. GLEA won't fracture. Not if I'm there to stop it happening.'

'The Chippers are not the only obstacle standing between you and the captain.' There was a singsong undercurrent to those words.

'What do you mean?' Kieran asked, unable to stop himself turning around.

The Desine tossed a bitter laugh down at him. 'She won't stay with you. Not once she knows.'

Kieran refused to rise to the bait this time. He didn't have to.

'You see, my son...' The god's voice tapered off as his human form dissolved, vanishing from the roof. A gust of wind fell heavy on Kieran's shoulder, as though someone was pressing down on it. The Desine switched to using mind-speech. *Any being you choose to marry will become immortal. Because that's what you are. Immortal. Do you think she can handle that? Do you think she'll still want you?*

'You underestimate her.'

You don't see the danger she poses to you! She will chain you to this body. She will force you to remain a mere man.

'I *am* a mere man,' Kieran told him.

You are my son!

'Do you even hear yourself? You're not my father. You're a god who manipulated, tormented, and isolated me instead of just *telling* me what was going on. We could have had...' Kieran shook his head. 'I don't know. I'll never know.'

The Desine hesitated, clearly thrown. *Had what?*

'Nothing. Go away! Just go away! Before I cast you out again.'

A howl of tortured wind—and then the god was gone.

The ensuing silence ate away at Kieran as he stormed back to the fortress, desperate for the false comfort that its walls could give him. He wanted to feel safe, even if it was only a lie. But he paused at the gated entrance, sensing the lifesigns inside the building, sensing how finite their lives were compared to his.

Immortal...

I don't even want this. How could Ami bear it?

Kieran covered his eyes with his hands and begged the tears to stay where they were.

He was fervently glad that Ami hadn't let him propose back at the cave (had it only been a handful of days since then?), because he hadn't truly known what that question—and her answer—really meant for them both.

'Kieran! What happened?' Avurn burst out of the fortress and came towards the gate. 'That sandstorm over the tower...you didn't renege on the deal you made with the Desine, did you?'

Kieran pushed past him. 'I need to put my uniform on.'

Avurn spun around and matched his pace as they entered the fortress, both of them tearing through the corridors. 'You listened to me, Kieran. You were there for me. I'm willing to return the favour, if you need me to perform that service. I cannot promise I will be any good at it, given my relative inexperience...'

For a moment, Kieran was sorely tempted.

But this was his burden and he had no right to push it onto the shoulders of a boy who was still vulnerable, still reeling from his own battles.

His decision had *nothing* to do with his fear that Avurn would point out the obvious.

Kieran entered their shared quarters and discarded the clothes the Desine had given him. Pulled on the purple jumpsuit. Ignored the accusatory look when Avurn noticed the gold stoke on the shoulder. Left before the boy could take him to task.

But Avurn's thoughts followed him. *Kieran! What have you done? You made a deal! Conveniently forgetting the fact that the Desine could pulverise you...how can you learn to use your powers if you refuse his help? You're a danger to everyone around you! Do you want to hurt Ami? Or maybe you don't care.*

That uniform you're wearing will hurt her more than any sandstorm ever could. And you know it.

Kieran lengthened his strides and burst into a run.

FORTY-SEVEN

Ami stood on the semi-spherical mezzanine that kept her above and apart from the festivities, trying not to pace. She didn't want anyone to think she was lurking by the doors for a reason.

Like she was waiting for someone.

The floor below her was grey, soulless concrete, but tonight it was obscured by a crowd of beings who were wining and dining, walking and talking, smiling and exchanging pleasantries. Though the many different species in attendance added colour to the proceedings, it was the bright purple uniforms that stood out the most. Chippers. Apparently, they were about to make some sort of grand announcement.

Whatever. Better that they snapped up all the attention so no one would notice Ami wearing the slightly too-tight dress that Avurn had acquired from a mediaist. The fabric was green silksein and the tag revealed that a famous Jezlo designer was to blame for the ruffles on the hemline. Pricey. She hadn't dared to ask what Avurn had bartered in return.

Despite her physical discomfort, Ami found herself smiling.

The Rochaccia of her childhood no longer existed, which meant that there was nothing left for her to flee. She could now run *towards* something.

'But I'm not done atoning,' she murmured and rested her arms on the metal railing that rimmed the stairs leading down into Neffron's 'concert hall'. Not that it had ever hosted a concert. Her father had preferred to stage military parades in this space and had recorded them to watch at his leisure.

'Ami?' a soft voice called.

She turned towards the main steel doors and saw no one there, but he was nearby. She could *feel* him. Behind those crimson velvet curtains, maybe? They were the only decorative touch in the entire hall and hung down the bland concrete walls at precise intervals, looking like an afterthought. Token window dressing on top of a brutal design. But Ami knew what they were hiding: multiple entrances that fed into Neffron's secret passages. She'd used them often enough as a child, though they weren't much of a secret now that she'd told Goss and her crewmates about them.

Ami had wanted to use the main doors tonight, so that everyone would see her on Kieran's arm. That didn't seem to be in his plans, though.

Frowning, Ami slid behind the nearest curtain and barely had time to gasp before Kieran spun her around, walking her backwards until she was pressed against the wall. Closing her eyes and locking her lips with his, Ami lost herself to that wild, searing scent he'd carried with him ever since their time together in the cave. It suited him. *Really* suited him.

Her whole body trembled with anticipation as one of his hands travelled up her bare arms to anchor her wrists above her head.

'*Stark*,' Ami breathed. 'I knew I didn't put on any underwear for a reason.'

He chuckled against her neck, sending a cascade of pleasure

tumbling through her, right down to her toes. Heat unfurled in her abdomen when his other hand began to stroke her breast, rhythmically grazing her nipple with the soft silksein. Not content to let him do all the work, Ami slid her thigh between his legs and pressed just so. A distracted groan was the response. She took advantage of his loss of focus and yanked hard on her arms. His grip gave.

Ami teased her fingers along his jaw and then down this throat, a much lower destination in mind, but his hand swiftly closed over her own, halting her progress. Something was wrong. Was that—a *zipper?*

She opened her eyes and blinked rapidly until her vision adjusted to the gloom.

Her heart plummeted. 'Why are you wearing that?'

He cupped her face, guilt warring with hope in his shadowed eyes. The words escaped him in a whisper. 'I'm not leaving GLEA.'

'You're joking.'

'No. I'm serious.' His thumb stroked her cheek. 'I know I should have talked to you about this beforehand, but—'

That's when she noticed the gold stripe on the shoulder of his jumpsuit.

'They promoted you,' she said dully.

There was a roar of voices inside the hall, followed by a burst of enthusiastic applause. Kieran jerked away from her. 'Stark. They're announcing me. I have to—Ami, please, I'll explain later.'

He strode towards the curtain and slapped it aside. The harsh ceiling lights that caused Ami to wince didn't even slow him down for a nanosecond. Arms raised in triumph, Kieran descended the stairs and then comfortably assimilated into the crowd. Hands clapped his shoulders, agents shouted his praises, and mediaists' voices grew breathy as they trained their vidcams on him.

This was the Chipper, not the man who had bargained with a god, not the man who had almost asked her to marry him. He just couldn't give up that purple jumpsuit, could he? Stark. Had he completely forgotten about the Desine?

Ami backed away from the curtain, breathing hard—and then jumped when someone touched her elbow.

She whirled towards the intruder, fingers wrapped around her new lasgun (small and light enough that she'd clipped it onto the ruffly hemline that sat halfway up her thighs) but she did not draw it. Not because she had good reflexes; no, her thumb seemed incapable of performing the right flick that was needed to unfasten the strap across the handle.

Goss Kwon dutifully put his hands up in the air.

Sighing, Ami loosened her hold on the lasgun. 'Goss. Shouldn't you be down *there*, celebrating?' She waved vaguely at the gap Kieran had left in the curtains.

Goss didn't even glance in that direction, clearly unbothered. 'Chippers just stole the spotlight, didn't they? They'll have a full hour to show the galaxy just how useful they are. They'll parade Krendasta around in front of the mediaists, rebrand him as their galactic poster boy, announce their sudden surge of new enlistments —and *then* they'll ask for donations.'

'You agreed to this beforehand?' Ami asked.

'Got an extra year of their protection out of the deal,' Goss said, his smile showing teeth. He tipped his head towards the entrance he'd used to sneak up on her, the sliding door almost impossible to see once it had shut. 'Captain, I'd like to steal a few moments of your time. If you aren't otherwise occupied.'

Ami savagely yanked the curtain back into place, then turned to Goss. 'Steal as much time as you want.'

'I suspected you would not need much convincing,' Goss remarked. 'Avurn told me you could use a distraction, which I am happy to provide. He also said he would eject Krendasta into a sun, if desired. I can't say I endorse this suggestion.'

'I did wonder where Avurn had got to,' Ami said. 'I hope he's not bothering you.'

'Bothering? No, he's quite fascinating. You're lucky to have him on your crew.'

'Yeah, I know. Avurn's a good kid.'

Goss offered her a suit-clad arm. Ami had to admit that he scrubbed up very well and his appearance was further enhanced by that dusting of hair on his jaw (he seemed to be growing a beard). Once she'd looped her arm through his, Goss escorted her along the dimly lit passageway, his expression solemn and his steps slow and graceful, as though they were joining the party instead of retreating from it. His past in politics was undeniable during moments like these.

'Are you sure you want the Chippers to stick a temple next door to your government headquarters?' Ami asked, barely noticing the doors and junctions they were passing.

Goss shrugged. 'Seems only fair, given what they're doing for us. Though they may be disappointed by how many of their potential worshippers choose to follow the Desine instead. Religion will play an integral role in helping my people move forward with their lives.' His lips firmed. 'Taylar and Neffron did terrible things to us—and they also made us do terrible things to each other. We could not control our actions, but that doesn't mean we can absolve ourselves. We need a way to find forgiveness. I'm sure you know what that's like.'

Ami grimaced. She *did* know. 'I wasn't under any outside influence when I ordered the bombardment of those outposts, the deaths of those mercs. I'll have to live with that.'

'Rochaccia appreciates the difficult choices you have made for us, Captain.' Goss drew up short in front of a door that was so overengineered it could have kept out the vacuum of space. He met and held Ami's eyes. 'You gave us our lives back—and then you gave us a future. Do not tell me you regret your actions, when they have done so much for so many.'

Goss slapped a sensor pad on the wall. The horizontal panels forming the door gaped a little and then whirred, as though pondering what they were supposed to be doing. Smiling serenely, Goss kicked the panels. They dutifully sprang apart, revealing what appeared to be a private hangar.

There was only one ship inside; large, looming, and yet somehow still elegant, its gently arcing hull reminded Ami of a bird in flight. It was a spectacular work of art, accentuated rather than interrupted by the five protruding lascannons that were spaced evenly from wing to wing. Gorgeous. And deadly. Very deadly. Ami couldn't stop herself imagining all the pirates and slavers she could scare into submission with a ship like this.

'It's yours,' Goss said.

The metallic gold lettering on the side clearly read '*Free Ride II*', courtesy of Avurn and his small army of painters, but it still took several seconds for Goss' words to register.

Ami violently shook her head. 'No. I won't take it. Goss, you need this for Rochaccia—'

She broke off when she noticed the ground crew moving crates into the generous hold, which could have easily fit her old ship inside it. The crew wouldn't take long to finish their work, thanks to the large exterior hatch set into the hull. Ami was pleased to see that the hold had interior access as well, the steel door on the far wall ostensibly opening out into a corridor in the ship's lower levels—but wait.

'What are they loading?' she demanded.

'Your father had considerable wealth on hand,' was the evasive reply.

'Goss!' Ami exclaimed. 'This vessel belongs to your planet, your people. Neffron's fleet was destroyed and you can't defend—'

'Captain.' The firm, unyielding tone that Goss now wielded told Ami that he was speaking to her as a planetary leader, not as a friend. 'This is not a gift. It's an investment. You'll be using this ship, and these coin-chips, to liberate those who would otherwise be lost —and then you will give them the option of coming to Rochaccia. We are in great need of more skilled and unskilled workers. And there are many beings in great need of a safe landing.'

Ami opened her mouth, then shut it. Goss would have encountered resistance when he'd suggested this use of the ship to his people. Which meant he had worked hard to convince them.

This was important to him. It was also his way of saying thanks.

'Are you seriously going to refuse?' Avurn swung a glare at Ami, his dark jumpsuit smeared with gold paint. So he'd managed to find something in *his* size, huh. 'I've already spent hours making my own modifications to the ship. If you don't want it, I'll take it.'

'I think you'd better accept my offer before he does,' Goss told Ami, his eyes dancing. 'How do you plan on rescuing all those countless beings who need saving if you don't have a ship?'

'That's not fair,' Ami said. 'I don't know your weakness but you know mine. And you're exploiting it.'

'Do you know what is truly unfair, Captain? That there are so many evils in our galaxy that will never meet justice.' Goss gestured loosely towards the hanger door set into the ceiling. 'You knocked out one major contributor to the slave trade, just one—well, two I suppose,' he conceded. 'But there are more. Many more. Go. Do what you do best.'

Ami raised her eyebrows at him. 'Am I going to cause a galactic incident if I refuse your *investment*?'

Goss chuckled. 'No. But since you're currently stranded, I might have to convince you to take an active role in my government. And we both know you're not suited for it.'

'Then I guess I better accept and get the stark out of here,' Ami said, unaware that her feet were moving until she was standing beside the gleaming hull. She ran her palms over the reflective chrome, wincing when she saw the sweaty handprints that she'd left behind. Glancing around at her audience, she grabbed a handful of ruffles from her dress and wiped the smudges away, barely remembering to pull the hem down to a decent level before she turned back to Goss. 'I might have to take on more crew...this ship is too starking big for me and Avurn.'

'What about your Chipper?' Goss asked.

'I doubt he'll be riding with me after this. They promoted him.'

Goss watched her for several long moments, a frown threatening to creep across his carefully crafted expression. 'Do they know about him working with the Desine?'

'Nope,' Ami said as she marched towards the entry ramp, dodging the people in her way. 'But that's not my problem. It's his. Right now, I want a tour of my ship—and I want to know the full specs.'

Goss allowed the change of topic and didn't ask about Kieran again. Ami was glad. She didn't have any answers for him. What the stark was Kieran doing? It was one thing to ditch her for GLEA, quite another to ditch the Desine.

Even my fancy new ship is no match for a god, she thought, biting her lip.

FORTY-EIGHT

The nearest star had been idling above the open hanger door for three Old Earth hours when Kieran finally came for her.

Catching sight of him at the bottom of the boarding ramp, Ami supposed there was no hiding from someone who could sense her lifesign anywhere in the galaxy. Though, judging by the fact that Kieran had not appeared any earlier, she suspected that Avurn had headed him off and only released him after receiving a satisfactory explanation for his recent behaviour. Ami vowed that she would not be so easily swayed.

'Captain, I need to speak to you,' Kieran called.

She sighed and wiped her hands over her jeans (which, despite being black, were starting to show the grease stains). While Goss had found a seemingly inexhaustible supply of socks and olive-green military uniforms, casual clothes that suited Ami's fuller figure were scarce in the fortress.

'Are you sure you want to have this conversation?' Ami asked.

'Yes,' Kieran said simply.

Mindful of the ground crew still going over the hull to check its integrity, Ami waved for Kieran to follow her inside the ship. He obeyed. As soon as they were safely out of sight, Ami turned to face him, planting herself in the middle of the corridor and giving him her best, most deadly glare. 'Kieran. I'm really angry with you right now and I'm probably going to say something I'll regret—'

Ami broke off when he moved forward and took her hands in his. Stark. How could she yell at him when he was gazing at her like that? Like she was his entire universe.

'I'm sorry I didn't consult with you beforehand. I should have.' Kieran lifted her fingers to his mouth and delivered small, glancing kisses to each and every knuckle. Once he was done, he added, 'I won't make any other decisions of that magnitude without first consulting you. I promise.'

'Kieran...' Her voice steadied on command, but her heart refused to comply. 'I know you wanted this—GLEA listening to you, accepting you, giving you a rank without you having to marry someone. And I'm thrilled they finally got off their butts and gave you what you deserve. But you can't have it. You don't seriously think the Desine will forget that deal you made, do you?'

His smile was strange, secretive. It worried her. 'I do not have to honour it—and he won't speak to me unless I allow him to. He's desperate to gain my favour.'

'*Okaaay*,' Ami said slowly. 'So he's agreed to train you and leave you alone all those other times? When GLEA needs you?'

'I don't want him to come anywhere near me!'

'Really? You're so set on avoiding him that you'll let your powers get out of control?'

'There's so much...' Kieran visibly swallowed. Unable to stop herself, Ami reached out and cupped his cheek, her thumb brushing the lip he'd pulled between his teeth. He leaned gratefully into her touch. 'There's so much I want to know. So much he can tell me.'

'You don't have to like him in order to learn from him, Kieran.'

Kieran nodded. 'Yes, I know. But...I'm wondering if there's a chance we can have a more meaningful relationship. The one we could have had. If circumstances were different.'

Ami's head gave an insistent throb. She felt sure she was missing something here. But if that was deliberate on his part, she knew it wasn't because he didn't trust her. He was having trouble processing something. She'd just have to wait him out.

Ami slid her other hand down between his shoulder blades and seated it at the small of his back, drawing him in close—though she was sorely tempted to throw him out the nearest airlock. There was breathable air on the other side of the hull, so all he'd suffer was some indignity. But still.

'Does he deserve that relationship, though?' Ami wondered.

Kieran's chin drooped to his chest. 'I don't know. He hurt me because he was hurting. That's no excuse, even if it helps me to make sense of his actions. I think...I think I want to give him the chance to apologise, to atone. And I want to *try* to have a relationship with him.' Then Kieran smiled and kissed her, quick and gleeful. 'He just has to accept that I'm only ever going to wear purple jumpsuits.'

'So if that works out...you're not going to choose,' Ami murmured. 'You're going to learn from the Desine. And stay with GLEA.'

'Yes,' he said.

Ami looked down at his new boots. They were so shiny she could see her own reflection in them. Her feet were bare. She preferred that on this ship, probably because the floors were heated, an extravagance the first *Free Ride* had been without.

'Ami, what happened in the cave...it was...' His voice faltered.

Just get this over and done with, Kieran, she thought, struggling to see him through the film of tears filling her vision. *Stop making it hurt so starking much.*

'Ami, you don't understand.' Kieran pulled her into a deeper, more luxurious kiss, one that would have completely consumed her if she'd let it. The words he then gave her made her traitorous heart leap. 'I can't go back to how things were before. Not when I know how much I love you, how much I need you.'

Ami felt her forehead bunch down to her eyebrows. 'But if you're with GLEA...'

'It's now obvious that I must become the full version of me,' he told her calmly. 'Not just the part that belongs to you, the Desine, or GLEA—I had to use every piece of me to save an entire planet and help prepare it for the future.' He held her eyes. 'Don't ask me to give you up. I can't. If we stay together, we'll have to be extremely careful and keep our feelings hidden when we're in public. I know I'm asking a lot. I know it's not what you wanted. But this is who I am and I think the galaxy *needs* me to be complete.'

Ami's shoulders lost their tension and their height. She leaned into him, breathing in the scent that made her think of wild wind and blistering sands and—*home*. But she didn't allow herself to get comfortable. Not yet. 'So what happens when GLEA outright orders you to marry a fellow agent? They will, you know. If you make them wait too long. And what happens when they find out about us? Because these kinds of things...they tend to get out. Every mediaist this side of Sundafar knows your name and what you look like. They'll be watching us everywhere we go.'

'It's only a matter of time,' Kieran agreed. 'I will just have to make the best of what time I have. I'll keep earning ranks. Maybe I'll get high enough in the Agency that I can convince them to change the rules. And if I fail? I remember someone telling me they'd find a way for me to save the galaxy regardless. I truly believe you could do it.'

Ami hesitated. 'I don't have your visions...'

'I did not see this in any vision,' Kieran said. 'It's what I want. And I want you.'

She pillowed her head against his chest, listening to the heart that beat only for her. 'I want you too. The full version of you.' She turned her smile up at him. 'You belong to me, Kieran, first and foremost. Don't you dare forget it. But if the galaxy needs you that badly...then I'm okay with sharing you. This kind of sharing I can do.'

'God, Ami, I love you. Thank you for listening to me.'

'You did nearly go out the airlock, mind.'

Kieran laughed and rained kisses down upon her, peppering them over her forehead, her cheeks, her lips. He found the edge of her shirt and began lifting it, his fingers eager and roaming, leaving sparks everywhere they went. A moan parted her lips.

Regaining herself, Ami swatted him away. 'Easy there. I want to show you the captain's quarters—I've been upgraded to a *double* bed. Very handy, since I'm going to need the extra space from now on. For some reason.'

'Can't imagine what that reason is,' Kieran murmured.

He tugged the zipper of his jumpsuit down his torso with excruciating slowness, micrometre by agonising micrometre. Ami felt the growl vibrate in her throat before it escaped her. She grabbed his uniform and pulled it down past his shoulders in one rough motion, then ducked forward to lick and nibble her way across his exposed chest until he gasped her name. Smirking, she yanked at the zipper and rendered him nude in record time.

Ami stepped back, admiring the view, enjoying the evidence of just how much he desired her. Gods, that was hot. Kieran just standing there, arms spread, offering himself. Waiting for her to make the next move.

She turned and made him chase her through the ship, towards her quarters.

He caught up to her there and threw her onto the bed, worshipping her thoroughly. Ami let the tears of joy fall once he was inside her, their bodies moving as one, their minds united by love and pleasure. But she couldn't shake the feeling that there was something he still wasn't telling her—and she wouldn't ask, didn't want to ask. Not when he was dozing, his face sporting a slack, satisfied smile.

Ami slid out of bed, made herself presentable, and left the ship in search of Goss and Avurn. She had both a farewell and a summons to deliver.

THE RETURN TRIP to Ilbb took several days. Compared to the weeks they'd been away, it should have passed in the blink of an eye. But the time dragged.

Kieran dedicated himself to exploring the *Free Ride II* but, even with its considerable size, he managed to memorise the contents of every cupboard in every compartment inside a day. Training Avurn filled some of the endless hours and yet offered minimal relief. Most of the exercises they performed together were repetitive and did not allow him to forget his situation, not for even a nanosecond.

Nights, by Old Earth reckoning, were more bearable. That's when Kieran would enter Ami's—*their*—quarters and lie on the side of the bed that belonged to him. Sometimes they entwined, fully clothed, whispering and laughing until one of them had to leave to replace Avurn on watch. Other times Kieran watched over Ami while she slept, kissing her forehead whenever he saw the frightening darkness of oblivion seize her mind, slowly easing her into more pleasant dreams.

When she was on the bridge, Ami was prone to sitting very still, chin propped up in her hand as she became lost in thought. Her new captain's chair was elevated, the better for her to keep an eye on her crew and the various controls she had at her command.

'We should get our stories straight before we return,' Avurn spoke up from his sunken compartment. He didn't oversee a mere console; he was now surrounded by vidscreens and constantly blinking sensors. There were even two spare seats in there with him. The weapons system was largely automated and Avurn had already tweaked it to his liking, but he'd remarked that he didn't trust a machine to make life-or-death decisions in his place.

'We've got plenty of time to cook up a story,' Ami said. 'I'd rather Kieran and I had a chat about whatever's on his mind.'

Kieran hesitated. 'Ami...'

She deserved to know, but he couldn't tell her. He couldn't. Not until he knew what it meant for him. And if he didn't figure that out, then he would never know what it meant for *them*.

Ami raised her eyebrows. He looked away, hating that he did so.

Avurn sighed deeply and spun around in his chair, facing his crewmates. 'Whatever Kieran is brooding about, I have no sympathy for him. That lucky starker has two sets of powers and he was just *given* them! The rest of us enjoy no such privilege. I do not even know where to begin to create a tech substitute for the Magic. Surely there is another method I can use to procure it, some way that doesn't involve being born in a desert. Perhaps if I were to ask the Desine...'

'Don't you dare!' Ami snapped. 'It's too dangerous.'

Avurn performed a pout worthy of a child vidstar. 'But, *Ami...*'

The ensuing argument went on for a good half hour. Kieran flashed Avurn a grateful look and the boy winked in response. Avurn had clearly felt his discomfort through their link and had decided to change the topic.

Later, after Ami had retired from the bridge, Kieran approached

Avurn. 'Do you have Micadei's communicator details? I think the Head General attached them to that list of safe planets he sent us.'

'The real question is why you would need said details,' Avurn said, eyeing him. 'It's not as if we have any passengers to offload. I also seem to remember us leaving Bagaran in a hurry—I was under the impression that you wanted no further contact with Micadei.'

'It's important that I speak to him,' Kieran said.

Avurn frowned. 'This is to do with you and Ami, isn't it. Something that's getting in the way.'

'Yes.'

'Very well.' Avurn gave a decisive nod. 'I'd rather not waste my time trying to contrive some way to punish you for hurting her. It would be difficult, considering your powers. And I have far more important things to do.'

Kieran laughed and thanked him. Avurn left soon afterwards, since it was Kieran's turn to stand watch on the bridge. Kieran stayed in one spot for at least an hour, watching the constant glow of leapspace in the viewport, breathing deeply as the energy of passing planets and people washed over him.

Finally, he braced himself and activated his communicator. He didn't have to wait long for the verbal link to be accepted.

'Kieran! Are you sure we should be talking?' Micadei blurted.

'I don't know,' Kieran said honestly. 'But I'm glad that we are. I was wondering if I could get your perspective on something.'

'Sure! Ask me anything.'

'You live with your parents, correct?'

'Yes...' Micadei's voice became guarded.

'What's that like?' Kieran swallowed. 'I mean, what's it like to grow up knowing you'll live forever? Doesn't it...frighten you?'

'Ohhh. *Oh*. You know! Oh cool. We're cousins, by the way.'

It was hard not to smile in response to Micadei's enthusiasm. Kieran reached out across the distance between them and found his cousin's lifesign: an unwavering beacon of hope and light. Micadei immediately sensed Kieran's probe but didn't withdraw, cheerfully inviting him in instead. Kieran's smile grew. He could easily see himself becoming friends with his cousin.

Micadei hummed thoughtfully. 'Immortality doesn't frighten me. I guess because I *did* grow up knowing about it—wow, this must be really confronting for you! But I definitely think eternity would be awesome if I had someone to share it with. When I see Mum and Dad together, they're so sweet and it's so obvious they're perfect for each other. Dad says she makes him a better god. And a better man. You know, it's pretty common for our aunts and uncles to get married. Most mortals don't care what they are.'

'Most mortals,' Kieran repeated. 'So there are those that do care.'

'Oh, um, that's not my story to tell. Anyway! Kieran, I can totally see myself becoming friends with you too. You really need to learn how to shield your thoughts.'

'I'll work on it,' Kieran said tightly. 'Thank you. We'll speak again, I promise.'

Micadei, predictably, was delighted to hear this.

Avurn returned to the bridge for watch duty some hours later, relieving Kieran. Perturbed and wondering about the story that his cousin had refused to tell him, Kieran drifted through the corridors until he reached the quarters he shared with Ami. He wasn't surprised to find her still awake, sitting up in bed with an adventure zine loaded on her techpad while she waited for him.

'Ami, I...I can't tell you what's on my mind,' he said softly. 'Not yet. I'm not ready.'

'But you will, when you are?'

'Yes,' he vowed.

She didn't ask any more questions or tell him to revoke his presence from her mind, as he'd feared she would. Instead, she curled up beside him and took his hand to her abdomen, sighing as his warmth began to counter her cramps. Avurn hadn't been able to source her usual meds on Rochaccia, though he'd managed to find a less-potent organic remedy. Ami was happy to have anything at all—and Kieran was happy to help her in any way that he could.

'Take your time, Kieran,' she murmured sleepily. 'I'll always be here for you.'

But would she still say the same thing when she knew what 'always' entailed? Kieran hoped so. He was always going to need her.

For the rest of his long life.

FORTY-NINE

Kieran knelt, the *Free Ride II*'s shadow shielding him from Ilbb's three suns, and scooped some sand into his hands. The whispers abruptly rose into a crescendo. He hesitated. Smiled. And then accepted the greeting the desert had given him.

Despite the blazing starlight, most of Carton City's denizens were in bed. Ami's crew had only just touched down on Ilbb and it was too late for them to officially announce their arrival, though Avurn had headed off to the bar to see if Tends needed him to cover a shift. Ami remained in her onboard quarters, claiming that she intended to finish her latest zine, but Kieran could see that her mind was filling up with lists: planets that needed help, planets she could *actually* help, notable suppliers of the galactic slave trade, notable suppliers who *might* be easier targets.

When the last of the soft sand had trailed away between his fingers, Kieran finally spoke. 'I'm ready to talk to you, Desine. If you are ready to accept me as I am.'

Barely a heartbeat later, he felt the god's presence at his back.

Hotter than the most barren deserts, as eternal as the stars—and always heralded by a howl of tortured wind. Kieran stood and turned, nodding his head at the Desine. The hood was down around the god's shoulders again. It revealed nothing this time.

The Desine stayed very still, an impassive, silent statue. His mind was an impenetrable fortress and there would be little warning if he chose to attack. Kieran straightened, uncowed. He would defend himself—and Carton City—if he had to.

'There...' The Desine swallowed. 'There are things I wish to say.'

'I'm not leaving GLEA,' Kieran said flatly. 'I won't let you control me or undermine my decisions, no matter what blood we share.'

The Desine shook his head, a haunted cast falling over his face. 'You remind me of...well, me. Back when I spoke such defiant words to my own father. He made a puppet of me and I refuse to do the same to my son. I may not like your decisions, Kieran, but I'll support them. I'll always support *you*. I lost you once, years ago. I saw myself losing you again, over and over in so many visions, and I was desperate to avoid that future. So desperate, so consumed, that I did not respect your agency or your feelings. As I should have. I cannot undo my actions but I am sorry for them. I am so sorry.'

Kieran exhaled deeply. It might have been a sigh of relief. The Desine gave him a faltering smile, one that grew stronger when Kieran managed to twist his own lips upwards in response.

'Do you still intend to learn how to use my powers?' the god asked slowly, cautiously, as though afraid to know the answer.

'It would be foolish not to—I don't want to endanger the people around me,' Kieran said and gestured loosely towards Carton City, which seemed a lot smaller now that it was dwarfed by Ami's newer vessel. 'And I can't achieve my aims if I ignore even one side of me.

What Ami and I accomplished on Rochaccia...we could not have done it without GLEA's help.'

'You liberated Rochaccia with *my* help,' the Desine reminded him.

'Were you the one who helped Goss and his people set up a new system of governance? Did your presence make them look legitimate to the rest of the galaxy?'

'No,' the god conceded. 'But know this, your achievements are not as important to me as your happiness. Kieran, if being with GLEA makes you happy...and if Captain N'uni makes you happy...'

'She does,' Kieran cut in. 'If you want anything to do with me, you'll also accept the part of me that belongs to her.'

'Very well.' A long pause, laden with longing. 'It seems I have a long way to go before I earn your trust. But I am willing to do it. I hope you will consider...visiting me? At the rock? Not just for lessons—but so we can talk. Partake in family bonding. Whatever it should be called.'

'I will. Visit you, that is. And—thank you.'

The Desine blinked once, twice. 'For what? Hurting you? Making you hate me?'

'For acknowledging what you did, for apologising, for giving us this chance.' Kieran swallowed the lump in his throat. 'For not abandoning me when I needed you.'

'I will always be here for you, in whatever capacity you desire,' the Desine vowed. He looked away abruptly, but Kieran could see the tears beading in the corners of his very similar eyes. 'I must go. My domain requires my full attention. We'll speak again. Soon.'

'Soon,' Kieran agreed.

'...AND we commend the crew of the *Free Ride II* for their assistanccce in thisss matter,' Major Yetz droned on. 'As for you, Lieutenant Krendasssta, your recccent conduct has been exemplary and you have been jussstly rewarded...'

Lieutenant Sies Ryn stamped the heels of her boots, her knees bouncing in agitation. 'Yes, *exemplary* conduct that saw him making decisions on a galactic scale without consulting a more senior agent, decisions that risked the lives of civilians—including a minor who was clearly incapable of consenting to taking part in a planetary liberation!'

Ami smothered the laugh too late.

'Do you think it's funny to endanger a *child*?' Ryn demanded.

Ami shook her head, trying to appear appropriately contrite, but this was nearly impossible when Avurn was giving her one of his patented smirks. He found the whole farce as ridiculous as she did. But she knew he wasn't going to speak up and bail her out; undue attention was the last thing he wanted. He was keeping his arms pinned to his sides, as though worried that the Chippers could somehow see through the sleeve concealing his own chip.

'No,' Ami replied calmly. 'I find it funny that you assume Lieutenant Krendasta could have done any of his great deeds without us civilians, minor included. I'm the one who did the endangering, by the way. I dragged my crew into my family drama. But that's not the main glitch here, is it? Kieran ignored the rules and showed you what GLEA is capable of when you hop into bed with people from outside the Agency. If you'd just get your heads out of your orifices'—not all of them were human, after all—'then you'd realise that you're becoming too insular. And you're so busy gluing tiny fractures you haven't even noticed that you're already falling apart.'

Silence fell over the room. Avurn was mouthing 'orifices' as if he couldn't quite believe she'd said that. Kieran's gaze was full of warning. Yeah, she shouldn't have said most of that—or any of it, really.

To her surprise, someone actually decided to back her up.

'Captain N'uni isn't wrong,' Ryn said, frowning. 'Major, if you could see how short-sighted this new mandate is, forcing agents to seek connections inside the Agency—'

Yetz's triangular head moved from side to side in a slow, mesmerising dance. Ze did not appear to be bothered by her outburst. 'Lieutenant Ryn. Please allow Lieutenant Krendasssta to deliver his formal report and do not interrupt the proccceedings any further.'

Ryn looked at Kieran, who very deliberately turned away from her, his eyes fixed on Major Yetz instead. Ryn's expression became pinched. 'GLEA is doomed if this carries on. You realise that, don't you, Krendasta? Or is your promotion blinding you? Can you really let them turn you into a *breeder*?'

'Kieran knows what he must do in service to the Creator God.' This was said by Pina-Sai, with a hand on Kieran's shoulder, as if Pina knew what Kieran wanted, what he needed.

Ami bit her lip. Hard.

Though she didn't possess Kieran's precognitive abilities, she suddenly saw her whole afternoon being swallowed up by an argument that she had no say in whatsoever—and if she was honest, the future of GLEA didn't matter to her. Kieran did. She loved him and supported his plan to change the Agency from within, but sneaking around in the shadows was going to get old. And fast. Sure, it was only a matter of time before Kieran either nixed the rules or got kicked out. But until then...

'C'mon, Av,' Ami said, snatching the sleeve of the boy's jumpsuit. 'We've got work to do. Someone has to look after the galaxy and it's obvious these starkers sure won't.'

Outside it was bright, painfully so. Ami blinked several times, annoyed to find her vision blurring. She made some sort of comment about the sand getting into her eyes, but Avurn immediately stopped and turned back around to face her.

He wasn't fooled for a nanosecond.

'If this charade of his begins to hurt you too much,' Avurn said, his dark eyes sharp and flinty, 'I will tell the Chippers about your relationship and force his hand.'

'Av! No! Don't you dare. Kieran doesn't need that kind of threat hanging over his head. He's got enough to deal with right now.'

Avurn clucked his tongue. 'Ah, Kieran and his foolish notion that he can keep the Chippers from self-destructing. There's no helping them. No matter what he says, Kieran would abandon the Agency if you but asked. I have felt his love for you in the link. You could do worse. Much worse. The name "Denton Dashing" springs to mind.'

Ami snorted with laughter. 'You know, Av, you can admit that you like Kieran.'

'I don't need to. He's already aware of this fact.' Avurn's lips curled briefly, then flattened out again. 'But I will admit to caring about you, Ami, if *you* admit that you should seek treatment for your cycle pain. I struggled to find your usual meds on Rochaccia and I do not want to fail you in this manner again. Besides which, those meds are dangerous in the long term.'

'Av—'

'No more excuses,' Avurn commanded. 'You have struggled for years, more years than I have known you I suspect, and you've always refused to do anything about it, ostensibly due to the prohibitive cost. I would have offered to obtain the necessary coin-chips from accounts that would not miss them if I didn't know how much that would horrify you. But now we have access to extensive, legitimate funds. If you still won't do anything about it, then I will know I am right about the real reason why.'

'I...' Ami wasn't sure what to say.

'You can atone without punishing yourself,' Avurn said bluntly.

Ami knew she couldn't blame the sand this time, especially when Avurn initiated a long, steady hug that was clearly as important to him as it was to her.

FIFTY

'Kieran, we should talk.'

The other agents had wasted no time in vacating the meeting room, some of them headed to the training course in the basement and others to Carton City's perimeter, but Pina-Sai had yet to remove his hand from Kieran's shoulder.

Pina had clearly been waiting for an opportunity to get him alone. Kieran shifted uncomfortably inside his uniform, which suddenly felt like an ill-fitting garment instead of a second skin. It—and that gold stroke on the shoulder—belonged to an agent who lied, who kept parts of himself hidden from the man who called him brother.

'About what?' Kieran asked. 'My promotion?'

'You deserve it,' Pina said, his smile dimming. 'But no. This is about...' His energy became laced with cobwebbed shadows; he was *suspicious*, Kieran realised. 'The others would not have noticed it, but I have spent the better part of a year linking up with you...and something is different about your lifesign. It concerns me. Your written report states that your chip wasn't damaged despite the injury you incurred, I know. But I still think you should get it checked.'

The rapidly fading scars on Kieran's temple began to itch. He resisted the urge to scratch them. 'It's fine. I'm fine. My powers are fine.'

'Kieran, please tell me the truth,' Pina pleaded. 'I'm your brother. You don't need to edit yourself when you're speaking to me.'

Kieran's laugh was hollow. 'Don't I?'

'I have faith in you, Kieran. I always have.'

'I needed more from you,' Kieran said. He swallowed, but the bite in his tone remained. 'You just sent me off the planet and hoped for the best. Didn't even bother to come with me. Or guide me. The Creator God never said you had to stay behind, did he? If you actually believed me about what happened on Fintaz, you'd have bothered—I was dangerously untrained and unanchored, Pina! I could have killed everyone I came into contact with. You weren't there to stop me if something went wrong. And things *did* go wrong. You abandoned me.'

Pina's grey eyes morphed from concrete into steel. 'I know what feels different. It's the captain, isn't it? You didn't listen to me. You pursued a deeper connection with her.'

'My chip would give me away if that was the case,' Kieran said, allowing a cocky grin.

'The chip only reads and reports on your desires,' Pina reminded him. 'Not your feelings. Though I do wonder if the desire to be with one specific person would be strong enough to come through...'

Kieran felt Pina reach out, attempting to create a link—and blocked him.

Pina's eyebrows shot upwards, sweeping clean the lines that had been crossing his forehead. 'Interesting. The tremendous power you're suddenly exhibiting...the potential damage to your chip...is it possible that you can now shield yourself so the server on Gerasnin receives nothing about your desires? Listen, Kieran, we need you. GLEA needs you. If you have to marry a fellow agent, for the good of the galaxy, then you must. You can't endanger whatever purpose the Creator God has for you.'

Kieran shook his head. 'It's not going to help, if people like Lieutenant Ryn and I capitulate. It won't stop agents leaving. I won't do it, Pina.'

'Don't be so selfish!' Pina barked. He drew a deep breath, but it didn't steady his agitated energy in the slightest. 'Alright. It seems that the duty of safeguarding the galaxy's future falls to me. If I find any solid proof that you and Captain N'uni are conducting a relationship, I will inform our superiors.'

Kieran stared at Pina. The betrayal was hot in his gut, searing his insides, forcing bile up his throat. He began to back away, towards the door. This method of attack had taken him completely off guard. He hadn't thought he needed to see into Pina's future, hadn't expected that he would ever need to. For all the secrets between them, they were *brothers*.

But then he looked at Pina again...

...and saw a Chipper in violet. A man who would never understand a god's son.

Ami would understand, Kieran realised, love filtering through him and laying down deposits in his bones. *I should tell her. Everything. Then we can make the decision together.*

Kieran, are you alright? the Desine asked. *I want to help you. Tell me what you need.*

Kieran's knees weakened and he nearly fell. He braced his hands against the wall, staggering his way down the corridor to the atrium, overwhelmed by the warmth of his father's presence. His father. The desert god, who had apologised, who had changed his ways accordingly, and who was determined to earn the right to be there for Kieran. Unlike Pina, who had stopped trying to accept Kieran as he was—if he'd ever really tried to begin with.

'Kieran?' Pina asked, following him. 'I—I didn't mean to upset you—'

'Yes, you did,' Kieran said, clenching his fists.

Stirring a sandstorm into existence was disturbingly effortless. The air in Carton City's streets became choked with dust. Wind howled. Waves of sand slammed against the walls of the outpost. Pina's eyes flicked to the exterior door, its small plexiglass panel showing him what was happening outside. Kieran could tear down this entire building if he wanted to and it was so hard not to give in. So hard not to submit to his immense powers. But he didn't. And even if he lost control, he trusted the Desine to stop him.

'You don't know me, Lieutenant Pina-Sai,' Kieran said roughly. 'Not anymore. I'm not your friend and I'm certainly not your brother.'

Pina took a step back. 'You don't mean that.'

Kieran laughed, feeling intoxicated by Pina's fear of the sandstorm. 'You have no idea who I am, what I want, or what I've been through. You'll never take me, all of me, as I am. Whatever kinship we had, it's gone.'

'Please, let me try to fix this!' Pina insisted. 'You've changed—change happens—but give me a chance to know you again.'

'No, Lieutenant,' Kieran said with a shake of his head. 'You'll just fail me again. I can *see* it—I can see a hundred possible futures and you fail me in every single one! But I don't need you, sir. I already have all the help and love I need.'

He turned towards the door, where the wild desert awaited him.

'Kieran, stop, it's not safe out there right now!' Pina cried. 'I won't tell anyone about you and Captain N'uni, I swear it—'

Kieran was outside mere nanoseconds later. The door slid shut behind him. He sensed that Pina was overwhelmed by despair, unable to force himself to follow Kieran into a deadly sandstorm, unable to deliver the feeble apology trapped in his thoughts.

But someone else had walked out into the swirling sands.

And she was not afraid of them—or the man who could create so much carnage.

'Want to trade your cramped bunk in there for my comfy double?' Ami shouted, her smile almost lost in the gloom.

She stood there in the centre of the so-called street, so full of casual confidence that anyone watching could have mistaken her as the progenitor of the storm. Above her, a dusty, turgid blanket of sand was blotting out the sky, twisting and spiralling as it formed the beginnings of a funnel, an invitation from the Desine. Kieran welcomed its appearance. He could ignore the vortex if he wished—or he could let it take him away from Carton City in an instant.

Kieran took unhurried steps towards Ami, knowing she was safe from the sands who understood how important she was to him. 'I'm about to visit the Desine. I'd really like it if you came with me.'

'You don't have to jump just because he tells you to,' Ami said.

When he drew closer, he saw that her smile had vanished.

'I know that, but I want to go,' Kieran told her. 'I want to see him.'

Her eyes searched his face. Kieran wasn't sure what she saw there. 'Why? And don't you dare tell me this about you learning to use your powers. Something else is going on.'

'Ami, he's my father.'

The vortex closed in around them, growing more frantic as it prepared to transport them across the planet. Ami didn't give it a second glance—or even a first glance. 'So? I know you have powers. It doesn't matter how you got them, gifted or inherited, because they're part of *you*. Stark, you were too afraid to check how I'd react in a vision, weren't you? Did you think I would stop loving you if I knew?'

'No, I...' Kieran grimaced. 'It's not that.'

'Then what's the problem?'

'I'm immortal, just like him,' Kieran whispered. 'And that means, if...if we marry, you will become immortal too.'

Ami opened her mouth, but her response was lost in the roar of the vortex as it swallowed them. Kieran wrapped his arms around Ami and held her close. She gave him a squeeze, her energy emanating such warmth, such love, that tears pricked his eyes. Kieran cradled the back of her head with his hands, unable to speak, unable to find any coherent thoughts to send to her.

The vortex fell away, leaving them standing in a still, silent night, the wavy dunes around them lit by a handful of moons and a dwindling fire. They were on the other side of the same planet, mere paces from the cave where so much had changed.

'Show yourself!' Kieran called.

A cocoon of sand rose from the ground before exploding outward, revealing the unhooded Desine at its centre.

Ami immediately headed him off, her cheeks tight, her stance stiff with defiance.

Kieran's chest ached. God, how he loved her.

He narrowed his eyes at the Desine, a reminder that his relationship with Ami was non-negotiable, and it seemed that this caused the god to re-evaluate his words, because there was a long pause before he finally spoke. 'Captain N'uni, you are faced with a choice. Either you force Kieran to watch you turn into bones and dust, or you agree to be bound to him forever. Frightening, isn't it? Kieran will outlive every mortal he meets. He'll outlive the Chippers, their entire Agency, and their ethos. And all the deserts, all the people living within them, will forever know him as the Sodesine, the son of the Desine. One day in the future, not so far away as you might think, Kieran will become the god they expect him to be. He will no longer be the man you see before you now.'

'Sodesine?' Kieran repeated.

His father nodded. 'That is your title in the Galactic Pantheon, derived from mine.' The god's lips twitched. 'Or did you think my name was "Desine"?'

Kieran shrugged, conceding the point, and looked back at Ami. She had the strangest look on her face.

He was afraid to ask. Afraid to even skirt her thoughts, in case...

And then she started laughing.

FIFTY-ONE

Ami clapped a hand over her mouth. Kieran's stupefied expression was priceless, but she knew she had to set him at ease. She cleared her throat. 'Kieran, don't you get it? Remember that vision you told me about, the one where GLEA wouldn't listen to *Kieran Krendasta?* Maybe they'll listen to the Sodesine instead!'

Kieran's burgeoning frown deepened. Ami could tell he wasn't convinced.

'Listen,' she said. 'If this guy's your father, then your grandfather must be the Creator God. GLEA is full of people who worship *him*, who have pledged themselves to *his* service. The Creator God knows the Agency is in danger of breaking apart and made it your job to stop that happening. Can't imagine he'd let them kick you out. And if they try, well, you can tell them who you are and see what happens then.'

'Can nothing I say dissuade you from this path?' the Desine demanded.

Ami speared him with her most blistering glare. 'No.'

But Kieran's brow was still heavy as he took a step back, towards the dark horizon. 'Ami, I can't...immortality is a big ask. I don't want to push that burden onto someone else's shoulders. I'm having enough difficulty dealing with it myself.'

'You don't have to deal with it by yourself, that's what I'm here for,' Ami said firmly. She refused to look away from Kieran, which seemed to make him even more uncomfortable, because his gaze slid to the sand at her feet.

'We haven't known each other that long...' Kieran fumbled.

Ami drew closer to him, until there was no more distance between them. 'I don't need any more time to think about it. I've made up my mind. I'm yours and you're mine. Forever.'

Kieran wet his lips. 'Ami...'

'I'm not going to get down on the ground like they do in the vids,' she went on. 'But I *will* ask that question if you don't beat me to it.'

The grin exploded over his face, chasing away the shadows that had gathered there and—Ami hoped—all of his reservations. Kieran dropped one knee to the sand, his hands enfolding hers. It was difficult to remember that they had an audience. Ami felt as though the world around them had fallen away, leaving them suspended alone in space.

A soft light filled Kieran's blue eyes. 'Captain Ami N'uni, will you marry a Chipper, a member of your crew, and a desert god's son?'

'Absolutely,' Ami said and fell into his waiting arms.

She knew that later they'd have to sit down and have a very serious talk about this and what it meant for them both, but for now she simply wanted to enjoy the moment. His kisses were deep and devastating, devouring her lips and her soul. Ami responded in kind. She tugged on his zipper, opening his jumpsuit just enough so she could slide her hand beneath the fabric. She felt the sparks ignite between their skin.

Kieran abruptly pulled away, frowning at the retreating back of the Desine. The god was trudging into the desert, his cloak billowing out behind him.

Kieran hesitated.

'Go on,' Ami said, making herself comfortable on the sand and crossing her arms behind her head. 'I'm not going anywhere.'

Kieran stayed just long enough to murmur 'I love you' against her forehead, then jogged off after his father. Ami watched him leave, smiling, knowing that he would always return to her. For the rest of their very long lives.

Ami, what the stark are you going to do with yourself for eternity? she wondered.

It suddenly occurred to her that she'd be able to save thousands —*millions*—more people than she'd originally thought she could. A lengthened lifespan definitely had its uses. And she'd always have the Sodesine with her, standing by her side, brightening her darkest hours. No one would be able to stop her.

At least now she had a decent enough ship, one that might last several decades (if she was careful). Still, even when the *Free Ride II* wore out, she'd keep going—she was sure Avurn could help her set up a bank account that earned her enough interest to buy the next ship.

I'm going to need a lot *of ships,* Ami thought.

PANTING, Kieran sprinted towards the Desine, then overtook him and whirled around, blocking his path. Kieran called on the sands, asking if they would stall his father for him—and they obeyed.

There was an amused twist to the god's lips as he looked down at the mound that had buried him up to his knees. 'I allowed this. You still have much to learn.'

'Ami's acceptance of me upset you,' Kieran blurted. 'Why?'

The Desine's gaze unfocused for several long moments, then sharpened again. 'You are aware of the time I lived on Yalsa 5, as a mortal.'

Kieran nodded mutely.

'My wife...' The god trailed off, canyons of sorrow digging deeply into his face, reminding Kieran of the ancient mountain ranges he'd seen on Rochaccia. He realised with a jolt that he had no idea how old his father actually was. The Desine cleared his throat. 'My wife would only stay with me if I renounced my godhood and remained a mere man. She could not accept...' He spread his hands. A sandstorm roared into the sky above them and hovered there, restless and roiling, blotting out the stars. 'This. And the duty that comes with it.'

Kieran's eyes itched. He felt the vision lurk, just out of view.

'Kieran,' his father pleaded. 'Don't look into my past. Please.'

'I won't,' Kieran said, blinking rapidly to stave off the images before they arrived. He didn't want to pry. What he had with this god was too new, too fragile. 'But you need to understand—Ami is not your wife. She will be mine.'

The Desine arched an eyebrow. 'And here I thought I was the one who should be doing the parenting.'

Kieran shoved his hands beneath his belt, feeling awkward. 'I don't know how to be a son.'

'I don't know how to be a father,' the god countered.

'Oh, this is perfect,' Kieran said with a laugh. 'We're going to make so many mistakes.'

'I look forward to making those mistakes. With you.'

They returned to the rock to find Ami waiting for them. She

stood, dusted herself off, and jerked her head at the Desine. 'Do we have to start inviting him over for dinner?'

Kieran was pleased to see the Desine's sombre expression break into a warm smile.

'Only if you'll have me,' the god said.

EPILOGUE

True night crept into Carton City, eagerly embraced by those denizens who only roamed the settlement's sandy streets under the cover of darkness. They didn't notice the boy slipping out towards the dunes, his black jumpsuit and his deliberate movements rendering him all but invisible. Once he was a safe distance away from the so-called city, Avurn chose a spot that looked comfortable and knelt down onto the sand.

'Lord Desine, god of the deserts,' he began, 'I know I am being forward, but I'm a trusted acquaintance of Kieran Krendasta's. I wondered if I might have a few moments of your time.'

A gust of wind was his answer, but it brushed past him and did not return.

Avurn sighed softly. He rolled off his knees and sat instead, crossing his legs underneath him. He would stay here for a while, not long enough to be mistaken for a fool, but long enough to know when all hope had been exhausted.

'I have not given you any reason to take note of me,' Avurn decided. 'Let me do so now. I was able to create my own chip, which conferred on me the powers of a Chipper, but I have an interest in obtaining a second set of abilities. I am not the only one who would benefit from your generosity. Teaching me to use the Magic will assist Kieran with his own training. This method has served him well before.'

The air remained still. The sand did not stir.

Avurn coughed and tried again. 'In return, I would serve you, of course.'

You will have to offer more than your worship to me, a voice cautioned him, underscored by wild, searing winds.

Avurn ran sums through his head until his heart settled. He was up to solutions that were six digits long when he finally managed to say, 'I'm sure we can come to some sort of arrangement. One that satisfies us both.'

Laughter rippled across the dunes. Avurn swallowed, but the saliva he desperately needed to soothe his parched mouth retreated in fear.

To his relief, the desert god seemingly decided to humour him. *If I grant your request, you must protect Kieran Krendasta's life with your own. Soon they will sense his powers. And they will come for him.*

Avurn tipped his head to the side, considering. Well, that wasn't so bad. He was already in Kieran's close orbit and any threat to the Chipper had the potential to endanger him as well.

Kieran was also, admittedly, his friend.

'I accept these terms,' Avurn said.

More laughter. This time it raised goosebumps. *What you have agreed to do is far more dangerous than you can possibly comprehend. And you have not heard the full details.*

Avurn forced his shoulders into a shrug. His bones ached against the tension in his muscles. 'I have my suspicions about those full details. I don't need you to confirm them—in fact, I'd rather you didn't, at least until I'm able to shield my thoughts from interested parties. And don't underestimate the lengths I'll go to in order to obtain more powers. I'm all in.'

You may come to regret this.

'Even if I do, I figure the rewards will be worth it.'

Very well.

Avurn's body jerked and rose into the air. A thick cloud of dust and grit howled as it descended on the boy, engulfing him—

—but Avurn kept grinning, even as his skin burned beneath the abrading sand. He could feel the god filling every crevice his mind and soul possessed, changing parts deep inside him. When his feet touched the ground again, Avurn was more powerful than nearly everyone else on the planet.

He believed Kieran to be the only exception. So too did the Desine.

They were both very, very wrong.

CURIOUS ABOUT THE DESINE'S PAST?

Discover how it all began in *The Tortured Wind*
Available now

Turn the page for a preview

The sun warmed Sandsa's back as he trudged away, wondering how to begin his task. He had searched his sprawling sands for anyone with her name and had failed...perhaps he would turn his eyes to the cities and the domains belonging to his brothers and sisters.

The taste of salt on his tongue gave him several seconds of warning before the Watine, the god of water, oozed into being.

'Pathetic mortals,' the Watine said in his low, sibilant voice. 'How they fall to pieces without us there to guide them through their wretched lives.'

Sandsa regarded his brother coolly and made no move to greet him. The Watine opened his tattered cloak and made a sarcastic gesture that could have been a wave or a threat. His hair, dripping with water and mucus, hung over his face; instead of hiding his permanently dour expression, the greasy strands enhanced it.

Sandsa held out his open hand. A whirling sphere of sand appeared on command, dancing above his palm; a not so subtle reminder for his brother not to test him. He allowed it to hover there for a moment, then extinguished it.

'Fayay,' he finally said, 'I have very little patience for your antics today.'

'You seem to have even less for the mortals,' Fayay noted. His cracked lips parted into a smile that revealed the fungus painting his chipped teeth. 'Are you punishing them? There are more delightful ways to do that. I can show you.'

Sandsa kept his face blank despite the disgust and anger he felt. That Fayay thought Sandsa was falling into his sadistic ways was bad enough; Fayay offering to show him how best to torture mortals was beyond insulting.

'I am no longer their god,' Sandsa said and continued to amble away, allowing his beige cloak to fly up into the wind, exposing the simple threadbare clothes he wore beneath it.

A column of briny water exploded out of the dune in front of Sandsa, halting his path.

'What are you saying, *Desine*?' Fayay called.

Sandsa smiled grimly and turned back around to face his brother. 'You know what I mean. Oh, how could I forget. You don't.'

Fayay cursed. He lacked the mind-reading abilities that many of their brothers and sisters possessed and Sandsa had always made a point of reminding him of this inadequacy.

'We have lived for millennia, you and I,' Sandsa said then patted four fingers to his mouth, as though smothering another yawn. 'And yet you do not understand. You never will.'

'You think you know more than me?' Fayay hissed. 'Do you perhaps presume to think you know more than *Father*?'

The laugh curdled in Sandsa's gut before it reached his lips. 'Father. Some father. The Ine is unfeeling. Uncaring. Their *Creator God*. He created this mess long ago. And now we must eternally clean up after him.'

Fayay's pale blue eyes narrowed. 'You are leaving the deserts to rot. What for? To live like some irresponsible mortal?'

'Ah, so you do not need to read minds to know my plans.' Sandsa clapped his palms together. 'You should congratulate yourself, Fayay.'

Fayay frowned in the direction of the two warring tribes as they shouted and killed each other, all in the name of their god. 'Do you envy these maggots?'

Sandsa laughed darkly. 'Envy the mortals? Of course I do! Do you know what it is they have? We can guide them but it is up to them whether or not they listen. Free will, that's what the Ine gave them. Free will. They get to do whatever they want.'

'Listen to yourself. Mortals are foolish, pitiful creatures and—'

'Then why do you keep looking after them?' Sandsa demanded. 'The mortals—they're *his* creation. It's not our fault the humans poisoned their planet then spread so far throughout the galaxy that he lost control of them. He made us, his children, just so we'd take care of the ones he couldn't! And instead of one god meddling with their lives, there are now more than fifty!' Sandsa drew a breath. 'Now there will be one less. It is time I left my people to fend for themselves.'

Fayay's tongue danced over his bottom lip, like some sort of slimy creature sneaking out of a cave. 'I care as little for the mortals as you do, Sandsa. But it is our duty to maintain Father's grand design.'

'I...' Sandsa hesitated. 'I have my reasons.'

'Does your favourite, Kuja, know your reasons?'

Kuja, their youngest brother and god of the rainforests, was the only sibling Sandsa could stand, the only other god who had felt the loss when their mother had left their father to live as a mortal. But no, this wasn't something Sandsa could share with Kuja.

Kuja wouldn't understand. None of them would.

Sandsa spread his arms, deliberately providing a tempting target to his brother. 'Admit it, Fayay. You despise being second best. If I leave, there will be no one to challenge you.'

The Watine's lips twisted. 'I will tell Father what you are doing. And he will punish you accordingly.'

'Hoping to impress him, are you?' Sandsa asked scornfully. 'Hoping he'll kill me because you never managed it? Do not bother, Fayay. He already knows. Don't you, Ine?'

Their father's presence bled into the landscape. Sandsa had the satisfaction of watching Fayay's already pallid face bleach even further. The Watine immediately exploded into wisps of water that evaporated in the arid climate as he teleported away.

Sandsa formed another sphere of sand in his palm and waited.

His father appeared in front of him. He was two heads taller than Sandsa and his body was so thin it was almost skeletal. His hair was a white crown, matched by a neatly trimmed beard, and his blue eyes were the twins of Sandsa's own. This was the Ine, the Creator God, the first deity that the humans had worshipped so many aeons ago, when they had been contained on one lonely planet, unaware that so many alien species shared the same god.

'We must talk, but not here,' the Ine said, his lips stretched into a genial smile.

His father touched his shoulder and the icy tendrils of a forced teleportation threatened to invade Sandsa's veins. He jerked away and threw the ball of sand he'd prepared; it shattered against his father's face. The Ine's apparent good will vanished. He clapped his hands and the rolling sand dunes around them disintegrated into blinding white walls and floors; with his love of the sun, Sandsa found this environment harsher and more cruel than any of his baked deserts. This realm, beyond the sight of mortals, was a boring cage, a palace of pain, not the home that the other gods seemed to think it was.

Standing there, on a walkway lined with pillars and his curious brothers and sisters, Sandsa howled a challenge then ran full tilt at the Ine. The columns of stone on both sides exploded into gritty tornadoes and twisted, spurred on by his fury. Balls of sand chased Sandsa, then overtook him. He threw everything he had at his father.

The Ine held up a hand. Sandsa froze in place and his control over the sands abruptly withered; his missiles dropped to the floor and the pillars became still and cold once more.

'Sandsa, my son,' his father began, 'you gave your people their own powers. You made them special compared to those that do not live in the deserts. That was no uncaring gesture.'

Sandsa pulled his lips back into a snarl. 'I only gave them power over the sand so they could protect themselves from the mortals who insist on inserting a chip into their flesh to talk to you!'

'Your people have "the Magic" so long as you are there for them. You are the source of their powers. What will protect them if you leave?'

'Nothing you say will keep me in your grasp,' Sandsa warned.

'If you abandon the deserts, my son, then you renounce your place among us.'

Sandsa felt the eyes of his siblings upon him and found himself unable to turn his head to regard them, to challenge them, to ask for their help. Kuja might try to intercede, but the young god would be too powerless to do anything. And Fayay...he would be loving this, anticipating the moment he became the most revered of all their siblings.

'One woman is not reason enough to turn away from your people,' the Ine told his eldest son.

Sandsa wet his lips. 'Father...'

'The woman in your dreams—do not let a reckless pursuit of her be your downfall.'

Sandsa's cheeks felt hot with anger and shame. So even his dreams were laid bare to the Ine. His father had watched them, had seen the woman that haunted him, called him, and offered so much more than anyone else could.

'I am a god, just as you are, Father,' Sandsa said lowly. 'But you forget. My mother was human, extended though her life was. You give the mortals the choice to obey or ignore us. Since part of me is human, I should be able to choose my fate. And I choose the woman in my dreams.'

'There is no choice to be made, Sandsa,' his father said. 'Do you not see this?'

Sandsa merely glared at him.

The Ine's expression remained infuriatingly calm. 'Then you

will ignore me, the deserts and your duty, and place your focus entirely on this woman.' Not a question. An acceptance.

'Sandsa, no!' That was Kuja, the Rforine, tearing free from the line of silent gods to stand between Sandsa and the Ine. 'I lost Mum. Don't make me lose you too.'

The rainforest god was only seventy years old, practically a baby. And it showed. Green eyes growing moist, long copper fringe flying back over his head, face dotted with freckles, Kuja repeated his entreaty, anguished.

'Do not pretend you understand what is going on here,' the Ine told Kuja, his voice measured and unhurried despite the muttering that passed through those standing around them. 'You cannot help him.'

'I'm sorry,' Kuja whispered, turning to show his tears to Sandsa.

Sandsa shook his head. 'You've done nothing wrong. I know you can't escape him. Goodbye, Kuja.'

Stepping aside, hunched in defeat, the Rforine briefly squeezed his brother's shoulder before rejoining the ranks of those who would never dare raise their voices against their father. Another hand replaced Kuja's, one of iron and aeons, and the Ine pushed his eldest son backwards, saying, 'Desine, god of the deserts, you are hereby outcast from this realm, an immortal wanderer with no home. May you find what you seek.'

And Sandsa fell. But not to the floor, where the impact might have shaken the fear from him.

He passed through a white shroud that ripped when he touched it, he sailed down past stars and planets dancing in their ancient patterns and, as he continued to fall, he saw her face, a smile tweaking her lips. But then she was gone, unreachable in the blackness of infinity.

ABOUT THE AUTHOR

Alyce Caswell lives in Sydney, Australia with one husband, one son, two wallabies, four kookaburras, and countless bush turkeys. When she isn't drinking her way through a giant pot of tea, Alyce is either buried in a Scottish romance novel, watching a Christmas movie, rocking out to New Wave music, or off exploring other galaxies.

You can contact her via email (alycecaswell@outlook.com) or on Twitter (@alycecaswell).

www.ingramcontent.com/pod-product-compliance
Lightning Source LLC
Chambersburg PA
CBHW060722190726
48285CB00001B/32